STAR WARS™

LES JEDI ASSIÉGÉS

AM

Titre original :
Jedi under Siege

Publié pour la première fois en 1996
par Boulevard/Berkley Books US, Inc.

Ce livre est publié sous la direction de
Jacques GOIMARD et Patrice DUVIC

Loi n° 49-956 du 16 juillet 1949 sur les publications destinées
à la jeunesse : mai 1998.

ISBN 2-266-09295-2

Kevin ANDERSON
Rebecca MOESTA

STAR WARS™

Livre 6

LES JEDI ASSIÉGÉS

Traduit de l'américain par
Rosalie Guillaume

POCKET
jeunesse

LE CYCLE DE

DANS L'ORDRE CHRONOLOGIQUE DE LA GUERRE

UNE NOUVELLE SÉRIE FRISSONNANTE !

1. Dévorés vivants
2. La cité des morts
3. Fléau planétaire
4. La machine à cauchemars
5. Le fantôme du Jedi
6. Armée de terreur

REMERCIEMENTS

Comme d'habitude, tous nos remerciements à Lillie E. Mitchell pour ses doigts de fée quand il s'agit de retranscrire ce que nous dictons. Son intérêt pour nos personnages et nos récits nous a aidés à les développer. À Lucy Wilson, Sue Rostoni et Allan Kausch de Lucasfilm pour leurs suggestions toujours bienvenues et leurs esprits ouverts ; à Ginjer Buchanan et toute l'équipe de Boulevard/Berkeley pour leur soutien inconditionnel et leurs encouragements ; à Jonathan MacGregor Cowan, notre plus avide lecteur-témoin et « remue-méninges ».

À Letha L. Burchard, supporter, fan et amie, qui « nous connaissait à l'époque où... » et qui n'a pas cessé de nous parler pour autant !

CHAPITRE PREMIER

À la lueur incertaine de l'aube, Jaina regarda son oncle, Luke Skywalker, amener le *Chasseur d'Ombres* dans le hangar de l'Académie Jedi, situé à la base du Grand Temple. Son père, Yan Solo, et Chewbacca, son copilote, étaient déjà partis depuis un moment.

L'Académie de l'Ombre se manifestait ; personne n'avait de temps à perdre.

Jaina éprouvait quelque peine à croire que Kashyyyk, deux jours plus tôt, avait été prise d'assaut par les forces impériales, sous la conduite de son ancien ami de Coruscant, Zekk, devenu un Jedi Obscur au service du Second Imperium. Quand elle avait affronté le jeune homme aux cheveux noirs dans les niveaux inférieurs de la forêt, il lui avait conseillé de ne pas revenir sur Yavin 4, car l'Académie de l'Ombre s'apprêtait à l'attaquer.

Selon Jaina, l'avertissement de Zekk signifiait que le jeune homme avait toujours de l'affection pour elle et pour son frère jumeau, Jacen.

Ses amis et elle étaient revenus sur Yavin 4 depuis quelques instants. Aucun des jeunes gens n'avait beaucoup dormi au cours du vol de retour, mais l'adrénaline les tenait éveillés. Jaina avait l'impression qu'elle allait exploser si elle ne faisait pas quelque chose immédiatement. Il y avait tant de préparatifs à mettre en œuvre, tant de points à planifier...

Jacen, debout près d'elle à l'entrée du hangar, lui flanqua un coup de coude. Elle se tourna vers lui.

— Tout ira bien, dit-il. Oncle Luke saura quoi faire. Il a déjà livré beaucoup de batailles contre les Impériaux.

— Tu ne peux pas savoir comme cela me rassure, répondit Jaina, sarcastique.

Jacen utilisa son arme favorite pour lui faire oublier ce qui les attendait.

— Tu as envie d'entendre une blague ?

— Oui, Jacen, répondit Tenel Ka, qui venait de les rejoindre. Je crois que l'humour nous serait utile en ce moment.

Après avoir passé les dix dernières minutes à courir dans le but de chasser sa tension, la jeune guerrière de Dathomir luisait de transpiration.

— D'accord, Jacen. Vas-y, dit Jaina, feignant de s'attendre au pire.

D'une seule main, Tenel Ka repoussa en arrière sa longue chevelure blond-roux. Elle avait perdu le bras gauche lors d'un entraînement au sabrolaser, et elle refusait d'accepter une prothèse biomécanique.

Elle fit un signe de tête à Jacen.

— Tu peux nous raconter ta plaisanterie, dit-elle.

— D'accord. Quelle heure est-il quand un walker impérial marche sur ta montre ? (Il leva un sourcil, attendant une réponse.) L'heure d'en acheter une nouvelle !

Après un instant de silence glacial, Tenel Ka déclara, d'une voix mortellement sérieuse :

— Je te remercie, Jacen. Ton humour était tout à fait adéquat.

La jeune guerrière n'esquissa pas l'ombre d'un sourire, mais Jaina crut détecter une lueur d'amusement dans ses yeux gris. Ne voulant pas décevoir Jacen, Jaina émit un gémissement comique.

À ce moment, Luke et Lowbacca, le jeune Wookie, sortirent du *Chasseur d'Ombres*.

Jaina se hâta de les rejoindre, sachant que le temps pressait. Son oncle semblait penser de même, car il parla à ses élèves sans aucun préambule.

— Le Second Imperium aura besoin d'un peu de temps pour installer les composants d'ordinateur qu'il nous a volés, dit Luke. Nous avons peut-être quelques jours devant nous, mais je ne veux pas courir le moindre risque. Lowie, Tionne et Raynar sont au lac pour une séance d'entraînement. Je voudrais que tu prennes ton skyhopper et que tu ailles les chercher. Nous devons tous nous mettre au travail.

Lowie meugla et courut jusqu'au petit T-23 que son oncle Chewbacca lui avait offert. De son emplacement habituel, à la ceinture de Lowie, DTM, le droïd-traducteur miniaturisé, couina :

— Oui, bien entendu, monsieur. Maître Lowbacca aura grand plaisir à vous rendre service.

D'un grognement, Lowie réprimanda le petit droïd, grand spécialiste de la traduction ampoulée.

Puis il grimpa dans le T-23 et ferma le cockpit.

Luke se tourna vers la jeune fille de Dathomir.

— Tenel Ka, réunis autant d'étudiants que tu peux et fais-leur un cours accéléré sur les méthodes de combat rapproché contre les terroristes. Je ne sais pas quelle stratégie l'Académie de l'Ombre utilisera, mais je ne vois personne de plus apte que toi à enseigner les tactiques de commando.

— Elle a fait des miracles contre les tueurs Bartokks, sur Hapès, dit Jacen.

Tenel Ka surprit Jaina en rosissant du compliment.

Elle partit au pas de course.

— Et Jacen et moi, oncle Luke ? demanda Jaina, impatiente. Que pouvons-nous faire ? Nous voulons vous aider !

— Maintenant que le *Faucon Millenium* est parti, nous devons remettre les nouveaux générateurs de bouclier en service afin qu'ils nous protègent des attaques aériennes. Venez avec moi.

Le bâtiment des nouveaux générateurs de bouclier était situé dans la jungle, de l'autre côté de la rivière, mais les champs de force étaient commandés à partir du centre de communication. Yan Solo avait récemment apporté les composants de Coruscant, la Nouvelle République se débrouillant pour rassembler une force de défense contre l'attaque imminente.

— Au fait, dit Jacen en s'asseyant à une console, ne devrions-nous pas envoyer un message à maman ?

— Pas avant d'en savoir plus, répondit Luke. Votre père et Chewie ont prévu de la contacter et de tout lui expliquer. Leia s'efforcera de réunir des troupes et de les envoyer nous protéger. En attendant, il nous revient de faire tout ce que nous pouvons pour nous défendre.

« Entre-temps, Jacen, surveille tous les canaux de communication. Vois si tu peux détecter des signaux, surtout ceux qui ont des codes impériaux. Jaina, occupons-nous de mettre en marche ces générateurs de bouclier.

— J'y travaille, oncle Luke, dit Jaina avec un sourire. Ça y est, les boucliers sont levés et fonctionnent à pleine puissance. Je pense qu'il vaudrait tout de même mieux que je fasse une vérification complète, pour m'assurer qu'il n'y a aucune faille dans nos défenses.

Jacen mit un casque et commença à scanner les différentes fréquences de communication. Il venait à peine de commencer quand son écouteur crépita ; une voix familière se fit entendre.

— ... demandant la permission d'atterrir, et tout le train-train habituel. J'arrive. *Bâton de Foudre*, terminé.

— Attendez ! cria Jacen d'une voix paniquée. Vous ne pouvez pas ! Il faut d'abord que nous baissions nos boucliers. Donnez-moi une minute, Peckhum.

— Vos boucliers ? De quoi parlez-vous ? demanda le vieil astronaute. Le *Bâton de Foudre* et moi, on fait ces livraisons sur Yavin 4 depuis des années. Je n'ai jamais eu besoin de m'inquiéter de boucliers !

— Nous vous retrouverons sur le terrain d'atterrissage et nous vous expliquerons tout, dit Jacen. Attendez une minute.

— Aurai-je besoin d'un code pour atterrir ? demanda Peckhum. Personne ne m'en a donné quand j'ai quitté Coruscant. On ne m'a pas parlé des boucliers.

Jacen leva les yeux vers Luke.

— C'est le vieux Peckhum et son *Bâton de Foudre*. A-t-il besoin d'un code pour se poser ?

Luke fit un signe négatif et indiqua à Jaina de baisser les boucliers. La jeune fille se pencha sur

16

la console de commande. Au bout d'un instant, elle annonça :

— Voilà, ça y est. Les boucliers sont baissés.

Jacen sentit un frisson courir le long de son échine à l'idée que leurs défenses étaient désactivées.

— D'accord, Peckhum, dit-il. Vous pouvez atterrir. Mais dépêchez-vous, pour que nous puissions remettre les boucliers en action.

Quand le vieil astronaute descendit de sa navette déglinguée, il avait le même air que lors de sa dernière rencontre avec Jacen : le teint pâle, les cheveux longs et rares, les joues ridées et la combinaison de vol défraîchie.

— Venez, Peckhum, dit Jacen, je vais vous aider à rentrer les fournitures. Nous devons nous dépêcher, avant que les Impériaux n'arrivent.

— Les Impériaux ? demanda l'astronaute en se grattant le crâne. C'est pour ça que vous avez des boucliers ? Quelqu'un nous attaque ?

— Tout va bien, dit Jacen, impatient de décharger le *Bâton de Foudre*. Les boucliers sont de nouveau en action, mais ils restent invisibles.

Le vieil astronaute leva la tête et scruta le ciel brumeux.

— Et l'attaque ?

— Nous avons entendu une rumeur... Assez fondée. (Il hésita un instant.) Zekk... C'est lui qui a conduit le raid sur les installations informatiques de Kashyyyk. Il a prévenu Jaina que l'Académie de l'Ombre est en chemin. Nous ferions mieux d'entrer dans le bâtiment.

Peckhum regarda Jacen, inquiet. Le jeune Zekk avait été comme un fils pour lui ; ils avaient vécu ensemble dans les niveaux inférieurs de Coruscant jusqu'à ce que Zekk soit kidnappé par l'Académie de l'Ombre.

Tandis qu'un frisson de peur prémonitoire parcourait Jacen, Peckhum murmura, en montrant le ciel :

— Trop tard. Ils sont déjà là.

CHAPITRE II

Du sommet de la tour d'observation la plus haute de l'Académie de l'Ombre, Brakiss, maître des nouveaux Jedi Obscurs, regardait une minuscule tache verte : la lune-jungle. L'assaut dévastateur était sur le point de commencer. Avant longtemps, Yavin 4 et son Académie Jedi seraient écrasées sous la puissance du Second Imperium.

Ce qui était dans l'ordre des choses.

À travers les couloirs métalliques de la station, les commandos marchaient vers leurs postes, les nouveaux pilotes de Tie effectuaient leurs vérifications avant décollage, et les étudiants Jedi Obscurs attendaient impatiemment de combattre et de remporter leur première victoire majeure.

La bataille finale serait un assaut double, mené à la fois par la plus puissante des Sœurs de la Nuit, Tamith Kai, et par le protégé de Brakiss, le jeune

Zekk aux cheveux noirs. Le désir de donner un sens à sa vie avait vite converti le garçon au Côté Obscur.

Brakiss ferma les yeux et inspira à fond l'air recyclé qui circulait dans les puits de ventilation. Ses robes argentées virevoltèrent autour de lui.

Il sentait les préparatifs fiévreux que chacun menait dans la station ; la tension montait, ainsi que l'envie de la bataille. Dans les courants de pensée qu'il captait, il percevait la dévotion des troupes au chef du Second Imperium, l'Empereur Palpatine, mêlée à de la peur concernant l'attaque imminente. Mais ça ne l'inquiétait guère. Un peu de crainte inciterait ses combattants à mieux utiliser leurs capacités et les rendrait prudents, sans pour autant les paralyser.

Brakiss avait hâte de vaincre Luke Skywalker. Des années auparavant, il avait infiltré l'Académie Jedi en se faisant passer pour un étudiant. Son but était d'apprendre les méthodes de formation de la Nouvelle République, puis de les communiquer à ce qui restait de l'Empire. Mais Brakiss n'était pas parvenu à berner Skywalker. Le maître Jedi avait tenté de le faire revenir du Côté Lumineux, minant sa dévotion au Second Imperium. Ce fou avait essayé de le « sauver », pensa-t-il avec un ricanement mental.

Brakiss s'était enfui.

Pourtant, grâce à ses aptitudes, et parce qu'il était prêt à utiliser le Côté Obscur de la Force, il en avait appris assez pour créer son propre centre de formation de Jedi Obscurs.

Et maintenant, on allait voir ce qu'on allait voir !

L'air frémit près de lui. Brakiss ouvrit des yeux calmes et pleins de satisfaction, percevant l'aura glorieuse qui entourait la projection de l'Empereur. Le mystérieux chef du Second Imperium flottait devant lui sous sa forme holographique, sa tête encapuchonnée aussi grande que Brakiss. L'image était impressionnante, avec ses yeux jaunes et ses joues ridées à demi cachés par les ombres.

— J'ai hâte de retrouver ma domination sur l'univers, Brakiss, dit l'Empereur.

— Et j'ai hâte de vous l'apporter, mon maître, répondit Brakiss en s'inclinant.

Arrivé dans une navette blindée spéciale et accompagné de quatre Gardes Impériaux, l'Empereur s'était récemment installé à l'Académie de l'Ombre. Les terribles soldats vêtus de rouge empêchaient les intrus d'approcher de l'Empereur, enfermé dans un caisson d'isolation opaque. Palpatine n'avait jamais parlé directement à ses loyaux sujets de l'Académie, pas même à Brakiss. Il n'apparaissait que sous forme de projection holographique.

— Nous sommes prêts à passer à l'attaque, seigneur, dit Brakiss. (Il leva les yeux vers l'impressionnante image.) Mes Jedi Obscurs nous garantissent la victoire.

— Parfait. Je n'ai nulle envie d'attendre davantage, répondit l'image de l'Empereur. Le reste de la nouvelle flotte n'est pas encore arrivé, mais cela ne devrait pas prendre plus de quelques heures. Nos vaisseaux de guerre sont en ce moment même équipés avec les systèmes informatiques volés sur Kashyyyk. Mes gardes me disent que de nombreux navires sont déjà opérationnels, et que le reste du travail sera terminé bientôt.

Brakiss s'inclina de nouveau, les mains croisées devant lui.

— Je comprends, mon seigneur. Mais nous devrions garder notre force de frappe en réserve pour notre prochain assaut contre les mondes mieux défendus de la Nouvelle République. Sur Yavin 4, nous ne rencontrerons que quelques Jedi gentillets et faiblards. Ils ne devraient poser aucun problème à mes soldats entraînés à utiliser la Force.

L'Empereur eut l'air sceptique.

— Ne vous laissez pas abuser par un excès de confiance.

Brakiss reprit la parole avec plus de conviction. Il laissa ses sentiments parler dans l'espoir de convaincre son chef.

— Avec cette attaque contre l'Académie Jedi, le Second Imperium deviendra autre chose qu'une bande de pirates indisciplinés volant du matériel. Nous avons l'intention de reconquérir la *galaxie*, mon seigneur. Ce sera une bataille de philosophies et de pouvoir. Il nous faudra imposer le mode de pensée *impérial* contre celui de la Rébellion. Il est juste que cette lutte oppose des Jedi : mes élèves et ceux de Skywalker. En quelque sorte, l'Obscurité contre la Lumière. Nous avons l'intention de les défier avec nos chasseurs Tie, mais le conflit principal sera direct et personnel. Nous voulons les écraser, non nous contenter d'entamer leurs défenses.

Brakiss sourit, levant les yeux vers l'Empereur.

— Et quand nous les aurons battus à plate couture, les autres Rebelles se disperseront et se cacheront, tandis que nous récupérerons ce qui nous appartient.

Le visage holographique de l'Empereur prit une expression inhabituelle. Les lèvres ridées se plissèrent pour former un *sourire*.

— Très bien. Il en sera fait comme vous le demandez, Brakiss : Jedi contre Jedi. Vous pouvez lancer l'attaque dès que vous serez prêt.

CHAPITRE III

L'Académie de l'Ombre baissa son bouclier d'invisibilité. Au moment où la station impériale apparut au-dessus de Yavin 4, deux chasseurs Tie spécialement équipés quittèrent son aire de décollage. Se déplaçant silencieusement, ils plongèrent dans l'atmosphère brumeuse de la petite planète.

Les chasseurs avaient été recouverts d'un blindage de coque spécial qui dissimulait leurs signatures aux radars, et diminuait les ondes émises par leurs doubles moteurs ioniques. Leur mission était de frapper en secret, non de démontrer la force de l'Empire.

Le commander Orvak plongea en piqué. Le second chasseur Tie, que pilotait son subordonné, Dareb, couvrait son flanc. Ensemble, ils firent le tour de la petite lune, descendant encore plus bas dans l'atmosphère. Ils décrivirent une spirale autour de l'équateur et remontèrent jusqu'aux coordonnées du temple en ruine où Luke Skywalker avait installé son Académie Jedi.

Orvak tenait fermement les commandes dans sa main gantée de noir. Il sentait le bourdonnement des moteurs du chasseur, comme s'il avait chevauché une bête indomptée. Il pilotait avec prudence et concentration, suivant les courants aériens. L'air chaud qui montait de la jungle secouait le navire.

— Reste tranquille, murmura-t-il au vaisseau.

Cette mission demandait la plus stricte précision et de grands talents de pilote. Orvak l'avait simulée de nombreuses fois, entraînant un certain nombre de jeunes élèves choisis parmi les rangs des nouveaux commandos d'élite.

Maintenant, il s'agissait de la *véritable* attaque. L'Empereur comptait sur lui.

Les arbres Massassi formaient un tapis vert au-dessous de lui. Leurs branches noueuses se dressaient dans la forêt comme des serres monstrueuses. Orvak fit glisser son appareil plus bas. Son passage en rase-mottes dérangea les créatures qui vivaient au sommet des arbres, et se hâtaient de fuir la chaleur des moteurs de son vaisseau.

Son collègue, Dareb, parla sur un canal à transmission strictement visuelle. Les mots étaient encodés et décodés par un système de brouillage spécial situé dans le cockpit d'Orvak.

— Les détecteurs à longue portée ont repéré le champ d'énergie protecteur, dit Darek. Les générateurs sont exactement là où nous le pensions...

— Cible vérifiée, dit Orvak dans le micro intégré à son casque. Le seigneur Brakiss a été obligé de passer un certain temps ici. Il en sait beaucoup sur les installations de l'Académie Jedi... À condition que les Rebelles n'aient pas tout déplacé.

— Pourquoi l'auraient-ils fait ? demanda Dareb. Ils sont trop sûrs d'eux. Nous allons leur montrer leur bêtise !

— Tant que tu ne me montres pas la tienne, je suis d'accord, dit Orvak. Assez bavardé. Dirige-toi sur la cible.

Les boucliers invisibles surplombaient une partie de la jungle où une rivière sinuait au milieu des arbres. Non loin de là se dressait une pyramide majestueuse. Orvak espérait que le Grand Temple de Skywalker ne serait plus debout à la fin de la journée.

Avant que l'Académie de l'Ombre puisse lancer l'assaut principal, Orvak et Dareb devaient accomplir leur mission préliminaire : détruire le générateur de boucliers et ouvrir la porte à une attaque dévastatrice.

Orvak vérifia les écrans. Grâce à ses détecteurs de fréquences, il apercevait les vagues ondoyantes du champ de force mortel qui protégeait l'Académie Jedi. À cause des arbres Massassi, le champ n'allait pas jusqu'au sol, s'arrêtant à environ cinq mètres des cimes. Cinq mètres... Ce n'était pas grand-chose, mais assez pour qu'un as du pilotage puisse passer. Çà et là, des branches approchaient d'un peu trop près le dôme d'énergie crépitante. Elles étaient carbonisées.

— Ce sera juste, dit Orvak. Prêt ?

— J'ai l'impression d'être capable de vaincre l'Alliance Rebelle tout seul, dit Dareb.

Orvak ne releva pas la confiance excessive de son équipier.

— Nous nous rapprochons, dit-il.

Il fit descendre plus bas le chasseur Tie camouflé, l'amenant à la limite des arbres. Les feuilles bruissaient, effleurant les ailes du vaisseau. L'air frémissait devant lui, indiquant la présence du champ d'énergie. Il espéra que les détecteurs ne se trompaient pas...

— Reste sur la cible, dit-il. Quand nous serons passés sous ce bouclier, notre véritable travail commencera.

Au moment où ils se faufilèrent sous la barrière invisible, Dareb vira sur le côté pour éviter une branche qui sortait de la frondaison. Le jeune pilote surcompensa et heurta une autre branche, qui le déséquilibra.

— Je ne peux pas redresser ! cria-t-il dans le système de communication. Le vaisseau n'est plus contrôlable !

Le chasseur Tie de Dareb monta en flèche vers le champ de force mortel. Il explosa à l'instant où il heurta le mur d'énergie. Concentré sur sa mission, Orvak continua sa course. Il jeta un coup d'œil à son écran arrière, où il vit les restes enflammés du chasseur de son équipier tomber vers la forêt.

Il serra les dents et inspira à fond à travers le masque à oxygène de son casque.

— Nous sommes tous sacrifiables, dit Orvak, comme s'il voulait s'en convaincre lui-même. La mission, voilà ce qui compte. Dareb était mon second. Maintenant, il ne reste plus que moi pour la mener à bien.

Il déglutit avec peine, conscient que les Rebelles devaient savoir ce qui se passait.

Sans s'arrêter, Orvak se dirigea vers la station des générateurs de bouclier. Isolée dans la jungle, celle-ci ressemblait à une série de grands disques à demi enterrés dans le sous-bois. Elle était entourée par une clairière artificielle. Le terrain dégagé était juste assez grand pour qu'Orvak puisse se poser. Au loin, il voyait la grande pyramide qui abritait l'Académie Jedi de Skywalker.

Il coupa les moteurs ioniques, ouvrit l'écoutille du cockpit, puis récupéra le paquet rangé à l'arrière du siège de pilotage qui contenait les explosifs dont il aurait besoin...

Orvak sortit de l'appareil, sautant sur le sol couvert de plantes et de mousse. La jungle l'entourait, chaotique et effrayante. Au-dessus de lui, il entendait le bourdonnement du champ d'énergie qui avait détruit son équipier.

Comparée à l'Académie de l'Ombre, propre et stérile, Yavin 4 était horriblement *vivante*. Elle grouillait de vermine, de végétaux à l'aspect bizarre, d'insectes, de petits rongeurs, de formes de vie qui rampaient partout et se cachaient dans tous les coins.

Le pilote aurait donné n'importe quoi pour être de retour dans les couloirs rectilignes de l'Académie de l'Ombre, où ses bottes sonnaient agréablement à ses oreilles sur les plaques métalliques du sol, où il sentait l'odeur de l'air recyclé passant par les aérateurs, où tout était réglementé et restait à sa place... Comme l'Empire le serait après sa victoire sur les Rebelles. Orvak se réjouit de sentir ses épais gants de cuir et le casque qui le protégeaient des créatures parasitaires de ce monde primitif.

Il courut vers la station des générateurs, portant le paquet qui contenait son équipement de démolition. La bâtisse se dressait devant lui, puissante mais sans défense. Condamnée.

Bien que les générateurs fussent manifestement neufs, des lianes, des branches et des fougères poussaient à profusion. Orvak vit des branches cassées et taillées là où quelqu'un avait élagué le feuillage pour ménager un accès à la station. La jungle, imperturbable, se contentait de repartir à l'assaut, sûre de son avantage. Orvak secoua la tête, effaré de la bêtise des Rebelles.

Quand il atteignit la station, il prit une attitude défensive et regarda à droite et à gauche, s'attendant à voir des Rebelles protéger les installations. Il ouvrit son paquetage, en retira deux des neuf détonateurs thermiques à haute puissance. Il placerait ces charges contre les cellules d'alimentation du générateur. Deux suffiraient à détruire le bouclier protecteur de l'Académie Jedi.

Le reste des explosifs servirait à la seconde partie de sa mission.

Orvak synchronisa les minuteries. Puis, sortant son compas, il regarda les coordonnées qu'il avait programmées. Il s'enfonça dans la jungle, se frayant un chemin dans le sous-bois en direction de sa deuxième cible, qui se trouvait à quelque distance, de l'autre côté d'une rivière.

Le Grand Temple.

Il s'arrêta un instant pour opacifier sa visière quand les minuteries annoncèrent « zéro ».

Les charges détonèrent.

Le bruit de l'explosion fut assourdissant. Un pilier de feu jaillit dans le ciel, carbonisant les arbres Massassi. Satisfait, Orvak se félicita d'avoir réussi un feu d'artifice des plus spectaculaires.

Mais le prochain serait encore plus beau !

CHAPITRE IV

Lowie ramena le skyhopper T-23 vers l'Académie Jedi, Raynar et Tionne serrés sur le siège arrière. Tandis qu'ils filaient à vive allure au-dessus des arbres, le Wookie leur expliqua la situation de son mieux. DTM traduisit.

— Et voilà pourquoi maître Skywalker a demandé que maître Lowbacca vienne vous chercher avec une telle hâte, conclut le petit droïd.

— Oui, oui, oui, fit Raynar d'une voix amère. Je suppose que vous pensez être des héros revenus sauver l'Académie Jedi. Je suis sûr que je m'en serais très bien sorti sans votre aide. Pendant que vous étiez partis vous amuser, j'étais occupé à m'entraîner avec Tionne.

Au ton de la voix du garçon aux cheveux blonds, Lowie comprit qu'il n'était pas très content d'avoir été fourré sans cérémonie dans le petit compartiment arrière, ses robes aux couleurs criardes entortillées autour de lui. Avant que la planète soit détruite par l'Étoile Noire, les parents de Raynar avaient été de petits monarques sur Alderaan. Ils étaient ensuite devenus de riches marchands. Raynar n'avait pas l'habitude d'être traité comme quantité négligeable.

— Non, Raynar, lui reprocha Tionne, clignant de ses yeux couleur de nacre. Personne ne se débrouille mieux seul contre un ennemi. Nous devons travailler ensemble à nous défendre. Sans préparation, une bataille est perdue d'avance.

Raynar ricana, puis il essaya de remettre de l'ordre dans sa tenue.

— Une bataille ? Nous ne sommes même pas sûrs qu'il va y en avoir une ! Pourquoi ferions-nous confiance à la parole d'un traître qui a pris fait et cause pour le Côté Obscur ? Zekk pourrait avoir menti pour nous inquiéter. Il est sans doute en train de se moquer de nous en ce moment !

Lowie grogna plus fort que le vrombissement du moteur.

— Maître Lowbacca tient à souligner, dit DTM, que Zekk a été l'ami de maître Jacen et de maîtresse Jaina pendant des années.

Raynar fit la moue.

— Dans ce cas, Jacen et Jaina Solo feraient bien de choisir leurs amis plus prudemment.

— Parfois, dit Tionne d'une voix ferme, la différence entre ami et ennemi n'est pas aussi grande que tu sembles le penser. L'aide nous vient souvent des sources les plus inattendues.

Lowie ne savait pas pourquoi, mais quelque chose le poussait à rentrer le plus vite possible. Le petit skyhopper frissonna et trembla quand il poussa les moteurs au maximum. Il volait parmi les arbres, sous le dôme mortel d'énergie qui protégeait l'Académie Jedi d'une attaque aéro-portée.

— Fais attention à cette grosse branche ! glapit Raynar quand Lowie vira sur le côté. Garde ton héroïsme pour le moment où l'Académie de l'Ombre se montrera... Si elle arrive jamais.

Lowie fut satisfait de voir que Tionne restait calme, et qu'elle approuvait la façon dont il pilotait le petit T-23.

Le Wokkie leva la tête et comprit tout à coup pourquoi il avait senti le besoin urgent d'accélérer. Il émit un aboiement bref, montrant l'anneau hérissé à peine visible à travers l'atmosphère.

— Maître Lowbacca dit... Oh, par mes circuits ! Il semble que l'Académie de l'Ombre soit arrivée !

Raynar se tut, ne trouvant plus rien à redire à la façon de piloter de Lowie. Peu après, un son aigu se fit entendre, suivi par le bruit de plusieurs explosions. À en croire les détecteurs de Lowie, le champ d'énergie protectrice venait de tomber en panne.

Il grogna la nouvelle.

Sans attendre la traduction, Tionne prit la parole :

— Nous pouvons quand même retourner à l'Académie, mais nous devrions laisser le T-23 à l'orée de la jungle. J'ai le sentiment qu'il serait dangereux d'approcher du terrain d'atterrissage ou du hangar. Ils doivent subir une attaque. (Elle se redressa.) C'est déjà commencé, j'en ai peur.

Le Grand Temple des Massassi était resté immuable pendant des milliers d'années. Les blocs de pierre qui le composaient paraissaient aussi solides que le jour où ils avaient été assemblés. Malgré tout, Jaina sentit une vibration dans le sol du poste de commande. Des alarmes clignotèrent sur la console des générateurs de bouclier.

— Nous avons un problème, oncle Luke, dit-elle. Une explosion dans la jungle... Oh, non ! Nos boucliers sont désactivés !

Luke se tenait derrière le fauteuil de Jacen, assis à la console de communication. Il fit un signe de tête à Jaina.

— Peux-tu remettre les boucliers en service d'ici ?

Jaina vérifia les connexions et bascula plusieurs commutateurs. Elle vérifia les écrans de diagnostic sans cesser de pousser des boutons.

— Je ne pense pas, dit-elle. L'alimentation est coupée. Il est possible que le générateur ait été entièrement détruit.

Jacen poussa un soupir et se leva.

— J'ai un mauvais pressentiment au sujet de tout ça, dit-il, passant les doigts dans sa chevelure châtain ébouriffée. Je parie que c'est un sabotage.

Luke regarda Jaina, puis Jacen.

Il prit sa décision.

— Nous tiendrons une réunion générale dans cinq minutes. Nous devrons peut-être évacuer le Grand Temple et nous cacher dans la jungle, où nous déjouerons l'attaque plus aisément. Envoie un message à ta mère et dis-lui que nous avons besoin d'urgence de renforts. Puis retrouve-moi dans la grande salle d'audience.

Jacen regarda sa sœur. Il semblait proche de la panique.

— Mes animaux..., dit-il. Je ne peux pas les laisser dans leur cage. Ils auront une meilleure chance de survivre si je les libère. Et si oncle Luke veut évacuer les étudiants...

— Vas-y, dit Jaina. Occupe-toi de tes animaux. J'enverrai le message à maman.

Jacen courut vers la porte, lançant au passage un bref « merci » à sa sœur.

Jaina s'assit à la station de communication, choisit une fréquence de transmission et essaya de contacter Coruscant. Elle ne reçut aucune réponse : seulement des parasites. Maudissant le comportement erratique de l'antique matériel, elle bascula sur une autre fréquence. Toujours rien.

Bizarre, se dit-elle. Peut-être l'écran principal de communication était-il en panne. Elle mit le casque et essaya une autre fréquence.

Des parasites encore. Elle commuta de nouveau. La « friture » se fit plus forte, comme si quelque chose avait *avalé* son signal. Bientôt le crépitement devint si aigu que Jaina grinça presque des dents. Elle retira le casque et le jeta en frissonnant.

— Nos communications sont brouillées !

Elle vérifia les relevés de la console de communication. Leurs transmissions à longue distance étaient bloquées par l'Académie de l'Ombre.

Elle devait en informer immédiatement Luke.

Dans sa chambre, à l'intérieur du temple, Jacen ouvrit les portes des cages qui contenaient sa ménagerie. Il constata que Tionne avait bien soigné ses protégés pendant son séjour sur Kashyyyk. Le serpent-cristal presque invisible scintillait de satisfaction, mais la famille d'araignées sauteuses pourpres de la cage voisine bondissait dans tous les sens.

— Tout va bien, dit Jacen, envoyant en même temps un message mental. Restez tranquilles. Vous serez en sécurité dans la jungle.

Une des cages abritait deux stintarils, des rongeurs aux yeux protubérants et aux dents aiguisées. Dans un enclos humide, de petits crabes sortaient timidement de leurs nids de boue. Des salamandres roses à l'aspect gélatineux émergèrent de leur aquarium, prenant une forme plus solide à mesure qu'elles séchaient. Des scarabées-piranhas bleu iridescent s'agglutinaient contre les fils de fer robustes de leur cage, les mâchouillant pour se libérer.

Jacen fit sortir ses amis un par un, après les avoir portés jusqu'à la fenêtre avec une hâte précautionneuse. Il venait de libérer la dernière créature, son favori, un lézard des souches, quand il entendit un grondement wookie suivi par la voix de DTM.

— Oh, que le Grand Circuit en soit remercié ! Nous ne sommes pas seuls dans le temple !

Jacen se retourna. Lowie, DTM, Tionne et Raynar se tenaient sur le pas de sa porte.

— Les autres sont-ils partis sans nous ? demanda Raynar, l'inquiétude et la tristesse se lisant sur son visage.

— Tout le monde est dans la grande salle d'audience, répondit Jacen. Nous devons y aller le plus rapidement possible. Maître Skywalker va nous donner ses dernières instructions.

Quand ils arrivèrent à la salle d'audience, Jaina s'y trouvait déjà, parlant à mi-voix avec Luke et Tenel Ka. Les autres étudiants étaient assis sur les gradins, silencieux et angoissés.

Luke eut l'air soulagé de voir Lowie de retour, sa mission accomplie. Tionne tendit la main à Luke, qui la serra brièvement.

— Je suis content de vous savoir saine et sauve, dit-il.

— Qu'a répondu maman ? demanda Jacen à sa sœur.

Jaina se mordit la lèvre inférieure. Tenel Ka parla à sa place.

— L'Académie de l'Ombre brouille nos transmissions. Nous n'avons pas pu envoyer le signal de détresse.

Jacen sentit le sang déserter son visage. Combien de temps faudrait-il aux renforts pour arriver, s'ils ne pouvaient même pas les prévenir du danger ?

Luke parla d'une voix puissante, s'adressant à tous les étudiants Jedi.

— Nous ne pouvons compter sur aucune aide extérieure pour nous sauver. Nous devons livrer seuls cette bataille. Je pense que le Grand Temple sera la première cible. Tenel Ka vous a déjà appris les tactiques de commando. Nous allons déplacer le théâtre des opérations vers la jungle, où le terrain nous est familier. Nous affronterons les Jedi Obscurs en combat singulier.

« Il faut évacuer immédiatement l'Académie Jedi.

CHAPITRE V

Dans le hangar bondé de l'Académie de l'Ombre, Zekk observait les derniers préparatifs de la bataille. Les troupes s'agitaient en tous sens. Zekk percevait leur colère sourde et leur avidité de destruction. Cela le galvanisait. Il avait l'impression que les lignes de Force qui l'entouraient brûlaient du désir de combattre.

Le centre de l'activité était une immense plate-forme qui dominait le hangar. Spécialement fabriquée pour l'assaut contre les forces de l'Alliance Rebelle, la structure tactique mobile était hérissée d'armes. Les commandos grouillaient sur sa surface blindée, préparant le décollage. Sous la houlette d'une Sœur de la Nuit, Tamith Kai, le dispositif servirait à coordonner les combats singuliers, Jedi contre Jedi, qui auraient lieu sur Yavin.

L'imposante sorcière était debout devant le poste de navigation de la plate-forme, ne songeant qu'à la vengeance. Sa longue cape noire virevoltait autour d'elle avec un bruit semblable au sifflement de serpents venimeux prêts à attaquer. Des épines arrachées à la carapace d'un insecte géant tueur d'hommes ornaient les épaules de sa tunique. Sa chevelure d'ébène s'enroulait autour de son visage, crépitante et frémissante de Pouvoir Obscur, comme si chaque mèche était vivante et animée d'intentions maléfiques.

Les yeux violets de Tamith Kai brûlaient de haine quand elle ordonna aux commandos d'embarquer sur la plate-forme de bataille. Son armure noire en écailles de lézard moulait son corps musculeux et bien bâti. Son attitude proclamait sa confiance en elle, ainsi que la soif de sang et de destruction qui l'animait.

Zekk effectuait les tâches qu'on lui avait assignées. Il était la cible des soupçons de Tamith Kai, et il le savait. La Sœur de la Nuit n'avait pas confiance en lui. Elle estimait que sa dévotion au Côté Obscur n'était pas assez forte, qu'il se laissait aveugler par son ancienne amitié avec les jumeaux Jedi, Jacen et Jaina Solo.

Zekk avait été formé par le seigneur Brakiss en personne. Il avait vaincu le protégé de Tamith Kai, Vilas, lors d'un duel à mort.

À cette occasion, il avait gagné le titre de plus Obscur des Chevaliers Obscurs. Depuis, Tamith Kai le quittait rarement des yeux, soit parce qu'elle était mauvaise perdante, soit parce qu'elle sentait les doutes qui l'assaillaient parfois.

Mais c'était à Zekk que Brakiss avait confié le commandement des nouvelles troupes de l'Académie de l'Ombre, avant-garde de la bataille pour la galaxie. Il conduirait personnellement les nouveaux Chevaliers Jedi Obscurs.

Ils fondraient sur leurs ennemis comme la peste, balayant les étudiants Jedi de la surface de Yavin 4.

Zekk inspira à fond. Il sentit l'odeur métallique de l'air froid.

Il entendit les réfrigérants circuler, les moteurs ronronner, les armures des commandos cliqueter, les signaux indiquer que les systèmes étaient verrouillés.

Ils étaient parés pour le décollage.

Zekk se tourna vers son groupe de guerriers adeptes de la Force. Il portait sa cape noire doublée de rouge et son armure de cuir ; son sabrolaser, accroché à sa ceinture, était prêt à servir. Sa longue chevelure noire était nouée en queue de cheval.

Ses yeux émeraude parcoururent les troupes rassemblées autour de lui.

— Laissez la Force couler à travers vous, dit-il aux étudiants.

Ils le regardèrent, mâchoires serrées, vifs, résolus au combat. Leur entraînement les avait préparés pour cet instant.

Il montra la plate-forme ; les Jedi Obscurs montèrent à bord, leurs mouvements souples et fluides comme à l'accoutumée.

— Nous devons frapper l'Académie Jedi maintenant, avant de perdre l'avantage de la surprise.

Le casque du pilote s'adaptait parfaitement à sa tête aux cheveux gris. Équipé du masque respiratoire, des lunettes, de la combinaison de vol noire, des gants épais et des lourdes bottes, Qorl se sentit ramené à une autre époque... Un temps où il était le premier pilote de l'Empire.

Des années auparavant, il avait décollé de la première Étoile Noire à la tête d'une escadrille de chasseurs Tie. Il traquait les ailes X de l'Alliance Rebelle, lancées dans une fuite désespérée. Abattu en vol, il avait atterri en catastrophe dans la jungle de Yavin 4.

Quand il avait levé les yeux, Qorl avait vu exploser l'invincible Étoile Noire. Cette catastrophe le laissait naufragé sur la misérable petite lune.

Après s'être remis de ses blessures, Qorl avait vécu en ermite pendant plus de vingt ans, jusqu'à ce que quatre jeunes étudiants Jedi le découvrent et déclenchent la série d'événements qui l'avaient ramené au sein du Second Imperium.

À présent, Qorl embarquait de nouveau sur un chasseur Tie et décollait d'une station. Prêt à battre les Rebelles ! Mais cette fois, il était sûr que les choses se termineraient différemment. Car l'Empire ne commettrait aucune erreur.

Qorl commandait une escadrille de douze chasseurs Tie. Les petits appareils étaient rangés dans un coin de la baie de lancement, serrés les uns contre les autres, prêts à partir dès que la plate-forme de bataille serait en position. Le pilote se tourna vers ses troupes, des combattants novices choisis parmi les meilleurs élèves-commandos. Aucun ne s'était battu autrement qu'en simulation, mais Qorl savait qu'ils avaient hâte de se retrouver au cœur de l'action.

Les hommes étaient debout devant leurs vaisseaux, vêtus de combinaisons de vol noires et de casques similaires à ceux du vieux combattant.

Un des pilotes sautillait sur place. Jetant des regards langoureux à son chasseur Tie, il caressait des yeux les tourelles des canons laser. Il avança d'un pas, retira son casque et le tint contre sa poitrine. Avant d'avoir vu le visage carré du jeune homme, Qorl sut qu'il s'agissait du robuste Norys, l'ancien chef de la bande Génération Perdue.

— Excusez-moi, monsieur, j'ai une suggestion à faire, dit Norys. Étant donné mes performances exceptionnelles au tir pendant les simulations, j'ai pensé que je devrais être nommé chef de cette escadrille.

Qorl tenta de dissimuler sa colère.

— Je comprends tes motivations, Norys, dit-il. Tu as fait de l'excellent travail lors de ton entraînement de commando et de pilote. Tu as hâte d'apprendre, et, je suppose, de servir le Second Imperium. Mais je suis obligé de refuser ta requête.

— Pour quelle raison ?

— Parce que Brakiss a cru bon de *me* désigner,

moi, dit Qorl, laissant la désapprobation percer dans sa voix devant le défi que lui lançait le jeune homme.

« Toutefois, si tu as décidé de ne pas obéir aux ordres de notre chef, libre à toi...

Qorl haussa les épaules, laissant Norys imaginer les conséquences de son insubordination.

Le jeune homme était grossier et indiscipliné ; s'il n'avait pas montré une exceptionnelle aptitude pour les armes et de grandes qualités de combattant, Qorl l'aurait consigné sur la station. Trop de choses étaient en jeu dans cette mission pour laisser un jeune ambitieux tout gâcher.

Norys rougit.

— Je crois que vous avez peur, Qorl. Vous êtes vieux, vous n'avez pas accompli de mission depuis des années. Vous dirigez l'escadrille pour couvrir votre médiocrité en nous empêchant de donner notre maximum.

— Ça suffit, dit Qorl d'une voix tranquille mais si menaçante que l'air vibra de tension. Je te donne le choix : dis un mot de plus, et je te renvoie à la station. Si tu tiens ta langue, tu pourras te battre pour l'Empereur.

Peu importait à Qorl la décision que prendrait le jeune homme. Il s'accommoderait d'une escadrille moins performante, si c'était la seule façon d'assurer la discipline au sein de ses troupes.

Norys fit un gros effort pour ne rien répliquer et remit brutalement le casque noir sur sa tête.

Qorl s'adressa à ses hommes, plus pour faire diversion que par nécessité.

— Nous sommes parvenus à brouiller les signaux de l'Académie Jedi. Nos ennemis ne peuvent pas appeler de renforts. Depuis que nos vaisseaux sont en orbite, les Chevaliers Jedi doivent penser que leurs pouvoirs et leur misérable bouclier d'énergie suffiront à les protéger.

« Si j'en crois nos systèmes de surveillance, notre équipe de commandos a réussi sa mission : éliminer les boucliers. L'Académie Jedi est sans défense.

« Quand Tamith Kai fera décoller sa plate-forme de bataille pour diriger l'assaut, le seigneur Zekk emmènera ses étudiants Jedi Obscurs affronter les Chevaliers Jedi en combat singulier. Notre escadrille effectuera des raids aériens. Nous sommes censés faire un maximum de dégâts. Mais n'oubliez pas que nous sommes une force de soutien, pas la première ligne d'attaque.

Les pilotes murmurèrent leur assentiment. Qorl ne put déterminer si la voix de Norys s'était jointe aux autres.

— Très bien. À vos vaisseaux !

Les pilotes entrèrent dans leurs cockpits. Qorl s'installa aux commandes du chasseur de tête. Il inspira à fond à travers le masque, sentant l'odeur familière de l'air mêlé aux produits chimiques de ses réservoirs.

Il sourit. C'était si agréable de voler de nouveau !

Campée devant la console tactique de la plate-forme de bataille, Tamith Kai hurla :

— Allons-y ! Nous reviendrons victorieux avant la fin de la journée !

Les grandes portes du hangar s'ouvrirent, révélant l'obscurité de l'espace où se détachait la sphère émeraude de la petite lune, derrière laquelle bouillonnait un immense chaudron orangé : Yavin, la géante gazeuse. La lune semblait minuscule ; c'était pourtant la cible de l'Académie de l'Ombre, destinée à devenir le théâtre d'une furieuse bataille dont l'Empire sortirait vainqueur.

Tamith Kai donna l'ordre de soulever la plate-forme avec ses moteurs à répulsion. Le vaisseau militaire était une barge à voile large. Les coins arrondis, elle était composée de deux niveaux. Le pont supérieur s'ouvrirait sur l'atmosphère dès qu'ils l'auraient atteinte. Les commandos et l'infanterie occupaient le niveau inférieur ; Zekk et ses Jedi Obscurs avaient pris position dans la baie, près des portes de débarquement.

La plate-forme descendit dans l'espace vers la fine couche d'air entourant la lune verdoyante.

Zekk faisait les cent pas, comptant les minutes. Il regarda à travers les hublots et vit la station, loin au-dessus d'eux, devenir plus petite à mesure que la vitesse du grand navire d'assaut augmentait et les rapprochait de Yavin 4.

— Vos paquetages sont prêts ? demanda Zekk

en ajustant l'équipement attaché sur son dos et sur sa poitrine.

Sa cape noire dansait autour de lui, le rouge de la doublure apparaissant par moments. Son escouade vérifia l'armement, une série de sabrolasers identiques fabriqués à l'Académie de l'Ombre. Les Jedi Obscurs réglèrent les générateurs de répulsion fixés à leurs épaules. Un par un, ils annoncèrent qu'ils étaient prêts.

Tandis qu'elle plongeait dans l'atmosphère, la trajectoire de la plate-forme zébra de brume blanche le velours noir de l'espace. Zekk sentit des vibrations quand le vent frappa les plaques de blindage.

La coque chauffa ; Zekk entendit le sifflement aigu de l'onde de choc. Mais il n'y avait pas lieu de s'inquiéter : Tamith Kai pilotait avec un talent consommé. Sans hésitation, elle allait droit vers leur but.

La voix basse et rauque de la Sœur de la Nuit jaillit des haut-parleurs.

— Nous approchons de la cible. Zekk, prépare tes Jedi Obscurs au débarquement. Les sas de largage aérien s'ouvriront dans une minute.

Zekk claqua des mains, ordonnant à son escadron de s'aligner.

— Les générateurs de répulsion vous soutiendront, dit-il. Mais utilisez la Force pour diriger votre descente. Nous devons frapper directement. Nos ennemis jurés nous attendent : les Chevaliers

Jedi de Luke Skywalker. L'avenir de la galaxie dépend de notre victoire.

Zekk regarda chacun des étudiants, essayant de leur insuffler sa détermination. C'étaient de vaillants guerriers, décidés à réussir.

Pourtant, le jeune homme n'avait pas réglé son propre conflit intérieur. Il savait que les doutes de Tamith Kai étaient fondés : il éprouvait encore une certaine sympathie nostalgique pour Jaina Solo et son frère Jacen.

Au plus profond des forêts de Kashyyyk, il avait conseillé à la jeune fille de rester loin de l'Académie Jedi. Il ne voulait pas qu'elle soit prise dans la bataille.

Il ne souhaitait pas sa mort.

Mais il était sûr que Jaina Solo, telle qu'il la connaissait et l'appréciait, ne resterait pas à l'abri en laissant mourir ses amis. Et il redoutait l'idée de la rencontrer de nouveau et d'avoir à se battre contre elle.

Zekk fut soulagé quand les portes de largage s'ouvrirent, l'arrachant à ses pensées. Une ligne étroite et brillante courut à leurs pieds, tel un sourire édenté. Puis la faille s'agrandit. Les arbres apparurent dans l'entrebâillement.

— Jedi Obscurs, cria Zekk par-dessus le gémissement du vent, le moment est venu ! En avant !

Conduisant l'assaut, il plongea dans le vide, puis activa son générateur de répulsion.

Il piquait sur l'Académie Jedi sans défense.

Derrière lui, les autres Impériaux se laissèrent

tomber de la plate-forme de bataille, rappelant des oiseaux de proie frappés en plein vol.

Avant d'atterrir, Zekk activa son sabrolaser et le tint devant lui comme une balise lumineuse. Il regarda vers le haut et vit ses hommes allumer leurs vibrolames, leurs capes volant derrière eux.

Une pluie de Jedi Obscurs s'abattit sur Yavin 4.

CHAPITRE VI

Le hurlement des moteurs ioniques déchira le silence de la grande salle d'audience. Les réflexes de Tenel Ka la firent réagir avant qu'elle reconnaisse le bruit. Elle courut à la meurtrière la plus proche, Jaina, Jacen et Lowbacca sur les talons. À travers la fente du bloc de pierre, elle vit des chasseurs Tie fondre sur l'Académie, mitraillant le sol sans interruption.

— Maître Skywalker, nous sommes attaqués ! s'écria-t-elle.

Luke Skywalker éleva la voix pour être entendu de chacun.

— Que tout le monde se cache dans la jungle et y reste jusqu'à la fin du raid. Battez-vous avec toutes vos capacités et tous vos talents. Souvenez-vous de votre formation... Et que la Force soit avec vous.

Une série d'explosions ponctua son ordre. Un craquement sonore retentit quand une bombe à protons frappa les niveaux inférieurs et creusa un cratère devant la pyramide.

Tenel Ka regarda les autres étudiants Jedi et estima que leur réaction aux ordres de maître Skywalker était bonne. Plusieurs avaient l'air surpris ; Tenel Ka capta des émotions conflictuelles : anticipation, nervosité, mal du pays, confiance en la Force, angoisse à l'idée qu'ils devraient tuer. Mais elle ne sentit ni confusion ni panique, et aucun refus d'affronter la situation.

Sans plus attendre, les étudiants quittèrent la grande salle. Luke Skywalker gagna la fenêtre où attendait le groupe de Tenel Ka. Il fit signe à Peckhum de se joindre à eux. Le vieil astronaute évita un nuage de poussière qui tombait du plafond.

Le maître Jedi lança une série d'instructions. Tenel Ka s'émerveilla de son calme apparent au milieu de la tourmente.

— Jacen, amène le *Chasseur d'Ombres* en orbite. Vois si tu peux traverser le brouillage et envoie un message à ta mère pour la prévenir que nous sommes attaqués. D2-R2 est dans le hangar, près du vaisseau. Tu n'auras pas besoin d'un autre copilote.

Jaina, qui adorait voler, était sur le point de protester quand Luke se tourna vers elle.

— J'ai besoin que tu traverses la rivière et que tu vérifies les générateurs de champ. Vois s'il y a moyen de réactiver nos boucliers. Lowie, toi et Tenel Ka...

Son comlink bipa, signalant un message urgent.

Plus proche que les précédentes, une autre explosion ébranla le Grand Temple. Dès que Luke eut allumé son comlink, les pépiements et les sifflements alarmés de D2-R2 en sortirent.

— Que dis-tu ? Calme-toi, cria Luke.

— Si vous me permettez, maître Skywalker, intervint DTM, j'ai pu faire l'analyse grammaticale du message de votre astrodroïd, et je suis capable de vous proposer une traduction. Je comprends couramment six formes différentes de communic...

— Merci, DTM, interrompit Luke. Cela nous serait fort utile.

— D2-R2 rapporte que... Oh, par le Grand Circuit ! L'avant du hangar a été touché ! L'entrée est bloquée par des débris. Aucun vaisseau ne peut sortir. Le *Chasseur d'Ombres* est prisonnier à l'intérieur.

— Par mon blaster ! dit Jacen après un instant de réflexion. Peckhum, qu'en est-il du *Bâton de Foudre* ? Il n'est pas dans le hangar, n'est-ce pas ?

Tenel Ka fronça les sourcils à l'idée que Jacen affronte les troupes impériales dans la vieille navette-cargo déglinguée.

— Le *Bâton de Foudre* n'a pas de blindage quantique, souligna Luke Skywalker.

— C'est trop dangereux, approuva Jaina.

— Nous sommes *tous* en danger ici ! s'écria

Jacen. Nous devons absolument transmettre ce message !

— Nous pouvons y arriver, dit le vieux Peckhum. J'ai appris quelques manœuvres militaires en mon temps... Assez pour nous amener en orbite sans que nous soyons pulvérisés, je crois.

Lowbacca poussa un glapissement et montra l'étroite fenêtre. Au-dessus de la jungle planait une plate-forme tactique hérissée d'armes. C'était une sorte de radeau spatial transportant les troupes ennemies.

Tenel Ka capta une présence hélas familière.

— Tamith Kai est à bord, je le sens, murmura-t-elle.

— Elle doit diriger l'infanterie depuis cette plate-forme, dit Luke.

— Alors, nous devons la mettre hors de combat, répondit Tenel Ka sans hésiter. Je me porte volontaire. La Sœur de la Nuit est mon affaire.

Lowbacca grogna un commentaire.

— Maître Lowbacca souhaite faire remarquer que son T-23 est toujours dehors, à l'orée du terrain d'atterrissage. Maîtresse Tenel Ka et lui pourraient atteindre la plate-forme en quelques minutes.

Luke fit un signe de tête approbateur.

— Nous avons tous une mission à accomplir. Je vais inspecter la pyramide pour m'assurer que personne n'y est resté. Je vous retrouverai aux points de rendez-vous, dans la jungle.

Tandis que les jeunes Chevaliers Jedi se précipitaient hors du temple, l'esprit de Tenel Ka se projetait déjà sur la confrontation à venir. L'adrénaline coulait à flots dans ses veines. Elle avait été élevée et entraînée pour la bataille.

Même si lutter avec un seul bras allait sans doute lui poser des problèmes, elle n'était ni anxieuse ni trop sûre d'elle, mais tout simplement *prête*. Un Jedi se devait toujours de l'être, elle le savait. Maître Skywalker et Tionne les avaient formés en ce sens. Tenel Ka avait son sabrolaser et la Force. En combinant les deux, elle était sûre de pouvoir vaincre n'importe quel ennemi.

Quand ils arrivèrent sur le terrain d'atterrissage, Jaina s'était déjà séparée du groupe, fonçant vers la rivière et les générateurs de bouclier. Tenel Ka fut étonnée de constater que le vieux Peckhum ne s'était pas laissé distancer lors du sprint vers la navette-cargo fatiguée.

Plongeant pour éviter les tirs de laser des chasseurs Tie, qui piquaient au-dessus d'eux, Tenel Ka et Lowbacca montèrent à bord du skyhopper, tandis que Jacen et Peckhum embarquaient dans le *Bâton de Foudre*.

Regardant Jacen gravir la rampe du *Bâton de Foudre*, Tenel Ka sentit un malaise qu'elle ne parvint pas à s'expliquer. Au même instant, Jacen ressortit la tête et la regarda d'un air grave.

— Je te raconterai une blague quand nous serons de retour. Une bonne, cette fois.

Il disparut à l'intérieur du vaisseau.

Quand Lowie activa les moteurs à répulsion du

T-23, Tenel Ka répondit, même si elle savait que Jacen ne risquait pas de l'entendre :

— Oui, Jacen, je serai heureuse de t'entendre raconter une blague. Dès que nous serons *tous* revenus.

CHAPITRE VII

Les moteurs du *Bâton de Foudre* gémirent quand l'appareil lutta contre la pesanteur. Aussitôt qu'ils eurent décollé, le vaisseau vibra violemment. Des alarmes se déclenchèrent dans la tête de Jacen.

— Nous avons été touchés ! cria-t-il sans prendre la peine de vérifier les écrans.

— Non, dit Peckhum d'une voix traînante. Le *Bâton de Foudre* fait ça depuis que j'ai connecté le couplage d'alimentation aux moteurs à répulsion arrière. Je suppose que je ferais mieux de vérifier mon branchement, un de ces jours.

L'information n'eut pas grand-chose pour rassurer Jacen.

— Euh... Jaina pourra peut-être vous aider, suggéra-t-il.

Un rayon d'énergie manqua de peu le vaisseau quand il croisa la route d'un chasseur Tie.

— Celui-ci n'est pas passé loin ! dit Jacen.

— Trop près à mon goût, fit Peckhum. Accroche-toi, jeune Solo, je vais essayer quelques-unes de mes manœuvres...

Lowie se concentra pour amener le T-23 à couvert. Du coin de l'œil, il vit les autres étudiants Jedi éviter le feu des chasseurs Tie et se précipiter vers la sécurité relative de la forêt.

Le jeune Wookie fit monter abruptement son skyhopper.

La frondaison avait toujours été synonyme d'abri pour Lowie ; il aurait aimé passer un moment de recueillement au sommet des arbres. Mais cette fois, ce n'était pas ce qui les attendait, Tenel Ka et lui...

Lowie serra fermement les commandes de son appareil et le fit zigzaguer au-dessus de la forêt, essayant de décourager leurs éventuels poursuivants. Aujourd'hui, les problèmes tombaient littéralement du ciel ; Lowie ne pouvait pas s'enfuir vers les hauteurs pour leur échapper. Sa meilleure chance était de rester près des arbres.

Un rayon laser passa près du T-23, soulevant un nuage de poussière et d'herbe brûlée.

— Que la Force te guide, Lowbacca, dit Tenel Ka, assise dans le siège du passager.

Lowie grommela et inspira à fond pour se calmer. Il laissa la Force diriger le vaisseau. Ils filèrent vers la rivière verdâtre au-dessus de laquelle ils avaient aperçu la plate-forme de bataille de la

Sœur de la Nuit. Même à cinq cents mètres de distance, ils voyaient des rayons laser jaillir du vaisseau blindé, carbonisant les arbres sur les berges du cours d'eau.

Tenel Ka poussa un cri de surprise.

— Regarde ! Ici !

Des silhouettes tombaient du ciel, tels des rapaces fondant sur leur proie. Les Jedi Obscurs descendaient en formation dispersée, leurs sabro-lasers brillant de mille feux tandis qu'ils contrôlaient leur chute avec des générateurs de répulsion.

Une alarme résonna au moment où Lowbacca détourna le regard pour observer ses ennemis. Une salve de canon laser venant d'un chasseur Tie les toucha. Un jet de fumée et d'étincelles sortit des moteurs du skyhopper. Le petit vaisseau vibra. Avec un bruit de métal arraché, un des ailerons se détacha.

— Par mes circuits ! Je ne peux pas supporter de voir ça ! couina DTM.

Lowie se battit avec les commandes pour garder le vaisseau en vol. Dirigée par la Force, une de ses mains aux griffes acérées se déplaçait à une vitesse incroyable sur le panneau de commande, tandis que l'autre guidait leur descente. La fumée envahit le cockpit ; le skyhopper crachota et toute sa carcasse trembla. Lowie coupa les moteurs principaux et laissa le petit vaisseau retomber vers le sommet des arbres. Pour amortir leur chute, il utilisa ce qui restait de puissance dans les moteurs à répulsion. Il espérait que cela suffirait.

Le T-23 s'écrasa sur les arbres géants.

Chaque inspiration déversait un torrent de feu dans les poumons de Tenel Ka. Près d'elle, le Wookie gémit, mais elle ne parvint pas à comprendre ce qu'il disait.

De plus, elle n'y voyait rien.

— Maîtresse Tenel Ka ! cria une voix électronique affolée. Maître Lowbacca réclame votre aide de toute urgence pour retirer la verrière du T-23 !

Tenel Ka essaya de regarder autour d'elle. Elle ne vit que des taches lumineuses, qui lui faisaient mal aux yeux. Et elle baissa les paupières.

Une voix assez puissante pour sortir un Maître Jedi d'une transe de guérison résonna de nouveau aux oreilles de Tenel Ka.

— Oh, que mon misérable processeur soit maudit ! C'est trop tard, elle est morte !

Lowbacca beugla de désespoir. Au même moment, quelque chose secoua violemment Tenel Ka.

— Non, croassa la jeune guerrière. Je suis vivante.

Lowbacca émit quelques aboiements décidés. Tenel Ka obéit à ses instructions avant que DTM en ait fourni la traduction.

— Maître Lowbacca vous demande de pousser la verrière, tout en faisant porter votre poids à bâbord. À gauche, donc.

Tenel Ka savait ce que voulait dire « bâbord ». En dépit de l'épais nuage de fumée montant des moteurs, elle se calma suffisamment pour laisser la Force couler en elle.

Même avec les yeux fermés, elle sut que DTM avait allumé ses détecteurs optiques aux rayons jaunes éblouissants.

— Il semblerait, continua le petit droïd, que la verrière du T-23 est coincée par une branche. Oh, nous sommes perdus !

À l'instant ou le traducteur miniature achevait ses lamentations, la verrière s'ouvrit. De l'air frais inonda le cockpit. Tenel Ka et Lowbacca débouclèrent leurs harnais de sécurité et sortirent de l'épave. Tandis qu'ils s'éloignaient de l'appareil, Tenel Ka porta la main à son sabrolaser pour s'assurer qu'elle ne l'avait pas perdu.

Il était toujours là.

— Oh, par mes circuits, gémit DTM. Maintenant, nous allons nous perdre dans la jungle et être capturés par des Woolamandres. Faites attention, maître Lowbacca ! Je n'ai aucune envie de revivre cette déplorable expérience.

En équilibre sur une branche, Lowbacca se tourna, regarda une dernière fois son T-23 démoli, et émit une note lugubre. Tenel Ka sentit que sa détresse n'avait pas pour cause les dangers de la jungle, mais la perte de son T-23. La jeune guerrière comprenait ce sentiment. Elle tendit la main et effleura le bras velu du Wookie, laissant la Force le réconforter. Puis ils partirent vers leurs objectifs : la plate-forme de bataille et la Sœur de la Nuit.

Au soulagement mêlé de surprise de Tenel Ka, Lowie était parvenu à poser l'appareil en catastrophe à moins de deux cents mètres de l'endroit où la plate-forme planait au-dessus des arbres Massassi. Avant qu'elle ouvre la bouche, son ami lâcha un bref aboiement d'avertissement et désigna le couvert des branches.

Tenel Ka comprit aussitôt et descendit dans l'enchevêtrement de feuilles pour s'y cacher. S'ils distinguaient la plate-forme, eux aussi étaient exposés aux regards de l'ennemi. Ils devraient avancer vers le vaisseau blindé en passant sous les arbres, comme des plongeurs dans l'océan.

N'ayant qu'un bras pour l'aider à garder son équilibre et à progresser, Tenel Ka devait se fier à la Force pour placer correctement ses pieds. Elle accepta de bon gré l'aide de Lowbacca pour négocier des branches plus étroites ou des passages dangereux.

Tenel Ka ne comprit pas pourquoi elle se sentit obligée de parler. Peut-être était-ce à cause de la tristesse de son ami Wookie.

— Nous aurons l'occasion de passer plusieurs jours ensemble à réparer ton T-23, Lowbacca. Quand la bataille sera terminée...

Le Wookie s'arrêta, la dévisagea d'un air intrigué, puis émit une sorte de rire.

DTM traduisit :

— Maître Lowbacca suppose que maître Jacen sera ravi d'avoir sous la main des... victimes à qui raconter ses plaisanteries...

À cette idée, Tenel Ka sentit son moral remonter. Ils avancèrent plus rapidement. L'esprit de la

jeune guerrière se concentra sur un seul but :
vaincre le Second Imperium.

Elle sentit un frisson courir le long de son
échine.

— Stop ! cria-t-elle.

Un chasseur Tie plongeait vers la mer de
feuilles, la faisant trembler sur son passage tandis
qu'il inspectait la carcasse du skyhopper. Lowbacca gronda ; Tenel Ka lui saisit le bras pour
l'empêcher de commettre une imprudence. Le
vaisseau impérial tourna autour de l'épave, comme
s'il cherchait des survivants. La guerrière espéra
que le pilote ne prendrait pas la peine de tirer sur
le petit vaisseau, le transformant en un tas de
débris fondus et fumants. Heureusement, après
avoir fait de nouveau le tour de l'épave, le pilote
remonta dans les cieux à la recherche d'une proie
plus intéressante.

Lowbacca et son amie se hâtèrent de traverser
les branches pour rejoindre leur cible.

— À moins que mes détecteurs ne soient totalement déréglés par le choc, dit DTM, nous
devrions nous trouver juste sous l'avant de la
plate-forme.

Lowbacca fit un geste de la main pour demander à Tenel Ka d'attendre. Puis il monta quelques
branches plus haut et vérifia leur position. Quand
elle entendit un bref aboiement de triomphe, Tenel
Ka le suivit et passa la tête au milieu des feuilles.
Dix mètres au-dessus du sommet des arbres, ils
découvrirent l'immense plate-forme. Immobile,

massive, elle était effrayante, blindée et hérissée d'armes.

— Il ne devrait pas être très difficile de la détruire, dit Tenel Ka.

Ils entendaient les ordres lancés aux troupes et le martèlement des bottes des commandos. Lowie pointa un index vers le haut et haussa les épaules, comme pour demander : « Et maintenant ? » La plate-forme était trop loin pour qu'ils puissent sauter, et ils n'avaient pas de générateurs de répulsion. Tenel Ka saisit sa corde et son grappin.

— Il nous faudra grimper, dit-elle.

Le navire ennemi était très haut, mais le grappin s'accrocha entre deux plaques de blindage dès le second lancer. La guerrière testa la corde de fibres en tirant dessus. Puis elle enroula ses jambes et son bras autour de la corde et entreprit de grimper, utilisant la Force pour léviter quand son unique bras ne lui fournissait pas un soutien suffisant.

À bord de la plate-forme, des commandos Impériaux, une batterie d'armes puissantes et la maléfique Sœur de la Nuit de Dathomir les attendaient.

Tenel Ka déglutit avec peine. Même si la Force était avec eux, les lois de la probabilité risquaient fort de pencher du côté ennemi.

CHAPITRE VIII

La rivière brun-vert qui coulait lentement à travers la forêt primitive était large, puissante, mais calme. L'onde ne montrait pas le plus petit signe d'agitation, car elle n'était pas affectée par la lutte titanesque qui opposait les forces du Bien à celles du Mal.

La rivière abritait de nombreuses formes de vie : du plancton invisible, des protozoaires carnivores, des plantes aquatiques, des arbres dont les racines plongeaient dans le courant, des prédateurs camouflés qui prenaient l'apparence de fleurs inoffensives...

Quand les tirs de blaster résonnèrent et que le bourdonnement des sabrolasers se fit entendre, d'autres créatures se faufilèrent entre les branches épaisses qui surplombaient la rivière : des prédateurs à deux pattes, habitués à utiliser la Force.

Des museaux reptiliens émergèrent de l'eau boueuse. Leurs fentes respiratoires se dilatèrent pour aspirer de l'oxygène. Les trois créatures écailleuses avancèrent si lentement que seules des ondulations, à la surface, signalèrent leur passage. Elles prirent position dans le fond boueux, à l'affût, tout près du chemin qui longeait la berge.

Leurs ennemis arriveraient bientôt.

Avançant furtivement, mais à l'évidence forts d'une grande confiance en eux, trois étudiants Jedi Obscurs se frayaient un chemin dans le sous-bois. Ils taillèrent les branches et les lianes avec leurs sabrolasers, atteignirent la berge et s'arrêtèrent pour se concerter.

— Les élèves de Skywalker sont des lâches, dit l'un d'eux. Pourquoi ne sortent-ils pas pour nous affronter ? Ils se cachent dans la jungle comme des rongeurs terrifiés.

— Comment n'auraient-ils pas peur de nous ? répondit un autre étudiant. Ils connaissent la puissance du Côté Obscur.

Après s'être consultés — de simples bulles d'air représentant leur moyen de communication — les disciples reptiliens de Luke Skywalker, des Cha'a, sortirent de la rivière, éclaboussant d'écume les trois élèves de Brakiss. Ils utilisèrent la Force pour créer une colonne d'eau bouillante et la projeter sur leurs ennemis. Le geyser se dressa comme un serpent avant de s'abattre sur les Jedi Obscurs, dont les sabrolasers crépitèrent et fumèrent.

Les trois Cha'a sifflèrent de rire.

Les Jedi crachaient et se débattaient, essayant d'appeler le Côté Obscur de la Force à leur secours.

À ce moment, un trio d'aviens emplumés quitta son perchoir et se laissa tomber sur eux, les assommant pour le compte. Les aviens pépièrent et criaillèrent, triomphants, tandis que les Cha'a sortaient de la boue et avançaient vers les trois captifs.

Les étudiants non humanoïdes de Skywalker coupèrent dans le sous-bois des lianes fines comme des fouets et attachèrent les bras et les jambes de leurs prisonniers. Un Cha'a ramassa les sabrolasers, puis étudia leur conception quelconque et leur finition bâclée. Il jeta ces armes médiocres dans la rivière, où elles sombrèrent sans laisser de trace.

Les aviens se penchèrent sur les captifs inconscients et sondèrent leurs esprits. Avec la Force, ils leur suggérèrent mentalement de dormir longtemps, très longtemps...

Tionne rejeta derrière elle sa chevelure d'argent. Elle avait besoin d'y voir clair, sans rien pour la distraire.

Elle regarda les étudiants Jedi de ses yeux couleur de nacre. Maître Skywalker lui avait confié la formation de ses élèves. Tionne devait maintenant livrer bataille. L'Académie avait souvent été la cible des forces du Mal, mais les Chevaliers Jedi l'avaient toujours emporté. Elle ne doutait pas qu'ils seraient de nouveau victorieux.

Ses étudiants et elle se tenaient autour de la dalle de marbre plate et des colonnes brisées qui avaient autrefois été un temple Massassi, avant que la jungle l'avale. C'était l'endroit qu'ils avaient choisi pour affronter l'ennemi.

— Êtes-vous prêts ? demanda Tionne. Souvenez-vous de ce que vous avez appris. *Nous ne pouvons pas nous contenter d'essayer.* Nous devons réussir à vaincre les suppôts du Côté Obscur.

Quand ses étudiants eurent crié leur accord, ils la regardèrent avec confiance. Une des jeunes femmes fit un signe à Tionne, prit une profonde inspiration et s'enfonça dans la forêt pour aller à la rencontre des forces d'invasion. Un instant plus tard, elle poussa un cri de défi en apercevant des étudiants de l'Académie de l'Ombre.

Tionne entendit un sabrolaser crépiter, des branches tomber... Puis des bruits de pas lui apprirent que l'ennemi fonçait vers le piège qu'ils avaient préparé. Tionne fit signe aux autres étudiants de se tenir prêts.

— Reviens par là, vermine Jedi ! cria un des Impériaux, caché par les bosquets.

Quatre Jedi Obscurs émergèrent de la jungle, déboulant dans la clairière où l'étudiante, haletante, s'était réfugiée de l'autre côté d'une grande dalle de marbre.

L'élève de Tionne avait l'air découragée.

Les envahisseurs avancèrent vers elle.

— Nous allons t'écraser ! rugit l'un d'eux.

— À l'attaque ! cria Tionne.

De leurs cachettes, dans les branches, quatre de ses étudiants invoquèrent la Force. Avec une puissance irrésistible, ils arrachèrent les sabrolasers des mains de leurs ennemis. Les Jedi Obscurs crièrent de surprise et d'inquiétude. Alors Tionne et ses étudiants sortirent des fourrés et les encerclèrent.

— Nous n'avons pas besoin de nos sabrolasers pour vous vaincre ! Nous pouvons vous réduire en bouillie avec le seul pouvoir de notre esprit, et de la Force Obscure ! cracha un de leurs adversaires, trop sûr de lui.

Les quatre Impériaux se mirent dos à dos, et levèrent les mains.

— À votre place, je ne ferais pas ça, dit Tionne, avec un léger sourire. Si notre concentration fléchit, cela se soldera par une défaite *écrasante* pour vous.

Elle regarda vers le haut. Ses quatre étudiants restèrent immobiles, les yeux fermés, tout à leur tâche.

Les Jedi Obscurs suivirent son regard et s'aperçurent que la dalle de marbre, qu'ils avaient prise pour le plafond écroulé du temple en ruine, flottait dans l'air sans soutien. Le rectangle de plusieurs tonnes était en équilibre au-dessus de leurs têtes, maintenu par la Force.

Les étudiants de Tionne ne se déconcentrèrent pas.

Les Jedi Obscurs déglutirent nerveusement.

— Vous pouvez tenter de fuir, si vous le souhaitez, dit Tionne. Vous avez peut-être assez de pouvoir pour nous vaincre tout en retenant la pierre. Prenez votre décision. (Elle haussa les épaules.) Moi, je ne m'y risquerais pas.

Les Jedi Obscurs échangèrent des regards déconcertés. Puis ils baissèrent les bras et se rendirent.

Tionne poussa un soupir de soulagement discret, mais venu du fond du cœur.

La forêt comptait un arbre de plus, de petite taille mais au tronc épais. Ses branches étaient disposées de telle façon qu'il avait une apparence presque humanoïde : il s'agissait d'une des élèves de maître Skywalker, une créature végétale aux mouvements lents et à l'espérance de vie fort longue.

Elle partait souvent passer des jours entiers au soleil, utilisant la photosynthèse pour *métaboliser* les minéraux, l'eau et le gaz carbonique.

Elle pouvait rester ainsi plusieurs jours dans un état contemplatif, méditant sur la Force et sur sa propre place dans l'univers. Les arbres n'accomplissaient guère d'actes auxquels ils n'avaient pas longuement réfléchi. Pourtant, à des moments comme celui-ci, elle avait la possibilité de bouger assez rapidement.

La créature était devenue étudiante pour mieux comprendre la Force et défendre le Côté Lumineux. Et voilà qu'elle se trouvait au milieu d'une bataille rangée contre l'Académie de l'Ombre !

Les ennemis fouillaient la jungle, cherchant des victimes. Mais maître Skywalker avait bien formé ses étudiants. Ils ne se laisseraient pas détruire sans combattre.

La Jedi végétale resta immobile, surveillant la jungle. Elle savait que ses ennemis viendraient à elle. Il lui suffisait d'attendre. Ses racines plongèrent plus profondément dans le sol pour aspirer toute l'énergie qu'elles pouvaient. Elle sentit la sève pulser en elle, lui donnant la rapidité dont elle aurait besoin pour l'acte qu'elle allait être obligée d'accomplir une seule fois... Du moins l'espérait-elle.

Elle avait bien choisi son emplacement, à côté d'un arbre Massassi immense mais malade, dont les branches se courbaient vers le sol. Le tronc était couvert de champignons parasites qui avaient enfoncé leurs racines dans le bois et commençaient à le ronger de l'intérieur.

La Jedi sentait que l'arbre existait depuis des centaines d'années. C'était le cycle de la forêt. Quand les plantes poussaient, elles portaient des graines pour se reproduire, puis elles se transformaient lentement en une matière organique qui servirait à fertiliser les nouvelles générations. L'étudiante observa la façon dont penchait l'arbre Massassi, la jungle environnante...

Silencieuse, elle attendit.

Elle envoya une sonde de Force si discrète que même les adeptes du Côté Obscur ne comprendraient pas qu'elle les manipulait. *Venez par là,*

répéta-t-elle mentalement. Un Impérial ne man-
querait pas de succomber à cette injonction. Il
penserait avoir localisé un ennemi.

Ce qui, en un sens, ne serait pas faux.

Après une période indéterminée (car la Jedi ne
mesurait pas le temps par petits incréments), elle
sentit une perturbation dans la Force. Deux élèves
de l'Académie de l'Ombre déboulèrent dans la
forêt, méprisants comme si ce délicat écosystème
n'était qu'une nuisance dont ils se débarrasse-
raient volontiers à l'occasion.

La Jedi attendit. Elle devait se concentrer, agir
au moment voulu sans se perdre en réflexions
inutiles.

Dans une de ses branches noueuses semblable à
une main, elle tenait un sabrolaser dont la forme
avait été étudiée pour s'adapter à ses membres de
bois.

Les deux Jedi Obscurs débouchèrent dans la
clairière et s'arrêtèrent.

— Je ne vois rien ici, dit le plus grand. Le seigneur Brakiss aurait honte de toi. Et Zekk te
confisquerait ton sabrolaser. Tu gaspilles les pouvoirs du Côté Obscur par bêtise !

— Je te dis que je l'ai senti, s'obstina le
second.

Il fit un pas, regarda d'un côté et de l'autre, étudia la jungle. Son compagnon ricana.

À ce moment, la Jedi utilisa ses réserves de
puissance et passa à l'action. Elle activa son sabrolaser et frappa.

— Je suis désolée, grand-père, dit-elle.

La lame de son sabrolaser traversa le tronc du vieil arbre Massassi, le séparant de sa base. La gravité dicta sa loi au géant déchu. Son sommet s'inclina et il s'écrasa sur les deux intrus.

Ils eurent à peine le temps de pousser un cri de surprise quand une avalanche de branches et de lianes les recouvrit.

La Jedi désactiva son sabrolaser. Son corps de bois fut agité de convulsions. En un seul geste, elle avait épuisé des mois, sinon des années de réserves d'énergie. Elle dressa ses branches vers le soleil et enfonça plus profondément ses racines dans le sol.

Il lui faudrait beaucoup de temps pour se remettre de cette journée...

CHAPITRE IX

Après avoir traversé la rivière, Jaina se fraya un chemin dans la jungle. Elle cherchait un sentier praticable dans le sous-bois. En ce moment, la forêt était son alliée. La protection qu'elle lui offrait était appréciable.

Jaina n'avait pas peur de combattre les Jedi Obscurs, mais elle devait accomplir une mission vitale qui convenait mieux à ses capacités.

Si le générateur se trouvait endommagé, les boucliers d'énergie n'étant pas opérationnels, toute la région deviendrait vulnérable aux attaques aériennes. Les étudiants de Luke Skywalker se défendaient bien... Si Jaina parvenait à réactiver le champ protecteur, ils pourraient s'occuper des ennemis un par un, sans craindre d'être pris à revers.

Jaina arriva dans la clairière où son père et

Chewbacca avaient installé le générateur. D'un coup d'œil, elle comprit que le système était fichu quel que soit son talent pour ce type de remise en état.

Elle pouvait réparer presque n'importe quoi. Mais dans ce cas, c'était impossible. Un saboteur s'était servi d'un détonateur thermique pour faire sauter la station. Il n'y avait plus rien à sauver car il ne *restait* plus rien.

L'attention de Jaina se détourna bientôt des ruines du générateur. Elle retint son souffle.

Dans la clairière, devant elle, il y avait un chasseur Tie en parfait état.

Depuis que Chewbacca avait offert à Lowie un skyhopper T-23, Jaina avait envie de posséder un vaisseau. C'était pour ça qu'elle avait tenté de réparer le chasseur Tie qui s'était écrasé dans la jungle de Yavin 4 — celui de Qorl.

Elle s'arrêta et regarda l'engin avec un mélange d'appréhension et d'enthousiasme. À part les sons étouffés de lointaines batailles, elle n'entendait rien.

Jaina sortit son sabrolaser et l'activa. Le rayon d'énergie jaillit, brillant d'une lueur violette électrique. La Jedi se glissa furtivement vers l'appareil, prête au combat si le pilote sortait, armé de son blaster. Mais elle ne vit personne alentour, et n'entendit aucun bruit en provenance du vaisseau.

— Hello ? Vous feriez mieux de vous rendre si vous êtes un Impérial ! (Elle se figea.) Il y a quelqu'un ?

Seuls les bruits de la jungle lui répondirent.

Poussée par le désir de s'approprier l'appareil, elle courut vers le chasseur Tie.

C'était un vaisseau sinistre : un cockpit rond suspendu entre deux unités d'alimentation plates de forme hexagonale, des moteurs ioniques et une batterie de canons laser.

Les idées et les plans se bousculèrent dans la tête de Jaina. Si elle pouvait piloter le vaisseau dans les rangs ennemis, elle passerait inaperçue. Les Impériaux découvriraient qui elle était seulement quand il serait trop tard.

Jaina désactiva son sabrolaser puis ouvrit le cockpit de l'appareil et embarqua. Elle avait étudié le fonctionnement des chasseurs Tie quand elle s'était occupée du vaisseau de Qorl. La jeune fille connaissait les touches du panneau de commande, et elle savait quels systèmes activer. Bien que le vieux pilote se soit enfui sans que Jaina ait eu l'occasion de piloter l'engin, elle était sûre qu'elle pouvait s'en sortir.

Elle s'installa dans le siège du pilote, nota l'odeur de lubrifiant rance, et poussa du pied les détritus divers que l'Empire ne se souciait pas de nettoyer. Un masque de respiration était suspendu à la petite console des systèmes environnementaux. Les cloisons mobiles du cockpit se refermèrent autour d'elle comme une coquille protectrice, lui laissant peu de liberté de mouvement, mais toutes les commandes à portée de main.

Jaina trouva le commutateur général et le bascula. Elle sentit les moteurs frémir, les systèmes se préparer, les batteries se charger. Tous les voyants du panneau clignotèrent. Elle inspira à fond, boucla le harnais de sécurité et saisit les commandes.

— Systèmes prêts au décollage, murmura-t-elle.

Elle regarda le ciel, cherchant d'autres Impériaux.

— Très bien, les gars, préparez-vous à avoir de la compagnie !

Le vaisseau impérial s'éleva dans les airs. Il dépassa vite le sommet des arbres. La jeune fille était ravie de voler.

Le chasseur se révéla incroyablement silencieux. Jaina se rendit compte que les moteurs principaux avaient été désactivés. Le chasseur volait avec autant de discrétion parce qu'il utilisait ses moteurs secondaires, beaucoup moins bruyants. C'était donc ainsi que le pilote était passé sous leur bouclier défensif !

Les systèmes d'origine étaient sans doute intacts, mais désactivés. De cette façon, le vaisseau ennemi s'était glissé dans l'atmosphère sans émettre le bruit familier — et assourdissant — des moteurs ioniques.

Super, pensa Jaina. Elle pouvait être silencieuse et dangereuse en même temps. Frôlant les arbres, elle étudia les environs pour repérer ses cibles. Elle accéléra, toute au plaisir du vol, tandis que le paysage défilait sous elle.

Droit devant, elle aperçut six chasseurs Tie en formation, qui tiraient sur la cime de la forêt et pilonnaient les temples, même ceux qui n'avaient jamais été utilisés par l'Académie Jedi. Le palais des Woolamandres, dont il ne restait déjà presque plus rien, fut rasé par des rayons laser. Pourtant, Jaina ne pensait pas que les Jedi y aient jamais mis les pieds.

Elle resta sur les fréquences de communication impériales, afin de pouvoir intercepter les commentaires échangés d'une voix rude par les pilotes. Ils discutaient de leurs plans, choisissaient leurs cibles, tiraient sur des silhouettes mobiles à demi dissimulées par les arbres Massassi...

Jaina laissa son micro débranché quand elle se joignit par l'arrière à la formation de chasseurs. Elle entendit quelqu'un saluer son arrivée sur la fréquence tactique. Plutôt que d'éveiller les soupçons avec la voix d'une jeune fille, elle tapota son microphone pour signifier qu'elle avait entendu.

Puis elle mit ses canons laser en batterie.

Un des pilotes déclara :

— Nous avons autant de cibles que nous voulons. Rasons-les !

Jaina se mordit la lèvre inférieure.

— Oui, marmonna-t-elle. Rasons-les !

Elle ferma à demi les yeux, et sentit la Force couler à travers elle. En dépit des détecteurs et des systèmes sophistiqués du chasseur Tie, rien ne remplaçait les perceptions Jedi pour déterminer ses mouvements. Elle devait viser et tirer, puis viser de nouveau, à la vitesse de l'éclair. Elle n'aurait qu'une seule chance.

Jaina saisit les commandes d'artillerie et se concentra sur le mécanisme de visée. Elle suivait toujours les Impériaux, qui ne se doutaient de rien. Il fallait les mettre hors de combat en utilisant un seul coup pour chacun. Elle ne pouvait pas tirer plusieurs fois sur la même cible, car elle soupçonnait que ses ennemis ne seraient pas ravis de son attaque... Pas question de leur laisser la possibilité de répliquer.

Jaina visa les endroits les plus vulnérables : les moteurs, et les joints qui reliaient les unités d'alimentation au corps de l'appareil. Si les chasseurs Tie se présentaient de profil, elle n'aurait aucun mal à faire sauter les ailes hexagonales, des cibles impossibles à rater.

Elle commença un compte à rebours silencieux. Puis elle pointa ses lasers sur le vaisseau le plus proche. *Qu'est-ce que j'attends ?* se demanda-t-elle.

Serrant les dents, elle tira, puis fit pivoter l'affût du canon laser, visant un autre chasseur Tie. Avant que son deuxième rayon d'énergie frappe le joint situé près du cockpit et détruise les unités d'alimentation, le premier Tie donna de la bande et tomba en tourbillonnant.

Jaina tira sur les moteurs arrière du deuxième vaisseau. Le chasseur explosa, l'aveuglant momentanément, mais elle détourna vivement les yeux. Quand elle eut une troisième cible dans la ligne de mire de ses canons, elle entendit les pilotes hurler de panique et de rage.

La formation commença à se séparer.

Elle n'avait pas beaucoup de temps devant elle.

Le troisième Impérial lui fit face. Jaina le mitrailla, frappant la verrière du cockpit. Le vaisseau tomba. Mais les trois autres avaient fait demi-tour et se dirigeaient vers elle.

Jaina cligna des yeux quand des salves de canon laser passèrent près de son appareil. Elle modifia la trajectoire de son chasseur. Utilisant la Force pour prévoir la direction des coups, comme le lui avait enseigné son oncle Luke, elle vira sur l'aile, puis essaya de s'éloigner à la vitesse maximale de son appareil.

Les trois Impériaux fondirent sur elle, la mitraillant sans relâche. Ils ignoraient leurs autres cibles maintenant qu'ils en avaient une de choix : un traître au sein de leur escadrille.

Jaina piqua pour éviter les coups. Elle ne prenait plus de plaisir à voler, car son attaque impulsive tournait au désastre.

Elle fila au-dessus de la jungle, les trois chasseurs Tie à ses trousses.

CHAPITRE X

La forêt ombragée, près du Grand Temple, était familière à Luke Skywalker. Au cœur de la bataille entre le Bien et le Mal, il trouvait apaisante l'ambiance de la jungle. Elle débordait de vie, glorifiant la Force qui lie tous les êtres.

Après s'être assuré que son sabrolaser était toujours attaché à sa ceinture, Luke invoqua la Force. Il la sentit couler dans son corps, puis s'en servit pour visualiser les escarmouches, tout autour de lui.

Ouvert aux émotions de ses étudiants, Luke envoya des pensées rassurantes à un jeune homme qui perdait confiance en ses capacités ; il prévint un autre élève d'une attaque imprévue, puis encouragea un troisième qui commençait à se fatiguer.

Un rayon laser provenant d'un chasseur Tie

jaillit à travers la forêt, et mit le feu au sous-bois. Luke fut obligé de battre en retraite derrière un fourré pour échapper à la fumée.

Il chercha mentalement le cœur de la bataille, l'endroit où il pourrait être le plus utile. Des dizaines d'années plus tôt, quand l'Étoile Noire était apparue au-dessus de Yavin 4, la mission de Luke avait été claire. Les super-lasers de l'immense station pouvaient désintégrer une planète. Il n'avait pas douté un instant que sa priorité était de détruire l'arme la plus puissante de l'Empire. Guidé par la Force, il avait réussi.

Mais la bataille d'aujourd'hui était différente. Elle n'avait pas de point central. Pas de super-arme à détruire. Les communications à longue distance de l'Académie Jedi avaient été brouillées, les boucliers défensifs sabotés. D2-R2 et le *Chasseur d'Ombres* étant bloqués dans le hangar, sous le Grand Temple, Luke n'avait aucun moyen d'aller affronter directement l'Académie de l'Ombre.

L'assaut était dirigé depuis la plate-forme géante qui planait au-dessus de la forêt, mais Luke devinait que cet aspect militaire de l'attaque était seulement une diversion.

Les chasseurs Tie avaient effectué une série de raids contre le Grand Temple. Pourtant, des fantassins et des Jedi Obscurs avaient été envoyés pour se battre en combat singulier contre les étudiants de Luke. Avec une stratégie différente, la victoire de l'Académie de l'Ombre aurait été bien plus aisée. Il semblait que Brakiss avait *choisi* la façon la plus difficile de combattre...

Luke était sûr que c'était bien ainsi que son ancien élève avait planifié les choses.

Son comlink bipa. Les étudiants de Yavin 4 portaient rarement des comlinks, mais le Maître Jedi en gardait toujours en cas de problèmes, afin de pouvoir être joint facilement. Même si l'Académie de l'Ombre avait brouillé les fréquences de transmission à longue distance, les signaux locaux de D2-R2 passaient toujours.

Luke activa l'appareil.

— Du calme, D2. Nous irons te récupérer dès que la bataille sera terminée.

Avant qu'il puisse ajouter autre chose, une voix d'homme sortit du petit haut-parleur.

— ... message pour Luke Skywalker. Je répète : message pour Luke Skywalker. Si quelqu'un m'entend, veuillez répondre immédiatement.

Luke regarda le petit appareil, puis il demanda :

— Qui est-ce ?

Avant d'entendre la réponse, ses sens de Jedi lui révélèrent l'identité de son correspondant.

— Vous pouvez m'appeler *maître* Brakiss, fit la voix. Dites à votre professeur que je transmets sur toutes les fréquences. Je ne doute pas qu'il souhaite me parler.

— Je suis Luke Skywalker. Si vous avez un message pour moi, Brakiss, vous pouvez me le communiquer directement.

Le cœur de Luke cognait dans sa poitrine, plus de surprise que de peur.

Un rire retentit dans le comlink.

— Mon très cher ancien professeur... L'homme que j'ai autrefois appelé *maître*. Je suis *ravi* de vous entendre.

— Que voulez-vous, Brakiss ? demanda Luke.

— Vous rencontrer. Face à face, sur un terrain neutre. En égaux. Nous n'avons pas eu l'occasion de terminer notre précédente... conversation, quand vous êtes venu dans mon Académie sauver vos Jedi.

Luke réfléchit un instant. Rencontrer Brakiss ? Peut-être était-ce la solution du problème qu'il avait essayé de résoudre. Après tout, qui d'autre était plus essentiel à cette affaire que le chef de l'Académie de l'Ombre ? Si Luke parvenait à raisonner Brakiss, à le détourner du Côté Obscur, la bataille pouvait être gagnée avant que trop de vies soient sacrifiées.

— Où, Brakiss ? Quel terrain neutre proposez-vous ?

— Votre Académie et la mienne sont hors de question.

— Je suis d'accord.

— Loin des affrontements. Au-delà de la rivière, dans le Temple du Bosquet des Feuilles Bleues. Mais vous devez venir seul.

— Et vous, en ferez-vous de même ? demanda Luke.

Brakiss eut un rire de gorge.

— Bien entendu. Je n'ai pas besoin de renforts. Et je sais que vous tiendrez parole.

Luke réfléchit un instant pour s'assurer que la Force guidait ses actes. Brakiss et lui étaient assez puissants pour sentir une trahison éventuelle.

— Très bien, Brakiss. Je vous y rencontrerai, seul. Nous réglerons nos comptes une fois pour toutes.

CHAPITRE XI

— Ce n'était pas si difficile, dit Jacen, se penchant dans le siège du copilote du *Bâton de Foudre*.

Le fauteuil gémit. Son rembourrage sortait par de nombreuses déchirures. Les moteurs toussotèrent et geignirent quand la navette-cargo s'arracha à l'atmosphère.

— Tu n'aurais pas dû dire ça, petit ! fit Peckhum quand les alarmes se déclenchèrent. Nous avons quatre chasseurs Tie aux trousses. On dirait qu'ils ont décollé directement de l'Académie de l'Ombre.

Jacen déglutit nerveusement. Il étudia les panneaux d'affichage et secoua la tête.

— Par mon blaster ! Nous ferions mieux de transmettre tout de suite le message de détresse, avant qu'ils nous descendent. Sinon, les renforts arriveront trop tard.

Peckhum le regarda, les yeux rouges, une expression grave sur son visage ridé.

— Il faut que tu te charges d'envoyer le message, Jacen. Je vais être pas mal occupé à réaliser mes exploits aériens... Si ce fichu tacot veut bien tenir le coup. (Il tapota les commandes.) Désolé de te faire ça, mon vieux, mais je ne t'ai pas appelé le *Bâton de Foudre* pour rien ! Faisons voir à ces Impériaux ce que nous avons dans le ventre !

Jacen testa le système de communication, qu'il ne connaissait pas. Il tourna des boutons, essaya de régler les fréquences, et se sentit complètement désemparé. Il aurait aimé que sa sœur soit là : c'était elle, l'expert en électronique ! Elle aurait su tout de suite comment éliminer les bruits de fond et le brouillage impérial.

Il envoya un message subspatial sur toutes les fréquences, à la puissance maximale que pouvait produire le *Bâton de Foudre* sans baisser ses boucliers.

— Ici Jacen Solo, dit-il.

Il s'éclaircit la gorge, ne sachant pas par où commencer. Mais les détails importaient peu.

— À l'attention de la Nouvelle République : nous avons une urgence. Jacen Solo, sur Yavin 4, demande une aide immédiate. Nous sommes attaqués par l'Académie de l'Ombre. Des chasseurs impériaux pilonnent l'Académie Jedi. Je répète, nous demandons une aide immédiate. Nos boucliers sont détruits. Nous avons besoin d'aide, le plus vite possible. (Il désactiva le micro et se tourna vers Peckhum.) Comment m'en suis-je tiré ?

— Parfaitement, mon garçon, dit Peckhum.

Il vira à tribord pour échapper aux quatre chasseurs Tie qui passèrent en tirant de tous leurs canons. Un coup atteignit le bouclier du *Bâton de Foudre* ; les autres passèrent à côté sans lui faire de mal.

— J'étais un sacré bon pilote autrefois, dit Peckhum. Et je le suis toujours... je crois.

Un chasseur se sépara des autres et décrivit un cercle plus serré, inondant l'espace de son feu mortel.

Peckhum piqua jusqu'à la lisière de l'atmosphère. La coque inférieure du *Bâton de Foudre* chauffa. Puis le pilote remonta, effectua un looping arrière et passa au-dessus du chasseur Tie, qui tirait toujours à feu continu. Des étincelles jaillirent du panneau de commande ; des voyants rouges clignotèrent sur les systèmes de diagnostic.

— Euh, Peckhum, que veulent dire ces alarmes ? demanda Jacen.

— Que nos boucliers sont en train de céder.

— N'avez-vous aucune arme à bord de ce vaisseau ? dit Jacen en cherchant des commandes de mise à feu.

Peckhum toussota et lança le vaisseau dans un plongeon vertigineux vers Yavin 4.

— C'est un cargo, mon garçon, et il est pas mal fatigué. Je ne m'attendais pas à me retrouver au cœur d'une bataille ! Diantre, il est déjà extraordinaire que les synthétiseurs de nourriture marchent encore !

Le reste de l'escadrille ennemie s'éloigna pour reprendre l'attaque contre l'Académie Jedi, mais le chasseur Tie continua à les harceler. Cette fois, il les avait dans sa ligne de mire : la majorité des rayons touchèrent le *Bâton de Foudre*.

— Ce type en veut réellement à notre peau, dit Jacen.

Peckhum poussa l'accélération au-delà des normes de sécurité. Le cargo gémit et craqua quand il s'enfonça dans l'atmosphère, malmené par les turbulences de l'air.

Jacen était secoué comme un prunier. Il saisit de nouveau le micro du système de communication.

— Ici Jacen Solo. Message de détresse personnel. Nous sommes en grand danger, pourchassés par un chasseur ennemi. Nous avons besoin de secours. Je vous en prie, quelqu'un peut-il nous aider ?

Peckhum le regarda.

— Personne n'arrivera ici à temps.

Jacen se souvint des récits qu'il avait si souvent entendus. Luke Skywalker s'était un jour trouvé dans la même situation, lors de la bataille de l'Étoile Noire. Il volait dans la tranchée de l'immense station, essayant d'envoyer une torpille à protons dans un minuscule port d'évacuation thermique. Son aile X se trouvait dans la ligne de mire de Dark Vador, et il n'était pas parvenu à échapper aux chasseurs et aux intercepteurs lancés à ses trousses. La situation semblait désespérée... Puis Yan Solo, le père de Jacen, était apparu de nulle part et avait sauvé la mise au Jedi.

Jacen ne pensait pas que son père fût dans les environs, et il ne voyait pas qui d'autre surgirait des cieux. Il ne pouvait pas compter sur pareille chance.

Il y eut un crépitement de parasites dans le système de communication, puis une voix se fit entendre, vibrante de méchanceté. Ce n'était pas celle d'un sauveur.

— Jacen Solo... Tu es un de ces marmots Jedi que nous avons rencontrés dans les niveaux inférieurs de Coruscant. Tu te souviens de moi ? Norys, le chef de Génération Perdue. Tu nous as volé notre œuf de faucon-souris... C'est le moment de régler nos comptes !

Jacen sentit un frisson lui parcourir l'échine quand il se souvint de la brute aux larges épaules. Norys continua :

— Le misérable ramasseur de poubelles, Zekk, a rallié le Second Imperium, mais toi, tu as fait le mauvais choix, petit ! Je voulais que tu saches qui allait te réduire en poussière.

— Je suis content qu'il ait choisi ce moment pour nous contacter, dit Peckhum, sarcastique. Je doute que nous tiendrons le coup longtemps. Ce type aurait détesté nous descendre avant de pouvoir nous faire ses adieux !

Peckhum était à bout de ressources. Il ne pouvait plus se livrer à des acrobaties. Tous ses talents de pilote étaient mobilisés pour éviter que le cargo se désintègre en plein vol.

Les moteurs du *Bâton de Foudre* commencèrent à fumer. D'autres alarmes se déclenchèrent. Derrière, le chasseur de Norys arrosait leur coque à feu continu, menaçant de faire exploser le vieux cargo.

Jacen jeta un coup d'œil à l'unité de communication. Il ne pensait pas utile de renouveler l'appel de détresse.

Les arbres défilaient sous eux à toute allure. Jacen regarda autour de lui.

— Je ne pense pas que ce soit le moment de vous raconter une blague, gémit-il.

Peckhum secoua la tête.

— Je n'ai pas très envie de rire pour le moment, petit...

CHAPITRE XII

La jungle humide et sombre se referma autour de Zekk, lui rappelant les niveaux inférieurs de Coruscant.

Il avait presque l'impression d'être rentré à la maison.

Ses Jedi Obscurs et lui étaient tombés du ciel, soutenus par les générateurs de répulsion. Arrivés dans les branches les plus hautes, ils s'étaient frayé un chemin vers le sol. Là, ils s'étaient dispersés pour affronter les étudiants auxquels maître Skywalker avait inculqué de force la philosophie des Rebelles.

Zekk ignorait tout de la politique. Il savait seulement qui était de son côté et qui l'avait trahi : Jacen et Jaina. Surtout Jaina. Il avait cru qu'elle était son amie. Pourtant, quand Brakiss le lui avait expliqué, Zekk avait compris ce qu'elle pensait vraiment de lui.

Jaina n'avait eu aucun mal à refuser de reconnaître son potentiel Jedi. La jeune fille n'avait pas même envisagé qu'il pût être son égal. Pourtant, Zekk avait ce potentiel ; il l'avait prouvé.

Il espérait quand même que Jaina et Jacen ne se battraient pas contre lui, car il serait forcé de leur démontrer sa puissance, et sa loyauté au Second Imperium. Il se souvint de son duel contre l'étudiant de Tamith Kai, Vilas, qui avait payé son échec de sa vie.

Un des Jedi Obscurs était coincé dans les branches supérieures d'un arbre. Zekk vit une lame de sabrolaser taillader les lianes, permettant au combattant de rejoindre le sol.

Au-dessus d'eux, une escadrille de chasseurs Tie traversa le ciel, tirant sur la forêt. Les Jedi Obscurs partirent à la recherche de victimes potentielles. Zekk prit trois hommes avec lui, et ils s'enfoncèrent dans les sous-bois.

Ils arrivèrent au bord d'une large rivière dont les courants brun-vert serpentaient à travers la jungle, agitant doucement les frondes qui pendaient dans l'eau. Plus bas, non loin du Grand Temple Massassi en ruine, il vit la plate-forme flottante de Tamith Kai.

Un des compagnons de Zekk désigna le ciel d'un index interrogateur.

— Oui, dit Zekk, je sais ce que vous voulez

faire. Invoquons un orage et une tempête pour ravager la jungle et débusquer ces couards de Jedi.

Il leva les yeux vers le ciel bleu et se concentra. Au fond de son cœur, il trouva la colère et le chagrin ressentis tout au long de sa vie. Il savait comment utiliser sa rage telle une arme.

Il s'en servit pour invoquer le vent et sentit que les autres guerriers du Côté Obscur faisaient de même, attirant les nuages jusqu'à ce que le ciel en soit rempli.

Le vent devint plus froid, chargé d'électricité statique. La cape doublée d'écarlate de Zekk vola autour de lui. Des mèches de sa chevelure noire lui fouettèrent le visage quand le vent les délogea de sa queue de cheval. Des éclairs zébrèrent le ciel. Le bruit de l'orage couvrit celui des chasseurs qui passaient et repassaient au-dessus d'eux.

Zekk sourit. Oui, un orage se préparait.

L'orage de la victoire...

Tandis que les nuages s'accumulaient, il entendit l'écho de plusieurs coups de canon laser. Il leva les yeux au ciel et vit qu'un combat inégal s'y déroulait : un cargo donnait de la bande au-dessus de lui, poursuivi par un chasseur Tie qui tirait sans arrêt sur sa proie.

Zekk reconnut le *Bâton de Foudre*, le vaisseau déglingué de son ami Peckhum, l'homme qu'il avait considéré comme un père pendant tant d'années.

Peckhum ! Ils avaient été proches l'un de l'autre, excellents amis malgré le peu qu'ils avaient en commun. Il se souvint, trop tard, que le vieil astronaute gagnait quelques crédits supplémentaires en faisant des livraisons à l'Académie de Skywalker. Son ami était donc sur la Yavin 4 quand l'attaque avait commencé ?

Son cœur se serra. Une angoisse déchirante le saisit ; sa concentration faiblit.

Les vents frappèrent furieusement les arbres les plus proches. Les autres Jedi Obscurs luttaient pour garder le contrôle de la bourrasque.

— Oh, non ! Peckhum ! s'écria Zekk, regardant le chasseur Tie mitrailler le vaisseau sans défense.

Il y eut une petite explosion sur la coque ; Zekk comprit que les boucliers avaient cédé.

Le *Bâton de Foudre* allait s'écraser... Et il ne pouvait rien faire.

Il entendit des cris de surprise quand les autres Jedi Obscurs perdirent le contrôle de l'orage. Les vents cassèrent des branches et déracinèrent des jeunes arbres, puis moururent quand les guerriers Obscurs cessèrent de manipuler le climat.

Leur attention avait été attirée par un jeune étudiant Jedi qui courait dans le sous-bois. Soit il était en train de se diriger discrètement vers eux, soit il fuyait, effrayé par l'ennemi.

Le garçon sortit des herbes sauvages, des cheveux blond paille hérissés autour de son visage empourpré. Ses vêtements étaient si ridiculement voyants qu'ils blessèrent les yeux de Zekk : rouge vif, doré, vert et jaune éclatants, violet... Comment le jeune homme avait-il pu rêver de se cacher en étant habillé comme ça ?

Le garçon avait l'air effrayé, mais déterminé. Il avança le menton et posa les mains sur ses hanches, ses robes multicolores virevoltant autour de lui au gré des derniers soubresauts du vent.

— Très bien, vous ne me laissez pas le choix. Je suis Raynar, Chevalier Jedi... euh... *étudiant*. Je vous ordonne de vous rendre. Sinon, je serai obligé de vous attaquer.

Deux compagnons de Zekk éclatèrent de rire, activèrent leur sabrolaser et avancèrent vers le jeune homme. Raynar recula jusqu'à heurter le tronc rugueux d'un arbre. Il ferma les yeux, essayant de se concentrer. Il retint son souffle jusqu'à ce que son visage devienne rouge vif, puis violet foncé.

Zekk sentit une faible onde de choc quand le garçon essaya d'utiliser la Force pour les repousser. Les deux autres Jedi Obscurs ne semblèrent pas s'en apercevoir.

Zekk s'aperçut qu'il n'avait aucune envie de faire un massacre. Le garçon avait l'air fier et impétueux, mais en même temps innocent.

Le jeune homme agit rapidement, avant que ses compagnons aient le temps de régler son compte à Raynar. Il projeta la Force vers le garçon, le saisit par ses robes multicolores et l'expédia dans l'eau. Raynar hurla quand il s'envola. Il tomba dans la rivière à plat ventre, le visage dans la boue.

Les deux Jedi Obscurs se tournèrent vers Zekk,

l'air furieux. Raynar pataugea dans le courant, ses robes couvertes de limon.

— Humilier un ennemi vaut mieux que se contenter de le tuer, dit Zekk doctement. Nous avons corrigé ce Jedi d'une façon qu'il ne risque pas d'oublier.

Les guerriers Obscurs ricanèrent ; Zekk sut qu'il avait réussi à les calmer. Pour le moment, du moins...

Il regarda le ciel, espérant apercevoir une trace du *Bâton de Foudre*. Il ne vit qu'un nuage de fumée en train de se dissiper. Il aurait voulu trouver un moyen d'aider son ami. Serait-il obligé d'ajouter la perte de Peckhum au prix de la victoire ?

Le vaisseau blessé était hors de vue. La fin de la bataille approchait : Zekk ne reverrait jamais le *Bâton de Foudre*, ni Peckhum.

CHAPITRE XIII

Le chasseur Tie de Qorl rasait la jungle, repérant des cibles pour les équipes d'assaut. Le reste de son escadrille avait reçu ses ordres, et volait suivant son plan d'attaque.

Pourtant, Qorl doutait que Norys obéirait aux ordres quand les rayons laser commenceraient à jaillir. La jeune brute irait de cible en cible comme un gundark fou, causant probablement autant de dégâts aux Impériaux qu'aux Rebelles.

Qorl sentit un frisson glacé parcourir son échine. Il s'était attendu à se réjouir de voler à bord de son chasseur Tie pour la gloire du Second Imperium.

Mais il avait nombre de doutes et d'arrière-pensées. Il craignait d'avoir pris la mauvaise décision avec Norys, le Second Imperium devant en payer le prix.

Norys s'était révélé une grosse déception. Quand Qorl avait choisi le jeune homme, il savait qu'il avait été endurci par des années de vie difficile, même s'il était sur Coruscant le chef de la petite bande de voyous appelée Génération Perdue. Le garçon aux larges épaules voulait devenir un Impérial parce qu'il était possédé par la soif de puissance. L'Empire avait besoin de gens comme lui.

Mais un soldat loyal doit aussi savoir obéir. Un serviteur de l'Empire ne pouvait pas être un loup solitaire, soumis à ses impulsions et non aux ordres de ses supérieurs. À mesure qu'il s'habituait à son nouveau statut, Norys était de plus en plus irrespectueux et indiscipliné.

Ce garçon était réellement assoiffé de sang ; il désirait dominer les autres, leur faire du mal, remporter la victoire à tout prix. Il ne luttait pas pour la gloire du Second Imperium ni pour instaurer un Ordre Nouveau dans la galaxie. Il se battait pour le plaisir.

C'était une attitude dangereuse.

Qorl vola en cercles, se rapprochant d'un feu de forêt allumé par un bombardier. Puis il alla vers la rivière, où planait l'impressionnante plate-forme de Tamith Kai. Il entendit un appel désespéré, émis sur toutes les fréquences, et reconnut la voix avant d'entendre le nom de celui qui transmettait.

— À l'attention de la Nouvelle République : nous avons une urgence. Jacen Solo, sur Yavin 4, demande une aide immédiate. Nous sommes attaqués par l'Académie de l'Ombre.

Qorl se cala dans son siège, régla son casque noir et continua à voler. Il se souvenait des jeunes jumeaux qui l'avaient aidé à réparer son chasseur, et qu'il avait gardés prisonniers dans son campement, au fond de la jungle. Ils lui offrirent leur amitié, et ils essayèrent de le convertir au Côté Lumineux. Mais il était trop bien endoctriné par l'Empire.

Se rendre, c'est trahir.

Qorl s'était enfui et il avait rejoint l'Académie de l'Ombre, où les jumeaux avaient été entraînés de force sous la tutelle de Tamith Kai et de maître Brakiss. Qorl fut troublé par la brutalité de leur formation et le mépris que les professeurs montraient pour la vie de leurs étudiants.

Personne ne découvrit jamais qu'il avait discrètement aidé ses jeunes amis à fuir. Ensuite, il fit de son mieux pour réparer la faute qu'il avait commise. Il effectua un raid sur un convoi rebelle, afin de voler des générateurs d'hyperdrive et des lasers pour équiper les nouveaux vaisseaux. Puis il travailla dur à la formation de Norys et des autres commandos.

Un vaisseau entouré de fumée passa au-dessus de lui. C'était une vieille navette-cargo déglinguée à la coque striée de brûlures de laser. Qorl reconnut le modèle, un navire non armé de conception ancienne, aux moteurs lents et aux boucliers insuffisants pour le combat.

Le navire était pourchassé par un chasseur Tie impitoyable.

Qorl eut honte de voir le Tie gaspiller ses munitions de la sorte. La navette exploserait bientôt.

Qorl contacta le chasseur.

— Pilote, identifiez-vous !

Qorl ne fut pas surpris outre mesure par la voix rude qui lui répondit.

— Ici Norys, vieil homme. Ne me dérangez pas, j'ai une cible dans ma ligne de mire.

— Norys, tu as déjà démoli ce vaisseau. Il n'est pas notre objectif principal. Le but de cette opération est de détruire l'Académie Jedi. Cette épave ne risque plus de nous causer le moindre souci.

— Laissez tomber, vieux croûton, dit Norys. C'est *ma* proie, et je vais lui faire sa fête.

Qorl essaya de contrôler sa colère.

— Nous ne sommes pas là pour nous amuser, Norys. Nous livrons cet assaut au bénéfice du Second Imperium, non pour ta satisfaction personnelle.

— Allez vous fourrer la tête dans une tuyère, dit Norys. Je ne vais pas laisser un vieux trouillard me dire ce que je dois faire.

Le garçon coupa la communication et plongea vers le vaisseau en flammes, tirant à feu continu.

La déception de Qorl se transforma en indignation. L'attitude du jeune homme était une insulte à tout ce que l'Empire avait d'admirable. Qorl se souvint de sa formation de pilote. Ses collègues de promotion et lui avaient travaillé ensemble comme une machine bien huilée : précis, respectueux, obéissant aux ordres, faisant de leur mieux pour promouvoir le mode de vie ordonné que l'Empereur imposait à la galaxie. Voilà qui valait la peine qu'on se batte !

Norys se fichait de tout, à part le plaisir qu'il prenait à faire le mal.

Le signal de détresse retentit de nouveau sur le système de communication.

— Ici Jacen Solo. Message de détresse personnel. Nous sommes en grand danger, pourchassés par un chasseur ennemi. Nous avons besoin de secours. Je vous en prie, quelqu'un peut-il nous aider ?

Qorl descendit, à la limite des arbres. Jacen Solo était un adversaire honorable, un garçon courageux, bien qu'il fût allié aux Rebelles et non au Second Imperium. Mais était-il vraiment à blâmer ? Après tout, sa mère était la Présidente de la Nouvelle République...

Norys avait eu le *choix*. Il savait pour quel but il avait été formé. Il avait accepté de bon cœur l'uniforme et le chasseur Tie... Mais il refusait de jouer le jeu.

Norys n'était qu'un tueur minable et amoral.

Le chasseur Tie continua de poursuivre le vaisseau endommagé. De la fumée noire sortait de ses nacelles. Qorl nota le moment précis où les boucliers s'effondrèrent.

Norys tira de nouveau, constellant la coque d'une série de marques noires.

Qorl activa ses canons laser et régla le système de visée. Le *Bâton de Foudre* exploserait dans quelques secondes. Qorl était sûr que le voyou continuerait de tirer sur les débris pour s'assurer qu'il n'y aurait aucun survivant.

Le dégoût le submergea. Il débrancha son système de communication et marmonna :

— Est-ce une entorse à l'honneur d'éliminer quelqu'un qui n'a ni foi ni loi ?

Qorl avait étudié la configuration des chasseurs Tie. Il connaissait leurs points faibles, et savait comment les détruire.

Il visa les réacteurs de Norys.

Ignorant les injonctions de son professeur, celui-ci tira de nouveau, plus lentement, comme s'il savourait d'avance la destruction du cargo.

Le *Bâton de Foudre* fit une embardée, ultime tentative pour échapper au feu des canons laser.

Qorl se rapprocha du chasseur de Norys.

Et il tira.

Le chasseur Tie explosa, détruit si rapidement et totalement que son pilote n'eut pas le temps de pousser un cri de surprise.

Honteux d'avoir trahi le Second Imperium, Qorl ne tenta pas de contacter le *Bâton de Foudre*. Il changea de direction et retourna vers le combat, tandis que la navette essayait de rester en l'air, ou au moins de se poser sans trop de dégâts.

CHAPITRE XIV

Tandis que la lutte faisait rage au-dessus de l'Académie Jedi et dans la jungle, le commando impérial Orvak avançait en silence, concentré sur sa mission.

Il avait abandonné son chasseur près du site des générateurs de bouclier, mais il y retournerait dès qu'il aurait accompli ce qu'il était venu faire. Depuis des heures, il progressait discrètement dans la forêt.

Plusieurs arbres étaient en feu. Des nuages de fumée montaient de la végétation humide. Il entendit des tirs de blaster et des cris, puis le bourdonnement lointain de sabrolasers. Ne voulant pas révéler sa position, il ne fit pas le moindre bruit.

Les Jedi de Skywalker avaient abandonné leur Grand Temple pour s'engager dans des escarmouches isolées. Ce qui lui laissait toute latitude pour accomplir son travail.

Aux abords de l'ancien édifice, Orvak vit des traces noires sur les murs épais, stigmates des lasers et des explosifs à protons largués par les bombardiers. Les lianes qui poussaient sur les flancs de la pyramide étaient tombées tout autour, carbonisées. Une explosion avait démoli la porte du hangar, empêchant la flotte de Skywalker de décoller.

Après tous ces millénaires, pensa Orvak, l'antique structure avait été endommagée. Mais c'était à lui que reviendrait l'honneur de donner le coup de grâce.

Il se faufila à travers le feuillage, déracinant des fougères et taillant des lianes pour se frayer un chemin. Il sortit finalement du sous-bois et arriva derrière le temple.

Les chasseurs Tie sillonnaient le ciel comme des oiseaux de proie. Orvak les regarda, encourageant mentalement leur assaut.

Sur un côté de la pyramide, il aperçut une cour dallée. De l'autre côté, au pied de la bâtisse de pierre, se trouvait une entrée obscure. Troublé à la pensée de la sorcellerie à laquelle avaient dû se livrer les étudiants Jedi, Orvak avança lentement.

Les herbes s'infiltraient déjà entre les dalles de la cour. La jungle envahirait probablement le site en quelques mois après la destruction du temple. Bon débarras ! À ce moment, Orvak serait revenu à l'Académie de l'Ombre, où, si sa mission se passait bien, il serait promu au rang d'officier sur un superdestroyer.

Quand les bruits de la bataille se firent plus proches, des bombes à protons explosant non loin de lui, Orvak agit. Il traversa rapidement la cour et pénétra dans le temple secret des Rebelles.

Il s'arrêta un instant, heureux d'avoir son casque, qui le protégerait des émanations mortelles, s'il y en avait. Qui savait quels pièges les sorciers Jedi avaient installés ?

Les détecteurs de son casque apprirent à l'Impérial qu'il n'y en avait aucun. Au fond, ce n'était pas étonnant : l'attaque de l'Académie était imprévue. Les Chevaliers Jedi n'avaient pas eu le temps de se préparer.

Orvak entra dans le temple Massassi, son paquetage sur l'épaule. Il courut dans les couloirs, cherchant quelque chose d'important à détruire. Il trouva des quartiers d'habitation, des salles à manger... Rien d'intéressant.

Il se dirigea vers le hangar, espérant y déposer ses détonateurs et détruire la flotte de Luke Skywalker. Quand il sortit de l'ascenseur et pénétra dans la baie, il n'en crut pas ses yeux : il n'y avait qu'un vaisseau, fin et élégant, tout en courbes et en angles. Rien de plus. Pas de flotte, aucune défense majeure. Orvak ricana, incrédule.

Les alarmes retentirent dans le hangar. Les lumières rouges blessèrent les yeux du commando. Un petit droïd en forme de tonneau se précipita sur lui, sifflant et criant. Des rayons d'électricité bleus sortirent du bras de soudure qui émergeait de son torse cylindrique.

Orvak se jeta dans l'ascenseur et appuya frénétiquement sur tous les boutons. Les Jedi avaient-ils une horde de droïds assassins pour défendre leur hangar ? Des machines mortelles hérissées d'armes, et qui ne manquaient jamais leur but ?

Quand les portes vitrées se refermèrent, la cabine s'ébranlant, Orvak jeta un coup d'œil et vit qu'il s'agissait d'un astrodroïd solitaire qui arpentait maladroitement le sol, et déclenchait les alarmes.

Personne n'était resté dans le temple pour lui répondre.

L'Impérial eut un rire nerveux. Un seul misérable astrodroïd ! Il détestait que les machines aient un sens trop aigu de leur importance. Mais il était désormais sûr qu'il n'y avait pas de piège.

Il fallait quand même chercher un autre endroit pour sa mission de sabotage. Un endroit plus *spécial*.

Orvak le trouva finalement, au dernier niveau de l'immense pyramide.

Il prit l'ascenseur jusqu'au sommet. Blaster prêt, le commando entra dans la grande salle d'audience.

Les murs étaient polis et incrustés de pierres multicolores. Sur la grande estrade, imagina Orvak, les Rebelles donnaient sans doute des conférences à leurs étudiants. Ils leur décernaient des médailles après des victoires contre les maîtres légitimes de la galaxie, se livrant peut-être à des rituels dégoûtants...

Oui, se dit-il. *C'est parfait !*

Le cœur battant de joie à l'idée d'accomplir la mission qui avait coûté la vie à son camarade Dareb, Orvak posa son sac sur le sol. Il retira son casque pour mieux profiter de la lumière diffuse qui filtrait par les dômes du temple.

La fumée noircissait le ciel, comme une épaisse peinture étalée dans l'air. Les bruits lointains de l'attaque résonnaient entre les murs de la grande salle. Mais le commando n'entendit rien d'autre et ne vit aucun mouvement. Le temple était vide ; il avait tout son temps pour travailler.

Orvak marcha jusqu'à l'estrade, ses bottes résonnant sur le sol de pierre. Oui, ce serait l'endroit idéal ! De là, l'explosion se répercuterait dans tout le bâtiment. Orvak retira ses gants épais afin de pouvoir préparer le délicat équipement électronique.

Il sortit les sept détonateurs thermiques qui lui restaient et les relia les uns aux autres. Puis il brancha les explosifs sur une minuterie centrale, et les répartit dans la grande salle d'audience comme les rayons d'une roue.

Cela ferait une superbe explosion !

Si tout se passait bien, quand les détonateurs exploseraient, ils feraient sauter le sommet du temple comme la calotte d'un volcan en éruption. L'onde de choc se propagerait vers les niveaux inférieurs et soufflerait les murs. La pyramide s'effondrerait et se transformerait en un tas d'antiques débris.

Ce n'était que justice !

Orvak revint vers l'unité centrale et programma les commandes. Il pensa avec satisfaction qu'aucun Rebelle ne donnerait de cours ici désormais. Nul Chevalier Jedi n'y recevrait les enseignements de la Nouvelle République. La pièce n'abriterait plus jamais de célébrations impies.

Bientôt, il n'en resterait plus rien.

Orvak tapa le code d'initialisation. Dans la pièce, les voyants des détonateurs virèrent au vert, prêts à recevoir l'ordre final. Examinant son travail, Orvak sourit et appuya sur le bouton « activation ». La minuterie commença le compte à rebours.

L'Académie Jedi n'avait plus longtemps à exister !

Orvak aperçut sur le sol un scintillement presque invisible. Quelque chose de transparent, mais de légèrement iridescent avait réfléchi un instant la lumière.

Il sortit son blaster.

— Qui va là ? dit-il.

Puis il aperçut de nouveau la forme mouvante, qui glissait vers lui.

Il la perdit de vue aussitôt.

Orvak fit feu, creusant des trous dans le sol. Des rayons d'énergie ricochèrent autour de lui. Il s'aplatit sur l'estrade, craignant une riposte. Il ne voyait plus la forme translucide, et se demanda ce que cela pouvait être. Un tour de sorcellerie, sans aucun doute. Il n'aurait pas dû baisser sa garde. Mais les Jedi ne l'emporteraient pas.

Orvak sentit comme une piqûre d'aiguille dans sa main. Il baissa les yeux, vit deux petites gouttes de sang perler sur sa paume, puis distingua la tête triangulaire d'une sorte de vipère transparente.

— Eh ! cria-t-il.

Avant qu'il ait le temps de réagir, le serpent cristallin se détacha de sa main et se glissa dans une fente du mur. Orvak vit un dernier scintillement.

L'Impérial avait sommeil, si sommeil...

La douleur de la morsure n'était plus qu'une pulsation sourde. Orvak pensa qu'un long repos l'aiderait à se remettre...

Il tomba, profondément endormi, juste à côté de la minuterie.

CHAPITRE XV

Tenel Ka se tenait sur le bord de la plate-forme de bataille, tous les muscles tendus, prête à l'action.

Elle enroula sa corde et la remit dans sa ceinture ainsi que le grappin. De son unique bras, elle saisit son sabrolaser et l'activa. Près d'elle, Lowbacca, sa fourrure rousse hérissée, retroussa les lèvres et montra les crocs. Le Wookie prit à deux mains son sabrolaser semblable à une massue et fit jaillir la lame couleur de bronze fondu.

Des commandos sûrs de vaincre marchèrent sur les intrus, blasters prêts à tirer.

DTM geignit :

— Par mes circuits, maître Lowbacca, nous aurions peut-être dû planifier un peu mieux notre attaque !

Lowie gronda. Tenel Ka se redressa de toute sa taille.

— La Force est avec nous, dit-elle. C'est un fait.

Un bombardier passa au-dessus d'eux, larguant des torpilles à protons dans la forêt. Le bruit des explosions retentissait tout autour d'eux.

Sur le pont de commandement surélevé de la plate-forme, Tamith Kai se dressait dans sa cape noire, tel un oiseau de proie. Elle se tourna, sa chevelure d'ébène crépitant, ses lèvres lie-de-vin retroussées sur un sourire méprisant. Tenel Ka et Lowie firent trois pas vers les commandos.

Un soldat en armure blanche, enragé par la vue des deux jeunes Jedi, tira au blaster. D'un revers de sa vibrolame, Tenel Ka intercepta le rayon d'énergie et le dévia vers le ciel.

D'un commun accord, la guerrière et Lowie chargèrent. Ils zébrèrent l'air de leurs lames, déviant le feu des commandos, que l'attaque plongea dans le chaos. Comme des tornades vivantes, Lowie et Tenel Ka se frayèrent un chemin à travers les soldats.

Tamith Kai se pencha pour observer l'escarmouche.

— La fille m'appartient. Je lui arracherai le cœur de mes mains !

Tenel Ka décocha un coup de sabrolaser qui faucha un autre commando. Elle se retourna vers la Sœur de la Nuit, le cœur battant, mais pourtant calme et résolue. Elle était prête à ce combat, sûre de ses capacités physiques.

Ce serait sa meilleure bataille.

— Je te laisse les commandos, Lowie, dit-elle, sautant sur le pont de commandement pour y rencontrer son ennemie.

Le jeune Wookie rugit, indiquant qu'il était prêt. DTM n'avait pas l'air aussi enthousiaste.

— Veuillez être prudent, maître Lowbacca. Il ne serait pas avisé d'entretenir des illusions...

Les commandos avancèrent, quinze contre un seul Wookie. Lowbacca n'avait pas l'air de penser que les chances étaient inégales.

Tenel Ka se campa devant la Sœur de la Nuit, grande et fière, son sabrolaser turquoise brandi. Elle se souvint de la fois où elle avait pris la femme par surprise, manquant l'estropier.

— Comment va votre genou, Tamith Kai ?

Les yeux violets de la sorcière lancèrent des éclairs. Elle secoua la tête, moqueuse.

— Tu ferais mieux de te rendre tout de suite, petite, dit-elle. Cela n'est pas digne de mes capacités : une gamine manchote qui ose penser qu'elle est une menace pour moi !

— Vous parlez trop, dit Tenel Ka. À moins que vous ayez l'intention de vous débarrasser de moi en me soûlant de paroles ?

— Tu es restée trop longtemps en compagnie de ces marmots Jedi. Ils t'ont appris à être impolie avec tes supérieurs.

D'un geste de la main, la Sœur de la Nuit

envoya un éclair bleu-noir vers la jeune guerrière de Dathomir.

— Je ne vois ici personne qui me soit supérieur, répondit Tenel Ka, avant de dévier le rayon d'énergie avec sa lame.

Elle utilisa la Force pour générer autour d'elle un cocon protecteur de pensées et de sentiments. La Sœur de la Nuit recula, surprise.

Un niveau plus bas, Lowbacca maniait sa lame couleur de bronze d'une main, projetant de l'autre un commando contre trois adversaires qui s'écroulèrent. Les Impériaux, trop nombreux pour se risquer à utiliser leurs blasters, semblaient avoir décidé d'arrêter le Wookie en le submergeant sous le nombre.

Grossière erreur !

Sur le pont de commandement, la Sœur de la Nuit tournait autour de sa proie. Tenel Ka tenait son sabrolaser prêt, ses yeux de granit rivés sur les iris violets de son ennemie.

Au-dessus d'eux, des bombardiers Tie descendaient en piqué, mais les pilotes s'intéressaient davantage au duel qu'à leur mission de bombardement.

La Sœur de la Nuit leva les mains ; une boule de feu bleue naquit dans chacune de ses paumes, gagnant de la puissance avec chaque seconde. Tenel Ka comprit qu'elle devait utiliser la concentration de son adversaire pour la surprendre.

Tamith Kai était debout près du bord de la plateforme ; Lowie et les commandos s'affrontaient au-dessous. La Sœur de la Nuit leva la main. Le feu crépita au bout de ses doigts, prêt à frapper.

Tenel Ka feinta une attaque classique, puis, sans avertissement, elle envoya une décharge de Force à son adversaire, suffisante pour la faire basculer par-dessus bord. Avec un hurlement sauvage, la Sœur de la Nuit tomba en arrière. Des éclairs bleus filèrent dans le ciel, manquant de peu un bombardier Tie.

La Sœur de la Nuit s'écrasa dans la mêlée. Lowbacca lui montra les crocs. Les commandos essayèrent de faire tomber le Wookie, mais Tamith Kai donna libre cours à sa colère, les envoyant tous bouler loin d'elle.

Tenel Ka leva les yeux et vit un bombardier Tie pointer ses canons sur elle. Les rayons d'énergie fusèrent, creusant à ses pieds des trous fumants.

La guerrière sauta d'un côté à l'autre afin d'éviter les décharges mortelles, utilisant sa symbiose avec la Force pour deviner où le prochain coup frapperait. Il lui était impossible de dévier le feu des armes à haute puissance avec un sabrolaser.

Elle faisait une cible facile, seule et sans protection.

La jeune Jedi n'avait pas le choix. Quand le vaisseau repassa au-dessus d'elle, elle projeta son sabrolaser sur la trajectoire adéquate. L'arme s'envola en direction du vaisseau ennemi.

La guerrière avait longtemps travaillé à améliorer ses performances, utilisant des lances et des couteaux. Elle ne ratait jamais son coup. Mais dans ce cas, la cible était lointaine et le temps limité.

Le bombardier gagna de l'altitude, virant pour revenir porter le coup final.

Le sabrolaser de Tenel Ka tournoya dans l'air. Avec un éclair turquoise aveuglant, il heurta le côté du bombardier. Il ne sectionna pas un panneau d'alimentation, comme elle l'avait espéré, mais arracha un stabilisateur et creusa un trou béant dans la coque. Puis il passa au travers du vaisseau et plongea vers la jungle, près de la rivière.

Incapable d'articuler un mot, la Sœur de la Nuit remonta sur le pont de commande avec un glapissement de rage. Sa cape noire claquait derrière elle comme les ailes d'un corbeau.

Les yeux de Tamith Kai étincelaient d'un feu violet.

Voyant la guerrière manchote seule et sans arme, la Sœur de la Nuit éclata d'un rire guttural plein de dérision.

— Maintenant, tu n'as même plus d'arme, se moqua Tamith Kai, regardant le moignon de son adversaire. Tu me fais perdre mon temps, gamine ! Pourquoi ne pas nous épargner du tracas à toutes les deux et te laisser gentiment tuer ?

Tenel Ka jeta un coup d'œil glacé à Tamith Kai. Elle avança d'un pas sans la moindre hésitation.

— J'ai perdu mon sabrolaser, mais je ne suis jamais *désarmée*.

Elle frappa du pied gauche, atteignant la Sœur

de la Nuit derrière le talon. Au même moment, elle lui flanqua un coup violent à la poitrine. Son adversaire tomba à la renverse.

Tenel Ka entendit les commandos hurler de panique. Puis elle perçut le bruit de ferraille d'un bombardier aux prises avec de sérieux problèmes.

Tenel Ka leva les yeux et réagit sans perdre un instant.

Le bombardier était revenu tant bien que mal, mais son compartiment arrière était en flammes. Hors de contrôle, donnant dangereusement de la bande, le vaisseau en perdition fondait sur la plate-forme.

Tenel Ka capta la terreur de son pilote. Il ne savait que faire, espérant seulement que la plate-forme serait l'endroit où atterrir en catastrophe. D'après la vitesse de sa descente et son manque de maniabilité, Tenel Ka comprit qu'un atterrissage était impossible.

Tamith Kai bondit pour attraper la cheville de Tenel Ka. La femme n'était pas consciente du danger venant du ciel.

Tenel Ka n'avait pas de temps à perdre avec elle. Elle libéra son pied botté et sauta par-dessus la Sœur de la Nuit.

Elle atterrit au milieu des commandos, près de Lowie.

Les soldats avaient repéré le bombardier Tie et se hâtèrent d'évacuer le pont.

— Lowbacca, nous devons partir tout de suite, dit Tenel Ka, le saisissant par un bras velu.

Il rugit. DTM intervint :

— Effectivement. Je pense que c'est une suggestion très raisonnable.

La jeune guerrière et le Wookie se précipitèrent au bord de la plate-forme et regardèrent en bas, vers la rivière et les arbres qui la surplombaient.

Sur le pont de commandement, Tamith Kai venait de remarquer l'approche du bombardier Tie à cause du bruit toujours croissant. La Sœur de la Nuit cria aux pilotes de la plate-forme d'activer les moteurs à répulsion pour fuir.

Ils n'y arriveraient pas, estima Tenel Ka.

Lowie et elle plongèrent, espérant atterrir à un endroit à peu près sûr.

Au-dessus d'eux, le bombardier Tie s'écrasa sur la plate-forme de bataille. Ses bombes explosèrent en même temps que les moteurs, creusant un cratère sur l'immense vaisseau plat.

Des plaques de blindage volèrent dans tous les sens, comme des flocons de neige métallique. Un torrent de feu et de fumée se déversa dans le ciel.

La plate-forme tomba telle une pierre.

La masse de débris explosa plusieurs fois encore avant de se jeter dans la rivière...

CHAPITRE XVI

Les rayons laser des Tie lancés à ses trousses zébrèrent la coque du vaisseau impérial dérobé par Jaina. Un coup toucha le coin d'une aile, faisant jaillir une volée d'étincelles.

La Jedi lutta pour garder le contrôle du vaisseau, qui menaçait de tomber en vrille. Elle perdit de la puissance, mais l'engin continua à voler, propulsé par ses moteurs auxiliaires. Ces engins étaient prévus pour des actions d'infiltration, pas pour une grande vitesse.

Les chasseurs Tie gagnèrent de la distance.

Jaina effectua des manœuvres acrobatiques, plongeant vers la jungle puis remontant. Elle avait l'espoir que les Impériaux feraient une erreur, comme par exemple heurter une branche d'arbre ou se percuter.

Mais elle n'eut pas cette chance.

Ses trois poursuivants allaient bientôt pouvoir tirer à bout portant ; Jaina n'avait plus qu'une chose à tenter. Utilisant son entraînement de Jedi, elle fit opérer un demi-tour en spirale à son chasseur Tie ; un instant plus tard, au lieu de s'éloigner de ses poursuivants, elle se dirigeait droit vers eux.

La distance diminua rapidement. Jaina ne pouvait tirer qu'une fois.

Elle ne rata pas son coup.

Le rayon de son canon laser décapita proprement un des chasseurs Tie, faisant éclater sa verrière. Le pilote passa par le trou, aspiré vers la jungle.

L'appareil de Jaina se glissa entre les deux ennemis restants. La Jedi filait aussi vite que possible. Les deux Impériaux furent plus longs à faire virer leurs appareils, mais ils reprirent quand même la poursuite.

Jaina examina le panneau de commande, cherchant quelque chose qui pourrait l'aider, une arme secrète... Mais elle doutait de trouver une astuce que ses poursuivants ne puissent imiter.

Son œil tomba sur un petit bouton marqué « désactivation des moteurs ioniques ». Elle comprit qu'il commandait la mise en service des moteurs normaux du chasseur Tie.

Elle bascula le bouton sur « zéro », réamorçant le système principal. Le chasseur Tie bondit en avant.

L'accélération la plaqua contre le siège et la fit

grimacer. Le vaisseau était plus rapide que tous ceux qu'avait pilotés Jaina.

Si elle pouvait prendre suffisamment d'avance et remonter en orbite, puis se cacher de l'autre côté de la lune, elle serait hors de contact visuel. Alors elle couperait ses moteurs et se laisserait dériver dans l'espace. Le blindage spécial du vaisseau l'aiderait à rester invisible.

C'était le seul moyen de se mettre en sécurité.

Elle fit monter le vaisseau en droite ligne, en direction de l'espace.

Les Impériaux la suivirent. Jaina ne savait pas si son accélération serait suffisante. Mais elle devait mettre tout son talent à creuser l'écart.

L'atmosphère se raréfia, devenant violet foncé. Puis le bleu nuit de l'espace la remplaça. Jaina vit que les Impériaux s'étaient rapprochés. Ils étaient de nouveau à portée de tir. Son plan ne marcherait pas : impossible de les éviter et de disparaître dans l'espace. Son blindage furtif serait inutile.

Elle se demanda si elle pouvait de nouveau affronter face à face ses adversaires. Elle pouvait certes abattre un chasseur avant qu'il ait le temps de tirer, mais deux ?

Pas la moindre chance...

Elle était perdue.

Jaina aperçut un scintillement sur le fond noir du ciel. Des vaisseaux quittèrent l'hyperespace. Les renforts ! La flotte de la Nouvelle République !

Son cœur bondit dans sa poitrine. C'était une

petite formation, mais bien armée et prête à affronter l'Académie de l'Ombre.

Avec un cri de joie, Jaina modifia sa trajectoire et fila vers les corvettes et les canonniers corelliens réunis en hâte par la Nouvelle République pour venir à la rescousse de l'Académie Jedi.

Le vaisseau de Jaina vibra quand elle poussa l'accélération bien au-delà des repères rouges. Elle perdait pourtant de la puissance à cause du mauvais état de son aile latérale.

— Vas-y, vas-y, murmura Jaina au chasseur.

Il ne lui fallait qu'un tout petit moment de répit.

La corvette corellienne de tête était de plus en plus proche. Mais les chasseurs ennemis collaient aux basques de Jaina, tirant toujours.

La Jedi évita les rayons laser jusqu'à ce qu'elle arrive enfin à portée des vaisseaux de la Nouvelle République. Ceux-ci tirèrent. Leurs coups passèrent si près de son navire que les rayons l'éblouirent.

Jaina réalisa que les canonniers lui tiraient dessus !

Elle comprit aussitôt pourquoi. Elle plongeait vers la flotte rebelle aux commandes d'un chasseur ennemi, deux autres Tie à sa suite. Les canonniers avaient dû croire que les trois vaisseaux accomplissaient une mission suicide.

Elle se hâta d'ouvrir le système de communication, puis émit à pleine puissance :

— À la flotte de la Nouvelle République. Ne tirez pas ! Ici Jaina Solo à bord d'un chasseur impérial capturé.

D'autres vaisseaux apparurent, un fatras d'engins lourdement armés, portant l'emblème de la station des Pêcheurs de Gemme qui orbitait autour de la géante gazeuse Yavin et appartenait à Lando Calrissian.

— Jaina Solo ? fit la voix de Lando. Ma petite demoiselle, que fais-tu là ?

— Je vais me transformer en poussière si vous ne vous occupez pas des deux Tie qui me talonnent !

La voix de l'amiral Ackbar retentit.

— Nous sommes en train de viser. Ne craignez rien, Jaina Solo.

— Je suis dans le chasseur de tête, rappela Jaina nerveusement. Ne vous trompez pas de cible ! Eh bien, qu'attendez-vous ?

Un feu nourri jaillit autour de Jaina. Les canonniers corelliens et la flotte privée de Lando Calrissian s'en donnèrent à cœur joie. Un instant plus tard, les deux chasseurs Tie s'envolèrent en fumée. Jaina lâcha un long soupir de soulagement.

L'amiral Ackbar lui envoya un signal, la guidant vers le dock arrière de la corvette.

— Soyez la bienvenue à bord, Jaina Solo, dit l'amiral. Nous vous offrons l'asile pendant la durée des combats aériens. Ça nous semble le meilleur moyen de protéger le personnel au sol.

— D'accord, dit Jaina. Mais dès que possible, je veux redescendre me battre à côté de mon frère et de mes amis.

— Si nous faisons correctement notre travail,

dit Ackbar, il ne restera plus grand-chose à combattre.

Dès qu'elle se fut posée, Jaina sortit, trempée de sueur et heureuse de quitter le vaisseau impérial. Elle n'avait plus très envie de voler à bord d'un de ces appareils. L'expérience avait été riche en émotions, mais elle ne se souciait pas de recommencer de sitôt.

Jaina salua les soldats de la Nouvelle République qui se trouvaient dans les docks. Elle passa une main dans ses cheveux, puis se précipita vers l'ascenseur le plus proche. Quand elle arriva sur le pont, elle rejoignit l'amiral Ackbar et regarda la flotte attaquer l'impressionnante station hérissée de pointes.

Les vaisseaux de la Nouvelle République harcelèrent le centre de formation des Jedi Obscurs en orbite autour de Yavin 4. Les boucliers de l'Académie de l'Ombre résistèrent, mais le bombardement fit quand même des dégâts.

Les vaisseaux de Lando Calrissian descendirent en piqué, ajoutant leur tir à celui des lasers de la flotte. Sous leur assaut combiné, l'Académie de l'Ombre serait détruite sous peu, pensa Jaina.

Ackbar envoya un message.

— Académie de l'Ombre, préparez-vous à vous rendre et à être abordée.

Jaina n'eut pas le temps de se détendre. La station ne daigna pas répondre. Un des officiers s'écria :

— Amiral Ackbar, nous détectons une fluctuation dans l'hyperespace, à tribord ! Il semble qu'une...

Des superdestroyers impériaux se matérialisèrent sur l'écran. Les vaisseaux semblaient avoir été montés et modifiés à la hâte, mais leurs armes étaient nouvelles et mortelles.

— D'où sort cette flotte ? demanda Lando.

Vaisseau après vaisseau, une escadrille apparut, armée jusqu'aux dents et dévouée à la cause du Second Imperium. À peine surgis du néant, les navires ouvrirent le feu sur les vaisseaux de la Nouvelle République.

— Remontez les boucliers ! ordonna l'amiral.

Il se tourna vers Jaina, le regard plein d'inquiétude.

— Il semble que les choses ne soient pas aussi simples que nous l'espérions, dit-il.

CHAPITRE XVII

Luke Skywalker arriva près des ruines Massassi connues sous le nom de Bosquet des Feuilles Bleues, une tour de pierre presque écroulée. Il était venu seul, espérant négocier, mais résolu au combat si nécessaire.

C'était l'endroit choisi par Brakiss pour leur confrontation. Leur duel, le cas échéant.

Luke écouta les bruits de la jungle : le babil des créatures dans les sous-bois, les oiseaux dans les branches... Et les coups de canon des chasseurs Tie dans le ciel. Il avait horreur de se trouver là au lieu d'être avec ses étudiants, luttant contre les forces du Côté Obscur.

Mais sa mission n'était pas moins importante. Il devait arrêter le chef des Jedi ennemis, son ancien élève...

Les branches d'un fourré s'écartèrent. Un

homme en sortit, bougeant avec une grâce fluide, comme s'il était fait de vif-argent. Un sourire se dessina sur son visage à la beauté de statue.

— Eh bien, Luke Skywalker, autrefois mon maître, j'espère que vous êtes venu dans l'intention de vous rendre ? De vous incliner devant mes capacités supérieures...

Luke ne lui rendit pas son sourire.

— Je suis là pour vous parler, comme vous me l'avez demandé.

— Je crains que parler ne soit pas suffisant. Vous voyez l'Académie de l'Ombre au-dessus de nous ? La flotte du Second Imperium vient d'arriver. Vous n'avez aucune chance de nous vaincre, malgré vos misérables renforts. Joignez-vous à nous immédiatement et évitez ainsi un bain de sang. Je sais quels pouvoirs seraient les vôtres, Skywalker, si vous vous autorisiez à *explorer* ce que vous avez toujours combattu.

Luke secoua la tête.

— Épargnez votre souffle, Brakiss. Vos paroles, pas plus que le Côté Obscur, ne peuvent avoir d'effet sur moi. Vous avez autrefois été *mon* étudiant. Vous avez vu le Côté Lumineux, et vous vous en êtes détourné comme un lâche. Mais il n'est pas trop tard. Venez avec moi : ensemble, nous découvrirons ce qu'il reste de lumineux dans votre cœur.

— Il n'en reste *rien*, siffla Brakiss. Je ne suis pas venu ici pour philosopher. Si vous refusez d'être raisonnable et de vous rendre, je devrai vous vaincre et prendre votre Académie Jedi par la force.

Il tira un sabrolaser de sous ses robes argentées. De longues pointes, semblables à des serres, entouraient la lame d'énergie. Brakiss poussa un soupir.

— Tout ça me semble un tel gaspillage d'énergie, dit-il.

— Je ne veux pas me battre contre vous, déclara Luke.

Brakiss haussa les épaules.

— Comme vous voulez. Dans ce cas, je vais vous découper en morceaux. Votre passivité me facilitera la tâche.

Les réflexes de Luke entrèrent en action au dernier moment. Il se projeta vers l'arrière, ajoutant de l'élan à son saut avec un rien de Force. Il atterrit en position de défense et tira son sabrolaser.

— Je me défendrai, Brakiss. Mais il y a tant de choses que vous auriez pu apprendre à l'Académie Jedi...

Brakiss lâcha un rire moqueur.

— Qui me les aurait enseignées ? Vous ? Je ne vous reconnais plus comme maître, Luke Skywalker. Quant à vous, il y a tant de choses que vous ignorez... Vous pensez que j'ai été lâche de quitter l'Académie avant d'avoir terminé ma formation. Qui vous autorise à en juger ? Vous n'avez reçu qu'un entraînement partiel, vous aussi. Un petit moment avec Obi-Wan Kenobi, avant que Dark Vador le tue, puis avec maître Yoda, que vous avez quitté... Vous êtes passé près de la vraie grandeur quand vous avez servi l'Empereur ressuscité. Mais vous avez reculé. Vous n'avez jamais rien *terminé*.

— Je ne le nie pas, dit Luke, portant son sabrolaser en position défensive.

Les lames se heurtèrent avec un crépitement. Les lèvres de Brakiss formèrent un sourire dédaigneux. Il se fendit de nouveau ; Luke para l'attaque.

— Votre enseignement soulignait que devenir un Jedi mène à la découverte de soi-même, dit Brakiss. J'ai continué depuis que je suis parti. J'ai abandonné vos enseignements, mais j'ai acquis un tel savoir ! Plus que vous, Luke Skywalker, bien plus, parce que vous vous êtes fermé beaucoup de portes. (Il prit un air de défi.) Moi, j'ai regardé derrière chacune d'entre elles.

— Une personne qui se précipite tête baissée vers un danger mortel ne doit pas être qualifiée de « courageuse », dit Luke, mais bien d'« imprudente. »

— Dans ce cas, *vous* êtes imprudent, dit Brakiss.

Il fendit l'air de son sabrolaser avec l'intention de couper les jambes de Luke. Celui-ci para, et obligea son adversaire à reculer. Les robes argentées du Jedi Obscur battirent autour de lui comme des ailes de papillon nocturne.

— Vous ne pouvez pas gagner, Brakiss, dit Luke.

— C'est ce que vous croyez, railla le maître de l'Académie de l'Ombre.

Il frappa avec une violence redoublée, laissant monter sa colère. Ses attaques se firent de plus en plus dures.

Luke garda son calme.

— Sentez la paix, Brakiss, dit-il. Laissez la douceur vous envahir... Tranquille, apaisante...

Brakiss éclata de rire, sa chevelure blonde emmêlée et collée par la transpiration.

— Skywalker, combien de fois tenterez-vous de me détourner de ma voie ? Vous m'avez pourchassé, alors que j'avais rejeté vos enseignements. Ne pouvez-vous accepter la défaite ?

— Je me souviens de notre affrontement, sur Telti. Vous auriez pu vous joindre à moi à ce moment-là. Il n'est toujours pas trop tard.

Brakiss ricana.

— Tout ça ne signifie rien pour moi. Ces événements n'étaient qu'une simple diversion. Jusqu'à ce que je trouve mon destin : la création de l'Académie de l'Ombre.

— Vous devriez peut-être embrasser une autre vocation, dit Luke.

Il para une attaque latérale de Brakiss.

Celui-ci changea de tactique. Au lieu de viser Luke, il frappa un des piliers du temple, une colonne de marbre gravée d'anciens symboles de la Sith. Des étincelles jaillirent quand la lame sectionna la colonne.

Luke se jeta de côté lorsque le pilier s'écroula. Le linteau avant du temple du Bosquet des Feuilles Bleues tomba sur le sol. Les pierres et les branches suivirent, volant dans toutes les directions. Luke s'écarta sans peine, évitant d'être blessé.

— Vous avez encore le pied assez léger pour un homme de votre âge, dit Brakiss, moqueur.

— Vous me semblez bien destructeur pour un homme du vôtre, répliqua Skywalker.

Il sauta par-dessus les décombres, toussa à cause de la poussière, puis croisa de nouveau le « fer » avec Brakiss.

— Vous devriez peut-être essayer de voir comment vos Jedi Obscurs s'en sortent, dit Luke. Mes étudiants sont en train de les battre à plate couture.

Dans la jungle, les luttes continuaient. Il avait hâte de retourner auprès de ses étudiants. Cette rencontre avec son ancien disciple n'avait servi à rien.

— Tout ça a duré assez longtemps, Brakiss. Vous pouvez vous rendre. Sinon je vous vaincrai, parce que j'ai d'autres choses à faire. Je dois retourner défendre mon Académie.

Brakiss parut surpris quand Luke plongea vers lui avec l'intention d'en finir. Luke frappa de nouveau, conservant sa résolution et sa concentration sans laisser la colère le dominer.

Le maître de l'Académie de l'Ombre se défendit. Luke vit l'occasion de frapper. Il changea légèrement la direction de son coup afin de ne pas toucher la lame elle-même. Il aurait pu viser plus bas et couper la main de son ancien étudiant, comme Dark Vador avait fait avec lui. Mais il ne voulait pas mutiler Brakiss. Il lui suffisait de détruire son arme.

Le sabrolaser frappa celui de Brakiss, à la jonction de la lame et de la poignée. Le sabrolaser mal conçu éclata, se séparant en deux parties fumantes.

Brakiss hurla et laissa tomber la poignée sur le sol, simple masse de composants détruits.

Le maître de l'Académie de l'Ombre recula en titubant, les mains levées.

— Ne me tuez pas, Skywalker ! Je vous en prie, ne me tuez pas !

Sa terreur semblait hors de proportion avec la menace. Le Jedi Obscur savait certainement que Luke Skywalker n'était pas de ceux qui achèvent un ennemi vaincu. Brakiss saisit ses robes argentées, tripotant les fermetures.

Luke s'approcha de lui, sabrolaser en avant.

— Vous êtes désormais mon prisonnier, Brakiss. Il est temps de mettre fin à cette bataille. Ordonnez à vos Jedi Obscurs de se rendre.

Brakiss laissa tomber ses robes autour de lui, révélant une combinaison de vol et un générateur de répulsion.

— Non, j'ai mieux à faire, dit-il en activant le générateur.

Devant les yeux ahuris de Luke, Brakiss monta dans les airs et se trouva rapidement hors d'atteinte. L'instructeur des Jedi Obscurs avait dû poser son vaisseau non loin, comprit Luke, et il allait rejoindre l'Académie de l'Ombre.

Déconcerté, Luke regarda son ancien étudiant

s'enfuir une fois de plus, vaincu, mais encore capable de faire beaucoup de mal.

La douleur de l'avoir perdu envahit l'esprit de Luke, presque aussi aiguë que le jour où Brakiss s'était enfui de l'Académie Jedi.

— Je ne suis pas parvenu à te sauver cette fois encore...

La taille de son adversaire diminua jusqu'à ce qu'il ne soit plus qu'un point minuscule semblable à une étoile de mauvais augure.

CHAPITRE XVIII

Dans l'espace, la flotte du Second Imperium se déchaînait.

— Tout le personnel aux postes de combat ! s'écria Ackbar. Levez les boucliers ! Préparez-vous à retourner le feu !

Les deux superdestroyers de tête tirèrent, leurs turbolasers jetant des éclairs. Des rayons d'énergie jaillirent, visant le vaisseau d'Ackbar.

Jaina était debout près du Calamarien. Elle ferma les yeux quand les tirs s'écrasèrent contre leurs boucliers avant.

— Le Second Imperium a dû construire sa flotte en secret, dit-elle. Ces vaisseaux donnent l'impression d'avoir été assemblés à la va-vite.

— Ça ne les empêche pas d'être mortellement dangereux, dit Ackbar en hochant la tête. Maintenant, je comprends pourquoi ils nous ont volé des

hyperpropulseurs et des lasers quand ils ont atta-
qué l'*Adamantin*.

Il se tourna vers les systèmes de communication, lançant des ordres de sa voix caverneuse.

— Changement de cible. La station de formation est moins dangereuse que ces vaisseaux. Que
chacun se concentre sur les superdestroyers !

Consternés, les officiers d'artillerie regardèrent
l'amiral.

— Monsieur, nos systèmes de visée refusent de
fonctionner, dit l'un d'eux. Les vaisseaux émettent
des signaux les identifiant comme des alliés. Nous
sommes dans l'impossibilité de tirer.

— Comment ? s'étrangla Ackbar. Mais nous
voyons que ce sont des ennemis !

— Je sais, amiral, s'écria l'officier. Mais nos
ordinateurs refusent de tirer. Ils pensent que ce
sont des vaisseaux de la Nouvelle République. Ce
blocage est inclus dans leur programmation.

Jaina comprenait ce qui se passait :

— Ils ont volé des systèmes de guidage et des
ordinateurs tactiques lors de leur raid sur
Kashyyyk. Ils ont dû les installer dans leurs vaisseaux, afin de tromper nos ordinateurs. Nous
devons changer les programmes de visée, sinon
nous ne pourrons pas faire feu. Le système d'iden-
tification nous en empêchera.

Lando Calrissian avait écouté sur la fréquence
ouverte. Sa voix retentit dans les haut-parleurs.

— Les vaisseaux de la station des Pêcheurs de
Gemme fonctionnent avec des ordinateurs diffé-

rents. Je suppose que l'honneur de tirer les premiers nous revient...

La flotte disparate de Lando se dirigea vers les superdestroyers, lâchant des torpilles à protons afin d'affaiblir les boucliers des Impériaux.

— Une petite astuce dont je me suis toujours souvenu, dit Lando. Tout ça me rappelle la bataille de Tanaab.

Il lâcha un glapissement de triomphe quand une autre salve de torpilles prit son envol. D'eux d'entre elles pénétrèrent les boucliers et laissèrent une traînée noire sur le flanc d'un superdestroyer.

Les vaisseaux de Lando continuèrent à tirer. Les Impériaux visèrent les petits navires, délaissant ceux d'Ackbar.

— Amiral, dit Jaina, si le Second Imperium est parvenu à retourner nos systèmes informatiques contre nous, je suppose que nous pouvons faire la même chose dans l'autre sens.

Ackbar se retourna, ses énormes yeux ronds fixés sur la jeune fille.

Elle se mordit la lèvre inférieure, et prit une profonde inspiration. Son idée était un peu folle, mais...

— Vous êtes l'amiral en chef de la flotte de la Nouvelle République. Il doit exister une programmation qui impose aux ordinateurs un signal prioritaire. Surtout dans les cas d'extrême urgence, comme celui-ci !

Ackbar la regarda, la bouche ouverte comme s'il avait besoin d'un verre d'eau.

— Par la Force, Jaina, vous avez raison !

— Qu'attendons-nous ? dit la Jedi en se frottant les mains. Reprogrammons les ordinateurs !

Après avoir détruit le vaisseau de Norys pour sauver Jacen Solo, Qorl ne ressentait plus rien, comme si son corps s'était transformé en un assemblage électronique, à l'instar de son bras gauche.

Après des années de service loyal, il avait trahi le Second Imperium. *Trahi*, lui ! Il avait laissé ses sentiments prendre le pas sur l'obéissance qu'il devait à son Empereur.

Le jeune Jacen avait été gentil avec lui. Il lui avait montré de l'affection et de l'amitié, bien que Qorl n'eût rien fait pour les mériter...

Il avait capturé les jumeaux, les avait menacés, puis forcés à réparer son chasseur Tie afin de pouvoir retourner au sein de l'Empire. Depuis il s'était autorisé quelques actions secrètes pour les aider, comme quand il leur avait permis de fuir l'Académie de l'Ombre en leur ouvrant discrètement les portes du dock. Mais tuer son propre élève pour les protéger...

Qorl avait commis une grave erreur en prenant des décisions *personnelles*. Ce n'était pas dans ses attributions. Il était un pilote de Tie, un soldat du Second Imperium qui aidait à former les autres pilotes et les commandos. Il devait obéissance et loyauté à l'Empereur. Les soldats n'avaient pas loisir de décider quels ordres suivre et lesquels ignorer...

Profondément troublé, Qorl amena son chasseur Tie en orbite. La plupart des membres de son escadrille s'étaient éparpillés. Les autres avaient été détruits par les défenses de Yavin 4. Il aurait dû rentrer et faire un rapport à ses supérieurs. Mais il avait à décider s'il lui fallait se rendre ou avouer ce qu'il avait fait et affronter la colère du seigneur Brakiss.

La mâchoire de Qorl se crispa. *Se rendre, c'est trahir.* Comment pouvait-il envisager une telle chose ? Les moteurs de son vaisseau hurlèrent quand il se dégagea de l'atmosphère et se dirigea vers l'Académie de l'Ombre.

À sa grande surprise, il s'aperçut qu'il arrivait en pleine bataille spatiale.

Des vaisseaux de la Nouvelle République étaient apparus, tirant sur l'Académie. La flotte de guerre du Second Imperium, des superdestroyers mal fichus et des croiseurs de bataille montés à partir de pièces de rechange et d'épaves, était venue à la rescousse. Par chance, ces rafiots étaient équipés des systèmes informatiques, de l'hyperdrive et des turbolasers volés aux Rebelles avec l'aide de Qorl.

La vue de la flotte emplit Qorl de consternation. Elle manquait de la grandeur et de l'impressionnante présence de l'armada d'origine de l'Empire. Qorl avait servi à bord de l'Étoile Noire, dans les rangs de la glorieuse armée commandée par le Grand Moff Tarkin.

Cette nouvelle force semblait un peu... désespérée,

comme si des hommes dont les rêves excédaient de beaucoup les moyens s'étaient joints au combat.

Qorl vit les vaisseaux du Second Imperium pilonner la flotte rebelle. Puis la situation changea : un vol de vaisseaux hétéroclites attaqua les superdestroyers.

Les boucliers des Impériaux tombèrent soudain en panne, comme si leurs ordinateurs les avaient coupés, et qu'ils aient accepté de se rendre.

Les croiseurs rebelles profitèrent de la brèche ; ils canardèrent la coque des nouveaux superdestroyers. Que se passait-il ? Pourquoi ses camarades ne remontaient-ils pas leurs boucliers ?

Pendant que Qorl volait vers la bataille, soucieux de faire quelque chose pour aider l'Empire, des chasseurs Tie sortirent des superdestroyers et entreprirent de mitrailler la flotte rebelle. Mais ils ressemblaient à de minuscules insectes, comparés aux vaisseaux d'Ackbar.

Qorl vit l'occasion de se racheter. Il avait déjà trahi ses amis de Yavin 4 *et* le Second Imperium. Quel que soit son choix, il serait maudit... Jamais il ne pourrait vivre avec ce qu'il avait fait.

Il lui restait la possibilité de se joindre au Second Imperium et de causer autant de dégâts que possible à la flotte rebelle. Il aurait peut-être la chance de mourir en combattant. Jadis, il s'était envolé de l'Étoile Noire, chargé d'une mission similaire. C'était sa chance de remettre les choses dans l'ordre.

Il arma les canons laser qui avaient tiré sur le

vaisseau de Norys pour empêcher la jeune brute de donner libre cours à sa folie meurtrière. Maintenant, il pouvait utiliser ses armes contre la cible qu'on lui avait désignée : l'Alliance Rebelle.

Son chasseur Tie débaula dans la bataille, comme venu de nulle part, et tira sur un des Corelliens, laissant une série de marques noires sur sa coque. D'autres chasseurs Tie se joignirent à lui, volant dans une formation d'attaque assez désordonnée. Ces pilotes étaient visiblement peu entraînés ; ils n'avaient pas dû faire assez de simulations. Le chaos environnant leur profita, leurs vaisseaux volant les uns autour des autres sans cible définie, mais avec l'objectif de faire autant de dégâts que possible.

La flotte de l'Alliance répondit par un feu nourri de turbolasers, arrosant l'espace dans toutes les directions. Un superdestroyer explosa, sa tourelle de commande en flammes. Un autre partit à la dérive, défenses détruites. Il fit demi-tour pour tenter de s'échapper. La flotte rebelle se lança à sa poursuite.

Le Second Imperium était en train de perdre la bataille !

Qorl pilonna les vaisseaux ennemis. Certains chasseurs Tie filèrent vers l'espace libre. Qorl se demanda où ils avaient l'intention d'aller. Leurs vaisseaux mères avaient été détruits et l'Académie de l'Ombre était sous le feu de l'ennemi. Entendaient-ils se rendre ?

— Se rendre, c'est trahir, murmura-t-il.

Puis il plongea vers le vaisseau amiral des Rebelles.

Des tirs de turbolaser passèrent non loin de lui, mais il les évita. Faisant feu de ses canons laser, il passa sous la coque du monstrueux vaisseau.

Il n'abandonnerait pas. Il connaîtrait sa fin dans un dernier moment de gloire.

Les Rebelles ajustèrent leur tir : un coup fit mouche. Qorl ferma les yeux, s'attendant à se désintégrer.

Mais le faisceau d'énergie avait seulement effleuré un moteur et endommagé une des unités d'alimentation.

Le chasseur de Qorl tomba en vrille, quittant le champ de bataille. Malgré son harnais de sécurité, le pilote fut ballotté de tous côtés dans son minuscule cockpit. Pendant la chute vertigineuse, Qorl pensa que le vaisseau allait exploser...

Puis il se rendit compte que le chasseur avait été pris dans un champ gravitationnel. Une fois de plus, Qorl allait s'écraser sur Yavin 4...

CHAPITRE XIX

À bord de sa navette monoplace, Brakiss s'éloigna de Yavin 4, se dirigeant vers sa précieuse Académie de l'Ombre. Il tapa les commandes qui ouvriraient automatiquement les portes des docks et lui permettraient d'accéder librement à la station.

La bataille spatiale ne le concernait pas. Ce n'était jamais qu'un événement de plus à avoir mal tourné...

Son cœur cognait toujours à tout rompre à cause du combat avec Sykwalker dans les ruines du temple. Les derniers mots de son ancien maître résonnaient sans cesse à ses oreilles. La colère et le désespoir tourbillonnaient dans son esprit.

Toutes les méthodes qu'il connaissait refusèrent de lui rendre le niveau de sérénité et de détachement dont il avait besoin pour utiliser pleinement ses pouvoirs.

Il essaya même d'avoir recours aux techniques

apaisantes que Skywalker lui avait montrées lors de son séjour sur Yavin 4.

Rien n'y fit.

Tout s'écroulait. Ses plans grandioses, ses Jedi Obscurs soigneusement formés, les troupes du Second Imperium... Tout avait échoué, à la veille de ce qui aurait dû être son triomphe, le coup final porté à la Rébellion. Se débarrasser de l'Académie Jedi aurait dû être une tâche aisée.

L'Empereur le tuerait pour cet échec. Mais Brakiss ne pensait qu'à une chose. Palpatine était leur dernier espoir. Leur *seul* espoir. Brakiss accepterait sa punition plus tard. Avant, il devait faire son possible pour assurer tout de même la victoire.

Il posa sa navette dans le dock presque désert, là où peu de temps avant chasseurs et bombardiers Tie se préparaient au combat. Tamith Kai était partie sur de sa plate-forme de bataille blindée, emportant les commandos et l'escadron de Jedi Obscurs de Zekk.

Ils étaient fiers, confiants, sûrs d'écraser les Jedi du Côté Lumineux...

Brakiss descendit de sa navette, essayant en vain de retrouver sa dignité. Pour ne pas rester sans arme, il prit dans un râtelier mural un des sabrolasers de série qui équipaient son Académie.

Mais comment ferait-il pour se défendre ? Il avait vu la plate-forme de Tamith Kai tomber vers la rivière, transformée en un amas de métal fondu. Les Chevaliers Obscurs de Zekk avaient été écrasés, les escadrilles de chasseurs Tie pratiquement détruites. Et la nouvelle flotte de superdestroyers était en train de se faire battre à plate couture par les Rebelles.

Brakiss quitta les docks et entra dans les couloirs presque vides de l'Académie de l'Ombre. Toutes les troupes valides avaient été envoyées au sol. Il restait à bord le minimum de personnel requis pour assurer la sécurité de la station.

Les couloirs auraient dû être le théâtre d'une célébration ; un silence sépulcral y régnait, comme à bord d'une épave abandonnée. L'Empereur devait trouver un moyen de les sauver afin que le Second Imperium règne sur la galaxie.

Palpatine avait échappé deux fois à la destruction. Après sa mort, à bord de la seconde Étoile Noire, lors de la bataille d'Endor, il était parvenu à ressusciter grâce à des clones. Bien que tous eussent été détruits, treize ans plus tard, l'Empereur était revenu d'entre les morts. Cette fois, aucune explication n'avait été donnée.

Un homme qui avait accompli de tels exploits trouverait certainement le moyen d'arracher la victoire à une bande de Rebelles et de criminels !

La tête haute, essayant de retrouver sa foi dans l'Empire, Brakiss avança le long des couloirs. Il devait voir l'Empereur ; cette fois, il n'accepterait pas de fin de non-recevoir. Le sort de la guerre reposait sur les minutes à venir.

Deux gardes étaient postés devant la porte scellée. Ils portaient des casques sinistres en forme de projectiles, avec une simple fente pour les yeux. Ils se raidirent en voyant Brakiss, et croisèrent leurs vibrolances pour lui barrer le chemin.

Brakiss alla vers eux sans hésiter.

— Place, dit-il. Je dois parler à l'Empereur.

— Il demande à ne pas être dérangé, dit un des gardes.

— *Dérangé ?* répéta Brakiss, sidéré. Il le sera bien plus s'il n'agit pas ! Notre flotte est en train de perdre ; les Jedi Obscurs ont presque tous été capturés ; la plate-forme de Tamith Kai s'est écrasée ; il ne reste quasiment plus de chasseurs Tie. Laissez-moi passer. Je dois absolument lui parler.

— L'Empereur ne parle à personne.

Les gardes avancèrent d'un pas, armes brandies.

Brakiss sentit sa colère croître. Elle lui donna de l'énergie. Le pouvoir coula en lui quand il puisa directement dans le Côté Obscur de la Force. Il comprit pourquoi la Sœur de la Nuit, Tamith Kai, vivait dans un état de colère permanente : l'expérience était fascinante.

Brakiss n'avait pas de temps à perdre avec des obstacles mineurs vêtus de rouge. C'étaient des traîtres ! Il laissa la Force lui dicter sa conduite.

Son sabrolaser venant se loger dans la paume de sa main, Brakiss appuya sur le bouton d'activation. Une lame d'énergie jaillit, mais il ne s'en servit pas pour menacer. Il en avait assez des menaces et des discussions. Il donna libre cours à sa colère.

— Cela suffit !

Il frappa sauvagement. Son champ de vision se

rétrécit, devenant un tunnel noir où se détachaient ses deux cibles. Les gardes tentèrent de se défendre. En vain. Brakiss était un Jedi puissant. Il connaissait le Côté Obscur ; les deux hommes n'avaient aucune chance contre lui.

Moins d'une seconde plus tard, ils gisaient tous deux sur le sol.

Brakiss activa le mécanisme de la porte. Les codes de sécurité essayèrent de l'empêcher d'entrer. Il fit sauter les circuits en utilisant la Force. De ses mains nues, il arracha les battants de la porte, puis il entra d'un pas décidé dans les appartements privés de l'Empereur.

— Maître, vous devez venir à notre aide ! s'écria-t-il.

La pièce était plongée dans la pénombre. Le Jedi Obscur cligna des yeux, n'y voyant goutte.

Il n'y avait personne.

— Empereur Palpatine ! La bataille tourne en faveur des Rebelles ! Vous devez faire quelque chose !

Ses mots résonnèrent dans la salle. Il n'entendit pas la moindre réponse, ne perçut aucun mouvement. Brakiss alla dans la pièce voisine, où se trouvait le caisson d'isolation aux parois noires. La porte blindée était fermée, les panneaux latéraux fixés par de solides rivets.

Brakiss savait que l'Empereur était dans le caisson, à l'abri des influences extérieures. Il avait craint que sa santé ne soit défaillante, et qu'il ait besoin de cet environnement spécial pour survivre.

À présent, il n'en avait cure, las de se faire claquer des portes au nez. Il était inconcevable que le maître de l'Académie de l'Ombre, un des membres les plus importants du Second Imperium, soit traité comme un vulgaire valet.

Il frappa à la porte blindée.

— Empereur, j'exige que vous me receviez ! Vous ne pouvez pas laisser cette défaite survenir ! Vous devez utiliser vos pouvoirs pour arracher la victoire à nos ennemis !

Aucune réponse. L'écho des coups mourut dans le silence de la pièce colorée de rouge sang par un éclairage étrange. Le cœur de Brakiss se glaça dans sa poitrine, comme une comète perdue aux franges d'un système solaire inconnu.

Si l'Empereur les abandonnait, ils étaient condamnés. Le Second Imperium était en train de se faire battre par les Rebelles ; Brakiss n'avait plus rien à perdre.

Il activa de nouveau son sabrolaser et frappa. La lame d'énergie étincela quand elle coupa l'épaisse plaque de blindage. Rien, pas même le fer mandalorien, ne pouvait résister au sabrolaser d'un Jedi.

Brakiss cisailla les charnières. Le métal fondu fuma et coula le long de la porte. Il frappa de nouveau, se ménageant une entrée en arrachant la cloison, comme un droïd-manutentionnaire démantibulerait un conteneur de marchandises. Il fit un pas de côté pour éviter un gros bloc de blindage qui tomba sur le pont avec un bruit assourdissant.

Brakiss attendit, figé par l'indécision. Quand la

fumée se dissipa, il leva son sabrolaser et pénétra dans le caisson.

Il ne vit pas l'Empereur. Pas de pièce richement meublée, pas même un appareillage médical complexe pour maintenir le vieux chef en vie.

À la place de Palpatine, il découvrit une supercherie...

Un troisième garde était assis derrière une console composée de trois ordinateurs entourant un fauteuil aux nombreux tableaux de commande.

Brakiss vit des vidéoclips holographiques de l'Empereur, filmés tout au long de son règne. L'accession au pouvoir du sénateur Palpatine, l'Ordre Nouveau, les assauts de la Rébellion... Des discours enregistrés, des mémos, pratiquement chaque mot que Palpatine avait prononcé en public, plus les messages privés. Des générateurs holographiques mélangeaient les clips et fabriquaient des images tridimensionnelles imitant la vie à s'y méprendre.

Brakiss regarda avec horreur.

Le garde se leva d'un bond, ses robes écarlates flottant autour de lui.

— Vous n'avez pas le droit d'entrer ici.

— Où est le Maître ? demanda Brakiss. (Mais il connaissait déjà la réponse.) Il n'y a pas d'Empereur, n'est-ce pas ? Tout ça n'était qu'un sinistre canular, une minable tentative pour vous approprier le pouvoir !

— Oui, dit le garde. Et vous avez joué votre rôle à merveille. L'Empereur est mort voilà bien des années, quand son dernier clone a été détruit, mais le Second Imperium avait besoin d'un chef. Quatre gardes parmi les plus loyaux de Palpatine ont décidé de créer ce leader.

« Nous avions tous les discours de notre Empereur. Nous avions ses pensées, ses enregistrements. Nous savions que le Second Imperium était viable, mais personne ne *nous* aurait suivis. Il fallait donner aux gens ce qu'ils voulaient : l'Empereur. Vous avez été facile à duper, car vous en aviez *envie*.

Le maître de l'Académie de l'Ombre avança vers le garde, son arme scintillant d'un feu glacé.

— Vous nous avez trompés, dit-il, toujours saisi d'une horreur incrédule. Vous m'avez trompé, *moi* ! J'étais un des soldats les plus dévoués de l'Empereur, mais je servais un mensonge ! Le Second Imperium n'avait aucune chance. Maintenant, nous allons être détruits à cause de vos plans ineptes ! Parce que le Second Imperium n'a pas de chef !

Aveuglé par la rage, Brakiss se jeta sur le garde, sabrolaser levé, tel un ange vengeur.

L'homme s'éloigna des écrans, cherchant une arme dans ses robes écarlates.

Brakiss ne lui en laissa pas le temps.

Il abattit le garde, qui s'écroula sur les commandes qui généraient le faux Empereur. L'illusion avait trompé Brakiss, l'Académie de l'Ombre et les Jedi Obscurs... Tous ceux qui avaient consacré leur existence à recréer l'Empire...

— L'Empire est vraiment mort, dit Brakiss d'une voix rauque.

Son calme et son apparence de statue l'avaient quitté.

Il entendit une voix de l'autre côté de la porte démantelée du caisson. Se retournant, il vit un éclair écarlate : le quatrième et dernier membre du groupe de « faussaires ». Brakiss avança lentement, raide et endolori, totalement découragé. Mais il n'était pas question de laisser un de ces chiens échapper à sa vindicte. Son honneur demandait que ceux qui l'avaient grugé périssent. Brakiss se précipita.

Le garde avait trouvé les cadavres de ses compagnons ; il savait que Brakiss était entré dans le caisson et qu'il avait vu les commandes holographiques.

Sans hésiter, le quatrième traître partit à la course.

Brakiss avait conscience que c'était la fin du rêve impérial. Ses Jedi Obscurs avaient perdu la bataille. Les chasseurs étaient écrasés par les Rebelles... Mais il ne laisserait pas cet imposteur s'en tirer vivant. Il se vengerait.

Le garde courait à une vitesse hallucinante, filant comme une flèche le long des couloirs vides de l'Académie de l'Ombre.

Brakiss courut aussi vite que possible. Mais le garde savait exactement où il allait, et il ne perdit pas de temps.

Le fuyard atteignit les docks et se rua vers la navette de Brakiss.

À la porte des docks, le Jedi Obscur cria : « Arrêtez-vous ! »

Il aurait souhaité que la Force lui permette d'obliger l'homme à obéir à son ordre.

Mais le traître n'hésita pas. Il entra dans la navette, activa les moteurs à répulsion et tapa les codes permettant de passer à travers le champ magnétique qui retenait l'atmosphère.

Brakiss écumait de rage. Il savait qu'il n'aurait pas le temps d'accéder à l'artillerie de la station et de faire sauter le vaisseau.

Il se sentit totalement seul. Sa vie entière était un échec. Tout ce qu'il avait essayé avait fait long feu. La supercherie était l'insulte finale : trompé par de simples *gardes* !

Un souvenir remonta à la mémoire de Brakiss. Lors de la construction de l'Académie de l'Ombre, prétendument sous l'aile de l'Empereur Palpatine, un mécanisme de protection avait été intégré à la structure : une énorme quantité d'explosifs reliés entre eux. De cette façon, si *Palpatine (pour employer ce nom)* s'était senti menacé par les nouveaux Chevaliers Jedi, il aurait pu actionner le détonateur et faire sauter l'Académie de l'Ombre où qu'elle se trouve.

Brakiss regarda la petite navette s'éloigner de la station. Horrifié, il se rendit compte que c'étaient les *gardes* qui possédaient les codes secrets de destruction.

Tandis que son vaisseau fuyait l'Académie de

l'Ombre et le système de Yavin, le dernier conspirateur réalisa que les forces qu'il laissait derrière lui allaient être totalement détruites. Le succès de la contre-attaque des Rebelles signifiait qu'il ne resterait sans doute aucun survivant.

Le garde devait préserver son secret et maintenir l'illusion que ses partenaires et lui avaient si soigneusement entretenue pour s'approprier le pouvoir. Il ne devait pas laisser l'Académie Obscure intacte s'il voulait couvrir ses traces. Avec un peu de chance, il retrouverait une place parmi les criminels qui pullulaient aux franges de la Nouvelle République.

Le garde envoya un bref signal codé. Un seul mot, qu'il avait espéré ne jamais devoir utiliser.

Destruction.

Quand son petit vaisseau plongea dans l'hyperespace, l'Académie de l'Ombre se transforma en une gigantesque boule de feu.

CHAPITRE XX

Zekk y voyait à peine à deux mètres dans les ténèbres de la jungle de Yavin 4. Les branches s'accrochaient à ses cheveux et à sa cape. Il haletait, le souffle court. Sa queue de cheval s'était défaite. Mais il continuait d'aller de l'avant. De temps en temps, il jetait un coup d'œil par-dessus son épaule pour voir si un des Jedi de Skywalker était sur ses traces. Il ne sentait personne, mais comment être sûr ? Ils pouvaient peut-être l'empêcher de détecter leur présence.

Il avait vu bien des choses étranges au cours de la journée. Des choses *horribles*. Peu lui importait que le chemin fût difficile et incertain : il ne s'en serait pas aperçu de toute façon. Son esprit était anesthésié par les abominations dont il avait été témoin : la destruction, la terreur, l'échec... La mort.

Zekk glissa sur des feuilles humides et tomba sur un genou. Il saisit une branche basse pour se redresser.

Désorienté, il regarda autour de lui.

Dans quelle direction allait-il ? Il savait qu'il marchait vers quelque chose... Mais quoi ?

Finalement, une partie de son esprit se souvint, et il repartit.

Devant lui, un rongeur de bonne taille jaillit du sous-bois, les griffes en avant. L'entraînement de Zekk lui permit de réagir automatiquement.

D'un mouvement souple, il tira son sabrolaser, puis se jeta hors du trajet de la créature, s'entaillant la joue en heurtant le tronc d'un arbre. Au même moment, il appuya sur le bouton d'activation de son sabrolaser. La lame rouge sang sortit de la poignée ; Zekk frappa, coupant le rongeur en deux en plein bond. Le cri de la créature mourut abruptement ; ses deux moitiés fumantes retombèrent sur le sol.

Cela lui rappela la façon dont il avait tué Vilas, l'étudiant de Tamith Kai, dans l'arène de l'Académie de l'Ombre. Ce n'était pas un souvenir susceptible de le réconforter.

Le sang coulait sur sa joue, mais la douleur était comme lointaine. La Force l'avait protégé. Mais qu'en était-il de ses compagnons du Second Imperium ? Qu'est-ce qui était allé de travers ? Il avait vu tous ses Jedi succomber ou se faire capturer par les étudiants de Skywalker.

Il avait le terrible soupçon d'être le seul encore en liberté.

Pourtant, le Côté Obscur avait remporté quelques victoires. Orvak avait réussi à détruire les générateurs de bouclier ; sans doute avait-il accompli aussi la deuxième partie de sa mission. Zekk percevait que certains élèves de l'Académie de l'Ombre avaient obtenu d'autres succès. Mais chacun avait été de courte durée.

Brakiss, Tamith Kai, ses compagnons et lui avaient tous été si sûrs d'un triomphe rapide ! Avec l'entraînement qu'ils avaient suivi, il n'aurait pas dû y avoir de problèmes.

N'était-ce pas ce que Brakiss leur avait inculqué ?

Quelques minutes plus tard, Zekk émergea dans une vaste clairière où la rivière coulait paresseusement entre les arbres. Reprenant un peu espoir, il s'approcha de la berge et se pencha pour boire.

Malgré les reflets verts de l'eau, il se voyait parfaitement dedans. Ses yeux émeraude enfoncés et entourés de cercles noirs le regardèrent. Seuls les vestiges de sa confiance en lui se voyaient sur ses traits. Des mèches hirsutes de cheveux noirs sales pendaient autour d'un visage aussi pâle que la lune de son monde natal, Ennth. Le sang suintait toujours de sa blessure à la joue, en un frappant contraste avec les bleus qui l'entouraient. Cela lui rappela Brakiss et son visage parfait de statue.

Un cri retentit dans l'esprit du jeune homme, si violent qu'il tomba à quatre pattes dans la boue.

Zekk se protégea les oreilles avec les mains. En vain.

— Brakiss ! hurla-t-il. Qu'est-ce qui ne va pas ?

Comprenant à peine ce qui se passait, Zekk leva les yeux vers le ciel. Un instant, il vit la station qui abritait l'Académie de l'Ombre, en orbite basse au-dessus de la lune-jungle.

Puis, sans que rien l'ait laissé prévoir, la station se transforma en une boule de feu. La mâchoire de Zekk béa à cette vue. Il n'avait pas cru possible de ressentir davantage de chagrin.

Mais il s'était trompé.

Brakiss. Zekk murmura mentalement ce nom. Il savait que son maître avait été à bord de l'Académie de l'Ombre au moment de l'explosion. Il l'avait *senti.* Brakiss l'avait formé, il lui avait donné un but, une place et des capacités dont il était fier. Zekk s'était senti *chez lui* à l'Académie de l'Ombre. Il avait été le plus Obscur des Chevaliers Obscurs.

Que lui restait-il ? L'idéal pour lequel il avait vécu avait disparu. Sa fierté, ses camarades, son avenir... Il ne faisait aucun doute que le Second Imperium avait aujourd'hui reçu un coup mortel ; maintenant, le seul homme qui avait jamais cru en lui était mort.

Non. Pas le *seul.* Le désespoir s'abattit de nouveau sur le Jedi Obscur. Le vieux Peckhum avait toujours cru en lui, et Zekk lui avait promis de ne jamais rien faire pour le blesser ou le décevoir.

Pourtant, il s'était battu du côté de ses ennemis. Malgré tous les défauts qu'il se connaissait, Zekk n'avait jamais menti au vieux Peckhum lors de leur cohabitation sur Coruscant.

La colère l'envahit. Contre lui-même, contre le fait d'avoir été forcé de combattre son ami. Il était injuste de devoir faire des choix aussi terribles. Ses muscles se raidirent jusqu'à ce que la tension devienne insupportable. Avec un cri de détresse, il plongea les doigts dans la boue. Elle était un sombre amas glissant.

Pourtant, c'était ce qu'il avait choisi : l'obscurité.

Ses camarades avaient descendu le *Bâton de Foudre*. Pour ce qu'il en savait, le seul autre homme qui l'estimait était mort. Les mains de Zekk se refermèrent sur la boue, qu'il frotta contre son visage. Cela réveilla sa coupure. Oui, il sentait de nouveau la douleur. Mais il s'en moquait. Il ne méritait que cela.

Il avait échoué. Il avait trahi Brakiss, les autres guerriers du Côté Obscur, le vieux Peckhum... et lui-même. Des larmes silencieuses coulèrent de ses yeux. Il continua à s'enduire de boue. Une boue noire comme son cœur.

Oui. Voilà ce qu'il était devenu. Après avoir choisi l'obscurité, il s'était immergé en elle.

Il en était souillé.

Trop tard pour revenir en arrière. Il avait fait ses choix, devenant un Jedi Obscur. Même si ses camarades avaient été vaincus ou capturés, et Brakiss tué, il ne pourrait jamais se débarrasser de cette souillure, aussi longtemps qu'il vivrait.

Jaina et Jacen, s'ils étaient encore en vie, ne pourraient pas lui pardonner. Si on comptait les batailles spatiales, les attaques au sol et la destruction de l'Académie de l'Ombre, Zekk était responsable, directement ou indirectement, de la mort de plus de cent personnes. Peut-être aussi de celle de Peckhum. Les jumeaux le savaient. Ils avaient toujours pensé que sa décision de rejoindre l'Académie de l'Ombre était erronée, car rien de bon n'en sortirait.

Mais il avait tranché et travaillé de son mieux. Sur Kashyyyk, il avait prévenu Jaina de ne pas retourner sur Yavin 4, dans l'espoir de la tenir loin de la bataille. Il doutait qu'elle l'ait écouté.

Il se leva péniblement et regarda une dernière fois son reflet dans les eaux paisibles de la rivière. Sa cape pendouillait lamentablement, sale et déchirée. Il était couvert de boue. Ses yeux émeraude avaient perdu leur éclat.

Sa tâche n'était pas terminée. Son sort importait peu, mais il avait encore des choix à faire.

Il montrerait aux jumeaux qui il était en réalité.

Le Jedi Obscur reprit la direction du Grand Temple.

Il lui restait encore une carte à jouer.

CHAPITRE XXI

— C'est là, fit Jaina, désignant la clairière que Luke avait choisie comme point de ralliement.

Sur le siège du pilote de sa navette personnelle, Lando Calrissian lui fit un grand sourire qui dévoila sa superbe dentition blanche.

— Oui, ma petite demoiselle, dit-il. Nous allons atterrir. On dirait qu'ils nous attendent. Les combats doivent être terminés.

Pendant que Lando posait la navette, Jaina essaya de se détendre avec des techniques Jedi. Mais elle n'y parvint pas. Ses muscles restèrent raides comme si elle était toujours aux commandes du petit chasseur Tie, luttant pour sa vie. C'était la première fois qu'elle se battait contre le Côté Obscur aux côtés d'autres Jedi.

C'était le but de sa formation.

Quand la navette toucha terre, Jaina ne perdit

pas de temps. Elle sortit du vaisseau aussi vite que possible et courut vers son oncle. Puis elle se jeta dans ses bras.

— Tu t'en es sorti ! Tu es vivant ! dit-elle, le soulagement et la joie la submergeant.

— Luke, vieux bandit ! fit Lando. J'étais venu te proposer mon aide, mais je vois que tu n'en as pas eu besoin !

— Oh, si, Lando, dit Luke. (Il serra Jaina dans ses bras et dit :) Nombre d'entre nous n'ont pas été aussi chanceux.

Réalisant qu'elle n'avait aucune idée de la façon dont les choses s'étaient déroulées au sol, Jaina se mordit les lèvres. Elle regarda autour d'elle, espérant apercevoir Jacen, Lowie et Tenel Ka.

Ce qu'elle vit la bouleversa. Aucun des étudiants de l'Académie Jedi ne s'en était tiré sans blessures. Plusieurs boitaient. Le bras droit de Tionne était en écharpe, et ses cheveux étaient roussis. D'autres avaient des égratignures, des bleus, ou des blessures plus sérieuses.

Jaina fut surprise de voir Raynar, le visage noir et les vêtements déchirés, marcher parmi les blessés en offrant son aide. Il semblait avoir perdu son arrogance.

Quand elle vit de qui il s'occupait, Jaina pâlit. Tenel Ka portait une mauvaise coupure juste au-dessus de l'œil droit. Une autre blessure, moins profonde, allait du haut de sa cuisse à son genou.

Raynar était en train de déchirer des bandes de tissu à peu près propres, sacrifiant sa tunique.

Jaina en fit un tampon et l'appuya sur la blessure de Tenel Ka pour étancher le sang.

Raynar pansa la coupure à la jambe.

Jaina regarda autour d'elle, cherchant toujours Jacen. À quelques mètres de là, elle vit Lowie allongé sur le sol. Se tenant le côté, il gémissait doucement.

Tionne, Luke et Lando aidaient les derniers blessés à rejoindre le camp. Il n'y avait toujours pas trace de Jacen.

— Lowie, ça va ? demanda Jaina.

Le Wookie grommela quelque chose et lui fit signe de continuer à s'occuper de Tenel Ka.

— Oh, maîtresse Jaina ! Que le Grand Circuit en soit remercié, vous êtes là ! s'écria DTM.

La voix du petit droïd paraissait bizarre. Jaina remarqua que la grille de son haut-parleur était tordue.

— Vous ne pouvez pas imaginer ce que nous avons vécu tous les trois aujourd'hui, continua-t-il. Maître Lowbacca et maîtresse Tenel Ka ont été obligés de sauter de la plate-forme de bataille pour éviter les bombardements. C'était une bonne idée, car la plate-forme a explosé peu après.

« Quand nous sommes tombés dans les arbres, maître Lowbacca a réussi à saisir une branche, mais maîtresse Tenel Ka s'est cogné la tête. Elle est tombée presque jusqu'au plus bas de la forêt. Maître Lowbacca a réussi à amortir sa chute en plongeant avec elle. Il l'a rattrapée par un bras et il a atterri à plat ventre sur une souche. Il a agi très bravement, maîtresse Jaina. Je ne suis pas un droïd médical, mais je crains que vous découvriez qu'il a une épaule démise et au moins trois côtes cassées.

Raynar appliqua une compresse propre sur le front de Tenel Ka, puis enroula un bandage autour.

— Va t'occuper de Lowie, dit-il à Jaina. Je finirai tout seul.

Quand deux autres étudiants blessés titubèrent dans la clairière, Jaina leva les yeux, pleine d'espoir. Mais aucun d'eux n'était Jacen.

— As-tu vu mon frère ? demanda-t-elle à Raynar.

Elle s'agenouilla à côté de Lowie et entreprit de l'examiner.

— Il est parti à bord du *Bâton de Foudre* avec le vieux Peckhum, continua Jaina. Il devrait être de retour depuis longtemps.

Raynar fronça les sourcils et secoua la tête.

— Ma foi... Il me semble avoir vu la navette de livraison. Je crois... qu'un des chasseurs Tie l'a touchée.

— Se sont-ils écrasés ? demanda Jaina.

Raynar détourna les yeux.

— Je ne sais pas. Le vaisseau semblait perdre de l'altitude, mais... (Il haussa les épaules, mal à l'aise.) De toute façon, ça s'est passé il y a des heures.

Jaina ferma les yeux, augmentant ses perceptions grâce à la Force.

— Il n'est pas mort, souffla-t-elle enfin. Mais

c'est tout ce que je peux dire. Je ne sens pas le vieux Peckhum, mais je n'ai pas avec lui un lien comme celui que je partage avec Jacen. Mon frère est quelque part dans la forêt, je le sais.

Un sourire de soulagement apparut sur les lèvres de Raynar.

— C'est une bonne nouvelle...

— Les derniers étudiants sont arrivés, je pense, annonça Lando en s'agenouillant à côté de Lowbacca. Comment vas-tu, mon garçon ? Tu as l'air d'avoir connu des jours meilleurs !

Lowie grogna qu'il était d'accord.

— Je crois que tous ceux qui étaient à proximité nous ont rejoints, ajouta Lando.

— Nous avons trouvé encore une étudiante, fit Luke en approchant.

Il montra le bord de la clairière, où Tionne s'occupait de la Jedi végétale. Un de ses « bras » était cassé.

Jaina leva la tête vers son oncle.

— Et Jacen ?

— Il est vivant, dit Luke. C'est tout ce que je sais pour le moment.

— Oui, dit Jaina. Mais où est-il ? Ne devrions-nous pas partir à sa recherche ?

— Il faut d'abord ramener les blessés au Grand Temple, répondit Luke. Si le vieux Peckhum et Jacen ont réussi à garder le *Bâton de Foudre* en état de marche, ils se seront sûrement dirigés vers le terrain d'atterrissage. Ils n'auraient pas pu se poser dans une clairière comme celle-ci.

C'était vrai. Jaina retrouva espoir. Elle se tourna vers Lowie.

— Peux-tu marcher ?

Lowie grommela une réponse affirmative.

— Maître Lowbacca estime être capable de se déplacer avec une assistance minimale, traduisit DTM.

— D'accord, répondit Jaina. Retournons à l'Académie Jedi.

Elle avait hâte de retrouver son frère et de savoir si tout allait bien pour lui.

Il leur fallut près d'une heure pour ramener les Jedi éclopés aux abords du temple.

À la consternation de Jaina, le terrain d'atterrissage était vide.

— Ne t'en fais pas, ma petite demoiselle, dit Lando. Je vais t'aider à les chercher.

Jaina soupira. Elle savait que Jacen était vivant, mais elle avait un mauvais pressentiment.

— D'accord, dit Jaina. Faisons d'abord entrer les blessés. Ils seront à l'abri dans le temple. Nous devrons passer par la porte de la cour, parce que celle du hangar est bloquée.

Rejoindre la cour dallée sembla prendre une éternité.

Puis l'entrée ne fut plus qu'à dix mètres. Voyant son but si proche, Jaina sourit et courut en avant.

Soudain, une silhouette dépenaillée sortit en titubant du temple.

Son visage ensanglanté et meurtri était couvert d'une épaisse couche de boue.

Mais Jaina l'aurait reconnu n'importe où et sous tous les masques.

Zekk leva fièrement le menton, barrant l'entrée.

— Personne ne pénétrera dans le temple, dit-il.

CHAPITRE XXII

Confrontée à son vieil ami, Jaina resta sans voix. L'air cessa de circuler dans ses poumons. Il lui sembla que ceux-ci étaient pris comme dans un bloc de glace. Son cœur s'affola et ses paumes se couvrirent de sueur.

Zekk ne bougea pas.

Luke avança près de Jaina. À demi soutenu par la jeune fille, Lowbacca émit un grognement sourd. Jaina sentit autour d'elle les esprits des autres étudiants Jedi. Pour eux, qui ne l'avaient pas connu avant la bataille, Zekk était un ennemi, rien d'autre.

Les yeux toujours fixés sur le visage couvert de boue de son ami, Jaina dit :

— Cela me concerne, mon oncle. Je dois m'en occuper seule.

Luke hésita un instant. Jaina savait que la situation lui posait problème. Quand il parla, sa voix était pleine d'incertitude.

— Ce n'est pas une machine détraquée que tu peux réparer avec tes trucs habituels, Jaina.

— Je sais, dit-elle doucement. Je ne suis pas sûre qu'il m'écoutera, mais je parie qu'il n'écoutera personne d'autre.

— Je me souviens d'avoir pensé la même chose, dit Luke, quand j'ai voulu ramener Dark Vador vers le Côté Lumineux. C'est une chose dangereuse... Et il est très rare de réussir.

Il soupira, comme s'il pensait à Brakiss.

Jaina détacha son regard de Zekk et se tourna vers son oncle.

— Je t'en prie, laisse-moi essayer.

Luke réfléchit un moment. Puis il lui fit signe d'y aller.

Jaina se concentra sur Zekk. Luke fit sortir Lowie de la cour. Jaina puisa de l'énergie dans la Force. Mais elle ne savait pas ce qu'elle allait pouvoir dire au jeune homme.

Par où commencer, quand on s'adressait à un Jedi Obscur ?

Il s'agissait de *Zekk*, se dit-elle. Son *ami*. Elle avança d'un pas et éleva la voix pour qu'il l'entende.

— La bataille est terminée, Zekk. Nous voulons simplement entrer et soigner nos blessés.

Zekk frissonna. Il recula d'un pas et écarta les bras pour bloquer l'entrée du temple.

— Non. Il y aura bien plus de blessés si vous ne restez pas là où vous êtes.

Jaina hésita. Il lui faudrait essayer une autre approche.

Les yeux de Zekk balayèrent la clairière, comme s'il évaluait la force des étudiants Jedi, handicapés par leurs nombreuses blessures. Il se demandait sans doute combien il pourrait en tuer avant d'être submergé.

— Je veux être de nouveau ton amie, Zekk, dit Jaina. Tu m'as manqué. (Il frémit comme si elle l'avait frappé.) Abandonne le Côté Obscur et reviens du Côté Lumineux. Souviens-toi que nous nous sommes bien amusés ensemble, toi, Jacen et moi. Tu te rappelles la fois où tu as récupéré ce vieux module, quand nous nous sommes branchés sur les ordinateurs du zoo holographique ?

Zekk fit un signe de tête circonspect.

— Nous avons reprogrammé tous les animaux pour qu'ils chantent des chansons à boire corelliennes, continua Jaina, avec un sourire mélancolique.

— Nous avons été pris, fit remarquer Zekk. Et le zoo a restauré la programmation d'origine.

— Oui, mais tant de touristes ont protesté quand ils sont revenus, que le zoo a ajouté nos animaux chantants au programme quelques mois plus tard.

Jaina pensa voir une étincelle d'amusement dans les yeux émeraude, mais ils se durcirent de nouveau.

— Nous ne sommes plus des enfants, Jaina. Et

nous ne pouvons pas le redevenir. Tu ne le comprends pas, n'est-ce pas ?

Son regard balaya la cour. Il se frotta les joues, étalant la boue.

— D'accord, dit Jaina. Je ne comprends pas. Explique-moi, alors.

Zekk prit une profonde inspiration et commença à faire les cent pas devant l'entrée obscure, semblable à une créature sauvage prisonnière d'une cage invisible.

— Ma place n'est plus nulle part, Jaina. L'Académie de l'Ombre était devenue mon foyer. Elle n'existe plus. Où puis-je aller ? Le Côté Obscur est désormais une partie de mon âme.

— Non, Zekk. Tu peux encore l'abandonner. Reviens vers la lumière.

Zekk rit. Son rire rauque vibrait de colère et d'un soupçon de folie. Il passa la main sur son visage et montra ses doigts boueux à Jaina. La blessure de sa joue se rouvrit, mais il ne sembla pas s'en apercevoir.

— Le Côté Obscur n'est pas semblable à cette boue, dit-il. Ce n'est pas quelque chose que tu peux laver comme le ferait un môme qui a joué dans la terre.

Zekk s'essuya la main sur sa cape en lambeaux.

— Je suis différent, maintenant. Je n'ai plus rien à voir avec le gamin sans éducation que tu as connu sur Coruscant. Je n'ai plus de place là-bas. Où pourrais-je aller ? J'ai été formé à devenir un Jedi Obscur. Maintenant, mon professeur est mort.

Il croyait en moi. Brakiss a donné un but à ma vie, et il m'a enseigné tout ce que je sais.

— Peckhum aussi a toujours cru en toi, dit Jaina d'une voix douce.

Zekk passa sa main boueuse dans sa chevelure emmêlée. Un éclair de folie passa dans ses yeux.

— Mais il est mort, lui aussi. J'en suis sûr. J'ai vu tomber le *Bâton de Foudre*.

Jaina eut l'impression qu'on lui enfonçait un poing dans l'estomac. Le *Bâton de Foudre* s'était écrasé ? Dans ce cas, Jacen devait être gravement blessé.

— J'ai trahi mon professeur et il est mort, dit Zekk. J'ai conduit les troupes de l'Académie de l'Ombre à la bataille, et tous mes camarades ont été tués ou capturés. Si Peckhum est mort, c'est aussi ma faute.

Les yeux de Zekk étaient vitreux et fiévreux, son souffle court et précipité.

Jaina serra les mâchoires avec détermination.

— Dans ce cas, Zekk, je ne veux plus voir personne mourir à cause de toi. Laisse-nous entrer dans le temple pour que nous puissions prendre soin de nos blessés.

Zekk cessa de marcher et fit face à Jaina.

— Non ! Restez dehors !

Jaina avança.

— Zekk, tu n'as plus de raison de te battre contre nous. Que peux-tu espérer ?

Zekk secoua la tête.

— Tu n'as jamais écouté mes conseils. Tu as toujours cru en savoir plus que moi.

Malgré son agitation, les mouvements du jeune homme étaient étonnamment précis quand il sortit son sabrolaser et activa la lame d'énergie rouge sang.

Si instinctivement qu'elle en prit à peine conscience, Jaina tira aussi son arme. La lame bleu-violet bourdonna et pulsa.

Un sourire sauvage naquit sur les lèvres de Zekk, comme s'il était content que les choses en soient arrivées là.

— Vois-tu, Jaina, dit-il en marchant sur elle, une fois que tu l'as laissé entrer, le Côté Obscur ressemble à une maladie contre laquelle il n'existe aucun remède.

Il plongea vers elle. Les deux lames se rencontrèrent avec un crépitement.

— Et la seule façon de supprimer la maladie, continua Zekk en attaquant Jaina, feintant tandis que celle-ci déviait ses coups, est de... (*feinte*) ... l'enlever... (*parade*) ... chirurgicalement.

Jaina s'éloigna, gardant un œil méfiant sur Zekk alors qu'elle attendait sa prochaine attaque. Du coin de l'œil, elle voyait Luke regarder la bataille avec un calme impressionnant.

Jaina se rendit compte qu'elle avait essayé de ramener Zekk de force vers le Côté Lumineux. Elle avait essayé de le « guérir ». Mais c'était impossible. Le choix devait venir de *lui*. Elle prit une profonde inspiration, laissant la Force couler en elle. Puis elle recula et baissa son arme.

— Je ne veux pas me battre contre toi, Zekk, dit-elle, désactivant son sabrolaser et le jetant au sol. Il reste de la bonté en toi, mais tu dois décider dans quelle direction tu veux aller. C'est à toi de choisir. Essaie de ne pas te tromper.

La surprise, la colère et la confusion se succédèrent sur le visage de Zekk.

— Comment sais-tu que je ne vais pas en profiter pour te tuer ?

Jaina vit Lowie approcher comme s'il voulait la protéger. Luke posa une main sur l'épaule du Wookie pour le retenir.

Jaina haussa les épaules.

— Je ne le *sais* pas. Mais je refuse de me battre. À toi de choisir.

Jaina repoussa des mèches châtain de son visage et regarda son ami dans les yeux avec une vraie assurance. Pas celle qu'il ne lui ferait pas de mal, mais celle d'avoir bien agi.

— Eh bien, qu'attends-tu ?

Avec une froide détermination, Zekk leva son sabrolaser au-dessus de la tête de Jaina.

CHAPITRE XXIII

Le commando impérial Orvak s'éveilla enfin, la tête lourde. Il lutta pour repousser les cauchemars qui l'assaillaient, emplis de crocs de serpents et de créatures invisibles se glissant dans les fentes du mur. Quand il secoua la tête, une vague de vertige le submergea, et la nausée souleva son estomac.

Orvak ne se souvint pas de l'endroit où il se trouvait ni de ce qu'il y faisait. Le sol de pierre était dur. Il était tombé dans une position inconfortable et avait dormi là pendant un certain temps. Sa main lui faisait mal. Il y vit deux petites blessures. Des morsures ? Sa vue se troubla et il se sentit dériver de nouveau.

Il avait dû enlever ses gants et son casque. Que faisait-il donc alors ? Et où se trouvait-il ?

Il n'entendit aucun bruit autour de l'Académie Jedi. Que se passait-il ?

Orvak se souvint d'être entré dans le temple pour remplir une mission importante... Il se remémora aussi le serpent quasi invisible qui l'avait mordu. Le venin l'avait plongé dans l'inconscience.

Il porta une main à ses yeux, mais il n'arrivait pas à voir nettement les objets. Oui, c'était une sorte de poison. Il avait été drogué, mais il était en train de se réveiller. Était-il prisonnier des sorciers Jedi ?

Orvak se mit péniblement en position assise. L'univers dansa autour de lui. Il s'appuya sur le sol. Il était venu dans le Grand Temple pour installer des explosifs, afin de faire sauter l'immense pyramide. Ainsi, chacun verrait la faiblesse de la Rébellion et de ses Jedi, et accueillerait à bras ouverts le Second Imperium.

Mais quelque chose était allé de travers.

Maintenant, il entendait un son. Un cliquètement. Secouant la tête, il regarda en direction de l'étrange bruit. Il venait de la minuterie qui se trouvait à quelques pas de lui, sur l'estrade de pierre...

Une minuterie !

Il cligna des yeux et parvint enfin à voir autour de lui. Ses yeux brûlaient, mais il distingua les nombres en train de décroître sur le cadran.

Douze... Onze... Dix...

Il se leva d'un bond. Le vertige le reprit.

Il replongea dans le néant.

Neuf... Huit...

CHAPITRE XXIV

Jaina n'entendait plus que le bourdonnement du sabrolaser de Zekk. Celui-ci abaissa lentement la lame vers son cou.

— Tu n'as jamais compris, Jaina. Tu ne peux pas... Tu as toujours vécu une vie si protégée... Le Côté Obscur est comme une cicatrice intérieure.

Les yeux de Zekk rencontrèrent ceux de Jaina. Sa main ne tremblait pas. Il parlait d'une voix basse, à peine audible.

— Certaines cicatrices sont inguérissables, continua-t-il. On peut les déguiser, mais jamais les effacer. Elles restent là où elles sont...

On eût dit qu'un essaim d'insectes passait à côté de l'oreille de Jaina. Mais ce n'était que le sabrolaser de Zekk, qui continua à descendre sans la toucher.

Dans la distance, Jaina entendit d'autres sons :

un crépitement de parasites, puis une voix tonitruante sortant d'un comlink.

— Ici le *Bâton de Foudre*. Évacuez tout le
monde du terrain d'atterrissage. Nous arrivons. Si
vous avez récupéré ces boucliers d'énergie,
veuillez les désactiver ! Nous avons déjà eu assez
de problèmes ! J'ai le bras cassé, et c'est le jeune
Solo qui pilote. Notre aile a été atteinte, et je ne
suis pas sûr de la maniabilité du vaisseau.

Le sabrolaser de Zekk s'éloigna de Jaina. Un
bourdonnement attira son attention. Jaina jeta un
coup d'œil derrière elle et vit le *Bâton de Foudre*
arriver au-dessus des arbres, crachotant et toussotant.

-— Allez-y, *Bâton de Foudre*, répondit Luke sur
son comlink. Vous pouvez atterrir.

Zekk regarda le vieux vaisseau déglingué, puis
il secoua la tête. Il tendit la main vers la jeune
fille.

— Jaina, je n'avais pas l'intention de...

À ce moment, une explosion déchira l'air,
oblitérant tout autre son. Le sol vibra sous les
pieds de Jaina comme lors d'un tremblement de
terre.

— Mets-toi à l'abri ! cria Zekk.

Jaina plongea vers le mur et se jeta sur le sol.
Elle fit un roulé-boulé puis regarda au-dessus
d'elle. Une explosion avait eu lieu dans le Grand
Temple. Des morceaux de blocs de pierre tombèrent de chaque côté de la pyramide.

Zekk essaya de se mettre à couvert, mais l'avalanche de pierres fut plus rapide que lui. Un gros

bloc le heurta à la tête. Le jeune homme aux cheveux noirs s'écroula sur le sol. En un éclair, Jaina
comprit : il savait.

Zekk *savait* que le temple allait exploser.

Il leur avait sauvé la vie à tous.

CHAPITRE XXV

Dans la jungle inexplorée de Yavin 4, sur la face de la lune opposée à celle où Luke Skywalker avait établi son Académie, de la fumée s'échappait du chasseur Tie qui s'était écrasé.

L'écoutille du cockpit s'ouvrit. Qorl sortit de l'appareil avec quelque difficulté. Son bras-droïd crépitait et lançait des étincelles : il avait été endommagé dans l'accident.

Pourtant, Qorl ne sentait pas la douleur, car il était toujours sous l'effet de l'adrénaline produite par le combat. Ses jambes étaient engourdies et raides, mais il n'était pas blessé. Il se laissa tomber sur le sol, et tituba à l'abri des arbres, au cas où le vaisseau exploserait.

Seul dans la jungle, Qorl regarda le Tie jusqu'à ce qu'il ait l'assurance qu'aucun des moteurs ne dépasserait le point critique. Le vaisseau sembla pousser son dernier soupir quand une ultime colonne de fumée s'en échappa. Puis il connut sa fin.

Les dégâts étaient importants. La coque avait été perforée par les branches des arbres Massassi. Les deux unités d'alimentation étaient tordues. L'une était cassée.

Tandis qu'il volait, mitraillé par les forces Rebelles, évitant les tirs de turbolaser de son mieux — jusqu'à celui qui lui avait coûté le contrôle de son vaisseau —, Qorl avait vu la déroute des superdestroyers. Il avait été témoin de l'explosion de l'Académie de l'Ombre.

Désormais, tout espoir était perdu pour le Second Imperium. L'Empereur était à bord de la station ainsi que le seigneur Brakiss. Les Jedi Obscurs restant à la surface seraient sans nul doute capturés et conduits dans les prisons des Rebelles.

Qorl avait beaucoup de choses à regretter. Au lieu de laisser mourir un des jumeaux Solo, il avait choisi de sacrifier Norys. Une trahison dont il avait honte.

Se rendre aussi était trahir...

De sa vie, jamais Qorl ne s'était rendu.

Il était de nouveau perdu dans la jungle. Le Second Imperium était vaincu. Qorl n'avait plus d'endroit où aller, aucun ordre auquel obéir... Nul souci que de chercher un lieu où vivre.

Peut-être était-ce mieux ainsi.

Il se débrouillerait pour se faire un nouveau foyer dans la jungle. Il la connaissait. Il savait quels fruits étaient comestibles, quels animaux étaient les plus faciles à chasser. Quel que fût l'honneur de s'être à nouveau battu pour l'Empereur, Qorl réalisa qu'il avait pris plaisir à ses années de solitude dans la jungle.

En somme, décida-t-il, ce n'était pas un sort si terrible.

Il partit à la recherche d'un endroit où s'installer. Cette fois, il avait l'intention d'y rester jusqu'à la fin de ses jours.

CHAPITRE XXVI

Le matin se leva, frais et clair. En quelques heures, la chaleur fit son affaire à la brume qui s'accrochait à la base du Grand Temple et aux arbres. Au-dessus, la géante gazeuse emplissait une bonne partie du ciel.

Attendant en compagnie de Lowie et de Jacen sur le terrain d'atterrissage, Jaina pensa avec étonnement à quel point une bonne nuit de repos et un repas copieux changeaient sa façon de voir les choses. Après que Luke, Tionne, Lando et quelques ingénieurs de la station des Pêcheurs de Gemme se furent assurés que la structure des niveaux inférieurs du Temple demeurait saine, les jeunes gens et le reste de l'équipe étaient entrés dans la pyramide, récupérant au passage D2-R2, ravi de retrouver son maître. Les transporteurs de l'amiral Ackbar avaient évacué les étudiants les plus sérieusement blessés, tandis que ceux qui souffraient de traumatismes mineurs avaient été soignés et renvoyés dans leurs chambres.

Jaina était soulagée de s'être bien sortie de la bataille, même si elle se sentait un peu coupable. Elle avait seulement récolté quelques bleus quand les débris lui étaient tombés dessus après l'explosion.

Jaina examina son ami Lowbacca. Son épaule avait été remise en place. Son bras était soutenu par une large bande de tissu et ses côtes cassées avaient été pansées. Le Wookie ne portait jamais d'autre vêtement que sa ceinture en fibres de plante syren ; l'épais bandage blanc, autour de son torse, lui donnait un air étrange.

Jaina entendit un gargouillement et un bip derrière elle. Elle se retourna et vit D2-R2 et son oncle Luke traverser le terrain d'atterrissage. Le visage du Maître Jedi affichait une expression de sérénité et de détermination, mais ses yeux brillaient malicieusement.

— Je crois que j'avais l'air pire que lui après ma rencontre avec le Wampa des glaces, sur Hoth, dit-il.

— Peut-être, mais Lowie se sent beaucoup mieux ce matin, répondit Jaina.

Luke gloussa de rire.

— Je parlais du Grand Temple...

Jaina se retourna et examina l'antique pyramide Massassi. Le niveau supérieur s'était effondré ; une partie des flancs avait suivi. Les murs déchiquetés de la grande salle d'audience auraient pu être pris pour les créneaux de quelque ancienne forteresse.

— J'ai d'abord pensé que nous serions obligés de transférer l'Académie dans un autre temple, dit Luke. Maintenant, je ne suis pas sûr que ce soit nécessaire.

— Tu veux dire que nous pourrions reconstruire ? gémit Jacen. Génial ! Encore des exercices : soulever les rochers, équilibrer les poutres...

D2-R2 pépia et bipa comme si l'idée l'enthousiasmait. Lowie gronda d'un air pensif, puis grogna de douleur en se tenant les côtes.

— Oui, dit Luke. Nous avons tous été atteints par cette rencontre avec le Côté Obscur. Je pense que rebâtir le Grand Temple fera partie du processus de guérison de nos blessures.

— Comme Zekk, murmura Jaina, le cœur serré. Il a grand besoin de guérison.

— Au fait, oncle Luke, que vas-tu faire des étudiants Jedi Obscurs que nous avons capturés ?

— Tionne et moi travaillons avec eux. Nous tentons de les convertir au Côté Lumineux, mais si c'est impossible... (Il écarta les mains.) J'en parlerai avec Leia, et...

— Oh, maître Lowbacca, regardez ! s'écria DTM.

Jaina remarqua que la grille de haut-parleur du petit droïd avait été soigneusement redressée.

— Ils sont de retour ! s'écria Jacen.

Remorquant le T-23 abîmé de Lowie, la navette de Lando se posa sur le terrain d'atterrissage, à bonne distance de la coque noircie du *Bâton de Foudre*.

Poussant un cri de joie, Lowie flanqua une tape amicale à DTM.

— Eh bien, qu'attendons-nous ? demanda Jaina quand la navette et le skyhopper eurent atterri.

Jaina, Jacen et Lowie coururent vers les deux appareils. Quand ils arrivèrent, la rampe de débarquement s'était déployée. Lando en sortit, Tenel Ka à son bras. La cape de Lando flottait derrière lui.

Il fit son sourire le plus charmeur.

— Votre amie a une énergie de fer, dit-il d'un ton approbateur.

— C'est un fait, dit Tenel Ka sans une trace d'humour.

— J'aurais pu te le dire ! fit Jacen. L'as-tu retrouvé ?

Tenel Ka hocha la tête d'un air satisfait. Elle lâcha le bras de Lando et tira un objet de sa ceinture pour le montrer à Jacen. C'était le sabrolaser qu'elle avait perdu pendant son duel contre Tamith Kai.

— Cela n'a pas été aussi difficile que je le craignais, dit-elle. Peut-être parce que je connaissais le rancor dont provient cette dent. J'ai été capable de *percevoir* son emplacement.

Tenel Ka n'avait plus l'air mal en point. Jaina remarqua avec amusement que la jeune guerrière avait tressé sa chevelure blond-roux de telle sorte que le bandage ressemblait à un ornement.

— J'ai invité Tenel Ka à bord de la station des Pêcheurs de Gemme, dit Lando, car elle a manqué la dernière visite. Nous avons des cuves bacta qui guériront son front en un rien de temps. Lowbacca, il semble que quelques jours dans une cuve ne te feraient pas de mal non plus.

Lowie aboya son accord.

— Oh, ce serait extrêmement gentil, maître Calrissian, dit DTM. Maître Lowbacca a hâte de guérir et de commencer les réparations de son véhicule.

— Son petit skyhopper n'est pas le seul à être endommagé !

Jaina sursauta quand la voix tonitruante de Peckhum retentit derrière elle.

— Je comprends ce qu'il ressent. Le gamin et moi avons aussi hâte de commencer les réparations du *Bâton de Foudre*. Mais je crois que Zekk en a encore pour un moment avant d'avoir récupéré.

Le vieux Peckhum était debout près de son vaisseau, un bras autour des épaules de Zekk.

L'autre bras portait un pansement épais.

Le visage de Zekk était aussi pâle que les bandages qui entouraient son crâne. Ses yeux étaient étrangement vides, et son visage inexpressif. Il ne croisa pas le regard de Jaina.

— Je crois que vous avez deux candidats de plus pour les cuves bacta, Lando, dit Jaina. Jacen et moi pouvons aller aussi sur la station, oncle Luke ?

D2-R2 pépia.

— Oh, c'est une excellente idée ! s'écria DTM.

— Nous promettons de ne pas nous faire kidnapper cette fois, souffla Jacen avec un sourire en coin « à la Solo ».

Luke rit.

— D'accord, je crois que cela vous fera du bien à tous. Vous êtes plus forts ensemble, ne l'oubliez pas. Si vous prenez un peu de temps pour guérir, vous reviendrez en pleine forme, et nous rebâtirons l'Académie... Prêts pour un nouveau départ.

— Merci, oncle Luke ! lança Jaina.

— Jacen, mon ami, nous ferions mieux de partir immédiatement, dit Tenel Ka. Sinon, tous les étudiants blessés voudront venir avec nous, et ils guériront bien trop vite.

Jacen regarda Tenel Ka, intrigué.

— Que veux-tu dire ? Pourquoi serait-ce un problème ?

— Parce que, déclara Tenel Ka, un Jedi doit rester *patient* le plus longtemps possible.

Jacen cligna des yeux, ne sachant comment réagir. Puis un sourire naquit sur les lèvres de Tenel Ka.

C'était la première fois qu'il la voyait sourire aussi spontanément.

— Je n'arrive pas à y croire, dit Jacen.

Jaina secoua la tête, stupéfaite.

— Il me semble qu'elle vient de faire un bon mot.

— C'est un fait ! s'écria Jacen.

Lowie s'esclaffa.

Jaina gloussa.

Bientôt, le terrain d'atterrissage résonna des rires de toute l'assemblée.

À PROPOS DES AUTEURS

Kevin J. Anderson et son épouse, Rebecca Moesta, ont participé à de nombreux projets Star Wars. Ensemble, ils écrivent les onze volumes de la saga des Jeunes Chevaliers Jedi, destinée aux adolescents, ainsi que la série des Chevaliers Jedi Juniors qui s'adresse à de plus jeunes lecteurs. Ils ont également signé des livres animés ayant pour cadre la célèbre Cantine de Mos Esley et le Palais de Jabba le Hutt.

Kevin J. Anderson est aussi l'auteur de la trilogie de l'Académie Jedi — parue chez Pocket SF —, du best-seller *Le Sabre Noir*, et de la bande dessinée *La Guerre de la Sith*, chez Dark Horse Comics. Son roman de fantasy pour adolescents, *Born of Elven Blood*, écrit en collaboration avec John Betancourt, a été publié en 1995 par Atheneum. À l'occasion, Kevin coiffe la casquette de l'anthologiste, toujours dans l'univers de Star Wars. Citons par exemple les *Légendes de la Cantine de Mos Esley*, où une nouvelle porte la signature de Rebecca, et les *Légendes du Palais de Jabba*.

LA GUERRE DES ÉTOILES

De Kevin J. Anderson & Rebecca Moesta
Les jeunes chevaliers Jedi

1. Les enfants de la force

Depuis la défaite de l'Empire, les années ont passé. Jacen et Jaina, les enfants jumeaux de Leia et de Yan Solo, viennent d'intégrer l'Académie Jedi fondée par Luke Skywalker. Avec leurs amis Tenel Ka et Lowbacca, ils décident d'explorer la jungle. Un jour, les quatre adolescents découvrent l'épave d'un chasseur Tie. Par défi, ils entreprennent de le remettre en état. Dans l'ombre, on les épie, on attend cet instant depuis vingt ans…

2. Les cadets de l'ombre

Même vaincu, l'Empire ne désarme pas. Il garde une arme secrète : le Côté Obscur de la Force. Un ancien élève de Luke, Brakiss, forme un commando de Jedi Obscurs. Bientôt une superbe occasion s'offre à lui : enlever Jacen et Jaina Solo, rien de moins ! Parviendra-t-il à les rallier au Côté Obscur ? Ou Luke Skywalker, parti à la recherche des jumeaux, arrivera-t-il à temps pour les sauver ?

3. Génération perdue

Sur Coruscant, Jacen et Jaina savourent les joies des vacances en famille. Par hasard, ils rencontrent un de leurs « vieux » amis, Zekk. Orphelin, le garçon vit dans les rues où il goûte la liberté avec l'insouciance de l'adolescence. Face aux jumeaux, il se sent comme un sale gosse sans intérêt… Qu'il se détrompe ! Son potentiel est énorme, et il fascine une entité maléfique, un monstre qui sait attirer à lui ceux qui n'ont plus rien à perdre !

4. Les sabres de lumière

Luke Skywalker n'est pas homme à précipiter les choses. Et pourtant, que faire quand la pression de l'ennemi devient insupportable ? À contrecœur, le Maître décide d'accélérer la formation de ses étudiants… Sommés de fabriquer leurs sabrolasers, les jeunes Chevaliers vont devoir faire preuve d'ingéniosité et… de maturité.

5. Le chevalier de la nuit

La sœur de Lowbacca, consternée par la perte d'une amie, songe à accomplir le rite d'initiation le plus périlleux qui soit. Lowie s'inquiète : jusque-là, il est le seul à être revenu vivant de l'épreuve ! Très loin de là, devenu le premier des Jedi Obscurs, le jeune Zekk reçoit l'ordre d'attaquer la planète…

6. Les Jedi assiégés

L'Académie de l'Ombre attaque Yavin 4 ! Brakiss, Zekk et les Sœurs de la Nuit sont à leur poste de combat, prêts à semer la destruction et la mort ! Va-t-on revoir partout l'affreux sourire de Palpatine ? Sa main de fer se refermera-t-elle sur la galaxie ? Luke Skywalker et ses étudiants aimeraient mieux la mort qu'un nouveau plongeon dans les Ténèbres !

7. Le cœur d'Alderaan

Jacen et Jaina ont décidé d'offrir à leur mère un cadeau d'anniversaire inoubliable. Avec l'autorisation de Luke Skywalker, ils s'envolent pour le champ d'astéroïdes d'Alderaan. S'ils parviennent à récupérer un fragment de la planète natale de Leia — détruite par l'Empire – nul doute que ce présent touchera le cœur de la princesse. Mais le champ d'astéroïdes est devenu un repaire de pirates…

8. L'alliance de la diversité

Le père du jeune Raynar Thul a disparu. Jacen, Jaina, Tenel Ka et Lowie décident de se lancer à la recherche de cet homme traqué par tous les chasseurs de primes de la galaxie. A-t-il été enlevé ou se cache-t-il pour fuir la colère de Noola Tarkona ? A-t-il découvert quelque chose de peu glorieux sur l'Alliance de la Diversité ? De graves questions pour de si jeunes Chevaliers…

9. Illusions de grandeur

Soigneusement déguisé, Bornan Thul charge Zekk de transmettre un message codé à Raynar et à sa mère. Mais Zekk le reconnaît et se met à rêver de le dénoncer pour toucher la récompense promise par Noola Tarkona. Parallèlement, Jacen, Jaina, Lowie et Tenel Ka vont retrouver Tyko Thul, qui a organisé son propre enlèvement pour forcer Bornan à sortir de l'ombre…

De Paul & Hollace Davids
La saga du Prince Ken

1. Le gant de Dark Vador

L'empereur est mort, les Rebelles ont proclamé la république. Mais Kadann, le Prophète Suprême du Côté Obscur, prédit qu'un nouvel empereur se dressera bientôt. À la main, il devra porter le gant du Seigneur Noir. Et ce défi-là, Trioculus, le mutant aux trois yeux, est prêt à le relever.

2. La cité perdue des Jedi

Ken a douze ans. Élevé par deux droïds au fond d'une ville souterraine, il est heureux de rencontrer Luke Skywalker, qui promet de lui faire découvrir l'espace. Mais Kadann, le Prophète Suprême, a prédit qu'un jeune prince Jedi causerait la perte de Trioculus et l'imposteur, fou de rage, arrive pour éliminer le gêneur.

3. La vengeance de Zorba le Hutt

Yan et Leia ont des projets d'avenir. Mais Trioculus verrait bien la princesse en impératrice du Côté Obscur ! Là-dessus Zorba le Hutt, revenant sur Tatooine, apprend que c'est Leia qui, de ses blanches mains, a tué son fils Jabba. Le père monstrueux médite une atroce vengeance.

4. Le Prophète Suprême du Côté Obscur

Une planète qui meurt ; une prophétie mortelle pour l'Alliance... Sur le mont Yoda, dans leur forteresse, les Rebelles continuent la lutte. Mais un visiteur leur apporte une terrible nouvelle : Kadann, le Prophète Suprême du Côté Obscur, veut récupérer le corps congelé de Trioculus pour prendre le contrôle de l'Empire.

5. La reine de l'Empire

Yan Solo demande Leia en mariage. Mais Zorba le Hutt, toujours avide de vengeance, enlève la princesse et la livre à Trioculus, qui rêve d'en faire sa femme. Leia hésite. Pour devenir la reine de l'Empire, doit-elle céder au Côté Obscur ? La mariée est prête à dire oui — mais pour quelles noces ?

6. Le destin du Prince Jedi

Kadann poursuit sa conquête. Bientôt, il régnera sur un nouvel Empire. Mais les combattants de l'Alliance sont prêts à lui barrer la route. Dans la Cité Perdue des Jedi se joue le destin d'un prince à la recherche de son identité. Comme Luke, fils de Dark Vador, Ken devra apprendre à vivre avec son terrible héritage.

De Christopher Golden
Novélisation du jeu micro

Les ombres de l'Empire

L'Empire a réussi sa contre-attaque, Dark Vador va capturer Luke. Mais Xizor, parrain d'un syndicat du crime, veut être le premier à s'emparer du jeune Rebelle : dans cette chasse à l'homme, le vainqueur pourra liquider les derniers Rebelles... et conquérir la faveur de l'Empereur.

Achevé d'imprimer
par Maury-Eurolivres S.A.
45300 Manchecourt

Imprimé en France

Dépôt légal : mai 1998.

12, avenue d'Italie • 75627 PARIS Cedex 13

Tél. : 01.44.16.05.00

Penguin Books
Vienna 1900: Games with l

Arthur Schnitzler was born in Vienna in 1862 and died
there in 1931. He was a practising doctor in Vienna as
well as a successful dramatist and novelist. His brilliant
dramatic sketches, *Anatol* (1893), typified a decadent
era in the figure of the sophisticated philanderer; the
Casanova theme recurs in Schnitzler's work, together
with elements drawn from his medical research (he
wrote a thesis on hypnotic treatments) and his
knowledge of Freud.

Arthur Schnitzler

Vienna 1900:
Games with Love and Death

The stories which formed the basis
of the BBC TV serial devised and
dramatized by Robert Muller

Penguin Books

March 1977

Penguin Books Ltd, Harmondsworth,
Middlesex, England
Penguin Books Inc., 7110 Ambassador Road,
Baltimore, Maryland 21207, U.S.A.
Penguin Books Australia Ltd, Ringwood,
Victoria, Australia

'Mother and Son' was formerly published in English
in 1926 under the title 'Beatrice' by T. Werner Laurie Ltd
and was translated by Agnes Jacques.

'The Man of Honour' was formerly published in
English in 1929 under the title 'The Murderer' by
Constable & Company Limited and was translated by
Eric Sutton.

'A Confirmed Bachelor' was formerly published in
English in 1924 under the title of 'Dr Graesler' by
Chapman & Hall Ltd and was translated by E. C. Slade.

'The Spring Sonata' was formerly published in English
in 1914 under the title 'Bertha Garlan' by Max Goschen Ltd
and was translated by J. H. Wisdom and Marr Murray.

Made and printed in Great Britain by
Hazell Watson & Viney Ltd, Aylesbury, Bucks
Set in Linotype Times

Contents

The TV serial also included 'The Gift of Life'
('*Sterben*'), which is not available in translation.

Mother and Son

Part One

She thought she heard a sound in the next room. She left her half-finished letter, went softly towards the partly open door and peered into the darkened room, where her son lay fast asleep on the divan. As she stepped inside, she could see how Hugo's breast rose and fell regularly in the healthy sleep of youth. His soft, rather crumpled collar lay open at his throat; he was fully clothed, even to the heavy spiked boots which he always wore in the country. Obviously he had intended to lie down for just a short time during the heat of midday, and then to resume his studies, for his books and papers lay open around him. Now he threw his head from side to side as if trying to awaken, but he only stirred a little and slept on. The mother's eyes, by this time accustomed to the darkness, could no longer ignore the fact that the strange, painfully intent expression around the boy's lips that she had noticed again and again during the past days, did not leave him even in sleep. Beatrice sighed and shook her head. Then she went back to her room, shutting the door quietly behind her. She looked at the letter, but had no desire to go on with it. Dr Teichmann, for whom it was intended, was certainly not the man with whom she could speak unreservedly – in fact, she already regretted the all too friendly smile with which she had bidden him farewell from the train. For just now, during these summer weeks in the country, the memory of her husband, who had died five years before, was more than ever alive within her, and she laid aside all thoughts of the lawyer's wooing and the proposal of marriage – which he had not yet made, but which was bound to come – together with all similar thoughts concerning her own future. She felt she could speak of her concern for Hugo least of all with the man who would see in it not so much a proof of confidence as a definite sign of encouragement. Therefore she destroyed the letter and went irresolutely to the window.

The line of mountains across the lake dissolved in tremulous rings of air. Below, in the water, sparkled the reflection of the sun, broken into a thousand rays. Beatrice turned away her eyes, blinded by the light, after casting a fleeting glance over the narrow meadow land, the dust-exhaling country road, the blinking roofs of the villas, and the motionless field of young corn in her garden. Her glance rested on the white bench under her window – and she recalled the many times when her husband had sat there dreaming over some rôle, or dozing, especially when the air was so redolent of summer as it was today. She remembered how she would lean over the sill to stroke the grey-black curly hair and run her fingers tenderly through it, till Ferdinand, who though immediately awake, but feigning sleep so that he might not interrupt her caresses, would slowly turn around and look up at her with his bright child's eyes, which could look so heroic or heavy with death on those long ago, but never to be forgotten, magic evenings. She loved to think of those times, though she knew she should not, certainly not with those sighs which in spite of herself came from her lips. For Ferdinand himself – in the days that were past, he had made her swear to it – wanted his memory to be celebrated only by pleasant recollections, and by an untroubled acceptance of new happiness. And Beatrice thought: 'How dreadful it is to think that we could speak of such horror in such bright times, jokingly and lightly, as if it concerned only others and could never fall upon us. And then when it really comes, we do not grasp it – and yet we endure it – and time passes, and we live on, and we sleep in the same bed that we shared once with our beloved, drink out of the same glass that he touched with his lips, pick strawberries in the shade of the same pine where we picked them with one who will never pick them again – and still we never quite understand either the meaning of death or life.'

She had often sat on this bench at Ferdinand's side, while the child, followed by the loving glances of his parents, had romped in the garden with ball or hoop. But as well as she knew in her mind that that Hugo who lay asleep there on the divan, with the new painful expression around his mouth, was the same child that played in the garden but a few years ago, in her heart she could not comprehend it any more than that Ferdinand was dead – more truly dead than Hamlet or Cyrano or King Richard in whose masks she had so often seen him die. But that she would probably never quite grasp, for between the bright full present and the dark mystery of death, there had not even elapsed weeks or days of suffering. Healthy and happy, Ferdinand had left the house one day to attend a theatrical performance, and within an hour they had brought him back from the railroad station, where the stroke had felled him.

While Beatrice clung to these memories, in her heart she felt all the time some other ghostly tormenting thing which awaited her solution. It was only after much meditation, that she knew that the last sentence in her unfinished letter, in which she had wanted to mention Hugo, would not leave her in peace, and that she must think it through to the end. It was clear to her that something either had happened or was about to happen to Hugo, something she had long awaited, but still had not considered possible. In earlier years, when he was still a child, she had dearly cherished the thought that later she would be not only mother, but friend and confidante to her boy – and till just recently, when he would come to her with his tales of school mishaps or to confess his first boyish love affairs, she dared imagine that her wish might be gratified. Had he not let her read those touching childish verses which he had written to little Elise Weber, the sister of a school friend of his, and which Elise herself had never seen? And even last winter, had he not told his mother that a little girl, whose name he gallantly kept secret, had kissed him on the cheek during a dance? And last spring, had he not come to her much disturbed to tell her of two boys in his class who had spent an evening at the Prater in questionable company, and who had boasted of coming home at three in the morning? And so Beatrice had dared hope that Hugo would choose her as confidante in his more serious emotional experiences, and that she would be able by encouragement and advice to keep him from the many sorrows and dangers of youth. But now she saw that these had been the dreams of an over-indulgent mother's heart, for at the first real conflict of the soul, Hugo showed himself strange and taciturn and his mother remained shy and helpless before these new events.

She shuddered, for at the first breath of wind, like a sneering confirmation of the fear in her heart, she saw down in the valley the hated white banner fluttering from the roof of the bright villa on the lake shore. Rippling jauntily, it waved the importunate restless greeting of a depraved woman to the boy whom she wanted to ruin. In spite of herself, Beatrice raised a menacing hand, then hurried back into the room in eager haste to see her son and have it out with him at once. She listened at the connecting door for a moment, for she did not want to awaken him from his good sleep, and she thought she heard his regular boyish breathing as before. Carefully she opened the door, intending to await Hugo's awakening, and then, sitting beside him on the divan, with motherly tact to win his secret from him. But, to her astonishment, she discovered that Hugo was no longer there. He had gone out without saying even adieu to his mother, as he had always done before, and without the accustomed farewell kiss—evidently he, too, feared the question which for days had been visible on her lips and which, as she knew now for the first time, she had expected to put to him at that moment. Was he already so far from her, already torn away by restless desire? That was what the first hand-clasp of that woman had made of him, when he met her recently on the wharf. That was what her look had done to him yesterday, when she smilingly greeted him from the gallery of the swimming pool, as his glowing boyish body had come swimming up out of the waves. Of course – he was more than seventeen, and she had never imagined that he would be spared for one certain girl who was destined for him from the beginning of time, and who would meet him as young and pure as he himself was. But only this had she wished for him: that his youth should not fall a victim to the lust of such a woman, who owed her half-forgotten stage reputation only to a glittering wantonness, and whose life and calling had not been changed even by her late marriage.

Beatrice sat on Hugo's divan in the half-darkened room,

her eyes closed, her head in her hands, deliberating. Where might Hugo be? With the Baroness perhaps? That was unbelievable. These things could not develop so rapidly. But was there still any possibility of saving her beloved boy from this miserable affair? She was afraid not. For indeed she had forebodings: just as Hugo had the features of his father, so did his father's blood run through his veins, that dark blood of those men from a different world, a lawless world, where boys were inflamed with the dark passions of men, while their eyes even in maturity gleamed with childish dreams. Was it only the father's blood? Did hers run more coolly? Dared she say that, simply because since the death of her husband no temptation had come to her? And because she had never belonged to another, was what she had once told her husband therefore any less true: that he alone had filled her whole life for her, because when his features were veiled by night, he represented many different characters to her – because in his arms she was the beloved of King Richard and Cyrano and Hamlet and all the others whose rôles he played – the beloved of heroes and scoundrels, the blessed and the damned, the naïve and the sophisticated. In fact, in her early girlhood had she not wished to be the wife of the actor because union with him offered the only possibility for her to live the decorous life which her bourgeois upbringing had intended her for, and at the same time to lead the wild adventurous existence for which she longed in her secret dreams? And she remembered how she had taken Ferdinand not only against the wishes of her parents, whose pious bourgeois minds could not quite overcome a slight repugnance at the thought of the actor, even after her marriage had been consummated, but how she had won him besides from a much more dangerous enemy. For at the time when she met Ferdinand, he was in the midst of a liaison (which was no secret in the town) with a not very young but wealthy widow, who had assisted him greatly in his early days and who had often paid his debts. It was only lack of will power that kept him bound to her. It was then that Beatrice had made the romantic decision to free her hero from such unworthy bondage and to dissolve the ties of a relationship which, owing to its unstable foundation, was bound to break sooner or later, but which she feared might come too late for the good of the artist and his art. It was a never-to-be-forgotten occasion for her, and although she received a half insulting and joking refusal which she never forgot, and though it was a whole year till Ferdinand was really finally freed, still she could not doubt that that conversation was the first step towards the break. In fact her husband did the story full justice and boasted of it proudly even to people who were not in the least concerned.

Beatrice removed her hands from her eyes, and stood up in sudden passion. Almost twenty years lay between that madly bold adventure and the present – but had she become a different creature since then? Did she not dare to trust herself to steer the course of one who was so dear to her, as she saw fit? Was she the woman to stand humbly by, while her son's young life was being besmirched and broken, instead of acting as she had formerly acted with the other? She would go today to the Baroness, who after all was only a woman and must have somewhere, though it be in the nethermost corner of her soul, some understanding of the meaning of motherhood. And happy in her sudden decision, which came to her like a beam of light, she went to the window, opened the blinds, and, full of new hope, she greeted as a good omen the charming landscape before her eyes. And she felt that she must carry out her sudden decision immediately, while her determination was fresh and strong. Without further hesitation, she went into her bedroom and rang for her maid, whom she bade be especially careful in helping her dress that day. As soon as this was done to her satisfaction, she put on her broad-brimmed panama hat with its narrow black band, over her dark-blonde, thickly waved hair, chose the freshest of three red roses from a vase on her night table, slipped it into her white leather belt, took her slender mountain cane in her hand, and left the house. She felt young, happy, and sure of the outcome of her mission.

As she stepped out of the door, she saw Herr and Frau Arbesbacher at the garden gate. He was in a waterproof shooting jacket and leather breeches; she wore a dark flowered cotton gown which, in style and cut, was too matronly for her rather careworn but still youngish face.

'Greetings, Frau Heinold,' called out the architect, raising his green Tyrolean hat with its cockade of goat's hair, and holding it in his hand so that his white head remained uncovered for a moment. 'We have just come to call for you.' And to her inquiring look: 'Have you forgotten that today is Thursday, the day of the tarock party at the Director's?'

'Yes, that is so,' said Beatrice, remembering.

'We just met your son,' remarked Frau Arbesbacher, and over her faded features passed a tired smile.

'He went up that way, with two thick books under his arm,' finished the architect, pointing to the path which led over the sunny meadow, upwards towards the wood. 'An industrious boy!'

Beatrice smiled in unrestrained happiness. 'Next year he will finish the "gymnasium",' she said.

'How pretty Frau Heinold looks today,' remarked Frau Arbesbacher naïvely, in a voice that was almost humble with surprise.

'Yes, how are we going to feel, Frau Beatelinde, when we suddenly find we have a grown son who fights duels and turns the heads of the women?'

'But did you fight duels?' interrupted his wife.

'Oh, well, I've had my little battles. Those things come of themselves. You get into trouble either way.'

They walked along the road, which with its splendid view of the lake, led up past the town to the villa of Herr Welponer, Bank Director.

'Well – here I seem to be going along with you, when instead I should go down to the village first – to the post-office – in regard to a package which was sent from Vienna a week ago, and has not yet arrived. And it was sent special delivery too,' she added naturally, as if she believed the story which she had so suddenly invented, she knew not why.

'Perhaps it will come on this train – your package,' said Frau Arbesbacher, pointing down below where the little train came puffing pompously from behind the cliffs, up to the station, which was slightly elevated from the meadow land. Travellers put their heads out of the windows, and Herr Arbesbacher waved his hat.

'What are you doing?' asked his wife.

'There are surely friends of ours among them, and one must be polite.'

'Well, then, auf Wiedersehen,' said Beatrice suddenly. 'I'll come up directly, of course. Take them my greetings in the meantime.'

She departed quickly and went down the road she had just ascended. She felt that the architect and his wife, who had remained standing on the road, followed her with their eyes almost to the villa which Arbesbacher had built for his friend and hunting companion, Ferdinand Heinold.

Here Beatrice took the narrow wagon road which led steeply past unassuming country houses to the town, but she had to wait before crossing the tracks, for the train was just leaving the station. Now she realized that she really had nothing to do at the post-office, but had much more important work – to speak with the Baroness. But now that she knew her son was in the woods with his books, that did not seem so pressing as it had seemed an hour earlier. She crossed the tracks to the station and found the usual excitement which follows the arrival of a train. The two omnibuses from the Lake Hotel and the Posthof were just rumbling away with their passengers. Other arrivals, high-voiced and excited, followed by porters, and happy-go-lucky picnickers, crossed Beatrice's path. She watched in amusement a whole family, father, mother, three children, nurse, and maid, trying to get into one cab, together with trunks, satchels, bags, umbrellas, and canes, and a snapping little fox-terrier. From another cab, a young married couple – friends of the year before – waved to her with the irresistible good spirits of summer resorts. A young man in a light grey summer suit, a very new yellow leather bag in his hand, raised his straw hat to Beatrice. She did not recognize him and greeted him coolly.

'How do you do, Frau Heinold,' said the stranger, shifting his bag from one hand to the other and awkwardly offering Beatrice his free right one.

'Why, Fritzl!' cried Beatrice, suddenly recognizing him.

'Certainly, Frau Heinold, it's I – Fritzl himself!'

'Do you know – I really did not know you. You've become quite a dandy.'

'Well, that's not so bad, is it?' answered Fritz, changing his bag back again to the other hand. 'But didn't Hugo receive my card?'

'I don't know, but he told me recently that he was expecting you.'

'Naturally, it was arranged in Vienna that I should come here for a few days from Ischl. But yesterday I wrote expressly that I expected to arrive this afternoon.'

'In any case, he will be very happy. Where are you staying, Herr Weber?'

'No, no, please, Frau Heinold – don't say Herr Weber.'

'Well then, where – Herr – Fritz?'

'I sent my trunk on in advance to the Posthof, but as soon as I have seen to my affairs, I shall be free to make my head-quarters at the Villa Beatrice.'

'Villa Beatrice? There is no villa by that name here.'

'But what else can it be called when a person with such a charming name lives in it?'

'It has no name – I don't like such things – No. 7 Oak Road is its name – see – there it is – up there – with the green balcony –'

Fritz Weber looked thoughtfully in the direction designated. 'The view must be delightful – But I shall not stop longer now. In an hour I shall find Hugo at home, I hope?'

'I believe so. Just now he is in the woods studying.'

'Studying, is he? Well, we shall have to cure him of that habit as soon as possible.'

'Oho!'

'You see, I want to take trips with him. Do you know that I climbed the Dachstein recently?'

'Unfortunately not, Herr Weber. It was really not in the newspapers.'

'But, please – not Herr Weber.'

'I'm afraid it will have to be that, since I'm neither your aunt nor governess.'

'An aunt like you might not be a bad thing to have.'

'Dear me, what a gallant gentleman he is – and at his age too.' She laughed aloud; and instead of the well-dressed young man, the boy suddenly stood before her, the child whom she had known since he was twelve; and his little blond moustache looked as if it were pasted to his lip. 'Well, then, auf Wieder-sehen, Fritzl,' she said, holding out her hand. 'This evening at supper you'll tell us about your Dachstein party, won't you?'

Fritz bowed a trifle stiffly, then kissed Beatrice's hand, which she allowed as if in submission to the quick passing of time. Then he went away with heightened self-respect, which was evident from his carriage and walk. 'And he,' thought Beatrice, 'he is the friend of my Hugo. Of course he is a bit older – about a year and a half or two, at least. He was always in a higher class than Hugo at school,' Beatrice remembered, 'and he had to repeat one year.' In any case, she was glad that he was there and expected to go on excursions with Hugo – if she could only send the two boys immediately on a two weeks' walking tour! Ten hours' walking a day, with the mountain wind blowing through one's hair – evenings to fall exhausted on a straw pallet, and in the morning to start again with the sun! How excellent and wholesome that was! She was tempted to go with them. But that would not do. The boys would not wish to have an aunt or governess with them. She sighed gently and passed her hand over her forehead.

She walked down the street which ran along the lake. The little steamboat had just left the landing and was floating sprucely and brightly across the water towards the place known as Grassy Meadow, where a few quiet houses lay almost hidden under the chestnut and fruit trees, and where it was already almost dark. On the diving-board over the swimming pool, a lonely figure in a white bath-robe bobbed up and down. There were still some swimmers in the lake. 'They are enjoying them-selves more than I,' thought Beatrice, looking enviously at the water from which came a cool peace-bringing breath. But she quickly turned the temptation from her, and in firm determina-tion continued on her way, until she unexpectedly found herself before the villa where Baroness Fortunata was living this summer. Through the commonplace garden of bright mallow and gillyflowers, she could see the veranda extending all along the front of the house, and she caught the shimmer of white dresses shining through. Her eyes fixed straight ahead, Beatrice walked on past the white fence. To her shame, she felt her heart beating wildly. The sound of women's voices came to her ear.

Beatrice hastened her steps and suddenly found herself beyond the house. She decided to go first to the village grocery, where she usually had some purchases to make, and especially today, as she expected a guest for supper. In a few minutes she was in Anton Meissenbichler's shop, had bought cold meat, fruit, and cheese, and had given little Lisle the package and a tip with instructions to deliver it at once to Oak Road. 'And now what?' she asked herself as she stood outside in the church square, facing the open cemetery gate, where the gilded crosses glimmered reddish in the afternoon sunlight. Should she let her plans fall through merely because her heart had begun to beat faster? Never would she be able to forgive such weakness. And the punishment of fate – she felt it – would be upon her. Then there was nothing left to do, but to go back – and without further delay – back to the Baroness.

In a few moments Beatrice was down at the lake shore. Now she passed by the Lake Hotel, on whose high terrace guests sat drinking coffee or ices, then past two huge modern villas that she detested – and two seconds later her eyes met those of the Baroness, who lay on the veranda on a chaise-longue under a white sun-shade trimmed in red. Leaning against the wall, stood another woman, like a statue, with an ivory yellow face, in a billowy white dress. Fortunata had been speaking gaily, but now she was suddenly silent, and her features hardened. But her look immediately softened again, and she broke into a smile of greeting that glowed with genuine friendliness and welcome. 'You jade,' thought Beatrice, a bit indignant at her own expression. And she girded herself for the struggle. Fortunata's voice rang too happy in her ears. 'How do you do, Frau Heinold.'

'How do you do,' answered Beatrice in a voice that could scarcely be heard, and as if she cared little whether her greeting reached the veranda or not. Then she pretended to go on.

'Apparently you are out for a sun and dust bath today, Frau Heinold.' Beatrice did not doubt that Fortunata had only said this in order to start a conversation with her. For the friendship between these two was so superficial, that the joking tone did not seem particularly in place. Many years ago Beatrice had met the young actress, Fortunata Schon, a colleague of Ferdinand's, at a theatre party, and in the good fellowship of that festive evening the young couple had sat at the same table with her and her lover of that time, and had had supper and drunk champagne together. Later, there had been fleeting meetings in the theatre or on the street, but these had never led to real conversation even of a moment's duration. Eight years ago, after her marriage to the Baron, Fortunata had left the stage and disappeared from Beatrice's vision until she had met her accidentally, here at the watering-place a few weeks ago; and after that meeting, since she could hardly avoid it, she had exchanged a few words with her on the street, in the woods, or while bathing. But today it pleased Beatrice that the Baroness herself seemed disposed to start a conversation and so she answered as indifferently as possible:

'A sun bath? – The sun has already set, and in the evening it's not as sultry near the lake as up above in the wood.'

Fortunata had stood up; she leaned her slender, well-formed little figure over the railing and answered quickly that for her part she preferred walks in the wood, and that she found especially the one to the Hermitage quite impressive.

'What a stupid word,' thought Beatrice, and asked politely why the Baroness had not taken a villa at the edge of the forest, since she preferred it.

The Baroness explained that she, or rather her husband, had rented the house from an advertisement, and that besides, she was quite well satisfied in every respect. 'But why not end your walk, and drink a cup of tea with me and my friend?' And without awaiting an answer, she went toward Beatrice, gave her a smooth, white, somewhat restless hand, and led her with exaggerated friendliness to the veranda, where in the meantime, the other woman still leaned motionless against the wall in her billowy white muslin dress, in a sort of gloomy seriousness, that struck Beatrice as half sinister, half ridiculous. Fortunata presented her: 'Fräulein Wilhelmine Fallehn – Frau Beatrice Heinold. You must know the name, dear Willy.'

'I had the greatest regard for your husband,' said Fräulein Fallehn, coolly and in a dark voice.

Fortunata offered Beatrice an upholstered wicker chair, and apologized as she stretched herself out again as comfortably as before. Never had she felt so tired and languid as here, especially in the afternoons. Most probably it was because she could not stand the experiment she was making of bathing twice a day and remaining in the water an hour each time. But when one knew so many waters as she – inland lakes, and rivers, and seas – one must finally discover that each water had its own definite character. So she continued, carefully and too elegantly as it seemed to Beatrice, while she stroked her red-dyed hair with one hand. Her long white dress, trimmed with crocheted lace, hung down over both sides of the low chair to the floor. Around her bare neck she wore a modest string of small pearls. Her pale narrow face was heavily powdered; only the tip of her nose showed pink, and her frankly painted lips were a dark red. Beatrice could not help thinking of a picture in an illustrated magazine, representing a Pierrot hanging on a lamp-post, an impression that was strengthened by the fact that Fortunata kept her eyes half closed while she spoke.

Tea and pastry were served and the conversation continued, with Wilhelmine Fallehn, who now leaned over the railing, her cup in her hand, joining in the talk even more informally than before. The subject changed from summer to winter; they spoke of the city, of the theatre, of the stupid disciples of Ferdinand Heinold, and about his unfortunate and premature death. Wilhelmine expressed in measured tones her surprise that a woman could survive the loss of such a husband, whereupon the Baroness, noticing Beatrice's surprise, smoothly remarked: 'You must know, Willy, Frau Heinold has a son.'

At that moment Beatrice looked at her with unbridled hostility in her eyes and she returned the look with the wicked slyness of a malicious water-sprite; in fact Beatrice imagined that Fortunata exhaled a damp breath like that from reeds or water-lilies. At the same time, she noticed that Fortunata's feet were bare in their sandals and that under her white linen dress she had nothing else on. In the meantime the Baroness continued speaking, incessantly, in her smooth and well-bred manner. She believed that life was stronger than death, and that therefore it must always win out in the end. But Beatrice felt that this was a creature who had never loved a soul, man or woman.

Wilhelmine Fallehn suddenly put down her cup. 'I must finish packing,' she explained, said a curt farewell, and disappeared through the sun-porch.

'You see, my friend is going back to Vienna today,' said Fortunata. 'She is engaged – so to speak.'

'Ah,' said Beatrice politely.

'What would you take her for?' asked Fortunata with half-closed eyes.

'She is evidently an actress.'

Fortunata shook her head. 'She was in the theatre for a while. She is the daughter of a high official. Or rather – an orphan. Her father put a bullet through his head in grief over the life she was leading. That was ten years ago. Now she is twenty-seven. She can still go far – Will you have another cup of tea?'

'No thank you, Baroness.' She took a deep breath. Now the moment had come. Her face suddenly became so determined that Fortunata unconsciously half sat up. And Beatrice began with decision : 'It is really not an accident that I was passing by your house today. I have something to say to you, Baroness.'

'Oh,' said Fortunata; and a faint red showed under the powdered Pierrot face. She threw one arm over the back of the chaise-longue and twisted her restless fingers.

'Please allow me to be very brief,' began Beatrice.

'Just as you wish. As brief or as lengthy as you like, dear Frau Heinold.'

Beatrice was provoked at these rather condescending words and said sharply : 'To put it simply and briefly, it is this : Baroness, I do not wish my son to become your lover.'

She was very calm; yes, exactly so had she felt when, nineteen years before, she had taken her future husband from the elderly widow.

The Baroness returned Beatrice's look no less calmly. 'Oh,' she said, half to herself, 'you do not wish it? What a pity – Really, to tell the truth, I had not yet thought of it myself.'

'Then it will be all the easier for you to grant my wish,' answered Beatrice, a bit more heatedly.

'Certainly, if it depends on me alone.'

'Baroness, it depends only on you. You know that very well. My son is still only a child.'

A look of pain appeared around Fórtunata's painted lips. 'What a terrible woman I must be,' she said thoughtfully. 'Shall I tell you why my friend is leaving? She had intended to spend the whole summer with me – and her fiancé was to have visited her here. And imagine – suddenly she became frightened. Afraid of me. Yes, perhaps she is right. That is how I am. I cannot answer for myself.'

Beatrice sat motionless. She had not expected such frankness that was almost shamelessness. And she answered bitingly, 'Then, Baroness, since you feel that way, it will mean very little to you to –'

Fortunata rested her childish glance on Beatrice. 'What you are doing, Frau Heinold,' she said in a quiet new-found voice, 'is touching indeed. But clever, on my soul, it is not. Besides, I repeat that I had not even entertained the thought. In truth, Frau Heinold, I believe that women like you have no conception of women – of my kind. Look here – two years ago, for example, I spent three whole months in a Dutch fishing village – quite alone. And I believe I was never so happy in my whole life. And so it could have happened that this summer too – Oh, I want to think it possible – I never have schemed – never in my life. Even my marriage, I assure you, was a matter of pure chance.' And she looked up as if a sudden thought had come to her. 'Or perhaps you are afraid of the Baron – are you afraid that there may be some unpleasantness for – ah – for your son on that score? As far as that is concerned –' And she smilingly closed her eyes.

Beatrice shook her head. 'I had really not thought of anything of the sort.'

'Still, one might think of such things. There's no telling what husbands will do. But look here, Frau Heinold,' and she opened her eyes again, 'if that question has really played no part, then it is all the more incomprehensible to me – Seriously – if I had a son of the same age as your Hugo –'

'You know his name?' asked Beatrice severely.

Fortunata smiled. 'You told it to me yourself – recently at the pier.'

'Quite right. I beg your pardon, Baroness.'

'Well then, dear Frau Heinold, I wanted to say – that if I

had a son and he were to fall in love with a woman like you, for
example – I don't know – but I think I could hardly picture a
better début for a young man.'

Beatrice moved in her chair, as if to stand up.

'We are just two women among ourselves,' said Fortunata
soothingly.

'You have no son, Baroness – and then –' She stopped.

'Ah, yes, you mean that there would be another very great
difference. But that difference would make the affair – for my
son – even more dangerous. For you, Frau Heinold, would
probably take such an affair seriously. But I, on the contrary –
I – Really Frau Heinold, the more I think about it, the more it
seems to me, it would have been wiser of you to come to me
with the opposite request – if you had brought your son, so to
speak, to my very arms.'

'Baroness!' Beatrice was dumbfounded. She could have
screamed.

Fortunata leaned back, crossed her arms under her head,
and completely shut her eyes. 'Such things do happen –' And
she began to tell a story. 'Many years ago, somewhere in the
provinces, I had a friend, an actress, who was at that time about
as old as I am now. She played the heroic-sentimental rôles.
One day a countess came to her – the name does not concern
us – You see, her son, the young count, had fallen in love with
a girl of the middle classes, of good but rather poor family –
civil service, or something of the sort. And the young count
wanted to marry the girl at once. Besides, he was under twenty.
And the countess – do you know what that clever woman did?
One fine day she appeared before my friend and spoke with
her, and asked her – Well, to make it short – she arranged
it so that her son forgot the girl in the arms of my friend
and –'

'I beg you, Baroness, to desist from such anecdotes.'

'It is not an anecdote. It is a true story and a very moral one
besides. A mésalliance was prevented, and an unhappy marriage, perhaps a suicide, or a double suicide.'

'That may be,' said Beatrice, 'but all that does not concern
us. In any case, I am different from the countess. And for me,
the thought is simply unbearable – unbearable –'

Fortunata smiled and was silent for a while, as if she wished to force an end to the sentence. Then she said, 'Your son is sixteen – or seventeen?'

'Seventeen,' answered Beatrice, and was immediately angry with herself for having given the information so meekly.

Fortunata half closed her eyes, as if she were seeing a vision. And she said as if out of a dream, 'Then you must get used to the thought. If it is not I, it will be another – and who can tell you' – (out of the suddenly opened eyes came a green flash) – 'that it will be a better one?'

'Will you have the kindness, Baroness,' answered Beatrice with laboured superiority, 'to leave that problem to me?'

Fortunata sighed softly. Suddenly she seemed tired, and said: 'Well, then, why talk of it any more? I am willing to be agreeable. Your son has nothing to fear from me – or as we might also put it – to hope – if you are not' – (and now her eyes were large, grey, and clear) – 'entirely on the wrong track, Frau Heinold. For I – honestly, till now I had never thought that I had made any particular impression on Hugo.' She let the name slip slowly out of her mouth. And she looked innocently into Beatrice's face. Beatrice had blushed darkly, and speechlessly pressed her lips together. 'Then what shall I do?' asked Fortunata pitifully. 'Go away? I could write my husband that the air here does not agree with me. What do you think, Frau Heinold?'

Beatrice shrugged her shoulders. 'If you really are willing, I mean if you will really have the kindness not to concern yourself with my son, it will not be so very hard, Baroness – your word will suffice.'

'My word? Don't you think, Frau Heinold, that in such affairs words and oaths – oh, even of women different from myself – mean very little?'

'You do not love him at all,' Beatrice suddenly cried, losing all her self-control. 'It would have been a whim, no more. And I am his mother. Baroness, you will not permit me to have made this step in vain.'

Fortunata stood up, looked long at Beatrice, and offered her hand. She seemed suddenly to admit defeat. 'Your son, from this hour, does not exist for me,' she said earnestly. 'Forgive me for having caused you to wait so long for this self-evident answer.'

Beatrice took her hand and at that moment felt a sort of sympathy, even pity, for the Baroness. She almost felt as if she owed her an apology. But she restrained this impulse, even avoided saying anything that might be taken as thanks, and said instead, rather lamely, 'Then the affair is in order, Baroness.' And she stood up.

'Must you go?' asked Fortunata in her most proper voice.

'I have detained you long enough,' answered Beatrice equally politely.

Fortunata smiled, and Beatrice felt rather stupid. She allowed the Baroness to accompany her to the garden-gate, and gave her her hand once more. 'Thank you for your visit,' said Fortunata cordially, and added: 'If I shall not be able to return it in the near future, I hope you will not take it amiss.'

'Oh,' said Beatrice and returned again from the street the friendly nod of the Baroness, who remained standing at the gate. Involuntarily Beatrice walked more rapidly than usual and kept to the level road. She could turn off later to the narrow forest path that led steep and straight to the Director's villa. 'How do matters really stand?' she asked herself excitedly. 'Am I the victor? She gave me her word. Yes. But did she not herself say that the promises of women did not mean much? No, she will not dare. She has seen to what lengths I can go.' Fortunata's words kept ringing in her ears. How queerly she spoke of that summer in Holland! As if of a peaceful respite from a wildly sweet, but very difficult time. And she imagined Fortunata in a white linen dress over her naked body, running along the seashore, as if pursued by evil spirits. Perhaps it was not always pleasant, the life that was Fortunata's lot. In a way, as was the case with women of her sort, she was probably half-insane and hardly answerable for the harm that she did. Well, she could do what she wished, only she must leave Hugo in peace. Why did it have to be just he? And Beatrice smiled as she thought that she could have offered the Baroness as compensation a handsome young man, newly arrived, named Fritz Weber, with whom she would surely be just as well satisfied. Yes, she would have made the proposal. Truly, that would have put the proper spice into the conversation. What women there were! What a life they led! So that they had to go to Dutch fishing villages from time to time to recuperate. For others all life was just such a fishing village. And Beatrice smiled, but without real joy.

She stood before the gate of Welponer's villa and entered. From the tennis court, which was quite near the entrance, Beatrice could see white figures shimmering through the thin shrubbery and could hear familiar voices. As she came closer, she saw two couples standing facing each other. On one side stood the son and daughter of the house, nineteen and eighteen years of age, both resembling their father in their dark eyes and heavy brows, and betraying by features and bearing, the Italian-Jewish stock from which they came. On the other side played Dr Bertram and his slender little sister, Leonie, the children of a well-known physician, who also had a home in the vicinity. At first Beatrice stood off a little to enjoy the strong free movement of their young bodies and the sharp flight of the balls. The fresh grace of the battle refreshed and pleased her. In a few moments the set was ended. Both couples met at the net, racquets in hand, and stood there, chatting. Their features, earlier made tense by the excitement of the game, now melted into vacuous smiles; their eyes, which before had followed the spring of the balls so keenly, now met dreamily. Beatrice realized this with strange uneasiness: it was as if the atmosphere, formerly so clean and pure, had suddenly become stormy and misty, and she could not help thinking: 'How well this evening would end if suddenly, by some magic, all the inhibitions of society should be done away with, and these young people might follow without hindrance the secret, perhaps even unsuspected urge which impels them.' And suddenly she realized that there was a lawless world – that she had just stepped out of such a one, and that its breath still hung around her. It was only because of that, that she saw today what otherwise would have escaped her innocent eyes. Only because of that? – Had she not herself secretly desired these worlds? Was she not herself once the beloved of the blessed and the damned, the naïve and the sophisticated, of scoundrels and heroes?

She was seen. They waved their hands to her in greeting. She went closer to the wire-netting and the others walked towards her. She heard their light chatter around her. But she felt as if both young men looked at her in a new way. Especially young Dr Bertram had a sort of superior scorn about his mouth and looked her up and down as he had never done before, or at least in a way that she had never before noticed. And when she left them to go at last up to the house, he jokingly caught her finger through the net and kissed it long, as if he could never stop. And he laughed insolently as a dark look of displeasure appeared on her face.

Up above, on the roofed, almost too handsome, balcony, Beatrice found both couples, the Welponers and the Arbesbachers, playing tarock. She would not let them be disturbed, pushed the Director back into his chair when he tried to lay aside his cards, and then sat down between him and his wife. She said she wanted to look on at their game, but she hardly did – her glance soon wandered over the stone balustrade far over the hills which the sun was gilding. Here a feeling of security and fitness came over her that she had not felt out there among the young people – a feeling that rendered her calm, but at the same time sad. The Director's wife offered her tea in her rather condescending manner to which one had to become accustomed. But Beatrice thanked her: she had just had some. Just! How many miles away lay that house with its insolently fluttering flags? How many hours, or days ago, had she left that place for this? Shadows sank upon the park, the sun suddenly disappeared behind the mountains; from the street below, invisible from here, came indefinite sounds. Beatrice suddenly felt so alone as she had only felt in twilight hours in the country immediately after Ferdinand's death and never since. Even Hugo seemed suddenly to disappear into unreality and to be unattainably far away. She wanted him urgently and hastily took her leave of the party. The Director insisted on accompanying her. He went down the broad staircase with her, then along the pond, in the centre of which the fountain was now silent, then past the tennis court, where the two couples, in spite of the falling evening, still played so eagerly that they did not notice them as they went by. Herr Welponer threw a troubled look towards them, which Beatrice had noticed on his face before. But she felt that today she understood him for the first time. She knew that in the midst of the strenuous powerful life of a keen financier, the Director was disturbed by the melancholy fear of advancing age. And while he walked at her side, his tall figure bent forward slightly as if only in affectation, and while he conversed lightly with her about the wonderful summer weather, and about the excursions which they really must undertake, but for which the energy always failed them, Beatrice felt that they were both being enmeshed in an invisible net. And when he kissed her hand at the gate of the park, he left a feeling of gentle sadness upon her, that accompanied her all the way home.

At the door, the maid told her that Hugo and another young man were in the garden, and besides, that a package had been left by the postman. Beatrice found it in her room, and smiled with pleasure. Was it not a good omen that fate had made the truth out of her unnecessary small lie? Or should it be taken as a warning: this time you were lucky. The package was from Dr Teichmann. It contained books that he had promised to send her, the memoirs and letters of great statesmen, of people, therefore, whom the little lawyer tremendously admired. Beatrice merely looked at a title-page, took off her hat in her bedroom, threw a shawl around her shoulders and went into the garden. She saw the boys below near the hedge. Without noticing her, they continued to jump high up in the air like madmen. When Beatrice came nearer, she saw that both had taken off their coats. Now Hugo ran towards her and kissed her for the first time in weeks, childishly and stormily on both cheeks. Fritz quickly slipped his coat on, bowed, and kissed Beatrice's hand. She smiled. It seemed to her that he wanted to wipe away that other melancholy kiss by the touch of his young lips.

'What are you children doing there?' asked Beatrice.

'Contest for the world's championship in high-jumping,' exclaimed Fritz.

The high cornstalks on the other side of the hedge moved in the evening breeze. Below lay the lake, dull grey and misty. 'You might put on your coat too, Hugo,' said Beatrice, gently pushing his damp blond hair off his forehead. Hugo obeyed. Beatrice thought that her boy looked rather unkempt and childish next to his friend, but it pleased her at the moment.

'Just think, mother,' said Hugo, 'Fritz wants to take the half-past nine train back to Ischl.'

'But why?'

'There are no rooms to be found, Frau Heinold. There may be one in two or three days at the earliest.'

'But you are not going away just because of that, Herr Fritz? We have room for you.'

'I have already told him, mother, that you certainly would not object to his staying.'

'Why should I? Certainly you shall spend the night here, in the guest room. What is it for, if not for just such occasions?'

'Frau Heinold, I shouldn't like to inconvenience you in any way. I know that my mother is always much upset when we have unexpected house guests at Ischl.'

'Well, that is not the case here, Herr Fritz.'

They finally agreed that Herr Weber's baggage should be sent for from the Posthof where it had been checked, and that he should live from that time on in the attic bedroom, in exchange for which Beatrice solemnly promised to call him plain 'Fritz' without the 'Herr'.

Beatrice gave the necessary orders in the house, and feeling it more fitting that the young friends be left to themselves for a while, did not appear until supper was served on the sun-porch. For the first time in many days, Hugo was in the best of spirits, and Fritz, too, had given up playing the grown-up man. Two school boys sat at the table, and as usual began first to criticize all their teachers, and then to discuss the outlook for their last year in school and plans for the more distant future. Fritz Weber, who wanted to be a physician, had already visited the dissecting room one day last winter, and he implied that no one else could have had such impressive experiences as he. Hugo, for his part, had long ago decided to dedicate his life to archaeology. He already had a small collection of relics – a Pompeian lamp, a piece of mosaic from the Baths of Caracalla, a pistol lock from the French invasion, and a few other things. He was planning to excavate here at the lake shore, and of course, over in Grassy Meadow where the remains of lake dwellings had been found. Fritz did not conceal his suspicions as to the authenticity of Hugo's museum pieces – above all he had always been doubtful of the pistol lock which Hugo had found in the Turkish entrenchments. Beatrice said that Fritz was too young for such scepticism, whereupon he answered that it had nothing to do with age – it was just his natural tendency. 'I prefer my Hugo to this precocious cub,' thought Beatrice, 'but in truth, life will be much more difficult for him.' She looked at him. His eyes were staring far off into the distance, whither Fritz surely could not follow him. Beatrice thought further : 'Naturally he has no suspicion as to the kind of person this Fortunata really is. Who knows what he imagines about her? Perhaps to him she is a sort of fairy princess whom a cruel wizard holds in captivity. How he sits there, with his ruffled blond hair and his untidy neck-tie! He still has the child's mouth – the sweet red child's mouth – It is his father's – the same mouth and eyes.' And she looked out into the darkness that hung so heavy and black over the meadow that it seemed as if a deep forest stood around the windows.

'May I smoke?' asked Fritz. Beatrice nodded, whereupon Fritz took out a silver cigarette case with a golden monogram and offered it politely to his hostess. Beatrice took a cigarette and let him light it for her, and was informed that Fritz got his tobacco directly from Alexandria. Hugo smoked today too. It was, he said, the seventh cigarette of his life. Fritz had given up counting his long ago. Besides, he announced that these cigarettes were given him by his father, who, he said, had excellent business prospects for the next year. Then he told the latest news – that his sister was going to finish her 'gymnasium' in three years, and then would probably study medicine just as he himself was going to do. Beatrice glanced quickly at Hugo, who blushed slightly. Was it perhaps still the love for little Elise that he had in his heart, and which caused the painful look about his mouth?

'Couldn't we go for a little row?' asked Fritz. 'It's such a beautiful night, and so warm.'

'Why not wait for moonlight,' said Beatrice. 'It's gloomy, floating around out there on such a dark night.'

'I think so too,' said Hugo. Fritz's nostrils twitched contemptuously. But then the boys decided to celebrate the day by having an ice on the terrace of the Lake Hotel.

'You young scamps,' said Beatrice smilingly as they left.

Then she looked over the attic room to see that everything was in order, and attended to all her final housewifely duties before going to bed. She went to her room, undressed, and lay down in bed. Soon she heard voices outside – evidently those of the porters who were bringing Fritz's trunk, which was now being carried up the wooden steps. Then followed a conversation between the porter and maid that lasted longer than was absolutely necessary – and then – all was silent. Beatrice took up one of the books of heroes that Dr Teichmann had sent her and began to read the memoirs of a French general. But her mind was not on it – she was restless and tired, and she felt as if the very stillness around would not let her sleep. After some time she heard the front door open, then footsteps, whispering, and laughter. The boys! They tiptoed upstairs as quietly as possible. Then from above came sounds of movement, a clatter, a murmur – then footsteps descending the stairs. That was Hugo going down to bed. Now all was quiet in the house. Beatrice put aside her book, turned out the light, and fell asleep, calm, and almost happy.

Part Two

They had at length reached their goal. As all had prophesied, the journey lasted longer than the architect had said. But he countered with: 'Well, what did I say? Three hours from Oak Road. It's not my fault if we started at nine instead of eight.'

'But now it's half-past one,' remarked Fritz.

'Yes,' said Frau Arbesbacher sadly, 'that's always how he measures time.'

'When there are women about,' answered her husband, 'you always have to add fifty per cent. It's an old, old story, especially when you go shopping with them.' And he laughed dully.

Young Dr Bertram, who since the beginning of the excursion had steadily kept near Beatrice, spread his green coat out on the grass. 'Please, Frau Heinold,' he said, pointing to it with a gentle smile. His words and looks had been full of meaning ever since the day two weeks ago, when he had kissed her finger through the tennis net.

'No, thanks,' answered Beatrice, 'I have my own, you see.' And at a glance from her, Fritz flung open her Scotch plaid, which he had been carrying on his arm. But the wind was so strong up there on the mountain side, that the blanket flapped like a giant veil until Beatrice caught it at the other end, and with Fritz's help, spread it out on the ground.

'There's always a nice little breeze blowing up here,' said the architect. 'But what a pretty sight, eh what?' And he made a sweeping gesture over the whole landscape. They were on a broad, closely cropped meadow that sloped gently and left the view free on all sides. All of them contemplated the scene for some time in silent pleasure. The men had taken off their waterproof hats. Hugo's hair was more untidy than ever, the bristling white hair of the architect was stirred too by the wind, even Fritz's well-combed crop underwent some damage, and it was only Bertrams straight blond hair that the wind could not disturb, though it blew so steadily over the height. Arbesbacher named several of the mountain peaks across the lake, together with their respective heights, and pointed out one peak which, he said, had never been reached from the north. Dr Bertram said this was a mistake, for he himself had climbed it last year.

'Then you were the first,' said the architect.

'That's possible,' answered Bertram nonchalantly, and called attention immediately to another mountain that looked much less formidable, but that he had never dared climb. He knew just how much he dared attempt. Above all, he was not fool-hardy, and had no especial fondness for death. He pronounced the word 'death' very lightly, in the voice of the expert who disdains to speak seriously of his specialty before the layman.

Beatrice had stretched out on the plaid and looked up at the dull, blue sky over which thin white summer clouds were passing. She knew that Dr Bertram was speaking only to her – that he was placing at her disposal all his most interesting qualities – pride and knowledge, contempt of death, and love of life – to choose from as she would. But it had not the slightest effect on her.

The youngest members of the party – Fritz and Hugo – had brought the lunch in their packs. Leonie helped them unpack and then buttered the bread in her graceful, motherly way, not forgetting to take off her tan gloves and to slip them into her brown leather belt. The architect uncorked the bottles, Dr Bertram poured the wine and offered the full glasses to the ladies, looking past Beatrice with deliberate indifference, towards the mountain tops across the lake. They all found it delightful to be partaking of bread and butter sandwiches and tangy Terlan wine up there, with the mountain wind blowing around them. To finish off the lunch, there was a large cake that Frau Director Welponer had sent to Beatrice that morning, together with an apology for herself and her family, because they were unable to join them, although they would have enjoyed it so much. Their refusal was not unexpected. To pry the Welponer family loose from their garden was no easy task, as Leonie said. The architect took the liberty of reminding the honourable ones present that they too could not boast much of their enterprise.

How had they been spending these beautiful summer days? – 'lackadaisied', as he put it, around on the forest paths, or bathed in the lake, or played tennis and tarock – but how many plans and preparations had been necessary before they finally decided to undertake even this little excursion – which, all told, was but a short walk?

Beatrice thought to herself that she had only been here once before – with Ferdinand – ten years ago – the same summer, therefore, when they had moved into their new home. But it was hard to realize that it was the same meadow where she was today – in her memory it had been so different – so much broader and lighter. A soft melancholy crept into her heart. How alone she was amongst all these people! What did the happy chatter all around mean to her? There they all sat on the meadow, letting their glasses clink! Fritz touched his glass to Beatrice's; but after she had long emptied hers, he still stood motionlessly holding his in his hands and staring at her. 'What a look,' thought Beatrice. 'Even more enraptured and thirsty than those that he has been directing towards me for the past few days – or do I just imagine it, because I have drunk three glasses of wine in such quick succession?' She stretched out again on her plaid beside Frau Arbesbacher, who had fallen fast asleep, and looked blinkingly into the air, where she saw a tiny smoke cloud rising gracefully – probably from Bertram's cigarette, though she could not see him. But she felt his glance running along the whole length of her body to the nape of her neck, until she almost thought she felt his touch, but realized that it was only the long grass that was tickling her.

The voice of the architect came to her as if from a great distance, as he told the boys of the time when the little train did not yet come to the village below. And although hardly fifteen years had gone by, he tried to spread an atmosphere of grey antiquity over that period. Among other stories, he told one of a drunken coachman who had once driven him right into the lake and whom he had thrashed almost to death for it. Then Fritz related the following heroic anecdote in his best manner: once in the Weiner Wald, he had made a very timid boy take to his heels by merely putting his hand into his pocket as if he had a revolver there. For it was a question, as he took care to explain, not of the revolver, but of presence of mind. 'It's a pity,' said the architect, 'that one does not always have a six-barrelled, loaded presence of mind about one.' The boys laughed. How well Beatrice knew that laugh, that double laugh, that she could now enjoy so often at home during meal times and in her garden; and how happy she was that the boys got along so well together. Recently they had gone away together for two days, fully equipped, on an excursion to Gosauseen, as a preparation for the September tour that they were planning. Besides, they had been better friends in Vienna than Beatrice had known. She had learned from others something that Hugo had stubbornly kept silent – that some evenings, after an hour in the gymnasium, both would go to a coffee house on the other side of the village to play billiards. But in any case, she was deeply grateful to Fritz for coming to them at that time. Hugo's mood had become again as fresh and untroubled as ever, the painful look had left his face, and surely he did not think of the terrible woman with the Pierrot face and the red-dyed hair. And Beatrice could not deny that she had comported herself blamelessly. Just a few days ago she had by chance seen her standing near her on the gallery of the bath house, just when Hugo and Fritz had come racing in as usual from the open lake. They reached the slippery steps simultaneously, and, supporting themselves with one arm, they had splashed each other's faces, dived and appeared again far out in the open lake. Fortunata, in her white bath-robe, had looked on carelessly with an absent smile, as at the play of children, and then had looked again out over the lake with lost sad eyes, so that Beatrice in mild discontent, and with an almost guilty feeling, recalled the talk in the white-flagged villa, that was ever becoming dimmer and less important to her, and that the Baroness herself seemed to have long forgiven and forgotten. One evening Beatrice had seen the Baron seated on a bench in the wood. He evidently had come for a short visit. He had light blond hair, a beardless, wrinkled, and yet young-looking face with steel-grey eyes, wore a light blue flannel suit, smoked a short pipe, and had beside him on the bench, a sailor's cap. He looked to Beatrice like a captain who had come from a distant land, and who must immediately go back to sea. Fortunata sat beside him, small and well-bred, her nose pinkish as usual, with tired arms, like a doll that the distant captain could take out or put back into its case according to his pleasure.

All of this went through Beatrice's mind as she lay on the meadow, while the wind blew and grass-blades tickled her neck. Around her now everything was silent; all of them seemed to be asleep; only at a short distance away somebody was whistling. Unconsciously Beatrice looked with blinking eyes for the small smoke cloud, and immediately saw it rising thin and silver-grey into the air. Beatrice raised her head slightly – she saw Dr Bertram leaning his head on both arms, his eyes fastened on the low-cut neck of her dress. He was speaking and it was quite possible that he had been speaking for a long time, in fact that his speech had awakened her out of her half-sleep. Now he asked her whether she would be interested in a mountain climbing party, in a real climb, or whether she were afraid of dizziness – it didn't have to be a peak, it could be a plateau as well; only he wanted to go higher than the others, so much higher, that they could not follow. To look with her from a high peak into the valley – that would be divine. When he got no answer, he said: 'Well, Frau Beatrice?'

'I'm asleep,' answered Beatrice.

'Then allow me to be your dream,' he began, and continued – he could picture no more beautiful death than to jump into the deep – one's whole life would rush by in such frightful clearness, and it would naturally be more pleasant in proportion as to how one had lived, and if one had not the slightest fear, only a never before experienced thrill, and a sort – yes, a sort of metaphysical curiosity. And he buried his burned-out cigarette stub in the ground with quick fingers. Besides, he continued, he was not particularly interested in such an end. On the contrary, even if he were obliged to see so much misery and horror in his work, for that reason, he treasured everything light and pure in life all the more. Wouldn't Frau Beatrice like to see the hospital garden? There was a very curious and charming atmosphere about it, especially on autumn evenings. You see, he was now living in the hospital. And if Beatrice would like to take tea with him at the same time –

'You're quite mad,' said Beatrice, sitting up and looking with

clear eyes into the blue-gold atmosphere which the dull moun-
tain-peaks seemed to absorb. Drunk with the sun, a little weak,
she stood up, shook out her dress, and noticed, how, quite
against her will, she looked wearily down at Dr Bertram. She
quickly looked away towards Leonie, who stood quite alone at
some distance from them, like a picture, a fluttering veil thrown
about her head. The architect sat with crossed legs on the grass,
playing cards with the boys.

'I say, Frau Beatrice, soon you won't have to give Hugo any
more pocket money,' he called out, 'he can support himself
comfortably out of today's winnings in tarock.'

'Then it would be wise for us to start homeward before you
are completely ruined.' Fritz looked at Beatrice with glowing
cheeks. She smiled at him. Bertram stood up, looked at the sky,
and then down over her bit by bit. 'What is the matter with
you all?' she thought. 'And what is the matter with me?' For
suddenly she noticed that she allowed the lines of her body to
play as alluringly as possible. Seeking assistance, she turned her
look towards her son, who was playing out his last card, his
childish face aglow, his clothes unspeakably untidy. He won the
game and proudly collected one crown and twenty heller from
the architect. They got ready for the descent, all except Frau
Arbesbacher, who was still asleep. 'Let her lie,' joked the architect. But at that moment, she stirred, rubbed her eyes, and was
ready for the homeward journey long before the others.

For a while the path led sharply downhill, then it ran almost
level through young forests; at the next bend, they could see
the lake which disappeared at once. Beatrice, who at first had
joined Hugo and Fritz and had run ahead with them, soon
remained behind; Leonie came up to her and spoke of a sailing
regatta that was to take place soon. Beatrice still remembered
clearly the race seven years ago in which Ferdinand had won
second prize in his boat, the 'Roxana'. Where was she now?
After so many triumphs she led a lonely inglorious life down
there in the boat-house. The architect took advantage of this
opportunity to say that this year boating was as much neglected as all other sports. Leonie expressed the opinion that
there was some enervating influence coming from the Welponer
house, whose effect no one could escape. The architect, too,

believed that the Welponers were in no way suited to agreeable society, and his wife said it was due most of all to Frau Welponer's arrogance and because she had not the slightest need for amusement. They suddenly were silent, as they saw the Director sitting on a worm-eaten, broken-down bench at the turn in the road. He stood up; and his monocle on its narrow silk ribbon hung down over his white piqué vest. He said that he had taken the liberty of coming to meet them and invite them in the name of his wife to partake of a small 'Jause', which was awaiting the tired wanderers on the shady veranda. At the same time, he looked wearily at them all, and Beatrice noted that when he looked at Bertram, his face darkened; and she suddenly knew that the Director was envious of the young man. But she was immediately ashamed of such a foolish assumption. She lived on in the present, quietly and un-questioningly, in undisturbed faithfulness to him alone whose voice even now rang clearer in her memory than all the voices of the living, and whose eyes still shone brighter than all those living ones.

The Director remained behind with Beatrice. First he talked of various unimportant events of the day, of some friends who had recently arrived, of the death of the miller, aged ninety-five, about the ugly house that a Salzburg architect was build-ing in Grassy Meadow, and then, as if by accident, reminded her of the time when neither his house, nor the Heinold house had yet been built, and when both families had lived all summer in the Lake Hotel. He recalled several trips they had taken together on the then little known roads, and one sailing party in the 'Roxana', which ended in a terrible storm; spoke of the housewarming party at the Heinold house when Ferdinand had made two of his fellow-actors dead drunk, and finally, of Ferdi-nand's last rôle in a modern, rather tragic play, in which he had so perfectly played the part of a youth of twenty. What an inimitable artist he had been! And what an excellent man! A man of eternal youth, one might say. A wonderful contrast to that class of people in whose numbers he must unfortunately include himself, of people who were not made to bring either themselves or others happiness. And as Beatrice looked at him questioningly, he said: 'I, dear Frau Beatrice, I was born old, so to speak. Do you know what that means? I shall try to explain. You see, we who were born old – during our lives we let one mask after another fall from us, until, at the age of eighty or thereabouts, sometimes sooner, we show our real faces to the world. The others, the youthful ones – and such a one was Ferdinand (quite contrary to his habit he called him by his Christian name) – they always remain young, remain children, and therefore are obliged to put on one mask after another if they do not wish to astonish other people too much. Perhaps these masks come of themselves over their faces, and they do not know that they wear them, and only have a strange dark feeling that something does not fit in their lives – because they always feel young. Such a man was Ferdinand.'

Beatrice listened to the Director in surprise and with rising defiance. She could not help feeling that he had conjured up Ferdinand's shadow intentionally, as if he had been assigned to guard her honour, to warn her of some near danger, and to protect her. Really, he might have spared himself the trouble. What gave him the right, what grounds had he for appointing himself the representative and guardian of Ferdinand's memory? What was there in her actions that aroused such insulting suspicions in his mind? If she could play and laugh today and wear bright colours again, could any unprejudiced onlooker interpret it as anything but the necessity of living on in conformity with the others? But the thought that she might ever be really happy again, or might belong again to any man, filled her with disgust and horror; and that horror, as she learned in many sleepless nights, became only deeper, when some inexplicable flashes of longing rushed through her blood and passed by unfulfilled. And again she glanced quickly at the Director, who now walked silently beside her. But she was terrified to discover the smile on her lips, that in spite of herself, came from the depths of her soul, and that unerringly, almost shamelessly, said more plainly than words: 'I know that you desire me, and I am glad.' She saw his eyes suddenly flare up into a burning question, which he immediately controlled and quieted. And he addressed an indifferent polite word to Frau Arbesbacher, who was just a few steps ahead of them, for the small party, now that they were nearing their goal, had all come together again. Suddenly young Dr Bertram was at Beatrice's side, and by his bearing, look and speech, implied that the relations between him and Beatrice had become more closely bound on this picnic, and that she must admit the fact that she was beginning to yield to his graces. But she remained cool and distant and grew more distant at each step. And when they reached the gate of Welponer's Villa, she announced, to the surprise of everyone, including herself, that she was tired and would prefer to go home. They tried to dissuade her. But since the Director himself expressed only mild disappointment, they did not insist. She was undecided as to whether she would return for supper, which they had agreed to take together at the Lake Hotel, but had no objections to Hugo's joining them in any case. 'I'll take good care,' said the architect, 'that he does not drink himself silly.' Beatrice took her leave. A feeling of great relief came over her as she took the road homewards and she was happy in the prospect of the few undisturbed hours that were to be hers.

At home she found a letter from Dr Teichmann, and was mildly surprised, not so much that he again gave a sign of life, as that she had almost forgotten his existence in the excitement of the past days. It was only after she had removed the dust of the day's journey and was sitting before her toilet-table in a comfortable house gown, that she opened the letter about whose contents she was not in the least bit curious. The letter opened, as usual, with reports on business matters, for Dr Teichmann believed it his duty to serve Beatrice first of all as her solicitor, and he informed her with misplaced humour of the success of a little venture of hers in which he was able to gain quite a sum of money for her. Finally, he told her, in an elaborately casual tone, that his vacation journey that year would take him past Oak Road, and that he dared hope – as he wrote – that through the bushes he might catch sight of a gay garment, or that a friendly eye might smile at him and might invite him to linger, even though it be for just a moment's chat. He did not forget to send regards to the Arbesbachers and the 'noble Lord and Lady of the castle, together with their worthy offspring,' as he expressed it, and the other friends, whose acquaintance he had made last year when he spent three days at the Lake Hotel. Beatrice found it strange that last year seemed so far away and like a different period of her life, although it had been hardly any different from this summer. Even the flirtations on the part of the Director and young Dr Bertram had not been wanting. It was only that she herself had gone on unperturbed amongst all their looks and words; yes, that she had hardly noticed them, and was only now conscious of them in reminiscence. This might be due to the fact that she had very little to do with all these summer acquaintances in the city. Since the death of her husband, after she had broken connections with the circle of artists and theatrical people, she had led a retiring and monotonous life. Only her mother, who lived in a suburb in an old mansion near the factory that her father had once managed, and a few distant relatives, found their way to her quiet home which had become quite bourgeois and commonplace again. And when Dr Teichmann would appear for tea and a little chat, it meant a diversion to her, that gave her real pleasure, she realized now with surprise.

Thoughtfully shaking her head, she laid the letter down and looked into the garden over which the early August twilight was spreading. The comfortable feeling of solitude had gradually left her and she wondered whether it would not be wiser to go back to the Welponers, or later to go to the Lake Hotel. But then she restrained the impulse, a little ashamed that she should have succumbed so completely to the allurement of society and that the pensive magic of such solitary summer evenings that formerly had so charmed her, should have disappeared forever. She threw a thin shawl over her shoulders and went into the garden. Here the melancholy she had been seeking came over her, and she knew in the depths of her soul that she could never walk up and down these paths that she had so often walked with Ferdinand, on the arm of another man. At this moment, one thing above all was clear to her: if Ferdinand in those distant days had made her swear not to cast aside any opportunity for happiness, certainly he had not pictured a marriage with such a man as Dr Teichmann; any passionate, though perhaps merely passing adventure would be much more likely to win his approval in his celestial realm.

And with horror she realized that a picture had sprung up in her mind: she saw herself up on the meadow in the twilight in the arms of Dr Bertram. But she merely saw the picture, no wish accompanied it; cool and distant, it hung in the air like a vision and disappeared.

She stood at the lower end of the garden, leaned her arms on the fence, and looked downwards to the lights of the town blinking below. The voices of an evening boating party, singing out on the lake, came to her with startling clearness through the quiet air. The clock in the church tower struck nine. Beatrice sighed softly, then turned around and slowly went back across the lawn to the house. On the veranda, she found the table set with the usual three places. She let the maid bring her her supper and ate it without any particular relish, feeling a useless, aimless sadness. While eating, she picked up a book – it was the memoirs of a French general, which interested her today even less than usual. The clock struck half-past nine, and, loneliness depressing her more every moment, she decided to leave the house after all, and to find the party at the Lake Hotel. She stood up, put her long silk coat over her house gown, and started out. As she went past the Baroness's house at the lake, she noticed that it was completely dark; and she remembered that she had not seen Fortunata for several days. Had she gone away with the distant Captain? But as Beatrice looked back again, she thought she saw a light behind one of the closed blinds. Why did it trouble her? She didn't care any more.

On the high terrace of the Lake Hotel, whose electric arc lights were already out, she found her party, seated around a table, in the faint light of two wall brackets. Conscious suddenly of the too serious expression on her face, she forced an empty smile to her lips. She was greeted warmly, shook hands with all of them in a row, the Director, the architect, their wives, and young Fritz Weber. There was no one else present. 'Where is Hugo?' she asked, somewhat perturbed.

'He left this very moment,' answered the architect. 'Queer that you didn't meet him.'

Unconsciously Beatrice glanced at Fritz, who with an embarrassed, stupid, childish smile, twirled his beer glass and

averted his eyes with obvious intent. Then she sat down between
him and Frau Welponer, and in order to overcome the menacing thoughts that were arising in her, she began to talk with
exaggerated cheerfulness. She was very sorry that Frau Welponer had not been with them on the charming picnic; she
asked about the brother and sister, Bertram and Leonie; and
finally related that at supper she had read some French
memoirs and letters of great men. She found no pleasure in
novels and such things any more. It seemed that the others
agreed with her. 'Love stories are only for young folks,' said
the architect – 'I mean for children, for in a way, we are all
still young folks.' Fritz too said that he preferred scientific
works, or especially books on travel. While he spoke, he moved
quite close to Beatrice, and pressed his knee against hers as if
by accident; his napkin fell down, he bent down to pick it up,
and tremblingly stroked her ankle. Was the boy mad? And he
continued speaking, excitedly, with glowing eyes: as soon as
he was a doctor, he would join some large expedition, perhaps
to Tibet or darkest Africa. The others smiled indulgently at his
words; only the Director – Beatrice noted it well – looked at
him with sullen envy. As the party arose to go home, Fritz said
that he would first take a solitary walk on the lake shore.
'Alone?' asked the architect, 'that isn't so easy to believe.' But
Fritz answered that walking alone on summer evenings was one
of his particular passions; just recently he had come home
about one in the morning, and in fact with Hugo, who at times
accompanied him on these nightly jaunts. And as he saw the
restless, questioning glance that Beatrice turned to him, he
added: 'It is quite possible that I shall meet Hugo somewhere
down at the lake tonight, if he hasn't gone rowing as he
sometimes does.'

'This is interesting news,' said Beatrice, shaking her head
doubtfully.

'Yes, these summer evenings,' sighed the architect.

'What have you to say about it?' asked his wife enigmatically.

Frau Welponer, who had gone down the steps of the terrace
ahead of the others, remained standing for a moment and
looked at the heavens, as if seeking something. Then she let
her head sink again in a strange hopeless way. The Director

was silent. But in his silence, burned hatred of summer nights, youth, and happiness.

They had hardly reached the lake shore, when Fritz slipped away, as if in fun, and disappeared into the dark. The two couples accompanied Beatrice home. Slowly and with difficulty, they climbed the steep road up the hill. 'Why did Fritz run away so suddenly?' Beatrice wondered. 'Will he find Hugo at the shore? Did he ever go rowing with him in the evening? Is there a compact between them? Does Fritz know where Hugo is at this moment? Does he know?' And she had to pause a moment, for it seemed to her that her heart had suddenly stopped beating. 'As if I did not know where Hugo is! As if I had not known it for days!' ...

'I rather wish somebody would build a railway up this hill,' said the architect. He had taken his wife's arm, which, as far as Beatrice could remember, he had never done before. The Director and his wife walked together, in step, both bent and silent. As Beatrice stood before her door, she suddenly knew why Fritz had stolen away down there. He had wanted to avoid going alone into the house with her at night, in the presence of all the others. And she was grateful for the wise gallantry of the young man.

The Director kissed Beatrice's hand. 'Whatever may happen to you,' he murmured, half-trembling, 'I shall understand, and you will have a friend in me.'

'Let me alone,' answered Beatrice as silently as he. The two couples parted. The Director and his wife disappeared with strange suddenness into the darkness, where wood, mountains, and heaven all ran together. The Arbesbachers took the road towards the other side, where the path was more open, and over which the soft, blue, starry night spread on high.

When the door had closed behind her, Beatrice thought: 'Shall I look in Hugo's room? What for? I know that he is not at home. I know that he is there where the light shone from behind closed blinds.' And she remembered that just now, on her return walk, she had again passed the house, and that it had seemed a house in the dark to her, like the others. But she did not doubt any more that at this hour her son was in the villa that she had passed thoughtlessly, and yet full of foreboding. And she knew too that she was to blame – yes, she alone – for she had let it happen. With that one visit to Fortunata, she had imagined that she had fulfilled all her motherly duties; after that she had let it go on as it would – out of laziness, out of weariness, out of cowardice – she had seen nothing, known nothing, thought nothing. Hugo was at Fortunata's at this moment, and not for the first time. A picture came to her, that made her shudder and she hid her face in her hands as if to banish it in that way. Slowly she opened the door to her bedroom. A sadness came over her, a feeling that she had taken leave of something that would never return. The time was past when Hugo was a child, her child. Now he was a young man, one who lived his own life, of which he could no longer tell his mother. Never more would she stroke his cheeks and hair – never more could she kiss his sweet child's mouth as before. Now for the first time, since she had lost him, she was alone.

She sat on her bed and slowly began to undress. How long would he stay away? Probably the whole night. And in the grey of early morning, very quietly, in order not to awaken his mother, he would slip through the hall into his room. How often had it happened already? How many nights had he been with her? Many? No, not many. For a few days he had been on a walking tour through the country. Yes, if he had spoken the truth! But he had not been telling the truth lately. Not for a long time. In the winter he played billiards in a coffee house in the suburbs, and where else he might have been, who knew? And suddenly a thought made the blood run faster through her veins: Was he perhaps even then Fortunata's lover: On the day when she had paid her ridiculous visit to the villa down near the lake? And had the Baroness played a shabby trick on her, and then, heart to heart with Hugo, had she scoffed and laughed at her? Yes – even that was possible. For what did she know today of her boy who had grown to manhood in the arms of a wanton? Nothing – nothing.

She leaned on the sill of her open window, and looked into the garden and far away to the dark mountain peaks on the other side of the lake. Sharply outlined, towered the one that Dr Bertram had never dared attempt to climb. How did it

happen that he was not there at the hotel? If he had guessed
that she might return, he would surely have been there. Was it
not strange that they should still desire her, who was the mother
of a boy who already spent his nights with a mistress? Why
strange? She was as young, perhaps younger than, Fortunata.
And all at once, she felt the outlines of her body under her
light garment, with agonizing distinctness, and even a sort of
painful pleasure. A noise outside on the path made her jump.
She knew it was Fritz coming home. Where could he have been
all this time? Did he, too, perhaps have his little adventure
here in the country? She smiled wearily. No, surely not he. For
he was a little in love with her. And really – no wonder. She
was just at the age that would appeal to so green a youth.
Evidently he had wanted to cool his longing out in the night
air; and she was a little sorry for him because just tonight the
heavens hung so heavy and misty over the lake. And suddenly
she remembered such a sultry summer night a long time ago,
when her husband had forced her against her will to go with
him from the soft privacy of their chamber into the garden,
and there, in the dark black shadows of the trees, to exchange
wild and tender caresses. Then she thought of the cool morning
when a thousand birds had awakened her to a sweet, heavy
sadness, and she trembled. Where was all that now? Did it not
seem that the garden into which she was looking had preserved
the memory of that night better than she herself, and that it
might be able in some wonderful way to betray her to those
who understood the language of the dumb? And she felt as if
night in person stood out in the garden, ghostly and mysterious
– yes, as if each house, each garden, had its own night, that was
quite different from, deeper and more trustworthy than, that
meaningless blue darkness that spread above the sleeping world,
unattainably far away. And that night that belonged to her,
stood full of secrets and dreams before her window, and stared
into her face with blind eyes. She unconsciously put out her
hands as if to ward off the vision; then she returned to her
room, went slowly to her mirror, and with a tired droop of the
shoulders, began to take down her hair. It must be past midnight. She was very tired, and at the same time far too wide
awake. Of what use were all her meditations, all her memories,

all her dreams? Of what use were all her fears and hopes? Hopes? Where was there any hope for her? She went again to the window, and carefully pulled the blinds. 'Even from here, it shines out into the night, into my night,' she thought. She locked the door leading to the hall; then, according to her old careful habit, she opened the door into her little parlour for a last look. She drew back, frightened. In the semi-darkness, she saw the figure of a man, standing upright in the middle of the room. 'Who is there?' she asked. The figure moved. She recognized Fritz. 'What are you doing here?' she asked.

He rushed to her and snatched both of her hands. Beatrice pulled them away. 'You are not in your right mind,' she said.

'Pardon me, dear Frau Heinold,' he whispered, 'but I – I don't know what to do any more.'

'That is very simple,' answered Beatrice. 'Go to bed.' He shook his head. 'Go, go,' she said, and turned back to her room, and was about to lock the door behind her. Then she felt his arms thrust gently but awkwardly around her neck. She shrank away, but turned around involuntarily and put out her arm, as if to push Fritz back. He took her hand and put it to his lips. 'But, Fritz,' she said, more mildly than had been her intention.

'I shall go quite mad,' he whispered.

She smiled. 'I believe you are already mad.'

'I should have waited here all night,' he whispered again. 'I had not dreamt that you would open this door. I just wanted to be here near you.'

'Now, go to your room at once. Do you hear me? Or you will make me really angry.' He had taken both her hands.

'I beg you, Frau Heinold.'

'Don't be ridiculous, Fritz! That's enough. Let go my hands. That's right. And now, go.'

He had let her hands drop; and then she felt the warmth of his lips on her cheek. 'I'm going mad, I've been in this room before.'

'What?'

'Yes, I spent half of the night here recently, until it was almost light. I couldn't help it. I should like always to be near you.'

'Don't say such foolish things.'

He stammered on: 'I beg of you, Frau Heinold, Frau Beatrice – Beatrice!'

'That's enough – really you are – what is the matter with you? Shall I call? But for God's sake! Think then – think of Hugo.'

'Hugo is not at home. No one hears us.'

Quickly that burning pain again rose within her. Then suddenly, with shame and fright she realized that she was glad of Hugo's absence. She felt Fritz's warm lips on hers, and a longing sprang up in her which she had never felt to such an extent before, not even in those far-off days. 'Who can blame me for it?' she thought. 'To whom am I accountable?' And with desirous arms, she drew the glowing boy to her.

Part Three

As Beatrice came out of the dark shadow of the forest into the open, the gravel road stretched out before her, white and burning hot, and she was almost sorry that she had left the Welponers so early in the afternoon. But since Frau Welponer had departed for her usual after-dinner nap as soon as they left the table, and since her son and daughter had also disappeared without any apology, Beatrice would have been obliged to remain alone with the Director, a thing that she must avoid at all events, after the occurrences of the past few days. His attempts to win her favour had become altogether too open; in fact, he had dropped certain hints that gave her to believe that he would be ready to leave his wife and children at her will – and not only that, but that union with her would mean above all that wished for flight from unbearable household ties. For, with her lately acquired painful insight into the relationships of man, Beatrice had realized that that marriage had been deeply undermined, and that a collapse could follow at any time, unexpectedly and without any special reason. She had often noticed the exaggerated care with which the husband and wife spoke to each other, as if the hatred which lowered quiveringly in the hard lines around their mouths might break out at any moment into words that could never be made good again. But not until Fritz had told her last night of the almost incredible rumour, which she still did not believe – of a love affair between her dead husband and Frau Welponer, did she allow herself to take part with any real interest in the cause for the disturbance. And although the rumour had been troubling her even during dinner, while indifferent conversation went on around the table, now as she walked homewards down the path through the glittering summer air, from whose burning breath every living being seemed to have fled to the shelter of closed rooms, Fritz's rude intimations began to work with painful activity on her mind. Why, she asked herself, had he spoken of it, and especially that night? Was it in revenge because she had told him jokingly that he had better remain at Ischl with his parents, whom he was going to visit in the morning, instead of coming back the same evening as he had intended? Had a jealous suspicion awakened in him, that with all the charm of his youth, still he meant nothing to her but a handsome young boy, whom she could send home without further ado, when the game was at an end? Or had he only succumbed to his inclination to indiscreet talk, which she had been obliged to curb several times before, and even quite recently, when he evinced a desire to tell her about Hugo's relations with Fortunata? Or was the conversation between Fritz's parents, that he said he had recently overheard, just a child of his fanciful brain – just as his visit to the dissection room, of which he had told her on the day of his arrival, had recently turned out to be empty boasting? But although he had undertaken to tell of the talk of his parents in good faith, might he not have heard wrongly, or misunderstood? This last idea was all the more probable, since not the slightest whisper of that rumour had come to Beatrice before.

Busied with such thoughts, Beatrice reached her villa. Since Hugo had ostensibly gone on a tour, and the maid was having the day off, Beatrice found herself alone in the house. She undressed in her room, and submitting to the heavy weariness that often came over her these summer afternoons, she stretched out on her bed. Consciously enjoying the solitude, the peace, the very faint light, she lay there a while with open eyes. In the large mirror that hung opposite her, she could see the life-size bust-portrait of her husband reflected in faint outline from the wall over her bed. She could see clearly only a red spot that she knew represented the carnation in his button-hole. In the early days after Ferdinand's death, this picture had continued to lead a strangely personal life for Beatrice. She saw it smiling or sad, happy or distressed – in fact, at times, she imagined that in some way the painted features expressed unconcern or despair over their own death. In the course of years, however, it had become dumb and silent, and remained a piece of painted canvas and nothing more. But at this hour, it seemed to want to live again. And although Beatrice could not see very clearly in the mirror, it seemed to her that it sent an ironic look down over her; and memories awoke within her that, though they had seemed harmless, or even gay before, now came to her mind with a new bitter meaning. And in place of the one on whom her suspicions had been fastened, a whole row of women went by, whose features she had forgotten, but who, as she suddenly realized, had all been Ferdinand's loves – admirers who wanted his autograph or photograph, young actresses who took lessons from him, society women whose salons he and Beatrice had often frequented, fellow-actresses who had fallen into his arms as wives, brides, or betrayed ones. And she asked herself whether it were not his consciousness of guilt that had made him so mild and so wisely indifferent, as it seemed, to any unfaithfulness that Beatrice might commit against his memory. And all of a sudden, as if he had thrown aside the useless, uncomfortable mask that he had worn long enough, both alive and dead, he stood before her mind with his red carnation and all – a silly comedian for whom she was nothing but an industrious housewife, the mother of his son, and a woman whom one embraced once in a while when, on a mild summer evening, the magic of propinquity so disposed one. And like his picture, his voice suddenly changed mysteriously. It no longer had the noble ring that sounded more beautiful in her memory than the voices of all the living. It rang empty, affected, and false. But at once she knew that it was not really his voice that she now heard, but that of another who recently had ventured – here in her own house – had ventured to ape the voice, intonation, and actions of her dead husband.

She sat up in bed, threw one arm over the pillow, and stared in horror into the darkness of her chamber. Now for the first time, in this peaceful hour, she recalled that event in all its atrocity. It had happened a week ago, on a Sunday as today – she was sitting in the garden with her son and – she thought the word with a grimace – her lover. Suddenly a young man had appeared, tall and dark, with shining eyes, in a sports outfit, with a yellowish-red tie. She did not recognize him until the cheerful greeting of the others informed her that Rudi

Beratoner stood before her, the same young man who had visited Hugo several times the past winter to borrow books from him, and who, as she knew, was one of the two who Hugo had told her had spent that spring night in the Prater with the girls of questionable repute. He was just coming from Ischl, where he had looked for Fritz in vain at his parents' home. Naturally he was invited to dinner. He accepted gladly, a little too boisterously, and proved to be indefatigable in relating hunting stories and all sorts of anecdotes; and his younger friends, who seemed like children in comparison with his precociousness, looked at him in astonishment. He also showed a capacity for drink that was far beyond his years. Since the boys did not want to remain behind him, and since even Beatrice allowed herself to drink more than usual, the spirit in the house was much easier than was usual. Beatrice, who noticed with gratitude and emotion that in spite of all the gaiety her guest acted with great respect for her, imagined, as she often did in these days, that all that had happened recently, the truth of which she could not doubt, was only some sort of dream that could be repaired. For a moment, as formerly, she had put her arm around Hugo's shoulders and played with his hair, but she looked coquettishly at Fritz at the same time, and forthwith felt strange emotions over her own fate and the world. Later she noticed that Fritz was whispering very eagerly to Rudi and seemed to be persuading him to do something very important. She asked gaily what terrible thing the two young men were plotting; Beratoner did not want to answer, but Fritz explained – there was no reason for keeping it a secret – the fact was commonly known that Rudi could impersonate actors remarkably well, not only the living, but even the – but now he stopped. But Beatrice, very much excited and already slightly intoxicated, turned quickly to Rudi Beratoner, and asked somewhat hoarsely: 'Then you can impersonate Ferdinand Heinold too?' She pronounced the famous name as if it belonged to a stranger. Beratoner did not want to hear of it. He did not understand Fritz at all – formerly he had practised such tricks, but not for a long time now; besides, he naturally could not recall the voices of those he had not heard for a long time, and if he had to do something, he preferred to sing a couplet in the style of any comedian they might choose. But Beatrice would not allow any evasion. She wanted nothing more than to take advantage of this opportunity. She trembled with longing to hear the beloved voice, at least in reflected splendour. That that desire might mean something blasphemous did not strike her in her befogged state of mind. At last Beratoner let himself be persuaded. And with beating heart, Beatrice heard at first Hamlet's monologue, 'To be or not to be,' ringing through the free summer air in Ferdinand's heroic sounding voice, then verses from Tasso, then some long forgotten words out of a long-forgotten play – she heard the beloved voice, deeply booming and melting softly away. With closed eyes, she drank it in, full of wonder, until suddenly she heard, still in Ferdinand's voice, but now in his familiar everyday tone: 'Grüss Gott, Beatrice!' Then she opened her eyes in great fright and saw before her an insolent, spoiled face, around whose lips there still remained fading traces, like ghostly reminders, of Ferdinand's smile; she met Hugo's wandering glance and the half tragic, half stupid simper on Fritz's face; and heard herself saying as if from afar, a polite word of thanks to the wonderful mimic. The silence that followed was dark and oppressive; they could not bear it very long and soon gay words about summer weather and picnics were flying back and forth. But Beatrice soon arose and went back to her room, where she sank wearily into her armchair and then fell into a sleep from which she awoke hardly an hour later as if from an abysmally deep night. When she walked later in the garden, in the cool of evening, the young people had gone away. They came back soon without Rudi Beratoner, whom they took elaborate pains not to mention further, and it was deeply consoling to Beatrice to see how her son and lover tried with unusual consideration and delicacy to wipe away the distressing impression of the afternoon.

And now, in the quiet solitude of twilight, when Beatrice tried to recall the real voice of her husband, she could not do it. It was always the voice of that unwelcome guest that she heard, and she realized more deeply than ever what a crime she had committed against the dead man, worse than any that he could have committed during his life-time against her, more cowardly and inexpiable than unfaithfulness and betrayal. He was rotting deep in the ground and his widow allowed stupid boys to make fun of him, of that wonderful man who had loved her – her alone, in spite of everything that had happened, just as she had loved no other but him, and would never love any other. Now she knew it for the first time – since she had a lover. A lover! Oh, if he would never come back, that lover of hers – if he would only go away forever out of her sight and out of her blood, and if she could live again in her villa with Hugo in the quiet peace of summer, as before! As before? And if Fritz were no longer there, would she have her son back? Did she still have the right to expect it? Had she troubled much about him recently? Had she not been much happier that he went his own way? And she remembered how, recently, when she had been walking in the wood with the Arbesbachers, she had seen her son, hardly a hundred steps away, together with Fortunata, Wilhelmine Fallehn, and a strange man; and she had hardly been ashamed, only had talked more eagerly with her friends so that they might not notice Hugo. And in the evening of the same day, yesterday – yes, certainly it was only yesterday – how slowly time went by – she had met Fraulein Fallehn and that strange man, who, with his black shiny hair, his sparkling white teeth, his moustache cut English fashion, his pongee silk suit, and his red silk tie, looked like a circus rider, a swindler, or a Mexican millionaire. When Wilhelmine nodded in greeting with her never-changing deep solemnity, he had taken off his hat, bared his white teeth, and looked at Beatrice with an insolent smile that made her blush even in recollection. What a pair they were! She believed them capable of any vice, any crime. And these were the friends of Fortunata, these were people with whom her son now went walking and whose company he now frequented! Beatrice covered her face with her hands, sighed and whispered to herself: 'Away, away, away!' She said the word without really knowing what it meant. Gradually she began to realize its full meaning and thought that perhaps in it lay her and Hugo's salvation. Yes, they must go away, both of them, mother and son, and as quickly as possible. She must take him with her – or he must take her. Both of them must leave this place before something would

happen to them that could never be repaired, before she would
lose all rights of motherhood, before her son's youth would be
completely ruined, before fate would fall crashing down upon
them both. There was still time. No one knew of her own
adventure, otherwise she would have noticed it in some way,
at least in the actions of the architect. And the adventure of
her son was doubtless also not yet known. And if they did
know it, they would excuse it in so inexperienced a youth;
and they could not even reproach a mother who had been so
careless up to this time, if she should flee with him now, as if
she had just discovered it. Therefore it was not too late. The
difficulty lay elsewhere: to persuade Hugo to undertake such
a sudden journey. Beatrice could not guess how far the power
of the Baroness extended over Hugo's heart and mind. She
knew nothing, nothing about him, since she had her own love
affairs to worry over. But Hugo was clever, and he would not
deceive himself into thinking that his adventure with Fortunata
was to last forever, and so he could easily see that a few days
more or less did not matter. And in her thoughts, she spoke to
him: 'We cannot go directly to Vienna. Oh, we can't think of
it, my child. We will go South. We have been planning that
for a long time. To Venice, to Florence, to Rome. Just think,
you will see the old palaces, and St Peter's! Hugo, let's go
tomorrow! You and I alone. Another journey like that one
two years ago in the spring. Do you remember? Over Murren-
steig by carriage to Mariazell. Wasn't it beautiful? And this
time it will be still more beautiful. And if it'll be hard at first,
oh, God, I'll understand, and I'll not ask you anything and
you'll not have to tell me anything. But seeing so much beauty
and novelty, you'll forget. You'll forget very soon. Much
sooner than you think—'

'And you, mother – you?' She heard Hugo's voice saying it.
She shuddered. And she dropped her hands from her eyes as
if to assure herself that she was alone. Yes, she was alone, quite
alone in the house in the half-darkened room; outside, the
summer day breathed heavily and sultrily; no one would
disturb her. She had plenty of quiet and time to plan what to
say to her son. Of one thing she was certain: she need not fear
a response such as she had imagined in her excitement: 'And

you, mother?' That he could not ask. For he knew nothing – he could know nothing. And he would never know. Even if some suggestive whisper should come to his ear, he would not believe it. He would never believe anything like it of his mother. On that score she could be quite at ease. And she saw herself wandering with him through some fantastic landscape that she remembered from a painting – a greyish-yellow road with a town all in blue and with many towers swimming in the distance. Then she saw themselves walking in a large square under arched passages – strange people met them and looked at her and her son. They looked at her meaningly with bold teethy smiles, and as if they thought: 'Ah, she has brought a nice youth with her on her journey! She might be his mother.' What? Did the people take them for lovers? Well, why not? They could not know that the boy was her son, and they would know her for one of those over-ripe women who desire such young blood. And there they would be, walking around a strange city among strange people and he would think of his beloved with the Pierrot face, and she, of her sweet blond boy. She groaned aloud. She wrung her hands. Whither? Whither? All of a sudden, one of the love-words with which she had held him to her bosom last night slipped treacherously from her lips – the boy whom she would bid farewell forever and whom she would never – never see again. Yes, just once more, if he came back today. Or tomorrow morning. But to-night her door would be locked. It was over forever. And she would say at parting that she had loved him very much – with a love that he would never meet again. And with that proud feeling, he would realize all the more his gallant duty to eternal silence. And he would understand that it must be thus, and he would kiss her hand once more and would go. Would go. And then what? Then what? And she lay there with parted lips, her arms outstretched, her body trembling, and she knew that if he would come at that moment into the door, young and full of longing, she would not be able to resist him and would again belong to him with all the ardour that was now awakened in her like something long forgotten, in fact, like something that she had never before known. And now she knew too, in simultaneous agony and ecstasy, that the youth to whom she had

given herself would not be her last lover. Already hot curiosity
raged within her: who would the next one be. Dr Bertram?
She remembered an evening – was it three or eight days ago? –
she did not know – time dragged so – went by so quickly – the
hours melted into each other and meant nothing – it happened
in Welponer's garden – Bertram had suddenly run up to her on
a dark path, had drawn her to him, and embraced and kissed
her. And even though she had angrily pushed him away, what
did that matter to him, who in spite of that must have felt the
submissive pressure of her lips, so accustomed to kisses? That
was why he had immediately become so quiet and patient, as
if he well knew just where he stood, and she could read in his
look: 'Winter belongs to me, dear lady. We have been in agreement for a long time. We both know that death is bitter and
virtue only an empty word, and that one should let nothing go
by.' But it was not Bertram who spoke to her. Suddenly, while
she lay there with closed eyes, another face had pushed Bertram's out of the way, that of the circus-rider or gambler or
Mexican who had recently looked at her so boldly, just as
Bertram had done and every one else. They all had the same
look – all – and that look always said and wished and knew the
same thing; and if one gave in to one of them one was lost.
They took the one who happened to please them, and threw
her away again. Yes, if one let herself be taken and thrown
away. But she was not of that class. No, it had not gone that
far with her. Passing adventures were not her style. If she had
been created for that, how could she take the affair with Fritz
so much to heart? And if she suffered such pangs of remorse
and fear, it was only because that which she had done was so
much against her nature. She hardly understood that it all had
happened. There was no other way to explain it, than that it
had come over her like a disease in these unbearably hot summer days, and had left her defenceless and weak. And just as
the disease had come, so it would leave her again. Soon, soon.
She felt in all her pulses, all her senses, in her whole body, that
she was not the same as she had been formerly. She could
hardly collect her thoughts. How feverishly they ran through
her mind! She did not know what she wanted, what she hoped
for, what she regretted, hardly knew if she were happy or un-

happy. It could only be a disease. There were women in whom such a condition lasted a long time, and would hardly ever improve; such a one was Fortunata and that marble-white Fräulein Fallehn. There were others again whom it invaded or attacked and left soon after. That was her case. Most certainly. How otherwise could she have lived all these years since Ferdinand had gone, as chaste as a young girl and without desire? It only came over her this summer. All the women looked differently this year; the girls too – their eyes were brighter and bolder, and their behaviour was lighter, more enticing and seductive. And one heard such stories! What was that one about the doctor's young wife, who went out on the lake evenings with an oarsman and did not come home till the next morning? And about the two young girls who lay naked on the meadow just as the little steam-boat went by, and suddenly, before anyone could recognize them, had disappeared into the forest? Really, it was in the air this year. The sun had unusual strength, and the waves of the lake caressed her body more tenderly than ever before. And when that secret curse was lifted, would she again be as she had been, and could she slip through the hot adventures of these days and nights as if through an easily forgotten dream? And if she felt it coming again as she had felt it coming on this time, far in advance, when longing began to rage in her blood with dangerous intensity, she would be able to choose a much better and cleaner salvation than this time – she would marry again as other women did when they felt as she did. Then an ironic smile came to her lips, as if taken unawares. She thought of some one who had recently been there, one whom she credited with the most honourable intentions, the lawyer, Dr Teichmann. She saw him before her in a brand new green and brown sports suit, with a plaid tie, his green hat with the fur cockade placed dashingly on his head – in short an outfit by which he openly wanted to show that he knew how to look very fetching, even though he, a very serious man under ordinary circumstances, placed no worth upon such superficialities. Then she saw him sitting at dinner on the veranda between her son and her lover, addressing now one, now the other, with the seriousness of a senior assistant master, and saw him in his ridiculous innocence which had tempted her to exchange handclasps playfully with her Fritz under the table. He had left the same evening, since he was to meet friends in Bozen, and although Beatrice had not invited him to remain, he seemed very much puffed up and full of hope on leaving, for in the gay mood of that summer day she had not deprived even him of encouraging and exciting looks. Now she regretted it as she regretted so much else; and her next conversation with him appeared all the more uncertain because in the complete relaxation of that hour, she was more painfully conscious of the gradual weakening of her will-power. With a similar feeling of shame, she recalled the feeling of helplessness that had at times come over her during her last talks with Director Welponer, and then it seemed to her that if she were to choose, she could sooner think of herself as the wife of the Director – yes she must admit that the notion did not lack charm for her. Today she felt as if this man had interested her from earliest times. The things that the architect had told her about the grandiose speculations and battles of the Director, in which he had been victor over ministers and members of the court, were especially well calculated to arouse Beatrice's curiosity and admiration. Besides, Dr Teichmann, too, had called him a genius when speaking of him, and had compared him in the daring of his undertakings, which always meant everything to Teichmann, to a valiant cavalry-general. And so it flattered Beatrice a little that just this man seemed to want her, apart from the satisfaction that it would offer her of taking the husband away from the woman who had once robbed her of hers. 'Has robbed me of mine?' she asked herself in confused surprise. 'What is wrong with me? What am I thinking of? Do I believe it, then? It may not be true. Everything else, but not that. I should have noticed something of it. Noticed something? Why? Wasn't Ferdinand an actor, and a great one too? Why couldn't it have happened without my noticing it? I was so trusting, that it was difficult not to betray me. Not difficult – but that does not mean that it actually happened. Fritz is a gossip, a liar, and these rumours are false and stupid. And even though it did happen, it happened long ago. And Ferdinand is dead. And she who was once his love is an old woman. What does all the past mean to me? What is going on now between the Director and me is a new story, which has nothing to do with the past.'

And she thought further, that in truth it wouldn't be so bad to retire some day into the noble villa with its great park. What wealth, what glamour! What an outlook for Hugo's future! Truly, he was no longer young, and that must be considered to some degree, especially when one was as pampered as she had been recently. Yes, during this very summer, during these last weeks, he seemed to be ageing more rapidly than ever. Was not perhaps his love for her to blame? Well, what was the difference? There were others, younger ones, and he would be betrayed anyhow: it was evidently his lot. She laughed dryly: it sounded ugly and mean, and she jumped up as if out of a wild dream. 'Where am I, where am I?' she asked herself. She wrung her hands entreatingly. 'How deeply shall you let me sink? Is there no halting any more? What is it then that makes me so wretched and so contemptible? What makes me reach out into space, and to be no better than Fortunata and other women of her sort?' And suddenly, with a failing heart, she knew what made her so wretched: the foundation on which she had rested in certainty for years was trembling, and the heavens were darkening over her: the only man she had ever loved, her Ferdinand, had been a liar. Yes – now she knew it. His whole life with her had been fraud and hypocrisy: he had betrayed her with Frau Welponer and with other women, with actresses, and countesses, and prostitutes. And when, on sultry nights, the languid charm of propinquity had driven him into Beatrice's arms, then it was the worst and lowest of all his lies, for she knew that on her breast he had thought of the others, all the others, in lust and malice. But why did she know it all of a sudden. Why? Because she was no different, no better than he. Was it Ferdinand whom she held in her arms, the comedian with the red flower, who often enough came home from the public-house at three in the morning, smelling of wine, swaggering, and babbling empty and unclean things, the one who as a young man had subordinated his higher passions to the favour of an old widow, and who in gay company read tender little notes that love-sick fools had sent to his dressing-room? No, that one she had never loved.

She would have fled from that one in the first month of her marriage. He whom she loved was not Ferdinand Heinold: he was Hamlet and Cyrano and King Richard, and this one and that one, heroes and scoundrels, conquerors and martyrs, the blessed and the damned. And he who with strange fire had lured her into the summer night out of the secret darkness of their chamber to unutterable ecstasy, was not really he, but some sort of spirit full of hidden power out of the mountains, whose part he was playing without knowing it – for he always played a part, because he could not live without a mask, because he was afraid to see his real features reflected in her eyes. And so she had always betrayed him just as he had betrayed her and had constantly lived a life lost from the beginning, a life of fantastically wild lust – except that no one could have suspected it, not even she herself. But now it was revealed. She was destined to sink lower and lower, and some day – who knew how soon – it would be clear to the whole world that all her bourgeois respectability was a lie, that she was no better than Fortunata, Wilhelmine Fallehn and all the others whom till today she had despised. And her son would know it too; and if he did not believe the affair with Fritz, he would believe a next one – would have to believe it – and suddenly she saw him vividly before her with eyes wide open and full of pain, his arms outstretched in repulsion; and when she wanted to come near him, he turned around in horror, and hurried away with the fleetness of a dream. And she groaned aloud, suddenly wide awake. To lose Hugo? Everything, but not that. Better to die than to have her son no more. To die – yes. For then she would have him again. Then he would come to his mother's grave and kneel down and deck it with flowers and fold his hands in prayer for her. With that thought an emotion crept into her heart that was sweet and at the same time repulsive, and falsely peaceful. Still, deep within her, she heard a murmur: 'Have I the right to rest? Haven't I much more to think about? Certainly – tomorrow we shall start out on our journey. To-morrow – how much there is to do – so much – so much –'

In the quiet dusk that surrounded her, she felt that outside, the world, people, and the landscape had awakened from their afternoon drowsiness. All sorts of distant sounds, indefinite and confused, came to her ears through the closed blinds. And she knew that people were already wandering on the roads, were rowing on the lake, were playing tennis, and drinking coffee on the hotel terrace – yes, in her still half-dreaming condition, she saw swarms of happy summer-resorters, like tiny puppets, but real as life, bobbing up and down before her. The ticking of her watch on the night table sounded too loud in her ears, and like a warning. Beatrice was curious to know how late it was, but she still lacked the strength to turn her head or even to turn on the light. Some new, nearer sound, evidently from the garden, had become gradually more audible. What could it be? The voices of men, without a doubt. So near? Voices in the garden? Hugo and Fritz? How was it possible that they should both have returned so soon? Well, it was already evening, and Fritz had evidently been drawn back by his love. No doubt they had first rung the bell, and she had not heard it because she was asleep. Then they must have climbed over the fence; naturally they could not suspect that the mistress of the house was at home. Now one of the two was laughing out there. What laugh was that? It was not Hugo's laugh. But Fritz did not laugh like that either. Now the other was laughing. That was Fritz. Now again, the first one. That was not Hugo. He spoke. It was not Hugo's voice. Then Fritz was in the garden with someone else? They were quite near. It seemed as if both had sat down on the bench, on the white one under the window. And now she heard Fritz calling the other one by name. Rudi – Well, then, it was he who was sitting with Fritz under her window. But that was not so astonishing. Recently they had arranged in her presence that Rudi Beratoner should come back very soon. Perhaps he had been there earlier, had seen no one and then had met Fritz, whom love had brought back so soon from Ischl, at the railroad station or somewhere else. In any case, there was no reason why she should rack her brains about it. There they were, the two young men, sitting on the white bench under the window of the adjoining room. Now she must get up, dress, and go out into the garden. Why? Did she really have to go into the garden? Had she such a pressing desire to see Fritz again, or was she the least bit anxious to greet the shameless youth who recently had aped her dead husband's voice and facial expression with such disgraceful facility? Still there was nothing else for her to do, but to bid the young people good-evening. She couldn't keep so still for all the time that they remained out there gossiping about everything they pleased. That it could not be a very pure conversation, she could not doubt. Well, that did not concern her. They could say what they wished.

Beatrice had gotten up and was sitting on the edge of her bed. Then she heard a word with perfect clearness, the name of her son. Naturally, they were talking about Hugo, and what they were saying was not difficult to guess. Now they laughed again. But she couldn't understand the words. If she were very near the window, she might be able to understand the conversation, but perhaps it were better to forego that. She might experience some unpleasant surprises. In any case, it would be wisest to get ready as quickly as possible, and to go into the garden. But Beatrice was impelled to slip first very quietly to the closed blinds. She looked out through a small crack and could see nothing but a strip of green; then through another crack, a blue strip of sky. But now, she heard all the better what was being said on the bench. First, it was only the name of her Hugo that she could make out. Everything was so whispered and hushed, as if both of them had in mind the possibility of being overheard. Beatrice put her ear to the crack and smiled with a sigh. They were talking about school. Very clearly, she heard: 'That horrid chap would have liked to flunk him.' And then: 'A mean dog.' She slipped back, dressed quickly in a comfortable house gown; and then, driven by her uncontrollable curiosity, she went back to the window. And now she remarked that they were not talking any more about school. 'A Baroness, is she?' That was Rudi Beratoner's voice. And now – pah – what a disgusting word – 'He's with her all day long, – and today –' That was Fritz's voice. Against her will, she put her fingers to her ears, went away from the window and made up her mind to go immediately into the garden. But before she had reached the door, she was again driven to the window; she knelt down, put her ear to the crack, and looked out with wide-open eyes and burning cheeks. Rudi Beratoner was telling a story – at times he lowered his voice to a whisper, but from the single words that Beatrice gathered here and there, it became gradually clear to her what the affair was about. It was a love adventure of which Rudi was telling; Beatrice could make out French pet names which he pronounced in a sweet, gentle voice. Ah, evidently he was copying the manner of that person. He did that thing so remarkably well. Who slept in the adjoining room? His sister. Ah, it was the governess – More – more – how did it work? When the sister slept, the governess came to him. And then – and then – ? Beatrice did not want to hear it, and yet she listened on and on, with growing eagerness. What words! What a tone! So this was how these boys spoke about their sweethearts! No, no, not all, and not about all. What a woman that must be! Surely she deserved it, that they should speak like that about her and not otherwise. But why did she deserve it? After all, what crime had she committed? It was only loathsome when they spoke about it. When Rudi Beratoner held her in his arms, he was surely very tender and had pure loving words for her – as they all had at those moments. If only she could see Fritz's face! Oh, she could picture it. His cheeks would burn and his eyes would glow. Now there was silence for a while. Evidently the story was finished.

And suddenly she heard Fritz's voice. He was asking: 'What, must you know everything so exactly?' A heavy feeling of envy stirred in Beatrice. 'What, do you want an answer to that?' Yes, Rudi Beratoner was speaking. Well, then, speak louder at least. I want to hear what you are saying, you rogue, who have insulted my husband in his grave, and who now are betraying and reviling your beloved. Louder! Oh, God, it was loud enough! He was not saying anything now – He was asking a question – he wanted to know – if Fritz – had here in town – yes, you blackguard – run riot with your own profane words! It will not help you. You shall not learn anything. Fritz is hardly more than a boy, but he is nobler than you. He knows what he owes a respectable woman who has shown him her favour. Isn't that so, Fritz, my sweet Fritz? – You'll not say anything, will you?

What held her so firmly rooted to the floor, that she could not get up, hurry out, and put an end to the shameful conversation? But what would it have helped? Rudi Beratoner was not the man to be so easily satisfied. If he did not get his answer today at this time, then he would repeat his question on the following day. It was best to remain there and continue to listen – then one knew where one was, at least. Why so softly, Fritz? Speak out. Why should you not glorify your happiness? A respectable woman like myself – that's quite different from a governess. Beratoner spoke louder. Beatrice heard him say quite distinctly: 'Then you must be a regular idiot.' Ah, let them take you for an idiot, Fritz. Accept the title. What, you do not believe him, you rascal? You want to worm his secret out of him at all costs? Have you any suspicions? Has anyone told you already? And again she heard Fritz's whispering, though it was quite impossible to understand the words. Now again, Beratoner's voice, deep and coarse: 'What, a married woman? Go on – would such a one ever –' Will you not keep still, you wretch? She felt that never in her life had she hated anyone as she hated this youth who insulted her without knowing that it was she whom he was insulting. What, Fritz? For heaven's sake, louder! 'She has already gone away.' Ah, excellent, Fritz, you want to protect me from insulting suspicions. She listened. She drank in his words. 'A villa near the lake – her husband is a lawyer.' What a rogue! How deliciously he lied! She might really have enjoyed it, if not for the fear that agitated her. What? The husband was horribly jealous? He had threatened to kill her if he discovered anything? What? Till four o'clock this morning? Every night – every – night – Enough, enough, enough! Will you not be still? Aren't you ashamed? Why do you defile me? If your fine friend does not know that it is I of whom you are speaking, still you do know it. Why don't you lie instead? Enough, enough! And she wanted to stop her ears, but instead of doing so, she listened all the more attentively. Not a syllable escaped her any more. And in despair, she heard from the lips of her boy the detailed description of those holy nights that he spent in her arms, heard it in words that beat down upon her like the lashes of a whip, in expressions that she heard for the first time, but that were quickly understood, and that brought bloody shame to her brow. She knew that everything that Fritz was saying out there in the garden was nothing but the truth, and yet she felt that it had already ceased to be the truth, that this contemptible chatter had turned what had been his and her happiness into filth and lies. And to him, she had belonged! He was the first to whom she had given herself since she was free! Her teeth chattered, her cheeks and brow burned, her knees sank weakly to the floor. Suddenly she drew back – Rudi Beratoner wanted to see the house. And how did it happen that the people had already gone away in the finest part of the summer? 'I don't believe a single word of your story. A lawyer's wife? Ridiculous! Shall I tell you who it is?' She listened with her ears, with her soul, with all her senses. But no word came. But without looking, she knew that Beratoner was indicating the house with his eyes; he was pointing exactly to the window behind which she was kneeling.

And now came Fritz's answer: 'What's the matter with you? You are quite crazy.'

Then the other one: 'But you needn't say any more. I have already noticed it. Congratulations! Yes, not everyone has it so convenient. Yes – the – but if I wanted –' Beatrice could not hear more. She hardly knew how it happened. Perhaps it was the blood roaring in her brain that had drowned out Beratoner's last words. For a long time, the conversation outside was lost in this roaring, until she could again understand Fritz's words:

'Well, then, keep still. What if she's at home!' It's a little too late to think of that, my dear boy.

'Well, what if she is?' said Beratoner loudly and insolently. Then Fritz was whispering again in quick excitement, and suddenly Beatrice heard both of them getting up from the bench. For heaven's sake, what now? She threw herself flat on the floor, so that it would be impossible to espy her through the crack in the blind. Shadows passed before the blinds, steps crunched on the gravel path, a couple of muffled words, then a faint laugh farther away – and then nothing more ... She waited. Nothing stirred. Then she heard their voices dying away farther out in the garden – then nothing – for a long time – nothing, until she was certain they both were far away. They might have climbed over the fence as they had come, and might be telling each other their stories outside. Was there anything left to tell? Had Fritz forgotten anything? He would make up for it now. And in his delightful way, he would find a few more things to add in order to impress Rudi rightly. Why not? Yes, that was the gaiety of youth. One had his sister's governess, the other, the mother of his school friend, and the third, a Baroness, who formerly had been in the theatre. Yes, they had enough to say, these young men – they knew women and could rightly say that one was like the other.

And Beatrice wept silently to herself. She still lay outstretched on the floor. Why get up? Why get up now? When she would finally make up her mind to get up, it would be only to put an end to it all. Oh, to meet Fritz again, and the other one – She could spit in their faces, beat them with her fists. Wouldn't that be a solace and a joy? – to rush after them, to scream in their faces: 'You boys, you wretches, aren't you ashamed, aren't you ashamed?' But at the same time, she knew that she would not do it. She felt that it was not worth the trouble, since she had decided and must remain decided to go on a path on which no scolding and no derision could follow her. Never, never, could she in her disgrace look anyone in the eyes again. She had but one more thing to do on this earth : to take leave of the one who was dear to her – her son! Of him alone! But naturally, without his noticing it. Only she would know that she was leaving him forever – that she was kissing the brow of her dear child for the last time – How strange it was to think such thoughts, lying stretched and motionless on the floor. If someone were to come into the room now, she would be taken for dead without fail. 'Where will they find me?' she thought. 'How shall I do it? How shall I arrange it, that I shall be lying here senseless, never to waken again.'

A noise in the front room made her start. Hugo had come home. She heard him going down the hall, past her door, and opening his – and now there was silence again. He had returned. Now she was not alone any more. She got up slowly, with aching limbs. It was almost completely dark in the room and the air suddenly seemed unbearably sultry. She did not understand why she had been lying so long on the floor like that, and why she had not opened the blinds much sooner. She quickly did so now, and before her eyes spread the garden, the towering mountains, and the heavens darkening above her, and she felt as if she had not seen all this for many days and nights.

The small world spread out in the evening light, so wonderful and peaceful that even Beatrice felt its calm. At the same time, however, she felt a fear creep gently into her mind. She must not let herself be deceived and confused by this peace. And she said to herself: 'What I have heard, I have heard; what has happened, has happened. The quiet of this evening, the peace of this world, are not for me: morning will come, the noises of the day will recommence; people will remain malicious and mean, and love, a filthy joke. And I am one who can never forget it, not in the daytime or in the night, not in solitude, or in new pleasure, not at home or abroad. And I have nothing more to do in this world than to place a farewell kiss on the brow of my beloved son, and go – What can he be doing there alone in his room?' From his open window a faint light shone out over the gravel and turf. Was he already in bed – weary after the joy and exertion of his trip? A shudder ran through her body, strangely composed of fear, horror, and longing. Yes, she longed for him, but for a different one than the one who lay in his room and who had the breath of Fortunata's body about him. She longed for the former Hugo, for the fresh, clean boy, who had once told her about the kiss of a little girl at the dance, for the Hugo who had driven with her one beautiful summer day over the country-side – and she wished for that time to return, when she herself was different – a mother, worthy of that son, and not a good-for-nothing woman, about whom spoiled boys dared gossip lewdly, as about any wanton. Ah, if there were only miracles! But there were none. Never could that hour be unmade when, with burning cheeks, on aching knees, with thirsty ears, she had listened to the story of her disgrace – and her happiness. Even in ten, in twenty, in fifty years, as an old man, Rudi Beratoner would still remember this hour, when in his youth he had sat on a white bench in the garden of Frau Beatrice Heinold, and his school friend had told him how night after night, until early morning, he had lain in bed with her. She shuddered, she wrung her hands, she looked up to the heavens, whose clouds remained still as death and showed no surprise at her lonely agony. All sorts of noises from the street and lake came up to her in faint confusion; the mountains rose up darkly to the beckoning night, the yellow fields lay dully glowing in the twilight that was creeping in all around. How long would she remain here so motionlessly? What was she awaiting? Had she forgotten that Hugo might disappear out of the house just as he had come, to one who meant more to him than she? There was not much time to lose. Quickly she unbolted her door, went into the small salon, and stood before Hugo's room. For a moment she hesitated, listened, but heard nothing; then she opened the door hastily.

Hugo was sitting on his divan and stared up at his mother with wide eyes, as if he had been frightened out of a restless sleep. Over his face played strange shadows from the uncertain light of the electric lamp, standing with its green shade on the table in the centre of the room. Beatrice remained for a moment at the door, Hugo threw his head back; it seemed as if he wanted to get up, but he remained seated, his arms extended, his hands resting flat on the divan. Beatrice felt the tension of this moment with heart-rending pain. An unequalled fear gripped her soul; and she said to herself, 'He knows all ... What will happen?' she thought in the same breath. She went to him, forced herself to look happier, and asked: 'Were you asleep, Hugo?'

'No, mother,' he answered, 'I was just lying down.' She looked into a pale, miserable, childish face; unutterable sympathy, in which her own suffering was buried, arose within her; still trembling, she laid her hand on his tangled hair, then put her arm around him, sat down beside him, and gently began: 'Well, my child –' Then she did not know what to say next. His face was violently distorted; she took his hands, he pressed hers distractedly, stroked her fingers and looked away, his smile was like a mask, his eyes reddened, his breast began to heave, and suddenly he slipped from the divan, lay at his mother's feet, put his head in her lap, and wept bitterly. Beatrice, shaken to the very depths, and yet happy in a way, for she felt that he had not become estranged from her, at first did not say a word, let him weep while she played quietly with his hair, and asked herself in terror:

'What can have happened?' And she comforted herself immediately: 'Perhaps nothing unusual. Perhaps nothing except that his nerves are giving way.' And she remembered very similar convulsive attacks that her dead husband had suffered for seemingly negligible reasons – after the excitement of a great rôle, after an experience that had wounded his artistic vanity, or entirely without ground, at least without any that she could discover. And suddenly she began to wonder whether Ferdinand did not sometimes cry out on her lap the disappointments and griefs that he had suffered at the hands of some other woman. But why did that trouble her? What he had done, he had expiated, and all that was far away, so far away! Today it was her son who wept in her lap, and she knew that he wept because of Fortunata. With what pain did that realization grip her heart! Into what depths did her own experience sink when she found herself in the presence of her son's mental agony! Whither did her disgrace and pain and desire for death flee, before the burning wish to help her dearly loved child, who wept in her lap? And in overflowing desire to aid him, she whispered: 'Don't cry, my boy. Everything will be all right again.' And when he shook his head, as if in denial, she repeated in a firmer tone: 'It will be all right again, believe me.' And she realized that she had directed these words of consolation not only to her son, but to herself. If it were in her power to help her son out of his despair, to fill him with new courage for life, that promise and strength must arise out of this knowledge alone, and even more from his gratitude and the feeling that he could belong again solely to her. And suddenly the picture rose up before her of that fantastic landscape in which she had dreamed she was walking with Hugo, and a thought full of promise came to her: 'If I were to undertake the voyage with Hugo, that I had been planning before that dreadful hour – and if we were never to return home from that journey? – And if out there, in foreign lands, far from all whom we know, in a purer atmosphere, we were to begin a new, a better life? –'

Then he suddenly raised his head from her lap – his eyes wandered, his mouth was distorted, and he cried hoarsely: 'No, no, it will never be all right again!' And he got up, looked absently at his mother, took a few steps towards the table as if he were seeking something there, then walked up and down the room a few times with sunken head, and finally remained standing motionless at the window, his eyes turned to the night outside. 'Hugo,' called his mother, who had followed him with her eyes, but did not feel capable of getting up from the divan. And again, imploringly: 'Hugo, my boy!' Then he turned to her again with that forced smile that was more painful than his weeping. And tremblingly she asked again: 'What has happened?'

'Nothing mother,' he answered in a sort of exaltation.

Now she stood up decidedly and went over to him. 'Do you know why I came to you?' He merely looked at her. 'Well, guess.' He shook his head. 'I wanted to ask you if you wouldn't like to go on a short trip.'

'A trip,' he repeated, seeming not to understand.

'Yes, Hugo, a trip – to Italy. We have time; school does not open for three weeks. We can be back long before that. Well, what do you think of it?'

'I don't know,' he answered. She put her arms around his neck. How much like Ferdinand he looked! Once he had played the part of such a young boy and had looked exactly like him. And she joked: 'Well, if you don't know, Hugo, I do know very well that we are to take a journey. Yes, my boy, there's no more to say about it. And now dry your eyes, cool your forehead, and we'll go out together.'

'Go out?'

'Yes, certainly. This is Sunday and there is no supper at home. Besides, we are to meet the others down at the hotel. And the moonlight party on the lake, don't you know that it is to take place today too.'

'Won't you go alone, mother? I could come for you later.'

An extravagant fear suddenly seized her. Did he want her out of the way? Why? For pity's sake! She forced back the frightful thought. And controlling herself, she said: 'Aren't you hungry?'

'No,' he answered.

'Neither am I. How would it be to go first for a little walk?'

'For a walk?'

'Yes, and then take the little detour to the hotel.'

He hesitated for a while. She stood there in strained expectation. Finally, he nodded. 'Good, mother, get ready.'

'Oh, I'm ready, I only need to get my coat.' But she did not budge. He seemed not to notice this, went to his wash basin, poured water out of the pitcher into his hands, and cooled his forehead, eyes, and cheeks. Then he ran his comb quickly through his hair a few times. 'Yes, make yourself handsome,' said Beatrice. And she remembered sadly how often she had said these words in long past times to Ferdinand when he was preparing to go out – God knew where –

Hugo took his hat and said smilingly: 'I am ready, mother.'

She hurried into her room, got her coat, and didn't fasten it until she was again in Hugo's room. 'Now, come,' she said.

As both were leaving the house, the maid was just returning from her Sunday holiday. But although she greeted her mistress obsequiously, Beatrice noticed from the almost imperceptible way in which that person lowered her eyes, that she knew all that had been happening during the past weeks in this house – Still she cared little about that. Everything was indifferent to her now, next to the feeling of happiness, the long lost feeling, that she had Hugo at her side.

They walked on through the meadows under the mute blue night of the sky, close to each other, and as rapidly as if they had a goal. At first they said nothing. But before they entered the darkness of the forest, Beatrice turned to her son and said: 'Won't you take my arm, Hugo?' Hugo took her arm and she felt better. They walked on in the heavy shadows of the trees, through whose thick branches the light from some villa lying in its depths broke from place to place. Beatrice let her hand slip over to Hugo's, she fondled it, lifted it to her lips, and kissed it. He did not hinder her. No, he knew nothing about her. Or was he just making the best of it? Could he understand it, though she was his mother? Soon they arrived at a broad, greenish-blue strip of light that lay before the gate of Welponer's villa. Now they could see each other face to face, but they looked ahead into the dark that immediately swallowed them up again. In this part of the forest, the darkness was so thick, that they had to slow their steps in order not to stumble. 'Look out,' said Beatrice from time to time. Hugo only shook his head and they held firmly on to each other. After a while they reached a path that, as they well knew from happier hours, led down to the lake. They turned down this path and again came into a faintly lighted place where the trees stood back and left an open meadow over which hung the still, starless sky. From here, a weather-beaten wooden stairway, on one side of which an unsteady hand-railing offered some support, led down to the road below, that to the right lost itself in the night, but to the left led again to the town from which countless lights shone up to them. In mute agreement, Beatrice and Hugo turned their footsteps in this direction. And as if their walk together through the dark, though speechless, still brought her closer to him, Beatrice said in a light, almost joking tone: 'I don't like it when you cry, Hugo.' He did not answer, but looked absently away from her over the steel-grey lake that now seemed to extend like a narrow strip beneath the mountains. 'Formerly,' began Beatrice again, and there was a sigh in her voice, 'formerly you told me everything.' And while she said that, she felt again as if she were saying these words to Ferdinand and as if she would learn all the secrets of her dead husband, that he had so disgracefully kept from her, when he was yet on earth. 'Am I becoming insane?' she thought. 'Am I already mad?' And as if to recall herself to the present, she snatched Hugo's arm with such force, that he drew back frightened. But she went on: 'Wouldn't it be easier for you, Hugo, if you were to tell me about it?' And she clung to him again. But while her own question continued to sound within her, she felt that it was not only the wish to relieve Hugo's soul that put this question into her mouth, but that a peculiar kind of curiosity had begun to rage in her, of which she was deeply ashamed in her heart. And Hugo, as if he guessed the secret disgrace of her question, answered nothing, and in fact, let his arm slip out of hers again, as if by accident. Disappointed and left alone, Beatrice walked beside him along the gloomy street. 'What good am I on this earth,' she asked herself, 'if I am not his mother? Is today the day to lose everything? Am I nothing more than a loose word in the mouths of spoiled boys? And that feeling of belonging to Hugo, of our common safety up there in the gracious dark of the forest, was all that only an illusion? Then life is no longer bearable, then everything is really over. But why does the thought frighten me? Was it not long ago decided? Did I not make up my mind earlier to put an end to it all? And did I not know that nothing else remained for me to do?' And trailing behind her, like jeering ghosts, hissed the terrible words that she heard today through the crack in the blind, and that meant her love and her shame, her happiness and her death. And for a moment, she thought in sisterly fashion of that other one, who once had run along the sea-shore pursued by evil spirits, weary with tormenting lust.

They were nearing the village. The light that now fell over the water just a few hundred feet away came from the terrace where the lively party were eating their evening meal and waiting for them. To enter once more into such a gay circle seemed madness to Beatrice; yes, entirely out of the realm of possibility. Why was she walking down this road? Why did she still remain at Hugo's side? What cowardice had it been, that had made her wish to bid him farewell, him, to whom she was no more than a tiresome old woman who wanted to force herself in on his secrets? Then, suddenly, she saw his eyes again turned on her with a look of entreaty, that awakened new fears and hopes in her.

'Hugo,' she said.

And in tardy response to a question that she herself had already forgotten, he said: 'It cannot be all right again. Telling will not help. It cannot.'

'But, Hugo,' she cried, as if newly emancipated, now that he had broken his silence. 'Surely it will be all right; we are going away, Hugo, far away.'

'What good will that do us, mother?' Us? – Does that include me too? But isn't it better that way. Aren't we nearer to each other that way? He walked faster; she kept at his side – suddenly he stopped, looked out at the lake, and sighed deeply as if consolation and peace came to him from the solitude over the water. A few lighted row-boats were gliding out there. 'Might that already be our party?' thought Beatrice casually. Certainly tonight they would have no moonlight. And suddenly an idea came to her: 'How would it be, Hugo,' she said, 'if we were to go out rowing alone?' He looked up at the sky, as if seeking the moon. Beatrice understood the look and said: 'We don't need the moon.'

'What are we going to do out there on the dark water?' he

asked weakly. She took his head in her hands, looked into his eyes, and said: 'You shall tell me about it. You shall tell me what has happened to you, as you always have done formerly.' She guessed that out in the friendly silence of the dark lake, his shyness, that now kept him from telling his mother what had happened, would leave him. Since she felt no resistance in his silence, she turned in decision towards the boat-house where her boat lay. The wooden door was not locked. She went into the dark boat-house with Hugo, unchained the boat hastily, as if there were no time to lose, then she swung over into the boat, and Hugo followed her. He took one of the oars, pushed away with it, and a second later, the open sky was over them. Now Hugo took the other oar and rowed along the shore, past the Lake Hotel, so near, that they could hear voices on the terrace. It seemed to Beatrice that she could hear the voice of the architect above the others. But she could not discern single figures or faces. How easy it was to flee from humanity! 'What do I care what they are saying about me, what they think, or know – ? You simply push your boat away from the shore, you go so near to people that you can hear their voices, and – it already makes no difference! When one is not coming back –' It sounded deep within her, and she trembled a little – she sat at the rudder and steered the boat towards the middle of the lake. The moon had not yet come up, but the water around them surrounded the boat with a dull circle of light, as if it had preserved the sunlight within itself. At times a ray came from the shore, in which Beatrice imagined she saw Hugo's face becoming steadily fresher and freer from care. When they were quite far out, Hugo let the oars drop, took off his coat, and opened his collar. 'How much like his father he looks,' thought Beatrice in painful surprise. 'But I did not know him when he was so young. And how beautiful he is. His features are nobler than Ferdinand's – and yet I never knew his real features, nor his voice. They were always the voices and faces of others. Am I seeing him today for the first time?' And she shuddered violently. But Hugo's features, now that the boat was entirely in the black shadow of the mountains, began gradually to grow hazy. He began to row again, but very slowly, and they hardly moved at all. 'Now is the time,' she thought, but she did not know for a moment for what it was time, until suddenly, as if awakened out of a dream, the burning wish returned to her mind to know Hugo's experience. And she asked: 'Well, then, Hugo, what has happened?' He merely shook his head. But with growing excitement, she felt that he was no longer so firm in his refusal to speak. 'Just speak to me, Hugo,' she said. 'You can tell me everything. I already know so much. You can hardly imagine –' And as if she might banish the last trace of the spell, she whispered into the night: 'Fortunata.'

Through Hugo's body went a shudder, so powerful that it seemed to break the boat in two. Beatrice asked further: 'You were with her today – and is this how you come back? What did she do to you, Hugo?' He was silent, rowed on rhythmically, and gazed into space. Suddenly, Beatrice was enlightened. She pressed her hands to her forehead, as if she did not understand why she had not guessed it earlier, and bending close to Hugo, she whispered quickly: 'The distant captain was there, was he not? And he found you with her?'

Hugo looked up. 'The captain?'

Now for the first time, she realized that the man whom she meant was not a captain. 'I mean the Baron,' she said. 'Was he there? He found you? He insulted you? He beat you, Hugo?'

'No, mother, the one you mention was not there. I do not know him at all. I swear it to you, mother.'

'Then, what is it?' asked Beatrice. 'Doesn't she love you any more? Is she tired of you? Did she laugh at you? Did she show you the door? Is that it, Hugo?'

'No, mother.' And he was silent.

'Well, then, Hugo, what is it? Do tell me.'

'Don't ask me, mother, don't ask me any more. It's too horrible.'

Now her curiosity burst into flame. She felt that from somewhere in the confusion of this day so full of puzzles, so full of old and new questions, she must find the answer. She groped in the air with both hands, as if she wanted to gather something that was scattered there. She slipped down from the seat at the rudder, and sat at Hugo's feet. 'Now then, speak,' she began. 'You shall tell me everything. You need not be shy. I understand everything. I am your mother, Hugo, and I am a woman.

Can you realize that? You must not be afraid that you can wound me, or offend my modesty. I have experienced much these past days. I am still not an – old woman. I understand everything. Too much, my son – you must not think that we are so far apart, Hugo, and that there are things that you must not say to me.' She felt in her confusion how she was giving herself up, how she was decoying him. 'Oh, if you knew, Hugo, if you only knew –'

And the answer came: 'I know, mother.' . . .

Beatrice trembled. Yet she felt no shame, only a relieved consciousness of being nearer to him and belonging to him. She sat at his feet at the bottom of the boat and took his hands in hers. 'Tell me,' she whispered.

And he spoke, but told her nothing. With heavy incoherent words he merely declared that he could never be seen among people again. What had happened to him today threw him forever out of the realm of the living.

'What has happened to you?'

'I was not in my right mind – I don't know what happened. They made me drunk.'

'They made you drunk? Who, who? You were – not alone with Fortunata?' She remembered that she had seen him recently in the company of Wilhelmine Fallehn and the circusrider. Then were they there? And with choking voice, she asked again, 'What has happened?' But without Hugo's answer, she already knew. A picture painted itself before her eyes in the night, from which she wanted to turn in horror, but it followed her relentlessly and insolently behind her closed eyes. And in new, frightful suspicion she opened her eyes again, and turning them directly to Hugo sitting there in the darkness with tightly pressed lips, she asked: 'Is it only since today that you know? Did they tell you over there?'

He made no answer, but a shudder ran through his body, so wild that it threw him weakly to the bottom of the boat beside Beatrice. She groaned aloud once in despair; and trembling forlornly, she grasped Hugo's feverishly shaking hands that he had stretched out to her. Now he left them in hers, and that did her good. She drew him nearer to her, pressed against him, and an agony of longing came from the depths of her soul and flowed mystically over to him. And both of them felt as if their boat, though it stood almost still, were moving on and on in growing speed. Whither was it taking them? Through what dream without aim? To what world without law? Did it ever have to go back to land? Dared it ever? Together they were bound on their everlasting journey; Heaven held no promise of morning for them in its clouds; and weakly succumbing to the anticipation of everlasting night, they gave each other their dying lips. The boat glided on, oarless, to farther shores, and Beatrice felt that she was kissing one whom she had never known before, one who was her husband for the first time.

As she felt consciousness returning, she had enough strength of mind left to beware of a complete awakening. Holding both Hugo's hands tightly in hers, she stepped to the side of the boat. As it listed, Hugo's eyes opened in a look touched with fear that bound him for the last time to the common lot of man. Beatrice drew her beloved, her son, her partner in death, to her breast. Understanding, forgiving, emancipated, he closed his eyes. But hers took in once more the grey bank rising up in the menacing dusk, and before the indifferent waves pressed between her eyes, her dying look drank in the shadows of the fading world.

The Man of Honour

A certain young man, a barrister, who did not practise, without parents, comfortably off, and a popular and pleasant member of society, had for more than a year lived with a girl of humble origin, who, like him, had no relations, and did not need to consider public opinion. At the very beginning of the acquaintance, less from kindness or passion than from the desire to enjoy his happiness as far as possible undisturbed, Alfred had made his mistress give up her position as correspondence-clerk in an important Viennese shop. For a long time, flattered by her grateful tenderness, he had felt happier in the quiet enjoyment of their common freedom than in any previous liaison, but at last he grew gradually aware of that familiar feeling of restless anticipation that with him had always meant the end of such a relationship – an end that, in this case, however, could not at present be foreseen. He already imagined himself as the companion in misfortune of an old friend of his who had been entangled, years before, in a connection of the kind, and now was forced to live a retired and restricted life as a harassed father of a family: and many hours that, without such forebodings, in the company of a sweet, gentle creature like Elise, would have been hours of pure delight, he now began to find wearisome and painful.

He was the sort of man who was quite clever enough, and, he flattered himself, considerate enough, not to let Elise notice these feelings of his, but still they had the effect of making him once more frequent that comfortable middle-class society which he had almost deserted in the course of the last year. And when a very popular young lady, whom he met at a dance, the daughter of a wealthy manufacturer, treated him with marked friendliness, and he suddenly saw before him the promising possibility of an engagement suited to his position and his

means, he began to look on the other connection, which he had
begun as a cheerful inconsequent adventure, as a burdensome
fetter which a young man with his advantages should be able
to shake off without hesitation. But the smiling serenity with
which Elise always welcomed him, her never-varying devotion
during the hours, now fewer and fewer, that they spent together, the unclouded confidence with which she let him go
from her arms into a world unknown – all this not merely
silenced the words of parting on his lips every time he thought
he had firmly decided to speak, but filled him with a sort of
tormented sympathy, whose hardly realized expression could
but seem, to an utterly trusting creature like Elise, a new and
sincerer mark of his affection for her. And so it came about
that Elise never believed herself more passionately adored by
him as when he was fresh from some meeting with Adèle, when,
trembling still at the recollection of her sweet questioning
glance, her thrilling touch, and, later, by the fragrance of their
first secret lovers' kiss, he came back to a home consecrated to
him alone and to his faithless love: and every morning Alfred
left his mistress, not with words of parting that he had composed outside the door, but with fresh protestations of eternal
fidelity. And so the days went on, and so did Alfred's two
romances: at last the problem for decision really was, which
evening he had better choose for the inevitable explanation
with Elise – the one before or the one after his betrothal with
Adèle: and on the first of these two evenings (had he not
still a respite?) Alfred came in to his mistress, thanks to
the habit of his double life, with an air of almost unruffled
composure.

He found her paler than he had ever seen her before, leaning
back in the corner of the divan: nor did she get up as usual
when he came in, to offer her forehead and mouth for a kiss
of welcome: she looked at him with a tired forced smile, so
that, not without a feeling of relief, a suspicion came into
Alfred's mind that the news of his forthcoming betrothal had,
in spite of all attempts at secrecy, in the mysterious way of
rumours, found its way to her. But in answer to his hurried
questions Elise merely said that, though she had not mentioned it before, she suffered from time to time with heart-

attacks, from which she usually recovered quickly, but this time the after-effects seemed likely to last longer than ever before. Alfred, in the consciousness of his guilty purpose, was very much upset by this disclosure; he was all kindness and sympathy, and before midnight, without an idea how the thing had got so far, he and Elise had planned a trip together, which was to be a lasting cure for these unpleasant seizures.

Never had she been so tender to him, and never had he felt such tenderness for her as when he said good-bye that night; indeed, on his way home he seriously considered writing a letter of farewell to Adèle, in which he proposed to excuse his escape from betrothal and the bonds of marriage on the grounds that his vacillating character made him quite unfitted for a life of permanent and peaceful happiness. The artful turns of phrase haunted him even in his sleep: but with the light of morning, as it shone through the slits of the jalousies and flickered on his coverlet, he felt that his anxiety had been both foolish and superfluous. Indeed, he scarcely thought it strange that his suffering lady of the night before seemed like a dream, vanished and forgotten, while Adèle stood before his mind, glowing with the fragrance of his infinite desire.

At midday he made his proposal to Adèle's father, who was friendly but not entirely favourable. With a good-humoured and playful reference to the many temptations of a young man like himself, the father, on the contrary, insisted that Alfred should first travel for a year so that he might test the strength and endurance of his feelings at a distance, and he actually forbade the two young people to correspond, so that he might be certain there had been no opportunity for self-deception in this way. If Alfred were of the same mind when he came home, and if he then found that Adèle felt the same as she was sure she did today, then, so far as he was concerned, there would be not the slightest objection to the young couple's immediate marriage. Alfred made a show of reluctance in agreeing to these terms, but, in fact, he took them with an inward sigh of relief as giving him a further respite before the dreadful day; after a moment's thought he explained that in these circumstances he would like to leave at once, and so bring the period of separation all the sooner to an end. Adèle seemed at first hurt by this submissive attitude, but at the end of the short private talk allowed by her father she was full of admiration for her lover's good sense, and sent him, protesting his fidelity and with actual tears in his eyes, into the dangers of a distant separation.

Scarcely had he got into the street when Alfred began to think over in his mind all the possibilities that might, in the course of the year he had before him, lead to a solution of his relations with Elise. And his impulse to dispose of the most serious difficulties of life, without really facing them, was so overmastering that it not merely overcame his vanity, but even drew to the surface of his mind certain darker imaginings which in the ordinary way would have been quite abhorrent to his easy-going nature. Under the pressure of unusually close companionship, such as was inevitable on a journey, Elise's feelings might well, he thought, grow cooler, and she might gradually come to dislike him : and his mistress's heart trouble might also set him free in a manner that would, of course, be more unwelcome. However, he soon thrust both hopes and fears so violently from him that, finally, his only feeling was one of childish, delighted expectation of an agreeable trip abroad in the company of a pleasant and devoted creature: and on the evening of that very day he was talking away in the highest spirits to his guileless companion about the delightful prospects of the journey they were to make.

As the spring was drawing near, Alfred and Elise first visited the mild shores of the Lake of Geneva. Later on they went up to various cooler mountain resorts : they spent the late summer by the seaside in England : in the autumn they visited the Dutch and German cities, and last of all, when the dark days began to come upon them, they fled to the genial southern sun. Until then, Elise, who had never before left the neighbourhood of Vienna, had moved through that year of wonders like a beautiful dreamer led by a beloved guide: even Alfred, though he never forgot the future and the crisis he had but postponed, seemed under the same spell as Elise, and gave himself up, unreflecting, to the delights of the moment. And though, at the beginning of their journey, he had carefully tried to keep away from people he knew, and had, so far as possible, avoided showing himself with Elise on populous promenades, or in the dining-rooms of great hotels, later on he challenged fate almost of set purpose, and had he received a telegram from his betrothed accusing him of disloyalty, he would have been perfectly willing to give up a future that still attracted him if he might but rid himself of all doubt, disquiet, and responsibility. But no telegram, nor any news at all, found its way to him from home, for contrary to Alfred's conceited expectations, Adèle held as strictly as he to the undertaking on which her father had insisted.

However, the hour arrived in which – at least for Alfred – this wonder-year came to a sudden end, and seemed to stand for an instant suspended in time, bereft of its magic, more desolate than any he had known. This happened one day in late autumn in the Botanic Garden in Palermo, when Elise, who until then had been so fresh and lively and blooming, suddenly clutched with both hands at her heart, looked nervously at her lover, and then smiled as if she knew it was a duty not to cause him any inconvenience. But this, instead of touching filled him with bitterness, which he did in fact at first try to disguise under an air of concern. He reproached her, though he did not believe what he said, with having constantly concealed such attacks from him; told her he was very hurt that she obviously regarded him as heartless; made her promise she would go with him to a doctor at once, and was very glad when she refused, as she said she had no confidence in the local quacks. But when, as though in an access of gratitude and love, there in the open air, on that bench with people passing to and fro, she suddenly seized his hand and put it to her lips, he felt something like a wave of hatred surge through his veins, that actually surprised himself: but he soon found an excuse for it in the many hours of boredom and emptiness which (did he not know it?) had been all too frequent on that journey. So a burning desire for Adèle suddenly flamed up within him, and in defiance of his promise, he sent a telegram to her that very day in which he begged her to send him a word to Genoa, and which he signed 'Yours for ever.'

A few days later he found her reply in Genoa, which read: 'Yours for just as long.' And, carrying this crumpled sheet against his heart – for in spite of its sceptical mocking tone, it was the epitome of all his hopes – he set out with Elise on the journey to Ceylon, which they had left until the end, as they thought it would probably be the most delightful part of their trip. It would have taken a far subtler woman than Elise to guess that, on this journey, it was only Alfred's bold imagination that made her feel such rapture as she had never known in his love, and to realize that it was not she who lay in his arms in those dark and silent nights at sea, but a lady far away, whom his desire was able to conjure into a living presence. But after they had reached that burning island, in the dull monotony of the last part of their stay there, when he found that the image he had all too impetuously evoked now refused to serve him, he began to leave Elise alone, and was malicious enough to use a slight return of the heart trouble, which attacked her soon after she got ashore, as an excuse for his aloofness. She took this, like everything he did, as a sign of the love that had now become all the meaning and happiness of her existence. And when, under the glare of that blue and golden sky, she clung to his side as they drove through the rustling shade of the forests, she did not know that her companion was merely longing for that solitary hour when, undisturbed by Elise, his flying pen would scribble imploring passionate words to another of whose existence Elise did not yet know, and never was to know. In such hours of solitude he was filled with so vast a longing for the absent one that he could forget the features, nay, the very voice, of the woman at his side; this woman that was his, with whom he had wandered over the world for nearly a whole year. And when, the night before they were to start the voyage home, on leaving the writing-room, he found Elise stretched out on her bed, unconscious from another serious attack, he recognized with a feeling of mild, almost agreeable, horror, that what he had thought was a sensation of slight anxiety was, in fact, the inextinguishable darkly-glimmering hope of his very soul. However, it was in very real and painful agitation that he at once sent for the doctor, who soon appeared and relieved the patient with an injection of morphia. But he gave the supposed husband, who explained that he had serious reasons for not postponing a voyage on which much depended, a note recommending Elise to the special care of the ship's doctor.

In the very first few days the sea-air seemed to have a healing influence on Elise. Her pallor disappeared, her whole being unfolded, her manner was less constrained than Alfred had ever known it. And, while she had hitherto been indifferent, almost hostile, to any, even the most innocent, overtures from strangers, on this occasion she showed no signs of avoiding the casual conversation inevitable on board ship, and accepted with pleasure the respectful homage of a few male fellow passengers. A certain German Baron, in particular, who was trying to cure a long-standing lung trouble by a sea voyage, spent as much time as he could in Elise's company without becoming a nuisance, and Alfred would have liked to persuade himself that Elise's encouraging demeanour to this, the most agreeable of her admirers, was the welcome sign of a new and growing inclination. But when, with an appearance of anger, he tried to call Elise to account for her rather marked friendliness, she smilingly explained to him that all this forthcoming manner of hers was simply intended to arouse his jealousy, and she was delighted with the success of her little stratagem. This time Alfred could no longer conceal his impatience and disappointment. He replied to her confession, by which she had thought to soothe and please him, with a harshness she could not understand: she stood before him for a moment or two in dumb perplexity, and then suddenly fell unconscious on the deck, where they had been talking, and had to be carried below to her cabin. The ship's doctor, who knew what the trouble was from his colleague's letter, did not think a careful examination necessary, and temporarily relieved that tormented heart by the same means as before. But he was not able to prevent the occurrence of further attacks, without any apparent cause, on the next day and the day after, and although morphia never failed in its effect, he did not conceal his fear that the illness might have a fatal end, and warned Alfred, in appropriate but quite definite terms, to use every possible consideration towards his beautiful wife.

Alfred, in the throes of his dumb resentment against Elise, would have been very ready to take this advice in regard to one particular especially, as to which the doctor had been very emphatic, if Elise had not been overcome by her desire, one dark night of loneliness, and had succeeded in tempting him, in spite of his resistance, back into her arms, as though to make her peace by her endearments. And yet as she lay there in his embrace, exhausted and with half-closed eyes, and he watched the bluish glitter of the waves shimmering through the little port-hole window on to her moist forehead, he felt his lips curl into a smile; it came from the deepest recesses of his soul, and he knew it for a smile of contempt, nay – even of triumph. And while he became shudderingly conscious of this dark hope of his, he had to admit to himself that its fulfilment meant salvation to him and deliverance from all his troubles, especially as Elise, if she knew the end to be inevitable and were given a choice, would certainly wish for no other than to pass away beneath his kisses. And as she now, though fully conscious of the risk, seemed prepared, in ever more passionate self-abandonment, to die for love and in the act of loving, he too felt himself strong enough to accept a sacrifice by which, dreadful as it might seem, the complications of destiny might so work out as to make three human beings happy in the end.

But while, night after night, he watched with expectant dread the dull glitter in her eyes, her ecstatic gasps for breath, and then a minute later her awakening gaze lit up once more, the warm breath rose to her lips eager to meet his, he felt as though he had been cheated; his murderous malignity spent itself in sending a wave of fresh and lovely life pulsing through Elise's veins. And she was so sure of his love that in the daytime, when he left her alone or to the company of others, to go and cool his fevered forehead in the sea-breeze on the upper deck, she stayed behind without misgiving, and when he came back to her with his wild and wandering smile, she answered it with shining eyes, as though it had been a greeting of affection.

At Naples, where the ship was to call and stay a day, and then go on to Hamburg without any further stop, Alfred hoped to find a letter from Adèle – he had written from Ceylon imploring her to send one there. The stormy weather made it unnecessary for him to find a pretext for leaving Elise and going ashore with some casual acquaintances on one of the boats that lay near by. He drove to the post office, went up to the counter, gave in his name, but had to go away with empty hands. When he tried to console himself with the fact that Adèle's letter had not been sent in time, or had been lost, the feeling of desolation that came over him made him realize that a life without Adèle was for him unthinkable. He was now at the end of his powers of deception, and he first thought of telling Elise the brutal truth the moment he got back to the ship. But then he reflected that the consequences of such a confession could not be foreseen – Elise might drop dead on the spot, or it might drive her to madness or suicide, and the circumstances of such a mishap could not be concealed, and this might damage his relations with Adèle. He ran the same risk if he postponed his confession to the last moment – until they landed in Hamburg, or even until their arrival in Vienna. Full of these despairing thoughts and even now hardly conscious of their implication, Alfred wandered up and down the seashore in the burning noontide sunshine, when he suddenly felt giddy and almost on the point of fainting. He sank nervously on to a bench and waited until the spasm passed and the cloud faded from before his eyes. Then he drew a deep breath as though awakening from sleep. He became suddenly aware that in that instant when his perceptions had threatened to give way a decision had come to fulness in his mind, terrible and clear, that had long been maturing in his deeper consciousness. This awful, burning purpose, whose fulfilment he had tried for many days to bring forth from its cowardly concealment, he must now accomplish, without more delay, by his own will and by his own hands. And as though it had been the fruit of long reflection, a finished plan came forth into his mind.

He got up, and first went to an hotel where he ate his lunch with an excellent appetite. Then he called on three doctors one after the other, pretended to be subject to attacks of agonizing pain, and that his stock of morphia to which he had been accustomed for years had run out. He took the prescriptions for which he asked, had them made up by different chemists and when he went on board again at sunset, he was in possession of a dose that he was sure was more than sufficient for his

purpose. At dinner on the ship he gave an enthusiastic description of how he had spent the day in an excursion to Pompeii,
and with a positive lust for lying, as though to damn himself
more deeply, he dwelt on the description of a quarter of an
hour that he had spent in the garden of Appius Claudius in
contemplation of a statuette which, of course, in reality he had
never seen, but happened to have read about in a guide-book.
Elise sat at his side, with the Baron opposite her; their eyes met
and Alfred could not rid himself of the idea that these were two
ghosts glaring at each other from empty eye-sockets.

Later, as they had so often done before, he walked up and
down with Elise on the upper deck in the moonlight, while far
away the lights glittered on the coast. He felt himself weaken
for a moment, but he roused his determination once again by
imagining that it was Adèle's arm that pressed against his own;
and by the glow of passion that shot through his veins he
realized that the most terrible crime was not too high a price
to pay for the happiness that awaited him. At the same time
he felt a sort of secret envy of the young creature at his side
who was so soon to find release, without pain and without
foreknowledge, from the perplexities of living.

When they were in their cabin and he took Elise in his arms
for the last time, he saw her with an utter and almost unbearably intensified clarity of vision, and yet there was a
despairing passion in his embrace; but he felt as though he
were accomplishing a destiny in which his will no longer took
a part. It needed but one movement of his fingers to upset the
glass where it stood, glimmering with bluish iridescence on the
little table, and the poison drops could have trickled in harmless
moisture on to the indifferent floor. But Alfred lay motionless
and waited. He waited until at last, as his heart stood still, Elise,
with a movement that he knew so well, reached out her hand
with half-closed eyes, as she always did, for a glass to quench
her thirst before she slept. He did not stir: he watched her
with staring eyes as she raised herself slightly, put the glass to
her lips, and swallowed the contents at a gulp. Then she lay
down again with a gentle sigh, and laying her head on his breast,
as her custom was, prepared to sleep. Alfred heard a long dull
hammering in his temples; he heard Elise's quiet breathing;

he heard the waves beating as if in lamentation against the bows of the ship, as it glided forward; and time seemed to stand still.

Suddenly he felt a violent shudder pass through Elise's body. Her two hands clutched at his neck, her fingers seemed to be trying to pierce his skin, and then, with a long groan, she opened her eyes. Alfred freed himself from her embrace, sprang out of bed, watched her try to raise herself, fling her arms into the air, stare into the half-light with wild fluttering eyes, and then suddenly collapse full length and lie completely motionless except for short sharp gasps for breath. Alfred at once realized that she was quite unconscious, and coldly wondered how long it would be before the end. It also occurred to him that at this moment she might still be saved, and with an obscure feeling that he would in this way tempt fate once again – either he would destroy the fruits of what he had accomplished or by a bold stroke find atonement; so he ran to fetch the doctor. If the latter realized what had happened, then the game would be definitely lost; otherwise he was freed forever from guilt and from remorse.

When Alfred came into the cabin, Elise lay back, pale, with glazed and half-closed eyes, her fingers clenched in the coverlet, and beads of sweat glittering on her forehead and her cheeks. The doctor bent down, laid his ear to her breast, listened for a time, nodded gravely, drew back Elise's eyelids, held his own hand to her lips, and listened again; then he turned to Alfred and told him that the death struggle was over. With a wild look that was not dissembled, Alfred hid his head in his hands, sank down by the bedside, and remained for awhile with his forehead pressed against Elise's knee. Then he turned and stared helplessly at the doctor, who held out his hand to him in sympathy. Alfred did not take it, shook his head, and, his mind completely clear and composed, he added as though in self-reproach now that it was too late: 'If only we had followed your advice.' Then he buried his face gloomily in his hands. 'That is what I thought,' he heard the doctor say in a tone of gentle reproof, and in an overmastering sensation of triumph he knew his eyes were blazing behind their twitching lids.

The next day, in accordance with the instructions, Elise's

body was consigned to the sea, and Alfred, as the widower, felt himself surrounded by universal though silent sympathy. No one liked to disturb him when he walked up and down the deck for hours and stared into a distance that for him – though no one knew it – was hidden by a haze of joy to come. Only the Baron occasionally joined Alfred for a few minutes as he paced to and fro, and even so he carefully refrained from uttering a word about the tragedy. Alfred knew very well that the only reason that led the Baron to accompany him was his desire to feel the atmosphere of the dear dead woman about him once again. For Alfred these few minutes were the only times in which the past seemed at all to move him: otherwise he had completely raised himself above his act and what it might mean to other men. In the living present stood before him the image of the woman he yearned for, whom his guilt had won – and when he looked down into the water from the bow of the ship, it seemed as though he saw her gliding over buried worlds to which, in those slumberous depths, it mattered little whether they had foundered yesterday or a thousand years ago.

Only when the German coast came into sight did his pulse begin to beat faster. His purpose was to stay in Hamburg no longer than was necessary to pick up the letter that must be waiting for him, and then to take the next train home. The tedious business of disembarkation set him quivering with impatience; and he sighed with relief when his luggage was at last put on the carriage and he drove through the streets of the city to the post office under a sky dotted with the small pink clouds of a late spring afternoon. He gave his card to the clerk, watched him with greedy eyes as he turned over the letters, held out his hand in readiness, and received the answer that there was nothing for him – no letter, no card, no telegram. He put on an incredulous smile, and asked the official in an almost humble tone, of which he was instantly ashamed, to look again. Then Alfred tried to make out the address over the edges of the envelopes, and several times he thought he recognized his name in Adèle's handwriting, more than once he hopefully held out his hand – only to be told again that he was mistaken. At last the official put the packet back into the pigeon-hole, shook his head, and turned away. Alfred wished him good day with exaggerated courtesy, and the next minute found himself standing bewildered at the door. Only one thing was clear, and that was that he must stay where he was for the present – he could not possibly go on to Vienna without news of some kind from Adèle.

He drove to an hotel, took a room, and scribbled the following words on one of the forms that lay ready on the table:

'No word from you. Can't understand it. Quite distracted. Back day after tomorrow. When can I see you? Reply at once.'

He added his address and had it sent off reply paid.

When he came down into the entrance-hall, which was already lighted up for the evening, he was aware of someone looking at him – someone who, without getting up, greeted him gravely from where he was sitting with a newspaper on his knee; it was the Baron, to whom he had only had time to say a hurried good-bye before he left the boat. Alfred said he was delighted at this unexpected meeting, and really believed he was, and he told the Baron he intended to stay until the next day. The Baron who, in spite of his pallor and persistent cough, said he felt very well, proposed during dinner that they should visit a music-hall together, and when Alfred hesitated he added softly and with lowered eyelids that grief had never yet brought anyone to life again. Alfred laughed, and then was startled by his laughter, thought the Baron had noticed his embarrassment, and at once decided that the wisest thing he could do would be to agree. Soon after he found himself sitting with the Baron in a box, drinking champagne, and watching, through the smoke and haze, the tricks and antics of acrobats and clowns, accompanied by the vulgar din of a blaring orchestra, listening to half-naked women singing *risqué* songs, and with a kind of demented defiance pointing out to his silent companion the graceful legs and bosoms displayed upon the stage. Then he flirted with a flower-seller, threw a yellow rose at the feet of a dancer who shook her black hair at him invitingly, and laughed aloud when he saw the Baron's thin lips curl as if in contempt and disgust. Later on it seemed as though hundreds of people from the hall below were looking up at him with malignant curiosity, and as if all the murmurs and whisperings were meant for him alone. He felt a shiver of fear go down his back, and then it occurred to him that he had swallowed several glasses of champagne rather too quickly and he recovered his composure. He was delighted to notice that while he had been leaning over the edge of the box two painted ladies had drawn the Baron into a conversation; he breathed deeply as though he had escaped a danger, got up, and nodded to his companion as though to encourage him and wish him luck in his adventure; soon he was walking alone, along streets that he had never seen and never was to see again, whistling some tune or other, and with the feeling that he was wandering through a dream city in the cool night air, back to his hotel.

When he awoke next morning after a deep and heavy sleep, he had at first to remember that he was not on the moving ship, and that the white glimmer yonder was not Elise's morning wrap but a curtain over the window. By a tremendous effort of will, he thrust aside the tide of memory that threatened him and rang the bell. A telegram was brought to him with his breakfast. He left it on the tray so long as the waiter was in the room; and he had the feeling that such self-control deserved some reward. The door had scarcely shut when he opened the telegram with trembling fingers: at first the letters swam before his eyes, then suddenly they stood before him, stiff and huge:

'Tomorrow morning 11 o'clock. Adèle.'

He ran about the room, laughing to himself, and refused to be dashed by the curt, cold tone of the summons. That was her way. And even if he did not find everything at home just as he had been hoping – even if there were some unpleasant disclosures waiting for him – what did that matter? He would again stand before her, in the light of her eyes, in the fragrance of her breath; and his dreadful deed would not have been in vain.

He would not stay in the hotel: he spent the short time before the departure of his train in wandering about the city, with wide-open eyes that saw nothing – neither men nor things. At noon he left Hamburg, and stared hour after hour through the windows at the flying landscape: all the thoughts, and hopes, and fears that rose in his mind, he strained his now docile will to force into subjection: and if, so as not to look strange to his fellow passengers, he took up a book or a newspaper, he did not read it, he counted up from one to a hundred – five hundred – a thousand. When night fell, his devouring desire broke down all his efforts to keep calm. He called himself a fool for having misinterpreted the absence of news, and the tone of his last telegram, and realized that his only reproach against Adèle was that she had held to the agreement more honourably than he. But even if it had somehow come to her ears that he had been travelling with a woman, he felt himself strong enough in his love to win his injured lady back to him in spite of all his jealousy and fury. And so completely had he become the master of his waking dreams that in that interminable journey through the night he could hear her voice, see the outlines of her form and features, and even feel her kiss more burning sweet than any that her lips had ever given him.

At last he was at home. His house welcomed him with its friendly comfort. The carefully prepared breakfast looked excellently appetizing, and for the first time for many days, so it seemed to him, he thought with perfect calm of one who, freed forever from all earthly care, now slumbered in the silent sea. At one moment he felt as though that succession of hours from the time he landed in Naples until Elise's death might be a figment of his shattered nerves, and that the dreadful ending had been, as the doctors had foreseen, or rather predicted, the result of the normal development of her illness. Yes, the man who, in that sunny foreign city, had hurried so malignantly from doctor to doctor, and from chemist to chemist, and with such dreadful forethought had prepared the deadly poison, the man who had held his beloved in his arms for a last hour of sacrilegious pleasure before he sent her into the beyond, seemed to him a being quite other than himself who sat here drinking tea in this familiar room, and amid these unchanged, homely, comfortable surroundings: he seemed a being greater than himself, to whom he must look up in shuddering admiration. Yet later on, when he was getting out of his bath, and he saw his slim naked body in the mirror and became suddenly conscious that it was he who had done this unbelievable thing, he noticed a hard glitter come into his eyes, and he felt worthier than ever to clasp his expectant lady to his heart, and (with a curl of contempt upon his lips) more certain than ever of her love.

At the appointed hour he entered the yellow drawing-room, which he had left a year ago almost to the very day, and in the next moment Adèle stood before him, as unconcerned as though she had said good-bye to him the day before: she gave him her hand, and he kissed it and held it long. 'Why don't I take her in my arms?' he thought. Then he heard her speak in that husky voice of hers, which had come to him in his dreams that very night; and he was conscious that he himself had not said a word except to whisper her name when she came in. He must not mind, she began, that she had not answered his beautiful letters; but there were certain matters that could be better dealt with face to face than in writing. Her silence must in any case have prepared him for the fact that many things had changed, and the cool tone of her telegram was, as she wished to acknowledge at once, quite intentional. For about six months she had, in fact, been engaged to another. And she mentioned a name that Alfred knew. It was the name of one of his many good friends of old days, of whom he had thought as little in that past year as of most men whom he had met in his previous life. He listened calmly to Adèle, stared spellbound at her smooth forehead, then through her into nothingness, and there was a murmur in his ears as of distant waves surging over sunken worlds. Suddenly he saw something like a gleam of fear in Adèle's eyes; and he realized that he was standing before her, deadly pale, and with a frightful expression in his face, and he found himself saying, 'It isn't true, Adèle; you don't mean it; you can't do it.'

She was clearly relieved that he had at last found his voice. She smiled her charming smile again, and explained that he must understand she did mean it: that she could do it – she could do, in fact, as she pleased. She had not been engaged to him, they had been completely free when they parted, and without any obligation, she as well as he. And as she loved another now, and not him, the affair was at an end. He must realize that, and resign himself: otherwise she should regret not having followed her father's advice of that morning and simply not been at home to Alfred. And she sat down opposite him, her slender hands clasped on her knees and with a distant look in her shining eyes.

Alfred felt that he needed all his self-command not to do something ridiculous or dreadful. He did not know what he really wanted to do: seize her by the neck and strangle her or fling himself on the floor and cry like a child. But what was the use of thinking about it? He had no choice, he stood there stricken, and had barely the presence of mind to seize Adèle's hands as she was hastening away and hoarsely implore her to stay. Only a quarter of an hour! She must hear him! He had the right to ask that after all that had once passed between them. He had so much to tell her, more than she could imagine, and it was her duty to hear him. For if she knew everything, then she would also know that he was hers and hers only, and she was his alone. She would know that she could not belong to another, that he had won her in guilt and torment; that his lawful claims upon her must utterly sweep aside all others, that she was fettered to him irrevocably, forever and forever, and he to her. And, on his knees before her, clutching her hands in his, his eyes fixed on hers, he poured out his story, and told her all that had happened in the past year; how he had loved another before her; how he had gone abroad with her as she was ill and had no one on earth but himself; how the torment of his desire had nearly worn him out, but the other had clung to him helplessly and he could not go; and how, at the end of his endurance, for love of her – of *her* whose hands he held in his, for a love the like of which had not been seen on earth, he had killed that other, who could not and would not have lived without him – poisoned her, half in pity and half in hatred; how the poor creature now slept under the sea-waves far away, martyr to a happiness that was to be beyond all others, like the price at which it had been won.

Adèle had let him keep her hands and her gaze was still plunged in his. She listened to what he told her, but he did not really know how she took it – whether as a fairy tale about strange far-off beings or as an item of news about people that were no concern of hers. Perhaps she did not believe what he was telling her. But, in any case, she did not care whether what he said were true or false. He felt his impotence more and more. He watched the words fall from her like a chill unheeded shower; and at the last, when he would have learned his fate from her lips, she merely shook her head. He looked at her fearfully, knowing yet unbelieving, and with a wild questioning look in his twitching eyes.

'No,' she said, in a hard voice, 'it is over.'

And that 'No' meant, he knew, that all was forever at an end. Adèle's face was quite inflexible. There was no trace in it of past affection, no sign of horror – only a devastating expression of indifference and boredom.

Alfred bowed his head with a vacant smile as though he understood, let go her hands, which she dropped coldly at her side, turned and went. The door behind him was still open, and he felt a chill breath on his neck. As he went down the stairs he knew that there was nothing left for him to do but to make an end. And it was so decided; he set all his doubts aside, and sauntered quietly homeward through that lovely spring day as though he were going to the sleep he needed after some wild carouse.

But someone was waiting for him in his room. It was the Baron. Without taking Alfred's proffered hand he explained that he only wanted a few words with him, and, as Alfred nodded politely, he continued:

'I think it my duty to inform you that I consider you a scoundrel.'

'Good!' thought Alfred, 'that will be an excellent way out.' And he answered calmly: 'I am at your disposal. Early tomorrow morning, if that suits you . . .'

The Baron shook his head curtly. It became apparent that he had made his preparations as soon as they had landed. Two young gentlemen from the German Embassy were merely awaiting his further instructions: and he said that he expected that his adversary, who was at home here, would find no difficulty in arranging for the affair to be settled before that same evening. Alfred believed he could promise to do so. For one instant he thought of confessing the whole truth to the Baron; but from the terrible look of hatred that glittered from those cold eyes, he was afraid that the Baron, who perhaps suspected the truth, might hand him over to the police: so he decided to say nothing.

Alfred found the two men he wanted without difficulty. One of them was Adèle's fiancé, the other a young officer with whom he had spent many a gay time in earlier days. At sunset, in a meadow by the Danube, a favourite spot for such encounters, he stood facing the Baron. A sense of peace possessed him that, after the turmoil of the last few days, was almost happiness. As he looked down the barrel of the levelled pistol, and heard a distant voice rap out, one by one, those last three seconds, that fell like three chill drops from the silent evening sky, he thought of one unutterably dear to him, over whose mouldering body surged the sea. And when he lay upon the ground, and something dark bent over him, enfolded him, and would not let him go, he felt at last content that his atonement was accepted, and that he was disappearing for her sake, and to her, into that nothingness he had so long desired.

A Confirmed Bachelor

The steamer was ready to cast off. Dr Graesler and the hotel manager stood on the deck together, Dr Graesler in a grey overcoat with a black armlet on his sleeve, the manager with his head bared, his smoothly plastered hair scarcely stirred by the breeze.

'My dear doctor,' the manager was saying in the affable tone that Graesler found so irritating, 'let me repeat: we count upon your returning next year, in spite of the misfortune you had here – the deeply distressing misfortune.'

Dr Graesler made no answer. His eyes were moist as he looked shoreward, where the huge hotel, with white shutters closed to keep out the heat, glared in the sunshine. His gaze wandered over the slumbering yellow houses and dusty gardens which stretched beneath the noonday sun obliquely upwards to the remnants of the crumbling wall that crowned the hill.

'Our guests,' continued the manager, 'all think so highly of you, and many of them are sure to come again next season. We confidently expect you to occupy the little villa again' – he pointed to a modest but cheerful house adjoining the hotel – 'in spite of the painful memories it holds for you.'

Graesler shook his head sadly. He removed his hard black bowler and smoothed his hair. He had fair, wiry hair, which was beginning to turn grey.

The manager persisted.

'My dear doctor, time works wonders. Besides, if you dread the loneliness of the little white house, you have the remedy in your own hands. Bring a pretty little wife back with you from Germany.'

Graesler's only answer was a hesitating lift of his eyes. The manager went merrily on. His tone was almost imperious.

'Please think it over. A pretty little wife with golden hair –

or black hair if you like. The lack of a wife is probably the one thing that stands between you and perfection.'

Dr Graesler raised his brows. His eyes looked as if he were staring at the retreating images of the past.

'But no matter,' the manager concluded blithely, 'whether you come back married or single, you will always be welcome. You will be here, won't you, as we arranged, on 27 October? Communications are still so unsatisfactory that unless you come then, you can't possibly get here before 10 November. And since we open on the first' – the manager's voice turned a trifle harsh, like a drill-sergeant's – it always made Graesler wince – 'that would be rather inconvenient.'

Giving the doctor's hand a hard shake, a habit he had acquired in the United States, and exchanging a farewell glance with a passing officer of the ship, the manager stepped briskly down the companion. A moment later he appeared on the gangway, from which he nodded a final salutation to the doctor, who continued to stand gloomily, hat in hand, gazing over the bulwark. A few minutes later the steamer was under way.

On the homeward voyage, during which the weather was beautiful, the manager's parting words often recurred to Graesler. As he dozed in the afternoon in his comfortable long-chair on the upper deck, a rug over his knees, he sometimes had a dreamlike vision of a plump and pretty woman in a white summer dress gliding through the house and the garden. She had a pink doll's face, which came to him as the memory, not of anyone he had met in real life, but of some picture he must have seen in a book or an illustrated paper. His dream had the mysterious power of laying the ghost of his dead sister and so giving him the sense that she had left the world a long while before, and in a less unnatural way than the actuality. But there were other hours in which sad memories came fully awake and the terrible experience recurred with intolerable vividness.

It had taken place only a week before. As often happened, Graesler had fallen asleep in the garden after luncheon, over his medical journal. When he awoke, he saw from the lengthening shadow of the palm tree that he must have been asleep at least two hours. That annoyed him; he took it as a sign of advancing years – he was forty-eight. He rose, thrust the journal into his pocket, with an eager wish for the refreshing spring breezes of Germany, and walked slowly towards the little house where he lived with his older sister.

He saw her standing at one of the windows. That was strange: during the hot hours the shutters were usually closed. Then he noticed that Friederike, seen from closer by, was not smiling at him as he had thought; she had her back turned and was absolutely motionless. A trifle uneasy – why, he could not have told – he hastened into the house. He found his sister leaning, apparently, against the window-frame, still motionless, and he noticed with horror that her head was hanging forward, her eyes were fixed and staring, and round her neck was a cord fastened to the top of the frame.

'Friederike!' he cried.

He drew out his pocket-knife and cut the cord. The lifeless form fell into his arms. He shouted for the servant in the kitchen, who had no inkling of what had happened, and with her aid carried his sister to the couch. He did his utmost to restore her to life, and the servant ran to fetch the hotel manager. But even before he came Dr Graesler realized that all was over, and the manager found him on his knees beside his sister's body, weak and distraught.

Dr Graesler racked his brains in an attempt to account for his sister's suicide. It seemed almost incredible that she, a mature spinster, in comfortable circumstances, with whom he had lightly chatted at luncheon about the approaching voyage, should suddenly have gone mad. A more probable supposition was that Friederike had been troubled with suicidal impulses for a long time, perhaps for years, and had chosen this quiet afternoon hour for the carrying out of a plan that had ripened gradually. Occasionally it had struck her brother that perhaps her outward equanimity concealed a gentle melancholy; but his time and energy were too much taken up with his work for him to pay much attention to anything of the sort. Now, on reflection, he realized that since childhood he had hardly ever seen Friederike really cheerful.

He knew little of her younger days; he had been a ship's

surgeon, continually away from home. It was not until after their parents' death, in quick succession, fifteen years before, that Friederike left her old home in the little country town to keep house for her brother after he left the service of the Norddeutscher Lloyd. By then she was well on in the thirties, but still had a young and graceful figure, and her eyes gave an impression of enigmatical gloom, so that she had no lack of wooers, and Emil sometimes felt he had good reason to fear that one of them might some day deprive him of her company. The years passed, no wooer ever did carry her off, her last chances vanished, and she seemed to accept her lot without repining.

But now, on thinking matters over, her brother fancied he could recall numerous dumbly reproachful glances, as if she had held him partly responsible for the cheerlessness of her life. Perhaps the consciousness that her life had been wasted had grown constantly keener, especially as she gave no open expression to the feeling, until at last the gnawing ache of it had driven her to make a sudden end.

Her brother, who had so little suspected the approach of tragedy, had now to turn his attention to domestic details, of which Friederike had always relieved him, and that at a time in life when a man hates most to make a change.

Towards the end of his trip a feeling of estrangement towards Friederike crept into his heart, a little resentment – without prejudice to his mourner's mood – that she had gone without a good-bye, had left him quite unprepared and all alone in the world. It was a chill thought, yet somehow consoling.

After a brief stay in Berlin, where he paid his respects to a number of consulting physicians, Dr Graesler returned on a beautiful May day to the health resort at which he had practised for the past six summers. He was warmly welcomed by his housekeeper, an elderly woman, a tradesman's widow, and was delighted to see the simple wild flowers with which she had decorated the house for his reception. It was not without uneasiness that he entered the little room his sister had occupied during the previous year – he was less profoundly moved than he had expected.

Graesler soon settled down to life as he found it. The spa was a small place, engirdled with well-wooded hills. The skies were limpid, and the air had the genial warmth of spring. Often an unwonted sense of freedom from restraint came over him. At breakfast for instance. No one, to be sure, to save him the trouble of pouring coffee for himself, but also no hint of restriction at the dainty table set out on the little balcony and decked with its blue-flowered coffee service, which glistened in the morning sunlight.

His other meals he took in the principal hotel of the town, in the company of some of the leading residents, old acquaintances with whom conversation was easy and many times entertaining. His practice was soon all that could be desired, and there were no cases of exceptional gravity to trouble his sense of professional responsibility.

The early weeks of summer passed almost without incident when, one July evening, after a busy day, Dr Graesler was summoned to the ranger's lodge, an hour's drive from town. The doctor was not pleased; he was not eager for practice among the permanent residents; it brought him little either in the way of reputation or fees. Still, as he drove up the valley in the mild evening air, at first along the pleasant road bordered by charming country-houses, then between golden fields lying in the cool shade of the hills, his vexation soon passed away. An excellent cigar helped to soothe him, so that by the time the ranger's lodge came in sight, he almost regretted that the drive was over so soon.

He had the coachman wait in the main road and walked up to the house by the bridle path between the young pine trees. The lodge had a friendly air, with the huge pair of antlers over the front door, the setting sun reflected in the windows, and a red glow on the roof.

A young woman whose face seemed familiar to Graesler came down the porch steps to meet him and shook hands with him.

Her mother, she explained, had had an attack of acute indigestion.

'For the last hour,' she said, 'my mother has been sleeping peacefully. I am sure the fever must have gone, but at four this afternoon her temperature was still just over a hundred. She had been feeling poorly since yesterday evening, so I thought I had better send for you. I hope there is nothing serious the matter.'

She looked at him with an air of modest inquiry as if the further development of the ailment depended upon him.

He met her gaze with due seriousness.

Of course, he recognized her. He had often seen her in the town and supposed she was one of the summer visitors.

'Since your mother is sleeping so quietly,' he said, 'I do not think there can be any cause for serious anxiety. You had better tell me a little more about the trouble. I should not like to wake the patient needlessly.'

She invited him on to the veranda and motioned him to a chair, while she herself stood beside one of the posts of the doorway leading into the house. In the most direct and circumstantial manner she gave an account of the course of her mother's symptoms. Dr Graesler felt sure the trouble was only an upset stomach, still he had to ask her about a number of medical details, and was surprised by her simple frankness in referring to the natural processes. He was not used to such freedom from constraint in a girl. Would she have been equally unconcerned, he asked himself, had he been a young man?

He guessed her age to be about twenty-five, although her large, tranquil eyes gave her an expression of greater maturity. In her fair hair, piled up in plaits, she wore a plain silver comb. She was simply dressed, but her white belt was fastened by a handsome gilt clasp. What struck Graesler most of all, even to the point of making him feel a trifle suspicious, were her extremely elegant doe-skin shoes, light-brown in colour, precisely matching the stockings she wore.

She had not quite finished her report and Graesler was not yet at the end of his survey, when from within came a call for 'Sabine'. The doctor rose. Sabine ushered him through the large dining-room, already growing dark, into another and lighter room with two beds in it. The patient was sitting up in bed. She wore a white dressing jacket and a white cap and looked exceedingly well-nourished. Her eyes were clear and friendly, almost merry. They lit up with surprise at seeing the physician.

'Dr Graesler,' introduced Sabine, laying her hand tenderly on her mother's forehead.

'Delighted to make your acquaintance, Dr Graesler.' The mother shook her head disapprovingly and turned to Sabine. 'But why, dear . . .'

'My visit certainly seems superfluous,' remarked Graesler, shaking the patient's proffered hand and holding it to feel her pulse, 'especially as your daughter' – he smiled as he spoke – 'appears to have an amazing amount of medical knowledge. Still, now that I am here. . . .'

With a shrug of her shoulders the patient submitted, and Graesler made an examination, while Sabine looked on calmly and attentively. When it was over, he felt able to reassure both mother and daughter. But a difficulty was encountered when the doctor wished to impose a rigid dietary for the next few days. Sabine's mother protested vigorously.

'I used to take pork and sauerkraut to cure attacks like this, and a special sort of sausage, which alas! is not to be had in this neighbourhood. Today I let Sabine keep me from eating a hearty luncheon. That's why I had the attack of fever, I suppose.'

Graesler thought she was joking, then realized that the mother was the very opposite of the daughter; she had a thoroughly lay, in fact an heretical view of medical science. She made fun of the virtues of the mineral water of the health resort. Bottles for export, she said, were filled with ordinary water to which salt, pepper, and probably more dubious ingredients were added.

Graesler could not repress a sense of annoyance; he was always inclined to champion the reputation of the spa in which he practised, and felt himself partly responsible for its successes or failures. Yet he refrained from flatly contradicting his patient and contented himself with exchanging a smile of understanding with the daughter. That was enough to justify his own views and maintain his dignity.

After leaving the mother, Dr Graesler assured Sabine again that she had no cause to be uneasy.

'I thought her condition was not serious,' said Sabine. 'Still with people who are getting on in years there are possibilities that don't exist in younger persons. That was why I felt I had better send for you, especially as father is away.'

'Is he on a tour of inspection?'

'What do you mean?'

'On a tour of inspection through the district?'

Sabine smiled.

'My father is not a forest ranger. This house is still spoken of as the ranger's lodge because up to six or seven years ago the ranger did live here; and my father is called "the ranger" though he doesn't know a thing about forestry.'

'Are you an only child?' asked Graesler. Sabine was accompanying him as though it were a matter of course along the bridle path between the young pine trees.

'No,' she said, 'I have a brother. He is much younger than I, only just fifteen. When he is home for the holidays, he spends all his time, of course, in the forest. Sometimes he even sleeps in the open.' Graesler shook his head disapprovingly. 'Oh, that's nothing,' she protested, 'I used to sleep out of doors myself now and then – not very often.'

'Quite close to the house, I hope?' the doctor asked rather anxiously. 'Only when you were a little girl, I suppose?' he added hesitatingly.

'Oh no, I was seventeen when we first came to live here. Before that we were in the city – in different cities.'

Respecting her reserve, Graesler asked no further questions. They had now reached the carriage road; the driver was there, ready to start. Graesler was impelled to say one word more.

'I think we have met several times in the town?'

'Certainly we have. I have known you by sight for a long time. But weeks often pass without my visiting the town. Last year I exchanged a word or two with your sister when we met casually at Schmidt's. She has come back with you this summer, I suppose?'

The doctor looked down. His gaze happened to fall on Sabine's shoes; he turned his eyes away.

'My sister is not with me,' he said. 'She died three months ago in Lanzarote.'

It hurt, and yet there was a certain consolation in pronouncing the name of the distant island.

All Sabine said was 'Oh.'

They stood in silence for a while. Graesler forced his features into a rather formal smile and shook hands with her.

'Good-night, Dr Graesler.'

'Good-night,' he answered, and stepped into the carriage.

Sabine stood for a moment until the carriage had started, then turned to go. Graesler glanced back. With slightly bowed head, and without looking round, she glided between the pines. From the house a ray of light shone across the bridle path. A turn in the road, and the picture was blotted out. Graesler leaned back in the carriage and looked up to the heavens; scattered stars glimmered in the cool twilight.

He thought of the long ago, of gayer days when he had had the love of beautiful young women. There had been the civil engineer's widow from Rio de Janeiro. At Lisbon she left the steamer of which he was the surgeon, ostensibly to make some purchases in the town, and had never come back though she had had a ticket for Hamburg. He saw her in her black dress driving townward from the docks and nodding amiably to him from the street corner before she vanished for ever.

There had been the lawyer's daughter from Nancy. He had become engaged to her in St Blasien, the first health resort in which he had practised. Her father was suddenly recalled to France by an important lawsuit. The girl left with her parents, and Graesler never heard from her again.

Next came the memory of Lizzie, a friend of his student days in Berlin, who had shot herself, partly on his account. He remembered the reluctance with which she had shown him the powder blackened wound beneath the left breast, and how, far from being touched, he had felt only annoyed and bored.

He thought of the charming Henriette, whom for a number of years he used to visit in her cosy little quarters in the upper storey of the house overlooking the Alster. He went to see her whenever he returned to Hamburg after one of his long voyages, finding her always as bright, simple, and willing as when he had last seen her – though he never learned, and never troubled to inquire, how she spent the time between his visits.

Many other incidents passed through Graesler's mind, some not altogether agreeable, some even unsavoury, so that he could not but wonder that he had ever gone in for things of that sort. On the whole, though, his feeling was one of regret that youth had passed, and with it the right to expect that life would still lavish its beauties on him.

The carriage rolled on between the fields. The hills looked darker and higher than in the daylight; lights twinkled in the little villas. On a balcony a man and a woman embraced in a more intimate way than they would have allowed themselves in the light of day. From a veranda, where a small company sat at supper, came the sound of conversation and laughter. Graesler, beginning to feel hungry, looked forward eagerly to his own supper in the 'Silver Lion' and told the driver to hurry.

He found the acquaintances whom he usually joined at supper already at table, and drank an extra glass of wine to make life seem sweeter and lighter. For some reason he did not follow his impulse to speak of his visit to the ranger's lodge. The extra glass of wine failed of its usual effect. Graesler rose from the table feeling even more melancholy than when he sat down. A slight headache bothered him on his way home.

During the next few days Dr Graesler, in the vague expectation of meeting Sabine, went down the main street oftener than usual. Once, during his consultation hours when the waiting-room happened to be empty, he was seized with a sort of presentiment; he went downstairs and took a hasty but fruitless walk to the pump-room and back. That same evening at the supper table he remarked as if casually that he had recently been summoned to the ranger's lodge; then he listened eagerly and a trifle pugnaciously to see if any disparaging word would be let fall concerning Sabine – some such phrase as is apt to be uttered about a woman when men are alone together in jovial mood, though there may be no warrant for the insinuation. There was so little response that Graesler was convinced that none of his friends had the faintest interest in the Schleheim family. There was merely a casual mention that the so-called ranger had some relatives in Berlin, and that the daughter (who had obviously not made a deep impression on Graesler's table companions) used sometimes to stay with them during the winter.

A day or two later, when his work was done, Graesler decided to take a walk to the lodge. From the road he saw the house standing impassive at the edge of the clearing in the forest. On the veranda was a man whose features were not distinguishable at that distance. Graesler felt strongly impelled to go on up to the lodge, say he had happened to be passing that way, and enquire after Frau Schleheim's health. But that, he immediately realized, would hardly be compatible with his professional dignity and might arouse a false impression. So he returned from his excursion more tired and out of spirits than he would have thought possible from so trivial a disappointment.

More days passed, and still he did not meet Sabine in the town. He began to hope, in the interest of his own equanimity, that she had gone away for a time or even for good.

One morning, when he was breakfasting on the balcony with far less relish than during the first days after his return to the health resort, he was told that a young gentleman wished to see him. Hard upon this announcement a tall, handsome stripling in a bicycling suit appeared on the balcony. In carriage and features he so strongly resembled Sabine that Graesler could not help greeting him as an acquaintance.

'The younger Herr Schleheim?' he said in a tone rather of conviction than inquiry.

'Yes.'

'I knew you instantly from your resemblance to – your mother. Won't you sit down? As you see, I have not quite finished breakfast. What's the matter? Is your mother ill again?'

He felt as if he were talking to Sabine.

The lad remained standing, cap in hand.

'My mother's all right, thank you, Dr Graesler. She's been rather more careful since your scolding.'

Graesler smiled, realizing that Sabine, in order to make her own admonitions more effective, had delivered them as coming from the mouth of the doctor.

Perhaps Sabine was the patient this time!

From the unexpected quickening of his pulse Graesler became aware of how much the girl's well-being meant to him. Before he could put the question, the lad said:

'It's father this time.'

Graesler was relieved.

'What's the matter with him? Nothing serious, I hope.'

'That's what we want to know. He has changed a good deal of late. Perhaps it's not exactly an illness. You see he's getting on, he's fifty-two.'

Graesler involuntarily wrinkled his brow, and asked in a rather chilly tone:

'Tell me just what is making you anxious.'

'Father's begun to suffer from attacks of dizziness. Yesterday evening, when he was getting up from his chair, he nearly fell down, and had to save himself by holding on to the table. For a long time we've been noticing that when he picks up his glass to drink his hand is shaky.'

'Hm.' The doctor looked up from his cup. 'Perhaps your father handles a glass rather often, and I suppose there's something stronger than water in the glass . . . ?'

The young man was rather embarrassed.

'Sabine thinks that may have something to do with the trouble. Besides, father smokes from morning till night.'

'Age doesn't seem to have much to do with his case. Does your father want me to visit him?'

'The matter is not quite so simple. We don't want father to know that you are coming on his account; he won't hear of consulting a doctor. Sabine wondered whether the thing couldn't be arranged as if you saw him by chance.'

'By chance?'

'For instance – if you were to walk past the lodge as you did the other afternoon. Sabine could hail you from the veranda. Then you could come in and – and – oh well, we should see.'

The doctor felt his face flush. Stirring in his empty coffee-cup, he said:

'I have very little time for country walks. But you're quite right, I do remember having passed close to the lodge a few days ago.'

He recovered his self-possession, looked up, and was glad to see that the young man had apparently noticed nothing. He went on in a professional tone.

'If there is no other way out of the difficulty, I will do what you ask. But you must understand that we shall not get very far with a casual talk on the veranda. I shall need to make a thorough examination before giving an opinion.'

'Of course we know that, Dr Graesler. What we hope is that after a time father will come to consult you of his own accord. But if you could only see him first . . . Could you manage to come one day soon, directly you are free to get away – today, if possible?'

'Today! I can see her again today,' thought Graesler. 'Delightful!' He consulted his engagement book and shook his head as if faced with insuperable difficulties. Then, with an air of resolution, he struck out an imaginary entry, and on the next page wrote the name that was uppermost in his mind, 'Sabine'.

'Very well, today between half-past five and six,' he said coolly but in a cordial tone.

'Oh, thank you.'

Graesler rose, cutting the thanks short, asked young Schleheim to remember him to Frau and Fräulein Schleheim, shook hands good-bye, and went inside where he watched from the window as the youth came out of the entry with his bicycle, settled his cap more firmly, mounted his wheel, and disappeared round the next corner.

'If I were ten years younger,' thought Graesler, 'I could fancy that it's all a pretext in Sabine to see me again.' He sighed.

Soon after five Graesler started.

He was wearing a light grey suit and still had the mourning band round his left sleeve. He intended to drive to within a short distance of the ranger's house, then get out and walk.

But he had got only a little way beyond the region of the villas when, to his surprise and delight, he saw Sabine and her brother coming to meet him along the path that ran beside the road. He jumped out of the carriage, which was driving at a foot's pace up the hill, and shook hands first with Sabine, then with the lad.

'We're so awfully sorry,' began Sabine with slight agitation, 'we simply couldn't manage to keep father at home, and he's not likely to be back again until quite late. Please don't be angry with me.'

Graesler made an unsuccessful attempt to look annoyed.

'Don't worry,' he said lightly, but consulted his watch and wrinkled his forehead as though planning something else for the rest of the day.

On looking up he had to smile to see Sabine and her brother standing there in the footpath like two schoolchildren expecting a scolding. Sabine was wearing a white dress; a broad-brimmed straw hat hung by a yellow ribbon from her left arm. She looked much younger than the first time he saw her.

'On this hot afternoon,' said Graesler almost reproachfully, 'you walked so far to meet me. You really need not have troubled.'

'Dr Graesler,' said Sabine rather embarrassed, 'to avoid any misunderstanding – of course this is to be taken as a regular visit . . .'

Graesler interrupted her :

'That's for me to decide, my dear young lady. The fact is, that even if your scheme had worked, I should not have regarded my visit as a professional one in that sense. You must simply look upon me as a fellow-conspirator.'

'But if you take it that way, Dr Graesler, you will make it impossible for me . . .'

Graesler broke in again.

'I had intended to go out driving today any how. Perhaps you will let me drive you home? Then I can see how Frau Schleheim is getting on.'

Graesler felt himself to be quite the man of the world, and made the fleeting resolve to practise in a larger health resort next summer, though so far he had been unsuccessful in the larger places.

'Mother is getting on splendidly,' said Sabine. 'But if you really have nothing better to do this evening' – she turned to her brother – 'how would it be if we showed Dr Graesler our forest, Karl?'

'Your forest?'

'That's what we call it,' said Karl. 'It really is ours. None of the patients at the spa ever come so far out. Parts of it are lovely, just like a primeval forest.'

'I certainly ought to see it,' said Graesler. 'I shall be delighted.'

The carriage and the driver were left near the ranger's lodge, and the three started off Indian file along a path that led at first through a field of wheat as high as a man's head, then across meadowland into the forest.

'Although I've been practising here every season for six years,' said Graesler, 'I scarcely know anything of the neighbourhood. My fate. When I was a ship's surgeon, all I ever saw was the coast, or at most the seaport towns and their immediate environment.'

Karl questioned him eagerly about his sea voyages and the lands he had visited. This put Graesler in the position of an experienced traveller, and he answered with an animation and a fancy that were not always at his command.

It was decided to rest for a while in a clearing which afforded a charming view over the town, where the glass roof of the pump-room glittered in the rays of the setting sun. Karl flung himself on the grass, Sabine sat on a felled tree, Dr Graesler, afraid of soiling his light suit, remained standing, and continued to hold forth about his travels. His voice, usually rather husky despite frequent clearing of the throat, seemed to him to have acquired a new, or at least unwonted timbre, and his hearers listened to him with a sympathy that he had not enjoyed for many a day.

When the time came to return, he suggested his going back to the lodge and acting as if he had met Karl and Sabine by chance, so that if their father had come back it would be a simple way of opening up an acquaintance with him. Sabine gave a short nod. It was a characteristic little gesture that to the doctor expressed assent more decisively than words could have done.

The way took them down hill by a path which widened as it descended. Karl now did most of the talking, all about the travels and the explorations he intended to make. It was a boy's love of adventure showing itself under the influence of the books he had recently been reading. Graesler was amused, and sooner than he expected they reached the garden hedge of the lodge.

They approached the house from the back. Standing among the tall pines, the white building with its six narrow, uniform windows gleamed dimly through the gathering dusk. On the lawn between the lodge and the hedge stood a long table with a bench and chairs, all made of rough wood.

Karl hurried on to spy out the land, and Graesler was left alone for a time with Sabine, among the pine trees. They looked at one another. The doctor smiled; it was an embarrassed smile. Sabine's expression remained grave, and the doctor, slowly glancing around, remarked: 'How peaceful it is here,' and gently cleared his throat.

Karl beckoned from one of the open windows.

Graesler assumed a professional mien and followed Sabine

through the garden to the veranda, where Karl was telling his father and mother the story of the afternoon encounter.

Graesler, still misled by the designation 'ranger', had expected to see a bearded, stocky man in a shooting jacket, and with a pipe in his mouth. He was surprised to find a slender, smooth-shaven gentleman with black, carefully parted hair only just beginning to turn grey. Schleheim's manner was friendly but struck one somehow as histrionic.

Dr Graesler started a conversation – first about the beauties of the forest, then, by a natural turn, about how slow the health resort was in developing in spite of the loveliness of the surroundings – during which he steadily observed the master of the house. He could not detect anything of note beyond a certain restlessness of the eyes and a frequent twitching of the corners of the mouth as if in scorn.

When Sabine announced supper, Graesler got up to go. The ranger, with exaggerated cordiality, would not hear of his leaving, and he was soon seated with parents and children at the supper table, lighted by a green-shaded lamp hanging from the rafters.

Graesler asked Sabine whether she ever took part in affairs like the Saturday Club meetings which were soon to begin in the town assembly rooms.

'Not of late,' she replied. 'I used to when I was younger –'

At Graesler's smile of protest she added, meaningly it seemed to him:

'I am twenty-seven already.'

Herr Schleheim gibed at the petty scale of life of the health resort, and dilated with great animation on the charm of great cities and the busy life of the world. From certain of his remarks it became clear that he had been an opera singer until late in his married life. He spoke of actors with whom he had worked, of patrons who had thought highly of him, and of doctors to whose wrong methods of treatment he ascribed the premature loss of his baritone voice. While talking he emptied glass after glass, until suddenly he seemed tired and began to look like an old, worn-out man.

Graesler felt it was time to go.

v.–6

Sabine and Karl, who accompanied him to the carriage, anxiously asked what he thought of their father.

'I can't say offhand. I'd like to observe him soon again, or better still give him a proper examination. No conscientious physician will make a diagnosis without an examination.'

'Don't you think,' said Karl to his sister, 'that it is a long time since Father has talked as freely as tonight?'

'I do,' answered Sabine. With a grateful look at Graesler: 'One could see in a moment that he took to you.'

The doctor waved aside the implied compliment. At the young people's request he promised to come soon again.

The evening was cool, and the stars shone brightly on the homeward journey. Sabine's confidence in him filled Graesler with satisfaction, all the sweeter since, he felt, it was not inspired solely by his medical skill. Of late years he had often wearied of his work, had felt comparatively indifferent towards his patients, and had even lacked human sympathy with their troubles. Today, after a long interval, he had once again been inspired with a sense of the loftiness of his calling – the calling that he had, to be sure, chosen with enthusiasm in the far-off days of youth though he had not at all times remained inwardly worthy of it.

Next day, when Dr Graesler opened the door leading into his waiting room, he was surprised to see Herr Schleheim among the patients.

'Don't tell my family I have come to consult you,' he said the moment he was alone with Graesler in the inner office.

Graesler agreed, and Schleheim did not hesitate to tell of his troubles and submit to an examination. The doctor found no trace of serious bodily disorder, nor could he detect indications of psychical disturbance, though this would not have been surprising in a man compelled in his prime to forsake a brilliant vocation without finding compensation in family affection or in the resources of his own mind.

The opportunity of a frank, open talk obviously did Schleheim good, and he was delighted when the doctor, after telling him he could not be considered a patient, genially suggested he'd come for a visit and a chat at the lodge whenever he happened to be walking in that direction.

When Dr Graesler called the next Sunday morning, he found the singer alone on the porch. Schleheim hastened to explain that he had thought it better after all to tell 'the family' (he always spoke of them collectively).

'I had to,' he said, 'I had to tell them I had consulted you and you had found nothing seriously wrong with me. They drove me crazy with their worried looks and their tedious talk about my health.'

Graesler agreed that the young people's solicitude might have been a trifle exaggerated but praised them for their warmth of feeling.

'Yes, yes,' said their father, 'I didn't mean to imply that they were anything but good and kind. That is why,' he added, 'I don't think either of them will get much out of life. Very likely they will never learn anything about it.'

A pale memory of discreditable adventures in days long past gleamed in his eyes.

Soon the other members of the Schleheim family arrived, all more or less Sundayfied in their attire with an aspect of middle-class gentility that Graesler had not noticed before. Sabine, apparently conscious of this, hastened to remove her berib-boned hat with a sigh of relief, and smoothed her hair.

Graesler stayed to the midday meal. The conversation at table skimmed only on the surface of things. Mention was made of a sanatorium not far from the town whose superintendent meditated retiring. Frau Schleheim asked Graesler whether he wouldn't like the position, seeing it might give him an oppor-tunity systematically to enforce his famous abstinence cures.

Graesler smiled.

'I am not willing to give up my personal freedom,' he said. 'Though I have practised here for six or seven years in succes-sion, and shall probably continue to practise here several years more, a sense of compulsion would make the place distasteful to me; it would even disturb me in my work.'

By a barely perceptible nod, Sabine seemed to express sym-pathy with his point of view. It appeared, however, that she was well informed regarding the state of affairs at the sanatorium. She said that the superintendent was elderly, and had grown lax of late, but that the place could be made far more profit-able than it was.

'I should think,' she went on, 'that every doctor would prefer to practise at a sanatorium; it's the only way of ensuring a per-manent relationship between doctor and patient, and the only way of really controlling a cure.'

'There is certainly a good deal in what you say,' said Graes-ler, with the reserve in his tone that seemed appropriate for an expert in lay circles.

Sabine did not miss the note. She blushed slightly and was quick to answer:

'You know I worked for some time as a hospital nurse in Berlin.'

'You don't say so!' exclaimed the doctor, temporarily at a

loss as to his own attitude towards this revelation. He had recourse to vague generalization. 'A beautiful, a noble calling. But how dreary and difficult! Your home in this lovely forest must have lured you back soon again.'

Sabine made no answer. The others, too, were silent. Graesler felt that the key to the riddle of Sabine's life was almost in his grasp.

After the meal, Karl proposed a game of dominoes in the garden, as if it had been his chartered right. He challenged Graesler, and soon the game clattered on in full swing, while the mother reclined in a comfortable chair beneath the pines and dozed over her needlework. The doctor thought of the gloomy Sunday afternoons he had spent by the side of his melancholy sister – a marvellous escape from a tedious and irksome phase of his life! And when Sabine, noticing his distraction, reminded him by a smile or a gentle nudge that it was his turn to play, the intimate little act aroused in him a vague sentiment of hopefulness.

The dominoes were cleared away, a flowered cloth was spread on the table, and Graesler had a cup of coffee with the others before leaving.

As he walked home, he carried away the memory of a smile from Sabine and a gentle pressure of the hand, which would have charmed away tedium and vexation on even a dustier and hotter road.

Nevertheless, he thought he had better let a considerable interval elapse before revisiting the ranger's lodge. It was easier for him to wait than he had expected; his work had begun to mean more to him, and he was not only very careful in keeping the clinical histories of his patients, but he took pains to fill in the gaps that had gradually formed in his theoretical knowledge by studying medical books and periodicals. It was the influence of Sabine's personality working upon him. He knew it was, yet he would not allow himself to entertain serious hopes of winning the young woman for his wife. Whenever he dreamed of wooing and winning her and tried to picture life with her at his side, the disagreeable figure of the hotel manager at Lanzarote would come cropping up. There he'd be, welcoming the almost elderly doctor and his young wife with an impertinent smile. The spectre was persistent, as if Lanzarote were the one place in the world where Graesler could possibly practise in the winter, and as if the hotel manager were the one mortal who could imperil the happiness of his wedded life.

One morning at the end of the week Graesler met Sabine shopping.

'Why haven't we seen you for so long?' she asked.

'So few people come to the lodge, and those who do seldom have anything sensible to say. Next time you must tell us more about yourself and your adventures. We'd love to hear about them.' A look of quiet yearning lit up her eyes.

'If you think life out in the world so very interesting, then why do you shut yourself up here?'

'Things may change,' she answered simply. 'In fact my life was once a little different. Still at present I wouldn't want anything better.'

The light of yearning in her eyes died out.

Graesler prepared for his next visit to the ranger's lodge by searching his memory for incidents worth recounting. He was rather disappointed to find that a life that had outwardly seemed fairly eventful should be so barren of real content. Still a few things had happened that fairly resembled adventures and might make interesting stories. On a South Sea island there had been an attack by the natives and one of the mates of the steamer had been killed; a pair of lovers had committed suicide on the high seas; a cyclone had struck his steamer in the Indian Ocean; once he had landed at a Japanese port which had been devastated the day before by an earthquake; and once he had spent a night in an opium den. (The story of the wind-up of this episode would certainly have to be expurgated for the family circle.) Then there were a number of patients at various health resorts to tell about. He remembered them fairly well — bounders, eccentrics, a Russian grand duke who had been murdered and had had a presentiment of his end.

A chance question from Karl gave Graesler his opening. It was on a soft summer evening as he stood leaning idly against the porch railings at the lodge. Many of his fainter memories, he noticed as he talked, grew clearer and livelier, and all sorts of things that he had thought forgotten welled up from the depths of his being. Once he even had a shock of surprise to find himself exercising a hitherto unsuspected talent; he found himself inventing whenever his memory failed. Should he be glad or sorry? Well, he wouldn't blame himself too much. His little lies were bringing him a long-denied pleasure; he was for a time the central figure of a sympathetic circle; and in the dreamy peace of the ranger's lodge, his telling of the tales aroused in his own mind seductive echoes of vanished days.

On a subsequent visit, when Sabine and her mother were

receiving visitors in the garden – a rare occurrence – Graesler sat on the veranda with Schleheim, who rattled on in lively fashion concerning his former activities in municipal theatres and the opera houses of the lesser courts. Schleheim's persistent implication was that he had cause to regret the variety and splendour of his earlier life. After he had lost his voice, his father-in-law, a well-to-do wine merchant in the Rhineland, had given him the chance of going into business, but he had preferred a retreat to nature and solitude, where he would not be constantly reminded, as he would have been in a town, of what he had lost, and where there was nothing to hinder his enjoyment of all that was left to him. There in the lodge he could make the most of the pleasures of domesticity – he spoke with a tang of irony – and the admirable qualities of his children (which he again almost seemed to deplore).

'If only Sabine,' he said gloomily, 'had inherited my artistic temperament along with my talents, she would have had a splendid future.'

Graesler learned from Schleheim that for a time Sabine had made her home in Berlin with her mother's relatives – 'middle-class sort of people' – and had studied singing and dramatic art, but had given them up because she was disgusted by the somewhat loose moral tone of her fellow-students.

'Fräulein Sabine,' said Graesler, with an assenting nod, 'has a really pure soul.'

'Oh yes! But what good is it compared with the immense advantage of knowing life in all its heights and depths? Isn't that better than keeping one's soul pure?' Schleheim looked into the distance, and continued in a depressed tone: 'So, one fine day she threw over all her plans, or rather all my plans, for art and fame, and took up nursing – with a sense of the contrast, I'm sure. She was suddenly inspired with the belief that nursing was her peculiar vocation.'

Graesler shook his head.

'Nursing doesn't seem to have satisfied her either. I understand she gave it up too after a few years?'

'Thereby hangs a tale,' answered Schleheim. 'She became engaged to a young doctor, an able man, I believe, with excellent prospects. I never had the chance of meeting him –' Karl came to announce that coffee was being served under the pines – Schleheim ended rapidly under his breath: 'Unfortunately the young man died.'

'Died,' Graesler repeated, with not a trace of sympathy in his tone. He stared into space.

The doctor was introduced to the visitors, a widow and her two daughters, both younger than Sabine. They knew one another by sight, and a lively conversation set in over the coffee-cups.

'We see you go by every afternoon, Dr Graesler, punctually at a quarter to three,' said one of the girls. 'We'll be sitting at the window sewing, and you'll come out of the hotel, and take out your watch and hold it to your ear, and shake your head, and then hurry home.'

'What on earth is there so important for you to do?' asked the younger girl, her eyes dancing merrily. 'Don't tell me you always have patients waiting for you. I shan't believe it. Invalids never come to this so-called health resort. You know they don't. The interesting young man they wheel up and down in a bath-chair in front of the pump-room is hired by the management. He is really an actor from Berlin and plays the invalid here every summer in return for board and lodging. And the smart lady with the seventeen hats who's an American or Australian by the visitors' list, is just as good a European as the rest of us. When she was sitting on a bench in the public garden the other day talking to the officer in mufti who had come over from Eisenach to see her, she was not speaking English, but unmistakable Viennese.'

Graesler made no attempt to prove the genuineness of the American lady, who was the patient of another doctor, but he was able to vouch for a French married couple, who had travelled everywhere and thought this the most beautiful spot in the world.

That led to general praise of the loveliness of the forest and the hills, and the cosiness of the little town, which was at its best when the visitors had left.

'You really ought to spend a winter here,' said Frau Schleheim, turning to the doctor, 'then you'd know what a charming place it is.'

Graesler made no answer, but in his eyes were mirrored distant scenes which the others had not visited and were never likely to visit.

Some one proposed a stroll. On the walk, the others kept together at the outset; but soon, as if by design, Graesler was given a chance of going on ahead with Sabine, Herr Schleheim not being one of the party. He had preferred to stay at home and read a history of the French revolution – an epoch in which he claimed to have a special interest.

Graesler felt surer of himself today in Sabine's company, superior, more intimate. Having lost a betrothed to whom she might have been closer than her father and mother supposed, she might be looked upon as a young widow. That would help to bridge the difference in age between her and himself.

The pleasant day closed to the tunes from the town orchestra on the broad terrace outside the Kurhaus, where they took supper together. Herr Schleheim joined them at supper again, looking so elegant, in fact, so foppish that Graesler could not but feel an inconsistency with the Schleheim who was so deeply interested in the French revolution. Sabine's girl friends jokingly admired his appearance, while Sabine – if Graesler rightly interpreted her glance – did not find her father's garb wholly to her taste. But every one was in high spirits, and the younger girl had plenty of sly digs to poke at the other diners on the terrace. She promptly discovered the lady with the seventeen hats, who was seated at an adjoining table with three young men and one older man and nodded her head in time with a Viennese waltz in a way that was certainly not the custom in Australia.

When Dr Graesler felt a foot gently touch his for an instant he was almost startled. Was it Sabine? No, it could not have been; he was far from wishing anything of the kind. It must have been the merry girl opposite with a particularly innocent air. The soft contact was momentary, probably accidental. It was characteristic that Graesler preferred to accept this explanation, yet with little satisfaction. Excessive modesty, a certain self-deprecation was his worst fault; otherwise, at his age he would not still have been practising in a ridiculous little health resort; he would be holding an official position in a place like Wiesbaden or Ems. Though Sabine looked at him from time to time with obvious friendliness, and once raised her glass to him, smiling, the wine he drank again only increased his melancholy.

By degrees his low spirits seemed to infect the whole company. The two elder ladies showed signs of fatigue, the young girls' flow of conversation was arrested; the singer, in a brown study, silently smoked a big cigar. When the company finally broke up, Graesler felt he had never been so lonely in his life.

Frau Schleheim, as was to be expected, came back with an upset stomach from Berlin where she had gone to take Karl at the end of his vacation. Dr Graesler was called in again, with the result that he formed the habit of visiting the ranger's lodge every evening, and kept up the visits even after his patient had recovered. Often he spent hours alone with Sabine, sometimes in the house or out walking. Her parents, probably suspecting an understanding between the two that was by no means distasteful to them, usually kept out of the way.

Graesler talked to Sabine of his youth, of his native city, ancient, many-towered, and surrounded by a wall; of the house where his father and mother used to live, an old-fashioned place, where the rooms were always ready for him (and until recently had been ready for his sister) for a brief visit in the spring or autumn. Sabine listened sympathetically, and he could not but let his fancy play with the idea of how delightful it would be if he and she were to go back home together. He thought of how surprised his old friend Böhlinger, the lawyer, would be – the only person who still formed a sort of tie between himself and his native town.

Autumn began early that year, and with unusual vigour, and most of the health-seekers had fled. Graesler, finding that all the hours except those he spent at the ranger's lodge hung heavy on his hands, was so alarmed at the prospect of resuming his lonely, meaningless, barren, unsettled life, that he sometimes felt quite determined to make a formal proposal for Sabine's hand. Lacking the courage to ask her in plain terms, he chose a roundabout way. He set to work to make serious enquiries about Dr Frank's sanatorium. Sabine had mentioned it to him a second time. And he went to visit the proprietor, with whom he was acquainted.

Frank was an apathetic old fellow. He wore a dirty, yellow overall and looked, as he sat smoking a pipe on a white bench in front of the sanatorium, more like a queer sort of farmer than a doctor. Graesler asked him point-blank whether there was any truth in the rumour that he wanted to dispose of the institution. Frank, it seemed, had merely dropped a hint here and there of his intention to retire, and had really been waiting for a sign.

'The sooner I can get rid of the place,' he said, 'the better pleased I shall be. I haven't many years to look forward to, and I should like to spend them as far away as possible from real and imaginary invalids. I have had to tell a hundred thousand lies during my professional career, and I'm sick of it. You can take it on all right,' he continued. 'You are still a young chap' – an assertion which Graesler countered with a melancholy gesture of dissent.

Frank led him over the building. Graesler was sorry to find that it was even more neglected and decayed than he had feared. Worse than that, the few patients he met in the garden, the corridors, and the inhalation-room, had a discontented and unhappy look, and their attitude towards the superintendent seemed to be suspicious, if not positively hostile. But when he came to the little balcony of the superintendent's dwelling-house, looking beyond the garden across the charming valley towards the gently rising mist-clad hills on the other side (where the ranger's lodge lay), he suddenly felt his heart go out in yearning towards Sabine. For the first time he frankly admitted to himself that his feeling for her was love. How delightful it would be to stand with his arm around her on this very spot, and hand over to her as his wife and helpmate the whole property which by then he would have had renovated and embellished. He had to keep a tight hand on himself and leave without coming to terms with Dr Frank, who, for his part, preserved his wonted indifference in the matter.

At the ranger's lodge that evening, Graesler thought it best to say nothing of his visit to the sanatorium; but the very next day he asked his friend Adelmann, the architect who was one of his daily companions at supper in the 'Silver Lion', to come with him and give an expert's opinion on Frank's place. It proved that the repairs needed would be less extensive and less costly than Graesler had feared. Adelmann was confident that the sanatorium could be made as good as new by 1 May next year. In his attitude toward Dr Frank and his terms Graesler continued to hesitate, though Adelmann, when the two had come away together, strongly advised him to conclude the advantageous bargain.

That same evening, warm as summer again, Graesler was seated with Sabine and her parents on the verandah of the ranger's lodge. He began to speak, as if casually, of his conversation with Dr Frank, pretending that Frank had happened to come out of the gate of the sanatorium when Graesler and the architect were passing by.

Herr Schleheim also thought the terms excellent and advised Graesler to give up the idea of practising that winter in the south, and to concentrate his attention on the important affair here at hand. But Graesler would not hear of this. It would be impossible, he said, for him to wind up his affairs in Lanzarote without another visit; and he would have no anxiety about the repairs and renovations at the sanatorium if they were in the hands of anyone so trustworthy as his friend Adelmann.

Sabine intervened in her simple and direct fashion.

'Why shouldn't I supervise the work while you are away? I'd send you regular reports.'

Soon after this the parents, as if by concerted arrangement, disappeared into the house, and Sabine and Graesler, following what by now had become their custom, strolled up and down the avenue. Sabine had a number of excellent proposals to make regarding the renovation of the old building. Apparently she had been turning the matter over in her mind. 'You'll need a lady, a real lady,' she insisted, 'as matron of the establishment. That chiefly is what the place has lacked of late years – social supervision, the sort that only a true lady can give.'

Graesler's heart beat fast. The decisive word had been spoken; he had been given his cue. He believed he was about to make the appropriate response when Sabine, as if divining his intention, added rather hurriedly:

'An advertisement will be the best way of finding what you want. If I were you, I'd even go on a trip on the chance of securing the right person for so important a position. You've plenty of time on your hands just now. I suppose your patients have all gone home? . . . When are you yourself thinking of leaving?'

'In – four or five days. First of all, of course, I have to go home, to my home town, I mean. My friend Böhlinger, my lawyer, writes that there are several matters he must discuss with me regarding my sister's estate. Before I leave, I shall visit the sanatorium again and go into everything most carefully. But I shall not be able to come to a final decision without consulting Böhlinger.'

He went on talking at random, guardedly and awkwardly, and profoundly dissatisfied with his own behaviour. The occasion demanded clearness and resolution, he told himself. Sabine was persistently silent; so he thought it best to plead a professional engagement and leave. He held Sabine's hand a few moments, then raised it to his lips and kissed it fervently. She made no attempt to withdraw it, and when he looked up he thought her expression seemed more contented, even brighter.

He mustn't say anything more. He let go her hand, got into the carriage, wrapped the rug round his knees, and motioned to the driver to start. Sabine still stood where he had left her, motionless in the pale light. She wasn't looking at him as he drove off – was she? Apparently not. She seemed to be staring into the void of the night.

Next morning there was a cheerless drizzle. Joylessly, simply as a matter of duty, Graesler went to make a third inspection of the sanatorium. He was taken around by a very youthful medical assistant who was exceedingly polite out of respect, not so much to the senior colleague as to the person who seemed likely to be the new superintendent and proprietor. The young man seized every opportunity to indicate his familiarity with the most up-to-date therapeutic methods, and was loud in regrets that under present conditions there were no means of applying them in the institution.

To Graesler the whole place seemed even more neglected than it had done the day before, the garden even more of a wilderness. When he went to Dr Frank's office, he found the superintendent in a badly furnished room just beginning his breakfast, amid a litter of bills and other business documents. Graesler told him he couldn't come to a final decision that morning and matters would have to stand over for about three weeks until he returned from his home town. Frank listened with his habitual apathy, merely remarking that in that case he should naturally feel at liberty to entertain other offers.

Walking back to town through the rain Graesler had a sense of renewed freedom. His umbrella dripped, the hills were shrouded in fog, it was cold, his fingers were nipped, he had to put on his gloves – a rather awkward job when you're also trying to hold up an umbrella. He shook his head disapprovingly. Now that he had grown used to a southern climate would he ever be able to accustom himself to passing a whole winter in this miscalled temperate zone? He almost wished it were possible to tell Sabine that very evening that the sanatorium had been snapped up by a brisker purchaser – and that Graesler wished him joy of his bargain!

On his return to his rooms he found a letter addressed in Sabine's handwriting. His heart seemed to stop beating. What could she have to write to him about? There was only one possibility. She must be asking him to discontinue his visits. That kissing of her hand yesterday – he had been sure of it in an instant – had spoiled the whole affair. It was not the sort of thing that came gracefully from him. He must have looked a perfect fool. Hardly knowing how, Graesler opened the envelope, and read the letter.

Dear Friend, I may call you that, mayn't I? You are coming to see me again this evening, but I want you to get this letter first. For, unless I write to you, perhaps you will go away this evening again just as you have done all these days and evenings, and will go on your trip without having spoken a word, persuading yourself that you have acted wisely. There is nothing left but for me to speak – or rather, since I cannot bring myself to speak, for me to write out my mind to you.

Well, then, dear Dr Graesler, my dear friend Dr Graesler, here I am writing to you, and you will read what I have written, will perhaps find it not unwelcome, and will, I hope, not consider me unwomanly because I feel that I can write to tell you that I should not take it amiss were you to ask me to be your wife. There you have it in plain terms. I should like to marry you. I feel a great, cordial friendship for you such as I have not felt for any human being before. Not love – not yet. But something akin to love, and something which may very well grow into love. During these last days, whenever you spoke of your impending journey, I had quite a strange feeling at my heart.

This evening, when you kissed my hand, it was lovely. But then, when you drove away into the darkness, I felt as if all were over, and as if you were never coming back again.

Of course that mood has passed. Those were only night thoughts. I know you are coming again. You will be here tomorrow evening. I know, too, that you like me just as much as I like you. One feels such things before they have found expression in words.

But it seems to me sometimes that you are a little lacking in self-confidence. You are, aren't you? I have been wondering why. I think it must be because you have never struck roots anywhere, and because in your whole life you have never stayed anywhere long enough to allow some one to make a strong impression on your heart. I think that must be the reason.

But perhaps there is another cause for your hesitation. I don't find it easy to write about, yet, now that I have begun, I must go on. You know, I was once engaged to be married. Four years ago. He was a doctor, like yourself. My father probably told you about him. I loved him deeply. It was a terrible blow to me when he died. He was so young, only twenty-eight. I thought, as people always do then, that I should never get over it.

But he was not my first love. Before that, I had a passion for a singer. That was when my father, with the best intentions in the world, was trying to force me into a career for which I was not naturally fitted. My fondness for the singer was the most passionate feeling I have ever experienced. But "experienced" is not the right word; I ought to say "felt". The whole thing ended rather stupidly. The man fancied he had to do with the same sort of creature that he was used to in his own circle, and behaved accordingly. I refused to have anything more to do with him.

The strange thing is that I think of him much oftener than of my betrothed, of whom I was so fond.

We were engaged for six months. That brings me to something which I find it rather difficult to speak of. Do you know what I imagine? You suspect what is not true; that is why you hesitate. Of course, it is a proof of the depth of your feeling for me. But at the same time it is – forgive me – to some extent a sign of priggishness or vanity. Doubtless vanity and priggishness on this particular point are common in men. Let me assure you, you need not entertain the suspicion. Must I speak more plainly? Well – I have no confessions to make regarding my past. When I look back upon my relation with my betrothed, I realize it was rather a strange one. In the whole six months I don't believe he kissed me more than a dozen times.

In the night time, you see, one can write out one's heart to a good friend – especially when one reflects that the letter need not be sent after all. Besides, of what use would the letter be unless I were frank and wrote everything that came into my head.

I loved him dearly, for the very reason that he was so grave, so tinged with melancholy. He was one of those rare doctors to whom all the suffering they witness becomes matter for personal suffering. Seeing that he took life so hardly, how could he pluck up heart to be happy? My dream was that I should be able to teach him. Fate willed otherwise. You shall see his photograph. Of course I have one.

I have not kept the singer's photograph. He didn't give it to me. I bought it before I met him.

How I do run! It is past midnight. I am still sitting at my writing table with no wish to come to an end. I hear my father pacing the room below. He has such restless nights now. We have troubled ourselves very little about him lately. You and I, I mean. This must not continue.

Oh, here is another matter – a proposal you must take in the spirit in which it is meant. About the sanatorium. My father says that if you cannot at the moment put your hand on the purchase money, he is quite ready to help you out. In fact, I think he would like to have a share in the business.

While we are on the subject of the sanatorium, and if you understand what I am driving at in this letter (I have made my meaning fairly plain!), you can perhaps save yourself the trouble of the advertisements and the journeys; I can confidently recommend myself for the position of matron.

Don't you think it would be delightful, Dr Graesler, if we were to work together in the institution as comrades – I had almost written 'as colleagues'!

Let me confess, I have been interested in the sanatorium a long time. Longer than its future superintendent ... The position and the grounds are lovely. It is such a pity that Dr Frank has allowed everything to go to rack and ruin. Another mistake is that for some time he has been accepting any patients that offered, without caring whether they were suitable cases or not. It seems to me the place should be reserved for the treatment of nervous diseases – excluding serious mental cases.

Why should I write all this? These suggestions could very well wait till tomorrow, whether or not we come to an understanding upon the main point of the letter.

Perhaps you may make it one object of your journey to push the interests of the sanatorium in Berlin and other large towns. When I was a nurse, I got to know some of the Berlin consultants, and perhaps they will remember me. I can see you smiling at this. Never mind. My letter is no ordinary one. An ill-natured man might say something about a woman forcing herself on him, but you are not ill-natured and will not think the worse of me.

Though my feeling for you is not romantic, it is very real. Partly too, I am sorry for your loneliness. Most probably I should never have written you this letter if your sister had still been alive. And perhaps I am fond of you because I admire you as a doctor. Yes, I really do. Some people might find your professional manner a little cold. But that is only your way. Fundamentally, you are sympathetic and good. The essential thing is that you inspire confidence in your patients, as you did in Mother first, and then in Father – and that is how it all began!

When you come tomorrow, I will make it easy for you. You need merely smile, or kiss my hand again as you kissed it on parting this evening, and then I shall know it is all right.

Otherwise, if things are not as I fancy, say so bluntly. You need not be afraid. We shall shake hands on it. I shall cherish the memory of the pleasant hours we have had together this summer, and I shall tell myself not to be presumptuous, or to plume myself any longer on the idea of being Frau Doktor or even Frau Direktor – dignities which do not, in truth, allure me so very, very much.

Please note, too, that if you should marry some one else, if next year you should bring back from Lanzarote as wife some beautiful American or Australian (warranted genuine!), my offer to supervise the building work at the sanatorium holds good, should you take the place over from Dr Frank. These are two fundamentally distinct proposals.

Well, it is really time for me to stop. I am quite curious to know whether I shall decide tomorrow morning to send you this letter. What do you think?

Good-bye. Till we meet!

My love to you. Whatever happens, I shall still be

> Your friend,
> Sabine.

Dr Graesler sat long over this letter. He reread it, and then read it a third time, and was still uncertain whether its contents made him happy or sad.

This much was clear, that Sabine was willing to marry him. To use her own words, she almost forced herself on him. Yet, as she herself admitted, the feeling that moved her was not love. She regarded him with too discerning, he might even say, too critical, an eye. She had correctly observed that he was priggish, vain, cold, irresolute – qualities he didn't deny in himself, but Sabine would scarcely have noticed or spoken about them had he been ten or fifteen years younger.

He could not but ask himself:

'If my faults are so obvious to her at long range and she doesn't forget to touch upon them even in her letter, what will happen later, in the intimacy of daily life, when many other faults of mine inevitably come to light? I shall constantly have to be on the watch, minding my P's and Q's. I shall have to play a part; which at my age will be far from easy. And it won't be easy to transform a morose, priggish, comfortably set-in-his-ways old bachelor into a charming, gallant young husband. Things might go on all right for a time. Sabine is certainly sympathetic toward me, you might almost say maternally tender. But how long would that last? Not long. Until some devil of a singer, or a melancholy young doctor, or some other seductive male should turn up to win the favours of the pretty young wife. And the winning of the favours would be all the easier as marriage would have ripened her and given her experience.'

The clock struck half-past one – long past meal time.

'Bother!' thought Graesler, and conscious, with a fierce obstinacy, of his priggish exactness, he hurried to the inn. At table he found the architect and one of the municipal councillors sitting in their corner over the coffee and cigars. The councillor nodded meaningly to the doctor.

'I hear we have to congratulate you.'

'What for?' said Graesler, startled.

'You've bought Dr Frank's sanatorium, haven't you?'

Graesler gave a sigh of relief.

'Bought it? Not yet, nowhere near it yet. It depends upon all sorts of things. The old hulk is in terrible disrepair, it practically needs rebuilding. And our friend here' – he was studying the bill of fare and lightly indicated the architect – 'runs up the costs—'

Adelmann protested hotly: he didn't want to make money from the work, and the buildings were not as bad as Graesler represented.

'If the contracts are made at once, the place will be as good as new by 15 May at the latest.'

Graesler shrugged his shoulders. He reminded the architect that the day before he had said 1 May at the latest.

'Besides,' he said, 'you know as well as I do that building never proceeds according to programme. There are always delays, and the costs always mount higher than the estimate. I don't feel fresh enough to go in for such things. On top of it all, Frank is asking a ridiculous price. How do I know' – he meant this in fun – 'how do I know, Mr Architect, whether you aren't working hand in glove with him?'

Adelmann flared up, the councillor tried to smooth matters over, Graesler apologized, but harmony was not to be restored. The two men soon got up to go with a cool good-bye, leaving Graesler alone to his dissatisfaction with himself.

Graesler hurried back home without touching the last course. A patient about to leave the health resort was there awaiting final instructions for the winter. The doctor prescribed the regimen inattentively and impatiently, and when the fee was handed him he accepted it with an uneasy conscience, annoyed, not only with himself, but also with Sabine, because in her letter she had not omitted to accuse him of indifference towards his patients.

He went out on the balcony and relighted his cigar. The garden looked miserable, but there, in spite of the poor weather, was his housekeeper sitting on a white bench as she did every day at this hour, with her work-basket beside her and knitting in her hands. Three or four years ago the elderly person had certainly had designs upon him. At least, Friederike had repeatedly said so. But then Friederike had always believed that her brother was surrounded by maids and widows eager to marry who lay in wait to pounce upon him. Heaven knows he had had many a narrow escape.

But he was born to be a bachelor. All his life he had been an eccentric, an egoist, an old fogey. Even Sabine had become aware of this. Her letter showed she had, with compelling clearness, even though for various reasons, least among which was love, she had flung herself, metaphorically speaking, into his arms. But if she had really flung herself into his arms, the whole thing would have worn a different aspect. The letter rustling in his coat pocket was anything but a love letter.

The carriage that came every day to take Graesler to the ranger's lodge was announced. His heart beat faster. He couldn't conceal from himself that there was only one thing for him to do – go to Sabine as fast as he could, take the dear hands that had been so heartily and unreservedly held out to him, and ask the sweet creature to marry him – even at the risk of losing his happiness again at the end of a few years or even months.

But instead of rushing down stairs, he remained as if rooted to the spot. Something – something, he felt, must first be cleared up in his mind once and for all. What could it be? Ah, now he had it. He must first read Sabine's letter through again.

He went to the consulting room, where he could quietly let what she said work its influence upon him.

He read slowly, with strained care, and at every word felt his heart grow colder. Every thing warm and fond in the letter willy-nilly seemed cold, even mocking. When he came to the passages in which Sabine touched on his reserve, his vanity, his priggishness, she seemed intentionally repeating the things she had already reproached him with in the morning, unjustly and *ad nauseam*. How could it occur to her to call him a prig, an old fogey when he had been ready, gladly ready, to pardon her without question if she had been guilty of a digression from the straight path. So far from divining this in even the slightest degree, she attributed his holding back to just that. Shows how little she knew him! Exactly. She didn't understand him.

Here was a new light shed upon the whole riddle of his existence. No one had ever really understood him, neither man nor woman. Not his parents, nor his sister, nor his colleagues, nor his patients. His reserve was taken for coldness, his sense of order for priggishness, his seriousness, for dryness. That was why, being a man without either dash or sparkle, he was destined to life-long solitude. And just because he was that sort of man and because he was so many years older than Sabine, he neither could nor ought to accept the happiness she was ready to bring him – or believed she was ready to bring him – the happiness that would probably be Dead Sea fruit.

He snatched up a sheet of writing paper.

'Dear Fräulein Sabine,' he began, 'Your letter has stirred me profoundly. How can I thank you, I who am a lonely and elderly man ...'

'Nonsense!' he thought, tore up the letter and made a fresh start.

My dear Sabine:

I have received your letter, your good, lovely letter. It has moved me to the core. How can I thank you? You reveal the possibility of a happiness I had hardly dared to dream of. And not having dared to dream of it I don't dare either to grasp it – at least not right away. Give me a few days. Let me come to the consciousness of my happiness. And you, Sabine, ask yourself again whether you really and truly want to entrust your gracious youth to me, a mature man.

It is a good thing, perhaps, that I must go back, as you know, to my home city. I mean now to go sooner – tomorrow morning, instead of Thursday. So we shan't see each other for about two weeks. That will give time for everything to settle itself in your mind and mine.

Unfortunately I can't express myself as beautifully as you do. If only you could read my heart. But I know you won't misunderstand. I think I'd better not visit the lodge today. This letter will be my good-bye instead – my good-bye for a few days. May I write to you while I am away, and will you write to me? My address will be 17 Burggraben.

As I said, I will confer with my lawyer about the sanatorium. So for the present I won't take up your father's kind offer. Give him my sincerest thanks. Besides it may be well to get the advice of an outside architect. This is not a slur, though, on the one here. But all this can be considered later.

Good-bye, Sabine. Give my kind regards to your parents. Tell them an urgent telegram from my lawyer has called me away a few days earlier. In two weeks then. I hope to find everything unchanged when I come back. With what impatience I shall await your answer. Now I must close. I thank you. I kiss your dear hands. Till we meet again. To our next happy meeting.

Your friend,
Emil Graesler.

He folded the letter. Several times, writing it, he had felt tears in his eyes from a vague emotion on his own account and Sabine's. But now that he had reached a temporary decision, his eyes were dry, and he was perfectly composed when he handed the letter to the driver with instructions to deliver it at the ranger's lodge. From the window, he watched the carriage start off. He was about to call to the man to turn back, but the words died on his lips, and soon the carriage was out of sight.

Graesler then set about preparing for the journey. There was little time and so much to do and think of that his mind was wholly engrossed for a while; but when, a little later, it occurred to him that by now the letter must be in Sabine's hands, he had a real physical hurt at his heart. Would she send an answer right away? Or would she just get into the carriage and come to fetch her irresolute lover? Ah, then indeed she'd have to say that she really was throwing herself at him.

But her love wasn't strong enough to stand such a test. She did not come. Nor did an answer to his letter come. At dusk he saw the carriage drive by with a chance fare inside.

That night he slept badly, and the next morning it was a chilly, depressed Dr Graesler that drove to the station with the rain rattling down sharply on the hood of the open carriage.

An agreeable surprise was awaiting Dr Graesler at home. Though it was at the eleventh hour that he had sent notice of his coming, he found his rooms not only in perfect order, but far more comfortably furnished than at his last visit. He realized why. In the previous autumn Friederike had stayed alone in the apartment for a few days and later had told him that she had bought new furniture and had arranged with good workmen for decorations and repairs. Throughout the winter she had kept up a correspondence with Böhlinger about the execution of the orders. When Graesler went through the apartment the second time and came to the room giving upon the courtyard which had been his sister's, he sighed gently, partly in deference to his caretaker, a compositor's wife, who accompanied him, and also in honest mourning. What a pity, he thought, that his sister could not have seen the familiar room in its new pleasant furnishing and lighted by electricity.

Graesler unpacked, interrupting the work every now and then to roam through the flat, take down a book from the shelves, put it back unread, and look down at the narrow, almost deserted street, where the lamp at the corner was mirrored in the wet pavement. Then he sat down before the writing table in the chair that he had inherited from his father and read the newspaper. To his sorrowful surprise he found himself feeling far, far away from Sabine. Not only that he was separated from her by space. More than that – the letter in which she had offered herself to him and which had made him take to flight, seemed to have reached him, not yesterday, but many weeks before. When he took it out of his pocket, it seemed to breathe out something sharp and disturbing. It made him nervous. Afraid he might be tempted to read it again, he locked it up in a drawer.

Next morning he didn't know what to do with himself either that day or in the days to follow. He had long been a stranger in his native town; some of his former friends were dead, and the ties with those who remained had been gradually loosened, though his sister, whenever they came back, had usually gone to call upon the elderly folk who had belonged to their parents' circle. As a matter of fact, Graesler had no other business here than the talk with Böhlinger. But even that was not urgent.

The first thing he did was what he always did when he had been away a long time; he took a long walk all over the city. Usually, in fact regularly, he had experienced a sort of gentle, soothing melancholy. This time, under the grey leaden sky, no such feeling stirred him. With no emotion of any sort, he passed the house from whose tall, narrow turret window his boyhood sweetheart had greeted him with stolen nods and smiles as he went by on his way to the high school. The murmur of the fountain playing in the autumn-tinted park left him unmoved – the park he himself had seen developed from the old town moat. He visited the courtyard of the famous Town Hall, then rounded the corner to where in a narrow alley stood an ancient, dilapidated building. Yes, there was the place, with shades half drawn and the indicative red curtains behind which he had had his first pitiful adventure followed by weeks of terror. Nothing but dusty, misty shreds seemed to rise up from his boyhood days.

The first person he spoke to was the white-bearded tobacconist of whom he bought his cigars. The man in a long-winded way commiserated him on his sister's death. Graesler hardly knew how to answer. He left the shop in dread of meeting other acquaintances and having to listen to the same meaningless phrases. But the next friend did not recognize him, and the third friend, who looked as if he meant to stop and talk, received a hasty greeting that was barely civil.

After luncheon, which he took in a familiar old inn (now extravagantly redecorated), Graesler went to see Böhlinger. The lawyer, who had already been informed of his arrival in the town, greeted him with quiet friendliness, said a few words of condolence, and asked for details of Friederike's death.

Graesler lowered his eyes and told the story of the tragedy in a subdued voice. Looking up he was rather amazed to see a fat old man sitting opposite him. In the doctor's memory, Böhlinger's face had always remained youthful; now it looked sallow and worn. The lawyer was obviously moved. For a long time he sat silent, then shrugged his shoulders and turned to his desk as if to say that there was nothing for the living to do after such an awful event but to set themselves resolutely to the tasks immediately before them.

He took out Friederike's will and other important papers and proceeded to explain about her estate. Graesler was her sole heir, and her savings amounted to a good deal more than he had expected. As Böhlinger made plain, Graesler could, if he wanted to, be able from now on to live upon his private income modestly but comfortably without having to practise medicine.

The very disclosure of this possibility made the doctor realize that for him the day of retirement had not yet come; he felt he had been born with a vigorous impulse to activity. He said so to Böhlinger and told him about the sanatorium and how far the negotiations for its purchase had advanced.

The lawyer went into the matter in detail. At first he seemed inclined to approve the plan, then hesitated about advising Graesler to go ahead with it. More than mere medical skill, he pointed out, would be necessary. For one thing the head of the institution would also have to have ease of social intercourse. This he allowed Graesler possessed in an eminent degree. For another thing he required business ability, and business ability was something Graesler had not yet had the opportunity to display.

The doctor had to admit Böhlinger was right and wondered whether it would not be well to tell him about Miss Schleheim, who would be quite equal to the business end of things. But the old bachelor of a lawyer would be the last person in the world to understand so peculiar an affair of the heart. Graesler knew he never missed a chance to speak slightingly, even cynically of women, and he wouldn't trust himself to listen quietly to a flippant remark about Sabine.

Böhlinger had not kept secret from Graesler the reason why he had so low an opinion of women. Once a year a masked ball was held in the town at which burgher society rubbed shoulders with the stage and even with persons of a more dubious moral standing. At one of these balls, Böhlinger, quite casually, had enjoyed the last favours of a lady whom no one would have dreamt of suspecting of such wanton conduct. She kept her mask on even in the intoxication of passion and believed that the secret of her identity had been preserved. By a strange chance, however, Böhlinger learned who she was, but he kept the name of the fair one strictly to himself. Consequently there was soon not a girl or a woman in the town upon whom Graesler's suspicions had not lighted; and the more spotless the lady's reputation, the stronger his suspicions.

This adventure was responsible for Böhlinger's determination to shun marriage or an intimate relationship with any woman of his own town. So the highly esteemed lawyer in a city greatly prizing respectability had to gather the rest of his experiences away from the city. He made frequent short trips which served only to confirm him in his bitter attitude towards the sex.

It would have been unwise, therefore, on Graesler's part to draw Sabine's name into the conversation. Very unwise, especially as he may have, by releasing the sweet, pure creature who had thrown herself into his arms, lost her forever. He said little more about his plans, turning the matter off by saying he had decided to await further reports from the architect. He then invited Böhlinger less cordially than he had meant to, to look him up shortly at his house on the Burggraben. Mention of his house recalled to him that he owed Böhlinger thanks for his supervision of the renovating.

'Oh, never mind about thanks,' said Bölinger modestly, 'but I'll be glad to see the place again. It's filled with memories for me too, you know, of a past alas! rather remote.'

As the two shook hands good-bye the friends looked one another in the face. Böhlinger's eyes showed a tendency to turn moist, but Graesler could detect in himself no trace of the feeling he had been vainly expecting throughout the day. It might have taken the bad taste away from this hour and raised it to a higher level.

On the street Graesler's sense of inner emptiness amounted almost to torture. The weather had cleared, and it was not so cold. He walked down the main thoroughfare, and was glad – mildly glad – to see from the shop windows that even his home town was beginning to show clear signs of the influence of modern taste. He went into a haberdasher's shop to buy a hat and a few other trifles.

Instead of the stiff sort of hat that he was accustomed to wear, he chose a sombrero. The mirror assured him it was more becoming; and out on the street in the growing dusk, he felt certain he was not fooling himself when he thought that the women threw him friendly glances. It occurred to him that a letter from Sabine might have come, and he hurried home. There were quite a number of letters forwarded from the health resort – nothing from Sabine. He overcame his disappointment by telling himself he had expected the impossible.

He went out again, and resumed his aimless stroll. After a time he decided to board a tram. He remained on the back platform of the car, and noticed, for the first time with a touch of melancholy, that where there had been meadows and plough-lands in the days of his boyhood, there were now the houses of a suburb. After most of the passengers had left the car, it struck him that no conductor had come to collect his fare. Looking round for the man he encountered two eyes scanning him quiz-zically. They belonged to a young, rather pale-faced girl who had been standing beside him on the platform. She was dressed in a light dress, simple but tasteful.

'You are puzzled because the conductor does not come?' she said, glancing up with a gay smile from beneath the brim of her soft straw hat.

'Precisely,' he rejoined, a trifle stiffly.

'There isn't any conductor,' the girl explained. 'In front, at the driver's end, you'll find a box. You drop your money in there.'

'Thanks,' said the doctor, and did as he was told. 'I'm very much obliged to you,' he repeated when he returned to the platform. 'A very practical arrangement, especially for rascals.'

'Rascals wouldn't have a chance here. We are all honest people.'

'I am sure you are. What will the passengers have taken me for?'

'For what you are, a foreigner. You are, aren't you?' She looked at him inquisitively.

'You might call me that.' Graesler gazed into space, then faced round to his companion and asked: 'What sort of a foreigner do you take me for?'

'Now, of course, hearing you speak I can tell you are a German, perhaps even a German from near here. But first I thought you were from far away, from Spain or Portugal.'

'Portugal?' Graesler involuntarily put his hand to his hat. 'No, I am not a Portuguese. But I have been in Portugal.'

'I should have thought so. You must have travelled a lot?'

'A bit.' Graesler's eyes lighted up a little with the recollection of the strange lands and seas he had seen. It pleased him that the girl's expression now showed, besides curiosity, a certain admiration.

'I get off here.' The announcement came unexpectedly. 'I hope you have a pleasant stay in our town.'

'Thanks, many thanks,' said Graesler, raising his hat.

The girl left and nodded good-bye from the sidewalk – more familiarly than was to be expected from so brief an acquaintance. On a bold impulse, Graesler jumped off the car, which had already started, and went up to the girl, who stood still in surprise.

'You were good enough to wish me a pleasant stay here. Our acquaintanceship has begun so promisingly, and perhaps . . .'

'Promisingly!' interrupted the girl. 'What do you mean?'

That sounded like a genuine rebuff, and Graesler continued more modestly:

'I mean, your conversation is so charming, and it would really be a pity . . .'

She shrugged her shoulders.

'I am almost at home, and my people expect me to supper.'

'Just a quarter of an hour.'

'I really can't manage it. Good-night.' She turned to go.

'One moment, please,' exclaimed Graesler, almost with fear in his tone.

The girl waited and smiled. 'We don't want our acquaintanceship to end so abruptly.'

She looked up at him smiling from under the brim of her dark straw hat.

'Of course not,' she said. 'That would be impossible. We know one another now. If I should meet you anywhere, I should recognize you at once as – the gentleman from Portugal.'

'But I don't want to wait for a chance meeting. What if we were to arrange for another talk like this – about an hour together?'

'An hour? You must have a lot of time to spare.'

'As much time as you please.'

'Unfortunately the same isn't true of me.'

'Nor of me always,' said Graesler.

'Are you on a holiday?'

'In a way. You see, I'm a doctor. Allow me to introduce myself. Dr Emil Graesler – born here and living here,' he added, quickly as if excusing himself.

The girl smiled.

'Here!' she said. 'My, how you can sham! A person had better be careful of you!' She shook her head looking up at him.

'But when can I see you again?' urged Graesler.

She thought a moment.

'If it really won't bore you, you can see me home again tomorrow.'

'Delighted. Where shall I meet you?'

'The best would be for you to walk up and down opposite the place where I am employed, Kleimann's glove shop, 24 Wilhelmstrasse. We close at seven. Then, if you like, you can ride back on the tram with me.' She smiled.

'Is that really all the time you have to spare?'

'How can I help it? I must be home by eight o'clock.'

'Do you live with your parents?'

She glanced up at him again.

'I see I must tell you who I am. My name is Katharina Rebner, my father is a postal employee, we live over there in the second storey, where you see the open window. There are three of us, father, mother and myself. I have a sister, but she is married, and she and her husband are spending the evening with us; they come every Thursday. That's why I must go right home.'

'This evening, but surely not every evening,' Graesler put in quickly.

'What do you mean?'

'Surely you don't spend all your evenings at home? You must visit your girl friends sometimes, or go to the theatre?'

'Girls like me don't often have the chance.'

Katharina nodded to a man passing on the other side of the street. From his dress he seemed to be a workman of the better sort. He was not young and was carrying a parcel. Without seeming to notice Graesler he nodded in return.

'My brother-in-law. My sister must already be there. I really must go.'

'I hope my having come with you won't make trouble for you at home.'

'Trouble? I'm grown up, I'm happy to say, and my people know me by this time. Well, good-bye.'

'Tomorrow, then?'

'All right.'

'Seven o'clock in the Wilhelmstrasse.'

Katharina did not move away. She seemed to be turning something over in her mind.

'Yes, at seven. But –' she hesitated, 'you spoke of the theatre. You won't be cross with me . . .'

'Why should I be cross with you?'

'I mean for reminding you of what you said. If you were to bring tickets for the theatre along, it would be so nice. I haven't been for such a long time.'

'I'd be only too glad to. It'll make me happy to do that little favour for you.'

'But don't get expensive seats, the sort you're probably used to. I shouldn't have any fun sitting in expensive seats.'

'Don't you worry, Fräulein – Fräulein Katharina.'

'Then you're sure you're not angry with me?'

'But Fräulein Katharina, angry – !'

She held out her hand.

'I really must hurry now. Tomorrow I shan't have to get home so early.'

She turned and left so quickly that Graesler missed the expression of her face, but there was a hint of promise in her voice.

As soon as he was back in his rooms the thought of Sabine returned and awakened a keen yearning. He had an irresistible impulse to write her, if only a few lines. So he sat down and told of his safe arrival, that he had found his flat in perfect order, had had a long but not conclusive talk with his old friend Böhlinger, and intended to make good use of his time the next day by visiting the hospital, where a former fellow-student was in charge of a ward. He signed himself 'your sincere friend, Emil'. He hurried out once again to take the letter to the station himself so that it would catch the night train.

Next morning Graesler carried out the plan he had written Sabine, and visited the hospital. The physician-in-chief gave him a cordial welcome and permitted him to accompany the members of the staff on their rounds. His interest was gratifying to himself at least. In regard to some of the more notable cases he asked for fuller information as to the course of the trouble, and the treatment, and did not even hesitate to express dissent once or twice, though always with the deprecating reservation: 'As far as a health-resort physician like myself is competent to form an opinion, and to keep in touch with the advance of medical science.'

At luncheon he joined some of the assistant physicians in a modest restaurant opposite the hospital and enjoyed himself so much talking shop with his young colleagues that he determined to come often. On the way home he bought the tickets for the theatre. Back in his rooms again he turned over the pages of his medical books and newspapers. But as the hours passed, his attention wandered more and more, distracted partly by the expectation of news from Sabine, partly by vague imaginings of how the evening would go. To prepare for all eventualities he decided to arrange for cold cuts and a couple of bottles of wine in the flat – this would not commit him to anything. He made the necessary purchases, ordered them to be sent home, and a few minutes before seven was pacing up and down the Wilhelmstrasse – not with the romantic hat of the previous evening. For one thing, he did not wish to be conspicuous: for another he thought it would be a test of the genuineness of Katharina's feelings if he wore his usual hard black Derby.

He was looking into a shop window when Katharina's voice sounded behind him:

'Good evening, Dr Graesler.'

He turned round, shook hands with her, and was delighted with the charming, well-dressed girl who might have been taken to be a well-bred young lady of the middle class – which, as a matter of fact, she was, Graesler hastened to remind himself, her father being a civil servant.

'I say,' she said promptly, 'what do you think my brother-in-law took you for?'

'I have no idea. A Portuguese – he too?'

'No, no. He thought you were a musician, a band-master. He said you looked exactly like a band-master he once knew.'

'Well, did you tell him I was something better or worse?'

'I told him what you really are. Wasn't that all right?'

'I certainly have no reason to make a secret of my profession. Did you tell your people that you were going to the theatre with me this evening?'

'It's no business of theirs. Besides, they never question me, and anyhow I might have been going to the theatre alone if I liked, mightn't I?'

'Of course. But – I like this way better.'

She looked at him, putting one hand up to the brim of her hat, which was a trick of hers.

'Going alone's no fun. Theatre's nice only in company. Some one must sit beside you who laughs, and you can look at, and . . .'

'And what? Go on.'

'And whose arm you can press when it's particularly delightful.'

'I hope you find it particularly delightful tonight. At all events I shall be at your disposal.'

She laughed lightly and quickened her pace, as if afraid they'd come late.

'We're too early,' said Graesler, when they reached the theatre. 'It won't begin for another quarter of an hour.'

She didn't listen to him. With sparkling eyes she led the way to the upper circle, hardly noticing when he helped her off with her coat. Not until they were seated side by side in the third row did she give him a look of thanks.

Graesler glanced about the moderate-sized audience to see

if there was anyone he knew. Here and there he noticed a face he succeeded in remembering. But certainly in the dim light of the upper circle no one would be at all likely to recognize him.

The curtain rose. The play was a modern farce. Katharina found it most amusing. She often laughed out loud, but without turning round to Graesler. In the first interval, he bought her a box of sweets, which she accepted with a smile. During the second act, she nodded at him from time to time at parts that struck her as particularly amusing. Graesler was not attending much to the play and at one point became conscious of an opera glass levelled at him from one of the boxes. He recognized Böhlinger, and nodded to him frankly, completely ignoring his friend's bantering expression.

During the last interval he strolled up and down the foyer with Katharina. Suddenly he linked his arm in hers – she made no demur – and gave his opinion of the acting in a soft, insistent way as if there were a delicious secret between him and his charming companion. He was rather disappointed not to meet Böhlinger here.

The bell rang for the final act. When the two were back in their seats Graesler moved close to Katharina. Their arms touched, and as she did not draw away, he felt that a more intimate relationship between them was gradually being established; and when he helped her on with her jacket after the play, he ventured a fleeting pat of her hair and cheeks.

Outside, she looked up at him from beneath the brim of her hat and said in a tone that had a ring of pretence in it:

'Now I must be getting home.'

'But first,' he neatly interposed, 'you will do me the honour to take supper with me, won't you?'

She looked at him dubiously an instant, then gave a quick, earnest nod of assent, as if understanding more than the obvious meaning of his words. Like lovers whose footsteps are hastened by passion, they hurried, arm-in-arm, through the dark streets to his house.

When Graesler switched on the light in his study, Katharina looked round at the pictures and books with curious interest.

'Do you like the place?'

She nodded.

'It's a very old house, isn't it?'

'Three hundred years, at least.'

'But how new everything looks!'

He offered to show her round the other rooms. She liked the furniture and the way it was arranged, but looked at him with suspicious astonishment when she entered his sister's room.

'Don't tell me you are married and – your wife is away?'

He smiled, then, passing his hand across his forehead, explained in a low voice about how the room had been furnished and redecorated for his sister, who had died in the south a few months earlier. Katharina looked at him searchingly. She seemed satisfied and drew nearer, and took his hand and stroked it caressingly. It made him feel good.

They went into the dining-room, where Katharina was prevailed upon at last to take off her hat and coat. In a trice she was at home. Graesler started to lay the table. She would not allow him to. He yielded to her playful insistence and from a seat at the other end of the room watched, with some emotion, the housewifely way in which she prepared everything and moved about in the kitchen and dining-room as if she had been keeping house there a long time.

She served the food, he poured the wine. It was a little feast. She talked with delight of the way the evening had gone, and was amazed to learn from Graesler that he rarely went to the theatre, which to her represented the acme of earthly joys. He explained how his occupation gave him few opportunities for such amusements: he had to change his residence every half year, had just come from a little German health resort, and would soon be starting for a distant island where there was no winter, where tall palm trees grew, and where people drove in quaint little carriages through a yellow country beneath the burning sun.

'Are there many snakes there?'

'One can protect oneself against them.'

'When are you going back?'

'Very soon. Would you like to come along?' He spoke in jest, but felt, in spite of the mood brought on by several glasses of wine drunk in quick succession, that a hint of truth quivered in his joke.

She answered simply, without looking at him:

'Why not?'

He drew closer to her, and put his arm gently round her neck. She recoiled. It did not displease him. He rose, determined from now on to treat Katharina quite like a lady, and he politely asked her leave to smoke a cigar. Then, as he smoked, and walked up and down the room, he spoke seriously and impressively of the strange course of man's days, not one of which can be counted on in advance. He spoke of the numerous places in the north and in the south to which his work had led him. Sometimes he stood beside Katharina, who went on eating dates and nuts, and gently laid his hand on her brown hair.

Katharina listened interestedly, occasionally interrupting with eager questions. At times her eyes lighted up with a peculiar, mocking expression which made Graesler go on talking with even more circumstantiality.

When the clock struck midnight, Katharina jumped up as if it were the absolute signal for going. Graesler pretended to be quite upset though in the bottom of his soul he felt a certain relief. Before Katharina left, she cleared the table, pushed the chairs into their places, and tidied the room. At the door, she suddenly raised herself on tiptoe, and held up her lips to be kissed.

'Because you have been so well-behaved,' she added. Again there was that peculiar gleam of mockery in her eyes.

They went down the stairs by the light of a flickering candle, which Graesler carried. At the first corner was a cab. They got in. Katharina nestled up against Graesler, he put his arm round her neck, and they drove silently through the deserted streets, until, when they were near Katharina's home, Graesler drew the girl towards him more hotly and covered her mouth and cheeks with passionate kisses. At Katharina's request, the cab drew up at a little distance from her door.

'When shall I see you again?' he asked.

She promised to come next evening. She got out, and asking him not to accompany her to the door, vanished in the shadow of the houses.

Next morning, Dr Graesler felt not the least inclination to visit the hospital. Later, when he was walking in the park in the cool, clear autumn sunshine, at an hour when other people were all at work, he had some stirrings of conscience, as if he were responsible to someone beside himself. That someone, he knew, was Sabine. The thought of Dr Frank's sanatorium suddenly urged itself upon him. He began to turn over in his mind various alterations: considered the possibility of installing new bath-rooms, drafted prospectuses in far more convincing language than he had ever had at his command, and vowed that he would return to the health resort and settle the matter the instant he heard from Sabine.

If she did not answer his last letter either, then all would be at an end, at least between him and her. As for the sanatorium there was, of course, no reason why the purchase of it should be made contingent upon her attitude. In fact, it wasn't a bad idea, on the contrary a devilishly good idea to enter the place, all splendidly renovated, with another lady manager – if possible with one who did not consider him a bore of an egoist and prig. And, if it should please him to choose Katharina as his companion, then, certainly, no one could say he was a bourgeois and prig.

He sat down on a bench. Children at play ran about. The mellow sunlight glinted through the russet foliage. A siren in a distant factory was blowing for noon.

'This evening, this evening!' he thought. 'Is it youth cropping up in me again. Am I not too old for such an adventure? Oughtn't I be on my guard? Shall I go away? Right away – the next ship to Lanzarote? Or – back to Sabine? To the creature with the pure soul? Hm! Who knows what turn her life might have taken had she met the right man at the right moment – not necessarily a saucy tenor, or a hangdog doctorman.'

He betook himself for luncheon to the best hotel, where he would not be teased by the shop talk of the young physicians. After luncheon would be time enough to make up his mind.

In the afternoon he had just seated himself at his desk and opened a book on anatomy when someone knocked at the door. It was the compositor's wife, the woman who kept house for him. With profuse apologies, she asked whether Dr Graesler would spare her one or two pieces from his sister's wardrobe. Graesler frowned.

'She would never have had the cheek,' he thought, 'to ask such a thing if I had not had a lady visitor last night!'

He answered evasively that his sister had willed that all such things should be given to deserving charities. Anyhow, he had not yet had time to look into the matter, and couldn't promise anything for the moment.

The woman had come prepared with the key of the attic, and handed it to Graesler with an officious smile, thanking him as effusively as if her request had been granted.

After she was gone, leaving him with the key in his hand, it occurred to Graesler it was good for him to have found a way to pass the next hours, and he went up to visit the attic, which he had not entered since boyhood. The tiny window in the roof admitted so little light that it was some time before his eyes got used to the obscurity. Old forgotten useless odds and ends cumbered the dark corners; in the middle of the room stood boxes and trunks.

In the first case that Graesler opened were old curtains and house linen. It not being his intention to unpack and arrange all these things, he shut the lid and turned to a long coffin-like chest. Its contents seemed more interesting. There was a litter of manuscripts – legal documents, letters in their envelopes, and packets of various sizes tied up with string. On one of these he read: 'Some of father's papers.' It was a surprise to Graesler that his sister had kept things like this so carefully.

Another packet that he handled was sealed three times and was marked in large letters: 'To be burned unread.'

Graesler shook his head mournfully.

'My poor dear Friederike, your wish shall be fulfilled at the first convenient opportunity.'

He replaced the packet, which he thought probably contained her diary as a girl and innocent love letters, and opened a third box, filled with kerchiefs, shawls, ribbons, and lace yellow with age. Graesler recognized some pieces as having belonged to his mother and even his grandmother. Many had been worn by his sister, especially in earlier days. There was the beautiful Indian shawl embroidered with foliage and flowers that a wealthy patient had given him for his sister as a parting gift a good many years before, Friederike had worn it recently. It was quite unsuitable either for the compositor's wife or for a charitable institution. So were a good many of the other things. But they would do charmingly for a pretty young woman who was good enough to cheer a lonely old bachelor. He closed the chest with particular care, folded the shawl smooth, and carried it off on his arm from the attic.

He had not long to wait before Katharina arrived. She had come straight from the shop a few minutes ahead of the appointed time.

'Without even waiting to tidy myself up,' she remarked apologetically and merrily.

Graesler was glad she had come. He kissed her hand and with a humorous courtesy, handed her the shawl, which was lying ready on the table.

'What on earth is that?' she asked, with an air of surprise.

'Something to make a person look pretty,' he answered, 'even if she doesn't need anything to make her pretty.'

'How splendid!' she cried.

She shook the shawl out and studied the effect in the mirror, speechless with delight. Then she turned to Graesler, looked up at him, took his head in both her hands, drew his face down, and kissed him on the lips.

'A thousand thanks,' she said.

'That's not enough.'

'A million, then.'

He shook his head. She smiled.

'I thank you,' she said, and put up her lips for another kiss.

He took her in his arms.

'I went up to the attic this afternoon,' he told her, 'to pick the shawl out for you. There must be plenty of other things up there that will be just as becoming to you.'

She shook her head as if deprecating the idea of another costly gift.

'Did you enjoy yourself last night? And did you have to work hard today?' Graesler asked her.

She answered him, and he in turn told her what he had done since they saw each other as if they had been old friends.

'Instead of going to the hospital I lounged about in the park, thinking of long ago when I used to play under the grass-grown walls.'

He told of other memories, dwelling in especial – half by design and half by chance – upon the days when he had been ship's surgeon. Katharina plied him with a child's curious questions about the appearance, dress, and customs of the strange people, about coral reefs and cyclones. Subconsciously he felt that he had to elaborate things which he had narrated with good effect in higher circles, for a simpler and therefore more appreciative audience. Involuntarily he assumed the tone of an uncle who delights children in the dark with stories of adventure.

Katharina sat beside him on the sofa, her hand in his. After a while she rose to get supper, but just then the front-door bell rang. Graesler was startled. What could it be? His thoughts raced? A telegram? From the ranger's lodge? Sabine? Was her father ill? or her mother? Or was it something to do with the sanatorium? Perhaps an urgent inquiry from Dr Frank? There might be another purchaser in the field. It might even be Sabine herself at the door. Then what the devil should he do? Anyhow she couldn't take him for an old fogey any more. But young girls with pure souls don't ring at bachelors' doors too late in the evening.

The bell rang again, shriller than the first time. Graesler noticed Katharina's eyes upon him, questioning but undisturbed. Too undisturbed, it struck him. Perhaps she knew something about the visitor. Was it her father? Or her brother-in-law – her alleged brother-in-law? A put-up job? Blackmail?

It served him right. How could he have let himself in for such an affair! Old fool that he was! Well, they wouldn't get much out of him. He wouldn't let himself be intimidated. It was not the first time he had been in danger – not the first by a long way! A bullet had whistled past his ear in the affray in the South Seas. The mate – that handsome, fair-haired fellow – had been shot dead close beside him.

'Hadn't you better see who's there?' asked Katharina, showing surprise at his strange expression.

'Of course,' he answered.

'Who can it be, so late?' he heard her say – the hypocrite – as he left the room.

Closing the door behind him, he looked through the judas into the hallway. A woman stood there, bare-headed, with a candle in her hand.

'Who is it?' he asked.

'Excuse me, is the doctor at home?'

'What do you want? Who are you?'

'Beg pardon, I am Frau Sommer's maid.'

'Who is Frau Sommer? I don't know her.'

'The lady who lives in the first storey. Her little girl is very ill. Please, can I speak to the doctor?'

Graesler drew a breath of relief, and opened the door.

He remembered that a widow by the name of Sommer lived in the house. Her daughter was about seven years old. The mother must have been the pretty woman in mourning whom he had met on the stair yesterday. He had turned to look at her, almost without thinking.

'I am Dr Graesler. What do you want?'

'If you'd come to look at the little girl, sir. Her head is so hot, and she cries and cries.'

'I don't practise here; I am only on a visit. I would rather you sent for another doctor.'

'It's not easy to get anyone as late as this.'

A door opened on the landing below, and a light shone up the stairway.

'Anna,' someone called in a loud whisper.

'That's Frau Sommer,' said the servant.

She ran to the banister.

'Yes, ma'am.'

'Why are you so long? Is the doctor out?'

Graesler also stepped to the rail and looked down. The lady, whose features were indistinct in the half light, raised her hands as if to a saviour.

'Thank God! You'll come directly, won't you, doctor? My little girl – I don't know what is the matter with her.'

'I'll – I'll come. Of course I will. But just one moment. I must fetch my thermometer. One moment, please.'

'Thank you,' came the whisper, as Dr Graesler closed the front door behind him.

Katharina was leaning against the table awaiting him eagerly. He felt profoundly tender towards her, all the more because of his suspicions. She seemed to him like an angel.

'Rotten luck,' he said, stroking her hair. 'They want me to come and see a sick child in this very house. I can't possibly refuse. There seems nothing left but to put you in a cab . . .'

She gripped his hand, which was still resting on her head.

'You are going to send me away?'

'Most unwillingly, as you can imagine. Or – or – would you really be patient enough to wait for me?'

She caressed his hand.

'If you won't be too long?'

'I shall be as quick as possible. How sweet you are.'

He kissed her forehead, hastened to fetch the pocket case which was lying ready in the study, and asked her to go on with her supper. From the doorway he looked back. She gave him a friendly nod, and as he hurried down the stairs he was cheered by the thought that a dear girl was waiting to give him a loving greeting when he came back from the gloomy seriousness of a professional visit.

Frau Sommer was sitting beside the bed of her little girl. The child was tossing feverishly. After an examination, Graesler told the mother that a rash might be expected to break out shortly. She was in despair. She had lost her other child three years before, and her husband had died six months before while abroad on a business journey. She had never even seen his grave. What was she to do if the last that was left her was to be taken from her too?

'No need to be so alarmed,' said Graesler. 'It may be nothing more than a simple case of tonsilitis. But even if it is the beginning of something more serious, your child is so healthy-looking and well-nourished, I am sure it will be able to resist.'

The mother, Graesler was glad to see, was relieved by his sensible words. The maid was sent to the chemist's to have the prescription filled, and Graesler sat by the sick bed, feeling the child's pulse, or laying his hand on her dry, hot forehead, where it sometimes encountered the hand of the anxious mother.

After a long silence, she began again to put anxious questions. The doctor took her hand paternally, spoke kindly to her—thinking that Sabine would certainly be pleased with him now. At the same time, he did not fail to notice, in the subdued greenish light of the shaded lamp, that the young widow's wrapper draped a graceful figure. As soon as the maid returned, he rose, and reiterated what he had casually explained when he came, that he could not go on with the case, as he had to leave town in a few days. Frau Sommer begged him to keep on as long as he stayed; she had no confidence in the local practitioners, while he had inspired her with the most absolute trust; she felt certain that if anyone could save her darling child, Dr Graesler was the man. So he had to promise to come again in the morning. He watched quietly at the bedside a few moments longer, and when the child began to breathe more evenly, he pressed the mother's hand cordially and took leave.

On entering his dining-room he was surprised to find it empty.

'Lost patience,' he thought. 'It was only to be expected. Just as well, perhaps; the child downstairs is probably going to have some infectious trouble. Very likely the young woman thought as much. Sabine would not have run away. I see she's had her supper before going.'

He contemplated the table with the remains of the meal on it. His lip curled contemptuously.

'It would not be a bad idea,' he went on thinking, 'to go downstairs again and keep the pretty widow company.'

He felt that beside the sick child's cot the mother would

grant him anything he asked – and the depravity of the notion gave him a far from unpleasant thrill.

'But I shan't go down,' he said to himself, 'for I am and always will be an old fogey after all. This time Sabine would probably forgive me for it.'

The door into the study was open. He turned on the light. Of course, Katharina was not there either. Switching off, he noticed a gleam of light through the crack of the door that led into his bedroom. A faint hope stirred within him. He dallied a while; it did him good to savour the warmth of expectation. A rustling sound came from within. He opened the door. There was Katharina, lying or rather sitting up in his bed, reading.

'You won't be angry with me?' she said simply, looking up from the big volume that she was holding in both hands. Her brown, softly curling hair was loose and fell over her white shoulders.

How pretty she was. Graesler continued to stand in the doorway without stirring. He smiled, for the book lying on the counterpane was the work on anatomy.

'What's that you've got hold of?' he asked, drawing nearer almost bashfully.

'It was lying on your writing-table, dear. Oughtn't I to have taken it? Forgive me. But if I hadn't, I'd have gone to sleep, and then nothing would have waked me up.'

Her eyes smiled, not mockingly, but almost with an air of surrender. Graesler sat on the edge of the bed, drew her to him and kissed her throat. The heavy book went shut with a bang.

When Dr Graesler went to visit his little patient next morning, Katharina left, and reappeared early in the evening. To Graesler's surprise, she brought a suit-case along. The night before she had said to him: 'I haven't taken my holiday yet. It's as if I had known of this beforehand and saved up the holiday.' In the intoxication of the first embrace Graesler had promptly invited her on a little honeymoon trip. But now, when she arrived all equipped for leaving, and hailed him merrily: 'Here I am. If you like we can go straight to the station,' something in him revolted against this offhand way of taking charge of his life, and he was glad to be able to plead that the little girl turned out to have scarlet fever, and he could not go away.

Katharina did not seem greatly perturbed. She prattled of other things, made him admire her new brown shoes, and told him how the head of the firm had just returned with novelties from London and Paris. As she talked, she went about the room, replacing one or two books in the shelves, and tidying the writing-table, while Graesler stood at the window and contemplated her doings silently and not unmoved. His glance fell on the suit-case; it looked melancholy and almost ashamed as it stood on the floor. The thought that the good creature would have to take it away with her soon touched him with light compassion. He held back from saying anything of the sort, but later, when he had sat down in the chair at his desk and Katharina was sitting on his knee like a child, her arm around his neck, he said:

'Need it be a journey? Why not just spend your holiday here with me?'

'That would be impossible, wouldn't it,' she answered weakly.

'Why? Isn't it lovely here?' He pointed through the window

towards the range of distant hills, and added jokingly: 'You'll like your board and lodging, too.'

With sudden decision, he rose, offered Katharina his arm, and escorted her into Friederike's room. He switched on the red-shaded hanging lamp. The room was suffused with a soft light. 'Consider this your own, beloved,' he said with grave courtesy.

Katharina was struck dumb; she could merely shake her head earnestly.

'Wouldn't you like it?' Graesler asked tenderly.

'It's really impossible,' she answered softly.

'Why? It is quite possible.' As if her only objection could be a superstitious one, he went on: 'Everything is new, even the wallpaper. It didn't use to look half so nice.'

Katharina looked round the room, her face cleared, and she stroked the flowered chintz of the sofa at the foot of the bed. Then her eyes fell on the muslin curtains over the toilet-table, looked back to disclose a pretty toilet set and a number of cut-glass phials. Graesler left her to her absorption and returned presently with her little suit-case. She quivered, and smiled half incredulously. He nodded to her, she shook her head. Then, as if finally persuaded, she stretched her arms out to him. He put down the case, and with gratified pride clasped her to his breast.

Some wonderful days followed, such as Graesler had scarcely enjoyed even in his youth. Like a happy newly-married couple, they spent most of the day in their own quarters, assiduously waited upon by the compositor's wife, who accepted the rather unusual situation with all the more readiness because Graesler had gratified her cool request and had given her quite a number of articles from his dead sister's wardrobe.

In the evenings the young couple would walk arm-in-arm through the quieter streets. One sunny afternoon they made an early start, and drove into the country in an open carriage, quite undisturbed by the possibility that they might meet some of Katharina's relatives (who supposed the girl to be staying with a friend at a considerable distance).

One day when they were still at table, Böhlinger called. Graesler was dubious about admitting him. Afterwards he was glad that he had let him in. The lawyer treated his friend's charming companion most politely. He quickly explained the business that had brought him, and took leave with the easy grace of a man of the world, kissing Katharina's hand on parting. The incident enhanced Graesler's tender feeling for Katharina, who had played her part with social perfection.

Dr Graesler visited his little patient every morning, then went for half-an-hour's walk to minimize the risk of conveying infection to Katharina. The scarlet fever ran a mild course. When the alarm of the first days had subsided, Frau Sommer proved to be a very gay, sociable, talkative person, who, whether by chance or design, never seemed to notice whether the wrapper she received the doctor in was as carefully closed across the neck and bosom as was quite proper. She always inquired after Graesler's 'young lady friend', and asked whether he proposed to take his sweetheart back to Africa – this being the name she had hit upon for the region where the doctor practised in winter – or whether he had a charmer (a negress perhaps) already awaiting him there. She even wanted him to take a box of chocolates to Katharina as a little gift from herself, but he refused to from fear of infection.

Katharina, on her side, had a word or two to say about the young widow. Though jealousy was at the bottom of her irony, Graesler could not but feel that there was justice in what she said. It appeared that during her husband's lifetime Frau Sommer's reputation had not been wholly above suspicion. His work as commercial traveller entailed frequent and prolonged absences; her little girl had been born before the marriage, and it was not certain whether he was the father. All this gossip came to Katharina from the compositor's wife, with whom, during her lover's occasional absences, she talked more freely than Graesler found altogether agreeable.

Once, he tried to make her realize how unsuitable this intimacy was. She hardly seemed to understand his considerations, and he did not insist because he was loath to darken the few days of his happiness by discord. He was fully determined that the days should be only a few and merely an interlude, an adventure. Whenever she asked him, modestly but curiously, about his plans for the winter, what sort of climate Lanzarote had, and what sort of life there was there, he would answer as briefly as possible and turn the conversation to something else, not wishing to raise hopes he had no intention to fulfil. It was his one desire that these brief weeks should pass without a cloud, and so he asked her little about her past, content to live in the present, delighting in his happiness, and delighting still more in the happiness he was able to bestow.

Gradually, however, as the days and nights slipped by, a longing for Sabine began to stir within him, especially in the early morning when Katharina was still asleep by his side. How much happier he would be, what a much worthier exist-ence he would be leading, if, instead of this pretty shop-girl (who must certainly have had two or three lovers in addition to the book-keeper to whom she had been engaged for a time, who tricked her good parents, and who gossiped with his house-keeper), if instead of this insignificant creature – whose charm and kindness he did not for a moment underestimate – he had a very different companion. What if Sabine's head were resting on the pillow beside him – she who had so delicately offered to join her life to his, and whose advances he had spurned in an unwarrantable fit of self-distrust.

He did not deceive himself. She had taken his timid and foolish letter as a definite refusal. As a matter of fact at bottom that is what he had intended it to be. But could he not retrieve his blunder? Could he not atone for his awkwardness and precipitation? Was it likely that Sabine's feelings for him, which she had expressed in such considerate words, had been extin-guished never to be kindled again? In his own letter he had set a term. By not writing to him was she not merely complying with his request; and weren't her silence and her forbearance the very mark of what was noblest and truest in her?

And now if he were to return to her at the end of the set term and were to give her an absolute yes, a yes that was the result of mature consideration, would he find her a different person from the one he had left? In the peaceful retirement of the ranger's lodge, no new lover was likely to have approached her. Her pure soul would not have been perturbed either by his foolish though well-meant letter, or by the intrusion of another passion. The very thought that Sabine might have a new wooer was the expiring flicker of a mood due to loneliness and timidity in one to whom confidence and self-assurance had now been restored by a wonderful turn of fortune's wheel. More and more it seemed to him that Katharina's true mission had been to lead him back to Sabine, whose love was to be for him the real meaning of his life. And the more trustingly Katharina – with no ulterior end in view – offered him the treasures of her gay, young heart, the more impatiently and hopefully his deepest yearnings went out to Sabine.

External factors also began to impose a prompt decision as October drew to a close. Graesler thought it expedient to write to Dr Frank saying he hoped to call at the sanatorium in a few days and settle the affair. No answer came, and he wired to ask whether he could count on meeting him on a specified day. Even the telegram did not elicit a reply. This annoyed but did not alarm Graesler; he remembered what an old curmudgeon Frank was. As for writing to Sabine and telling her he was coming, that, he knew from his previous experience, was something he couldn't possibly do. He would simply go unannounced, stand before her, and take her hands in his. Her clear eyes would give him the redeeming answer.

The day Katharina's holiday ended and she was to return to her parents' home had naturally been fixed at the outset of her stay. As if by mutual agreement, however, they both avoided mention of it, and Katharina's whole manner betrayed so little thought of a separation that Graesler began to feel uneasy lest this clinging little creature, who had turned up uninvited one evening with her suit-case, contemplated spending the rest of her life with him. He considered the possibility of taking flight from the house and the town early one morning before she was awake, and began to make inconspicuous preparations for departure.

Besides the Indian shawl, he had given her a number of his sister's belongings, including a few trinkets. The more valuable pieces of jewellery he reserved for Sabine. He felt he must find one more memento for Katharina to salve his conscience and to comfort her a bit for his disappearing. So two days before his intended departure, on a rainy afternoon while Katharina, as she often did at that hour, was resting in her room, Graesler mounted to the attic again. Rummaging in the trunks and boxes, turning over silks, portfolios of pictures, veils, handkerchiefs, ribbons, and lace, he unexpectedly came across the packet which bore Friederike's inscription directing that its contents should be burned unread.

For the first time, as if suspecting that it might be long before he revisited this room, or even that he might never see it again, he felt the spur of curiosity. He laid the packet aside with the thought that he had better find a safer place for its disposal, and that a later heir, who would have no scruples regarding the wishes of an unknown person long deceased, would probably open it without hesitation.

For Katharina he chose a few pretty trifles, among them a

fine amber necklace and a piece of gold-embroidered oriental stuff – articles which, like many others in the trunks he had never imagined Friederike possessed. He took them along with the packet, and laid them on his writing-table before going to Katharina's room.

He found Katharina leaning back in the armchair, wrapped in a gift of his, a Chinese dressing-gown richly worked with gold dragons on a purple ground. She had fallen asleep over one of the serial numbers of an illustrated novel, her favourite literature. Touched at the sight and reluctant to wake her, Graesler returned to the study, sat down at the writing-table, and began to play heedlessly with the threads which tied up the packet, until the seals cracked and broke. He shrugged his shoulders.

'Why not?' he said to himself. 'She is dead. I have no belief in personal immortality. But if after all there should be immortality Friederike's soul on high will not take what I do amiss. Besides, there are not likely to be any dreadful secrets in these letters.'

The letters were carefully arranged with blank sheets between. The first that Graesler read dated more than thirty years back and was from a young man who signed himself Robert and evidently had the right to address Friederike in extremely affectionate terms. The letter showed that Robert had been a family friend. Graesler, however, couldn't remember him. There were about a dozen letters from him; love letters, but very innocent and of no great interest to Graesler.

Next came letters belonging to the period when Graesler was ship's surgeon and paid only brief visits to his home at two years' intervals. The letters were now in various handwritings, and it was some time before Graesler could make out what could be the meaning of all these passionate asseverations, oaths of fidelity, allusions to happy hours, ebullitions of jealousy, warnings, vague threats and fierce vituperations. He could not imagine what this amazing hotch-potch could have to do with his sister. He was on the point of deciding that the letters must have been addressed to some other person (perhaps to one of Friederike's women friends, who had entrusted them to Friederike for safe keeping) when he recognized a familiar handwriting, and from this and from other signs he knew that these particular letters were from Böhlinger.

The threads of the strange romance began to disentangle themselves. Graesler made out that his sister, more than twenty years earlier, when she had already been a fairly mature woman, had been secretly engaged to Böhlinger. Böhlinger, on account of one of Friederike's previous love affairs, had delayed the wedding. From impatience, caprice, or vindictiveness, Friederike then betrayed him, but later sought a reconciliation. Böhlinger merely replied with outbursts of mockery and contempt. The tone of his last letters was so immoderate, so abusive, that Graesler couldn't understand how in the end a tolerable relationship, in fact a sort of friendship could have been established between the two.

His feelings were rather of excitement than wonder. It was, therefore, with enhanced curiosity and not with any sense of shock, that he went on to find out what further secrets of Friederike's life the remaining letters would disclose.

There were not many left, and were in different handwritings; from which Graesler inferred that Friederike had now preserved only samples of her correspondence.

First came two or three written in a cipher of letters and figures. After a gap of several years followed letters from the period when Friederike kept house for her brother. Some of these were in French, some in English, and some in what Graesler supposed to be a Slavic language, though he had been quite unaware that his sister knew any such language.

Some of the letters were from wooers; others from the grateful recipients of favours, respectfully cautious, or else the unambiguous expression of love. In both kinds Graesler could occasionally glimpse the blurred image of one or another of his patients, whom he himself, in the unwitting rôle of pander, must have introduced to Friederike.

There was no doubt that the last of the letters burning with passion, chaotic, and filled with forebodings of imminent death, had been written by a lad of nineteen, a consumptive in the last stages of the disease whom ten years before Graesler had sent northward from Lanzarote to die at home. Perhaps, the doctor thought, Friederike, who had then seemed to him so quiet and good, but had now been revealed as a passionate woman with a wide experience of love, might have been responsible for the poor young fellow's premature end.

The shame with which it filled Graesler that his sister had considered him unworthy of her confidence, doubtless (like Sabine), looking upon him as an old fogey, rather marred his feelings for her, especially as it struck him that to some of the writers of the letters he must have seemed as ridiculous as a deceived husband. In the end, all this was outweighed by satisfaction that Friederike had tasted of the fullness of life and he was free from responsibility towards her. For it was now plain that she had given up life because it could no longer offer her the pleasure that she had once enjoyed in abundance.

As he fluttered the pages of the letters again and reread a passage here and there, it dawned upon him that the revelation was, after all, not entirely unexpected; and on reflection it seemed less enigmatic than at first. A number of incidents recurred to his mind. He recalled a little affair on the Lake of Geneva between Friederike and a French captain. One of the letters contained an allusion to it. At the time he had not understood the full significance of the incident, and had felt that it was no business of his to interfere with the freedom of a woman well on in the thirties. As for Friederike and Böhlinger he had been aware that the two as very young people had been greatly attached to one another, but circumstances had kept him from knowing about their later intimacy. Quite possibly the strange glances Friederike had sometimes given him in the last years had not been reproachful. On the contrary, they probably pled for forgiveness that she had lived with him as if with a stranger, and kept her feelings and experiences a secret from him. But still, he reflected, he himself had told Friederike only the most innocent of the adventures, while there had been a host of others that he had kept concealed which would have appeared just as questionable if written about in letters marked 'to be burned'. Consequently, he had no right to bear her a grudge for a reserve which he himself had been so careful to practise.

Katharina coming up from behind laid her hands on his forehead.

'You?' he asked, as if waking from a dream.

'I've been in twice before, but you were so absorbed I didn't want to disturb you.'

He looked at his watch. Half-past nine. Four hours wrapped in that life history.

'I have been reading some of my sister's letters,' he said, drawing Katharina on to his knee. 'She was a strange woman.'

For an instant he thought of telling Katharina the story in the letters, but it would have been wronging the memory of Friederike to retail her experiences to this girl who would probably trace similarities that in a higher sense were non-existent.

He pushed the letters aside with a gesture as if to say, the dead past must bury its dead, and, in the tone of a man emerging from dark dreams to a bright present, he asked Katharina what she had been doing with herself.

'Oh, I went on reading my novel for some time; then I cleaned the silver and the glass on the toilet-table, then I altered some of the fastenings on the Chinese robe. And then – oh, well, I spent half an hour on the stairs talking to the housekeeper. You know she's really quite a nice woman, even though you can't bear her.'

Graesler was not best pleased that Katharina should enjoy conversing with a woman in such a station and that she should show herself on the stairs in her Chinese dressing-gown. However, this episode in his life was nearly over. In a few days he would be back in a worthier and purer environment. He was never likely to see Katharina again. His future visits to his native city would be brief, for the sanatorium would demand his whole attention year in and year out.

Katharina was still sitting on his knee, and he went on mechanically stroking her cheeks and neck. Suddenly he noticed that she was looking at him attentively and with a sad expression.

'What's the matter?' he asked.

She shook her head, and tried to smile. He was distressed and astonished to see that there were tears in her eyes.

'You are crying,' he said gently, feeling at this moment surer of Sabine than ever before.

'Nonsense,' answered Katharina, and jumped up. Making a merry face, she opened the door into the dining-room and showed him that the table was ready for supper.

'Do you mind my having supper with you in this Chinese robe?'

This reminded him of the amber necklace. He clasped it round her neck.

'Still another thing?'

'Yes, but that's the last.' The moment the words were out of his mouth he was sorry. They sounded worse than he had meant them to be. 'I mean . . .', he said, trying to make amend.

She raised her hand as if to tell him to keep quiet.

They sat down to supper. After a bite or two, she suddenly asked:

'Shall you think of me sometimes when you have gone?'

This was her first allusion to the impending separation. Graesler was nonplussed. Noticing his discomfiture she added hurriedly:

'Don't say anything more than yes or no.'

'Yes,' he answered with a forced smile.

She nodded, and seemed perfectly satisfied, as she filled both their glasses. Now she went on prattling in her usual gay, naïve way, as if there were no parting in view – or else as if it didn't matter to her much that they were going to part.

She wrapped the Chinese garment, which was too large for her, tightly round her body, then let it fall free, pulled it up over her head, let it down again, and danced round the room, wine-glass in one hand, the gathered-up robe embroidered with golden dragons in the other hand, laughing gaily with languishing eyes.

Graesler took her in his arms, and half carried her into the dimly lighted room that had once been Friederike's. His ecstasy was tinged with a subflavour of dull anger against the sister who had lied and deceived him.

Graesler rose next morning while Katharina was still asleep, and went to pay a final visit to his little patient. She was getting on splendidly, but he was still keeping her in bed. He did not wish that any hint of his intention to leave so precipitately should reach Katharina's ears by way of the housekeeper, and he thought it best to tell Frau Sommer that he expected to stay a week longer. She smiled, saying:

'I can quite understand that you don't find it easy to tear yourself away from your young friend. She's a charming creature, and she looks perfectly lovely in that Chinese robe you gave her.'

Graesler frowned, and turned to examine little Fanny, who was arranging her doll's flaxen hair with all a child's seriousness.

A few days before he had begun to tell Fanny about some wild beasts for a menagerie that had been on shipboard on one of his homeward voyages. She gave him no peace; he must tell her exactly how the lions looked, and the tigers, and the leopards, which he had sometimes watched being fed between decks. But he cut the recital short, having a number of preparations to make for his departure on the morrow. He rose suddenly, to the little girl's great dissatisfaction, and made for the door. Frau Sommer detained him with a dozen questions regarding details of treatment – matters he had already explained time and again. Though noticing his impatience, she still kept him back, standing very close to him, as she always did, and gazing at him with an expression of sentimental gratitude. Finally he escaped and hurried out.

He had told Katharina that he had a great deal to attend to that day, and was obliged to visit the hospital, so that she should not get impatient and should leave him plenty of time to make preparations for the trip. He actually did go to the hospital and take leave of the senior physician, then he made a few purchases, arranged for the forwarding of his baggage, and went to see Böhlinger, with whom there were various business matters to be settled. Böhlinger seemed hardly to notice his friend's uneasiness. He gave Graesler cordial wishes for success in the negotiations with Dr Frank, and deliberately avoided all reference to private matters. It was not until after the two had parted that Graesler remembered he had been conversing with one of his dead sister's former lovers.

He now hastened home for his final luncheon with Katharina. He proposed to spend these last hours with her undisturbed, and would give no sign of his intention to leave next morning before she awoke. A letter containing a small gift of money would be sufficient farewell.

When he entered the dining-room, he found that the table had been laid for one only. The compositor's wife appeared and remarked, with a malicious assumption of regret, that by the young lady's orders she herself had laid the table, and the young lady begged to be excused. Graesler's fierce look drove her out of the room in alarm. He hurried into the study, where he found a sealed letter from Katharina.

My dear, dear Friend,
    It was so lovely with you. I shall think of you a lot. I know you're going away tomorrow, and I'd better not disturb you today. I hope all will go well with you. If you come again next year – but you'll have forgotten me long before then. I hope you'll have a pleasant sea voyage. A thousand thanks for everything.

Your loving
Katharina.

Graesler was touched by the lovingness of the letter and the clumsy, childish handwriting.

'She's a dear,' he said to himself. But he wouldn't be soft. He returned to the dining-room, rang for luncheon, and between the courses made entries in his engagement book so as to avoid exchanging a word with the housekeeper, whom he dismissed immediately after the meal.

Then he wandered over the flat. Everything was in perfect order. All Katharina's belongings had been removed. No trace was left of her beyond a subtle fragrance which lingered most in the room that had been hers the last three weeks.

To Graesler the whole place, although everything else was as usual, seemed intolerably chill and empty, and the loneliness that came over him made him wonder whether he shouldn't throw his other hopes and possibilities to the winds, and ask Katharina to come back to him. But no, he quickly told himself, that would be unwise, ridiculous, it would imperil his whole future, would destroy all chance of a happiness that seemed almost within his grasp.

All of a sudden the image of Sabine flashed up in his soul with wonderful brightness. There was nothing now to keep him from leaving that very evening; he would see Sabine early the next morning. However, he did not act on the impulse; he mustn't appear before his lady-love jaded after a sleepless night.

He would use the extra time at his disposal to write a letter announcing his return. It would prepare the ground for a favourable reception. But when he sat down at his desk and took up his pen, he found himself unable to put down a word that could give even approximate expression to his feelings. He contented himself with a couple of lines tossed off as if in the heat of passion:

I am coming tomorrow evening. I hope you will receive me kindly.
Longingly, E. G.

Next he wrote out a telegram to Dr Frank, saying he would be back early the next day, and asking him to send a message to his rooms stating whether it would be possible to begin the renovations on 15 November.

He himself dispatched the letter and telegram, returned home, arranged various belongings, and packed his valise, into which he put a small antique cameo with the head of a goddess set in gold. During the night he awoke with a start half a dozen times at least from nightmares in which it seemed to him that all would be lost. Sabine, and Katharina, and the sanatorium, and his property, and his youth, and the lovely southern sunshine, and the ivory cameo – were he to oversleep himself in the morning and miss the train.

It was a mild, sunny afternoon in the late autumn when Dr Graesler returned to the health resort. In front of the railway station were about half a dozen hotel omnibuses and two or three cabs. The hotel runners called out the names of their respective hotels half-heartedly, as few health-seekers visited the place at that advanced season.

Dr Graesler drove home and told the driver to wait. He asked for his letters, was annoyed to find that there was no answer from Dr Frank, and bitterly disappointed that there was no word of greeting from Sabine. He pumped his obliging housekeeper. No news of importance in the town, or neighbourhood, or – the ranger's lodge!

At last, not until nightfall, he drove along the familiar road past the village, now for the most part untenanted; up the valley between the gloomy hills and beneath a starless sky; onward to the place where (he knew now with a pitiless certainty what for days and until this last hour he had foolishly tried to conceal from himself) he was to make a desperate and probably vain attempt to regain the favour of the splendid being whose offer he had spurned partly from silliness, partly from cowardice.

He searched his mind unceasingly for words that would both justify him in her eyes and irresistibly convey his tenderness.

The carriage stopped as if at haphazard in the road. A ruddy gleam shot down the avenue. Apparently the lamps had only just been lighted in the lodge. Graesler got out and walked up the bridle path, slowly, to the still violent beating of his heart. The front door was opened promptly in answer to his ring. Simultaneously, the door of the living-room opened and Frau Schleheim appeared. Through the doorway Sabine was visible, seated at the table reading. She looked up from her book.

'It is good of you,' said the mother, holding out her hand cordially, 'to take pity on us poor forsaken women.'

'I ventured to let Fräulein Sabine know I was coming.'

'Welcome back,' said Sabine, rising and giving him a friendly handshake.

He tried to read her eyes. They rested on his unmoved, far too unmoved. He asked after Herr Schleheim.

'He is travelling,' answered Frau Schleheim.

'Where is he now?' asked Graesler, sitting down at Sabine's invitation. Frau Schleheim shrugged her shoulders.

'We don't know. He sometimes leaves us like that. In a week or two he will be back. *We* know, don't we?' she concluded with a meaning look at her daughter.

'Are you going to stay here long, Dr Graesler?' asked Sabine.

He looked at her. Her gaze left him unanswered.

'That depends,' he answered. 'Probably not very long – just until I have settled my affairs.'

Sabine nodded as if absent-mindedly.

The maid came in to lay the table.

'You'll stay to supper?' asked Frau Schleheim.

He hesitated. His look again questioned Sabine.

'Of course he will. We counted on his staying.'

Graesler felt: 'She is not loving, she is merely gracious.'

He accepted the invitation with a mute nod.

All three were silent, and as silence at the moment was hardest of all for him to bear, he began to speak briskly.

'First of all I must look up Dr Frank tomorrow. Would you believe it, he never took the trouble to answer my last letters? But I still hope we shall be able to come to terms.'

'Too late,' said Sabine coolly. Graesler was quick to realize that her tone conveyed a reference to something beside the lost business opportunity. 'Dr Frank,' she went on, 'has decided to keep up the place himself. Renovations have been going on busily for the last few days. Your friend Herr Adelmann is in charge of the work.'

'Adelmann is no friend of mine,' said Graesler. 'If he had been, he would certainly have let me know.' He shook his head heavily and slowly, as if he had suffered a serious disillusionment in the architect.

'Since the sanatorium is lost to you,' said Sabine politely, 'I suppose you will go south again?'

'Certainly,' answered Graesler promptly. 'To my good old Lanzarote. The climate here! Who knows whether I'd still be equal to a Central European winter.'

It occurred to him that on account of the few steamers going to Lanzarote he could not possibly get there before the middle of November and he might find his place filled, as he had not written one way or another.

Oh, well, he was no longer dependent upon his practice there. If he liked, he could take a holiday for six months or more, and if he was economical, he might even give his practice up altogether. The thought alarmed him. He was incapable of living without his profession. He had to make people well, lead the life of a fine, active man. That was probably his destined lot in life. And probably he was destined to lead this life beside this splendid woman. Maybe she was merely punishing him for his delay and putting him to the test again.

He explained that he had not yet made arrangements and was still awaiting a letter from Lanzarote, which might bring the acceptance of certain new advantageous conditions that he had proposed to the administration there. In the event of a refusal, he had decided to devote the ensuing winter to study at various German universities.

'I was far from idle during my stay in the city. I visited the hospital and I had some private practice. A chance case, to be sure. A dear little girl of seven, the daughter of a widow who lives in the same house as I do. I couldn't refuse. Scarlet fever. It was quite a serious case. But the child is out of danger now. Otherwise I could not have left.'

While speaking, Graesler tried to evoke the image of Frau Sommer. Instead he kept seeing the lady with the doll's face of the illustrated papers, the one that had come in his dreams during the voyage home. There must be a resemblance. Why, of course, unconsciously it had struck him immediately.

Sabine seemed to have listened with growing interest, but without much credence, he feared perhaps because of his uneasy conscience. Without apropos she began to speak of her two girl friends.

'You remember them. The younger one became engaged to a summer visitor here from Berlin.'

'We're going to Berlin for the wedding,' said Frau Schleheim, 'and mean to stay some time. That will give us a chance to see the city again.'

Once more and impatiently, almost imploringly, Graesler's eyes asked Sabine: 'How about us two?' But her eyes remained inscrutable. As the evening wore on she seemed to grow milder, more friendly. He felt that he had as good as lost the game. Still his pride rebelled against accepting the mute dismissal that she seemed to intend for him; and he was determined before leaving to ask her for a private talk.

When he rose and with assumed lightness spoke of the possibility of meeting at Christmas in Berlin, Sabine also got up from the table. Evidently she intended to accompany the guest to his carriage. They walked side by side under the pines as in happier days, but silently. Of a sudden, almost involuntarily, Graesler stopped, saying:

'Are you angry with me, Sabine?'

'Angry?' she answered tonelessly. 'Why should I be?'

'My letter, I know it, my miserable letter.'

In the dim light all he could see was that she winced and made a deprecatory gesture. He tried to explain, feeling that he was floundering more and more hopelessly.

'You misunderstood my letter – completely misunderstood it. It was my conscientiousness, my sense of duty that made me write it. Oh, if I had only done what my heart told me to do. I loved you, I adored you, from the first moment I stood opposite you at your mother's bed. But I was too craven to believe in my own happiness. After such a cheerless, lonely life as I have had, I had given up hope, I didn't dare to dream. An old man like me. Almost an old man. Of course it isn't years that make age. I came to realize this in those long weeks we have been apart. But your letter, your wonderful, heavenly letter – oh, I wasn't worthy of it.'

The words poured from his lips in a medley, and he knew all the time that the right ones wouldn't come simply because the way to her heart was barricaded.

'Forgive me, Sabine, forgive me,' he ended hopelessly in an almost stifled cry.

'I have nothing to forgive,' – he heard her as from a great distance – 'but it would have been better if you had not spoken. I had hoped you wouldn't. If I had known I would have begged you not to come.'

Her tone was so hard that suddenly Graesler took fresh hope. Wasn't it affronted love that made her so pitiless? *Affronted* love – but *love* which she still felt but of which she was ashamed? He resumed with fresh courage:

'Sabine, I'll ask this one thing of you, let me see you again next spring, and let me ask you once again.'

She interrupted him.

'It's rather cold here. Good-bye, Dr Graesler.' Even in the darkness, he thought he could discern a mocking smile on her lips as she added: 'I wish you all happiness in the future.'

'Sabine!' He took her hand and wanted to hold it. She withdrew it gently.

'A pleasant journey,' she said. There was back in her voice all the kindness that was now lost to him for ever. She turned, and resolutely, though without quickening her pace, walked back to the house and vanished through the doorway.

Graesler stood only a little while, then hurried to the carriage. As he drove homeward through the night, wrapped in cloak and rug, a defiant mood took possession of him.

'Very well then,' he said to himself. 'You will have it so, you yourself thrust me into another woman's arms. You shall have your way. More than that, you shall see for yourself. Before I go south, I shall bring her here for a few days and will go driving past the ranger's lodge. You shall make her acquaintance, shall talk to her. . . "Allow me to present my wife to you, Fräulein Sabine. Not so pure a soul as you, but not so cold either. And not so proud, but kind. Not so chaste, but sweet! Katharina is her name – Katharina . . ."'

He spoke the name out loud, and as the distance between him and the lodge increased, the hotter his longing for Katharina. Soon, soon – tomorrow, tomorrow evening – he felt it with real joy – he would hold his darling in his arms again.

How astonished she would be to find him waiting for her at

seven o'clock when she came out of the shop in the Wilhelm-strasse! And a still greater surprise awaited her. There was nothing of the old fogey about him. He had only one wish in the world, to be happy, and he would take happiness where it was offered him so warmly, so unqualifiedly, with such genuine womanliness. He would find happiness with Katharina ... with Katharina ... He was glad he had seen Sabine. He knew now for sure that Katharina, and no other woman, was the right woman for him.

Next evening, an hour after his arrival, he took up his stand at the street corner from which he could not fail to catch sight of Katharina directly she left the glove shop. The two other saleswomen who were employed at the same counter emerged and disappeared, the shutters were lowered; all the rest of the employees went away; the arc light was extinguished – and still there was no sign of Katharina. Strange, very strange. Her holiday time was at an end. What could be keeping her away from work? Graesler was suddenly fired with jealousy – she was with someone else! With some former acquaintance for whom she had time again, now that the old doctor from Portugal, the fellow with the Indian shawls and amber necklaces, had gone away. Or perhaps with some new friend. Why not? We can quickly take up with new friends, can't we, Miss Katharina, people like us?

Where are you? At the theatre, probably. That's the fixed order of things, isn't it? Theatre the first evening and supper together. The second evening – everything else! You've been through that sort of thing many a time, I suppose.

But that Katharina should link on with a new admirer the very day after leaving the old one, was really a little too much. It was more than a joke! The miserable creature, for whose sake he had lost a Sabine. Gone off with shawls, and hats, and robes, and trinkets. And making merry with the first young comer over the old fool from Portugal.

With deliberate self-torture, Graesler refused to consider other, more innocent possibilities for explaining Katharina's non-appearance.

Well, what had he better do? The most sensible thing, of course, would be to go home and have done with it all. But he couldn't conquer his feelings to such an extent. He went to the suburb where Katharina lived, intending to watch near her house and see if he would not soon discover whom she had picked up – unless, she had already installed herself in her new lover's quarters.

But no, that was not likely. There were not many fools to be found who would be willing to take such a baggage into their house, such an artful Miss, such a chatterbox, such an ill-bred, deceitful thing. There was no measure to his contempt for her. He gave himself up to it with a certain voluptuous satisfaction.

'Is that being a Philistine, my dear young lady?' He was suddenly apostrophizing Sabine, against whom he also felt his gall mounting again.

'Well, I can't help it. No one can get out of his own skin, man or woman. One woman is born to be a whore; another is doomed to be an old maid; a third, in spite of the best education in a good family, leads the life of a cocotte, humbugging her parents and her brother and hanging herself as soon as she is too old to attract lovers any more. As for me, I was created to be a prig and a Philistine. But, by God, there are worse things than being a prig. There are some women who, if you're not a prig with them, make a fool of you. The fact is, there is not enough of the Philistine in me. If a certain young lady had put off her appointment tonight and come out of the shop modestly at closing time, I should actually have been capable of taking her off to Lanzarote with me as my wife. That would have tickled you, Mr Hotel Manager. But no danger now. Thank goodness, I'm coming back as alone as I left, if I go back at all, which is still far from certain. Anyhow, I shan't be there according to your orders on 27 October, even if I still could. I'm going to Berlin first, then perhaps to Paris to have a thoroughly good time such as I've never had in my life.'

In imagination he saw himself in certain places of ill repute, dancing with half-naked women; he planned monstrous orgies as a sort of demoniacal revenge on the wretched sex that treated him so trickishly – revenge on Katharine, Sabine, Friederike.

All unwittingly he had arrived at Katharina's dwelling. An unpleasant wind had risen, and was driving the dust along the mean little street. Here and there windows were being hastily closed. Graesler looked at his watch. It was still a good while before eight. How many hours would he have to wait, and how on earth should he pass the time? The wench might not be back till ten, eleven, midnight, the small hours.

The thought of tramping up and down for an indefinite time in the wind and the rain (the first drops had already begun to fall) was exceedingly disagreeable. He began to pay heed to an inner voice which had been faintly trying to make itself heard for some time. Supposing Katharina were at home after all? She might have left the shop earlier than usual – though that was not likely on the first day after her holiday. Or perhaps her holiday was not yet over. She might be spending the last day of freedom with her family. He would not quite accept any of these conjectures. Yet they relieved his mind. Besides he could soon learn the true state of affairs. He had merely to go up to the second storey and ask at Herr Rebner's door whether Fräulein Rebner was at home. No one would take that amiss. A family in which the daughter came back from a visit with twice as much luggage as she had had when she left was not likely to be very particular. If she was out, it might be possible to learn under what pretext she was away. And if she was at home, all the better. Everything would be all right, then. He would be able to see her, and make the necessary arrangements for tomorrow, the day after tomorrow, and subsequent days. Everything that had been running through his head would turn out to have been nonsense. He would owe her a mute apology – though his thoughts had been the outcome of a fit of ill-temper for which another woman was far more to blame than Katharina.

So it was with the best intentions that he stood before the door of the flat.

He rang. A small, elderly woman, wearing an apron over her house dress, answered the door and looked at him in surprise.

'Excuse me,' said Graesler. 'Is this Herr Rebner's.'

'Yes, I am Frau Rebner.'

'Oh, of course. Er – er – I wondered if I could have a word with Fräulein Katharina? I had the pleasure –'

'Oh,' interrupted Frau Rebner, obviously pleased. 'I suppose you are the doctor Katharina met when she was staying in the country with Ludmilla – the gentleman who gave her the lovely shawl.'

'Yes, I am. My name is Graesler.'

'That was the name, Dr Graesler. She told us all about you. I'll find out if she can see you. She's in bed. She must have caught a cold.'

Graesler was startled.

'In bed? Since when?'

'She hasn't been up at all today. She seems to have fever with the cold.'

'Have you called a doctor, Frau Rebner?'

'Oh, no. She ate a hearty breakfast. She'll probably be all right again soon.'

'Since I'm here, perhaps you'll let me have a look at her. I don't think Fräulein Katharina will mind.'

'No. You're a doctor, and it may be very lucky for her.'

She led the way through a fairly large unlighted room into a smaller room, where Katharina lay in bed. The light from a candle beside the bed flickered on a wet cloth that covered the girl's forehead and hid her eyes.

'Katharina!' exclaimed Graesler.

With apparent effort, she pushed the napkin off her eyes. They were dull.

'Good evening,' she said. She smiled faintly, but seemed barely conscious.

'Katharina!'

Graesler quickly pulled down the sheet and slipped the night-gown away from her shoulders. A dark-red rash was visible. Her temperature was already very high; prostration was extreme; and no further examination was needed to tell Graesler that Katharina had scarlet fever.

He sank into a chair close to the bed and held Katharina's hand. He felt guilty and terribly distressed.

There was the sound of an exclamation at the front door. It was the father who had just come in.

'Why, children, what's all this fuss about? Have you really sent for the doctor?'

His wife went to meet him.

'Not so loud,' she said. 'Her head hurts. This is the doctor she met when she was staying with Ludmilla.'

'Oh,' said the man drawing nearer. 'I'm glad to make your acquaintance. Here I send my daughter to the country for a holiday, and it costs a whole lot, and she comes back sick. Well, I suppose it's nothing much, is it, Doctor? She probably sat out of doors in the evening in cold weather. Didn't you, Katharina?'

Katharina made no answer, and drew the cloth over her eyes again. Dr Graesler turned to the father. He was a short, stoutish man with dull eyes, almost bald, and with a grey moustache turned up at the corners.

'It's not a cold. It's scarlet fever.'

'But, doctor, how can it be? Only children have scarlet fever. Her sister had it when she was five. She ought to have had it then.'

The father's loud tones seemed to have cleared Katharina's mind a little.

'Dr Graesler must know better than you, father,' she said. 'He'll cure me. Won't you, Doctor?'

'Of course, Katharina, of course,' answered Graesler. He loved her at that moment more deeply than he had ever loved any human being in his life.

While he was giving his instructions, Katharina's sister appeared, followed by her husband. The man greeted Graesler with a wink, but when he realized the gravity of the situation, he disappeared with his wife into the adjoining room. Graesler explained to the parents that he would stay the night, because the first night was of critical importance, and if he watched by the patient, he might head off dangers of which the first signs would escape lay people.

'I say, Katharina,' said the father, coming close to the bed, 'you're a lucky one. Not many people have a doctor stay with them all night. But –' he drew Graesler towards the door – 'I had better tell you right away that we're not wealthy people. When she was in the country, it was only as Ludmilla's guest. You may have noticed it. We merely had to pay her ticket there and back.'

His wife told him to stop talking, and led him off into the

living room, so as to leave Katharina alone with the doctor.

Graesler leaned over the sick girl; he stroked her cheeks and her hair; he kissed her forehead; he assured her that she would be quite well again in a few days, and must come back to him. He would never let her leave him again, but would take her with him wherever fate led him. He had been drawn back to her by a tremendous force. She was his child, his beloved, his wife. He loved her as no one had ever been loved before.

She smiled contentedly, but as he went on he could tell that his words scarcely penetrated her consciousness. What was going on around her was to her no more than a succession of flitting shadows. He realized that this was to be the beginning of days filled with cruel dread for a loved being who was the prey of an invisible enemy drawing ever nearer. He must arm himself for a desperate struggle, a struggle that from the very start he knew was a hopeless one.

For three days and three nights Graesler watched almost without intermission at Katharina's bedside. She never regained full consciousness, and passed away on a gloomy November evening. Two days later, during which Graesler was completely occupied by all the dreary matters attendant upon a death, the funeral was held.

He walked behind the coffin. To Katharina's relatives he said not a word beyond what was absolutely necessary. In his grief they seemed far, far away. He stood beside the grave rigid until the coffin was lowered, then, without taking leave of the others, he stalked out of the cemetery and drove to his flat.

Till evening he lay on the sofa in his study, plunged in a heavy sleep. It was dark when he awoke. He was alone, more alone that he had ever been before, even after the death of his parents and sister. His life seemed to have lost all meaning.

He went out into the street, without knowing what to do or where to turn. He hated people, the city, the world, his profession – his profession which had killed the one creature who had seemed destined to bring happiness to him in his declining years. What was there left for him on earth? The one consolation seemed that he could, if he wanted to, abandon medicine and never exchange another word with a human being.

The streets were damp. A white mist lay on the lawn in the park where he was walking. He looked up. Torn clouds raced across the sky. He felt tired, tired of his aimless wandering, tired of his own company. He couldn't bear being by himself. It was impossible to go home and spend a desperately lonely night in the rooms where he had been so happy with Katharina, telling over his own fate in the same unmeaning phrases, without response from somewhere, without consolation or sympathy. If he were not to sob and scream and curse out there under the heavens, he knew he had to find some human being to talk to.

His old friend Böhlinger was the only one who would do. So he made for his old friend's house. Fortune favoured him; the lawyer was at home. Graesler found him seated at his desk, wearing a Turkish dressing-gown and veiled in tobacco smoke.

'You here again? What's up? A rather late visit!' He glanced at the clock. It was ten.

'I'm sorry,' said Graesler, in a hoarse voice. 'I hope I'm not disturbing you.'

'Of course not! Sit down. Have a cigar?'

'Thanks,' answered Graesler. 'I can't smoke now. I haven't had any supper yet.'

Böhlinger glanced at him with knitted brows. 'Something serious seems to have happened. How about the sanatorium?'

'Nothing has come of it.'

'Well, well. But that's not what has hit you so hard, is it? Tell me. Of course, I'm delighted to see you at any time, but your coming as late as this – I know there's a special reason. Go on, confess. Do you want advice? A woman in the case?' He smiled. 'Unfaithful?'

Graesler made a gesture of dissent.

'She is dead,' he said harshly. He sprang to his feet and paced up and down the room.

'Oh,' said Böhlinger. He was silent for a space. When Graesler passed him, he seized his hand and pressed it several times. Graesler sank into a chair. He put his head in his hands and wept bitterly, as he had not wept since childhood. Böhlinger waited and smoked. Now and then he glanced at a document on his desk and made a note or two in the margin. When Graesler began to recover his composure, he asked gently: 'How did it happen? She was so young.'

Graesler looked up, his lips drawn in a smile of derision. 'She certainly did not die of senile decay. It was scarlet fever. And it was my fault – my fault.'

'Your fault? Did you bring the infection from the hospital?'

Graesler shook his head, leapt to his feet again, and tramped the room, shaking his hands desperately.

Böhlinger leaned back, watching him.

'How if you told me about it,' he said. 'Perhaps it would make you feel easier.'

Graesler began to tell the whole story of the last few months, hesitatingly at first, inconsecutively, but growing more fluent as he went on. He told of Sabine as well as of Katharina; of his hopes and fears, of his renewed youth; of his dreams in the health resort and in his native town; and of how all had come to naught. Sometimes it seemed to him as if Sabine must be dead, too – that he had killed them both. Occasionally Böhlinger interjected an inquiry or a sympathetic word. When the story was complete he asked :

'Did you come back really intending to marry the girl?'

'Certainly. Do you think her past would have prevented me?'

'By no means. I know that women with a future are not always to be preferred.' He stared into space.

'You may be right there,' said Graesler. Looking straight at Böhlinger he added : 'There was something else I wanted to tell you . . .' He paused.

The tone of his voice surprised Böhlinger.

'What do you mean?'

'I have read your letters to Friederike – your letters, and other men's letters to her, too.'

'Have you really?' said Böhlinger, hardly perturbed, but with rather a wry smile. 'That is an old story, my friend.'

'Yes, it is an old story,' rejoined Graesler. Feeling the need to sum up his attitude towards the affair briefly and once for all, he added : 'Of course the letters made it clear to me why you did not marry her after all.'

Böhlinger looked at him uncomprehendingly. Then, his mouth twitching, he answered :

'You think it was because – because she deceived me? That's how the phrase runs. Good Lord, what a fuss one makes about those things when one is young. In reality, she only deceived herself, and I – I deceived myself. Especially the latter. Well, now it's too late.'

They were silent for a space.

'It is an old story,' repeated Graesler at length, as if in sleep. Intense exhaustion had overwhelmed him, he could hardly keep his eyes open. But he started up when Böhlinger took his hand

and cordially urged him to stay the night. He even offered him his own bed. Graesler preferred to lie down as he was, fully dressed, on the sofa in the study. Instantly a profound sleep took him. Böhlinger covered him with a rug, opened the window for a while to let out the fumes of tobacco, arranged the papers on his desk, and left Graesler to his slumbers.

When he awoke, he found Böhlinger standing over him with a sympathetic smile.

'Good morning,' said the lawyer, with a kind glance.

'Like a doctor,' thought Graesler, 'like a doctor when a child wakes up from the first healing sleep.'

The pale autumn sunshine was streaming into the room. Graesler realized that he must have slept a long while. 'What time is it?'

At that moment the midday bells began to chime.

He rose and shook his friend by the hand.

'Many thanks for your hospitality. It's time for me to be getting home now.'

'I'll go with you,' said Böhlinger. 'It is Sunday, and I have nothing to do in the office. But you must breakfast first, and the bath is ready.'

Graesler accepted his attentions gratefully. Refreshed by his bath, he went to the dining-room, where breakfast was already served. Böhlinger sat beside him and served him, telling him all the news in politics and municipal affairs, trying to keep his thoughts away from his troubles.

'What is the world to me?' thought Graesler, 'or the city or the people? Yes, if Sabine could be restored to life – Katharina,' he corrected himself, 'Sabine is still alive – after a fashion.' He smiled, scarcely knowing why.

The friends went out together. The streets were alive with people in their Sunday best, and Böhlinger exchanged numerous greetings. When they passed the glove shop in the Wilhelmstrasse, Graesler regarded its closed shutters with hatred and horror. At length they reached the house where Graesler lived.

'If you have no objection,' said Böhlinger when they reached Graesler's house, 'I will come up with you.'

Out of the front door came a woman plump, pretty, wearing widow's weeds, the gravity of which was modified by the smart tilt of her hat. She was holding a little girl's hand. Her face lit up with surprise and pleasure when she saw the doctor.

'Look! Who's that, Fanny?' she exclaimed delightedly.

But Graesler's eyes went wide as with horror and he gave the child one glance of uncontrolled hate. Without the faintest greeting he passed through the doorway.

Böhlinger noticed that the lady, still holding her daughter by the hand, stood looking after Graesler in amazement, almost in despair. With a displeased shake of his head, he followed him upstairs, determined to ask for an explanation. But before the door of the flat had closed behind them, Graesler burst out:

'That was the child, the mother and the child. It was the child's fault. Katharina had to die, and the child I cured.'

'You can't speak of fault,' rejoined Böhlinger. 'The child's not to blame, neither is the mother. The way you behaved must have been incomprehensible to her.'

'I know it,' said Graesler. 'And of course she doesn't know what happened since we last saw each other.'

'You stared at her as if she were a ghost. And the way you looked at the child! You should have seen the mother's face. She was frightened almost out of her wits.'

'I am sorry,' said Graesler. 'But she'll get over it. I'll explain the first chance I get.'

'You should.' In a merry tone, Böhlinger added: 'Especially as she's a very pretty, pleasant-looking little person.'

Graesler wrinkled his brows and made a gesture of warding off. He begged to be excused a few moments to look at his letters, which he had not seen since his return and might contain something important. The fact was, he could not suppress a faint hope that there might be a word from Sabine calling him back, though he realized the utter senselessness of such a hope. There was not a single communication of the slightest moment.

The friends went to a restaurant. Over a bottle of excellent Rhenish, in the dim light of a warm, cosy recess, Böhlinger advised Graesler not to give himself up to useless sorrow and to take up his work again as soon as possible. The doctor promised to write that very day to Lanzarote to say he would be back by the end of the month. He was confident that he would be welcome.

Over the coffee and cigars, they talked of Friederike. Böhlinger sat amid the smoke-wreaths and listened with half-closed eyes, while Graesler spoke of her with emotion, praising her thoughtfulness and loyalty. He even intimated that when she had her room redecorated and refurnished, she had not been thinking of herself, but, with a prophetic, self-sacrificing sense, of some other woman who might be destined to become her brother's helpmate and beloved.

Böhlinger merely nodded. Every now and then he gave Graesler, whom he had never known so garrulous before, a look of amazement not unmixed with pity. By and by his attention wandered; he even seemed a trifle impatient, and suddenly arose saying he had an engagement that evening.

Graesler walked home alone. As he paced his study, he felt his grief gradually turn into boredom. He sat down at his desk, and penned a letter to the hotel manager at Lanzarote, explaining that he had to postpone his coming this year, but felt sure it would not cause much inconvenience, since few visitors arrived earlier than the middle or even the latter part of November.

That was the end of his day's work. He took hat and stick, intending to go for another walk.

On the way downstairs passing Frau Sommer's door, he hesitated a moment, then rang the bell. The door was opened by the lady herself, who greeted him more cordially than he had any right to expect. He promptly apologized for his behaviour that morning. Perhaps Frau Sommer already knew what a disaster had befallen him – and be ready to forgive him.

'I have no idea what you are referring to,' she answered. 'Won't you come in and tell me all about your trouble?'

Graesler entered and told Frau Sommer that his dear little friend had died after a few days' illness; of what she had died he did not say until Frau Sommer expressed her condolence.

'There's been a great deal of scarlet fever,' he said, 'almost an epidemic. So I suppose there was no connection between Katharina's illness and little Fanny's especially as Fanny's illness was so mild that I have some doubt as to whether or not it really was scarlet fever.'

Fanny herself came running in. Graesler took her between his knees, stroked her hair, and kissed her forehead.

Tears came to his eyes. He wept quietly. When he looked up again he saw tears in the young widow's eyes.

Next day he visited Katharina's grave, accompanied by Frau Sommer and Fanny. While Graesler stood in silence with bowed head, and Frau Sommer read the inscriptions on the ribbons tying the few simple wreaths that still lay there, the little girl knelt down and prayed with folded hands. On the way back they stopped at a confectioner's, and Fanny returned home with a large box of sweets.

Henceforth Frau Sommer looked after the bereaved bachelor with unostentatious kindness. He spent much of his time, in fact every evening, in the widow's flat. He grew fonder and fonder of the little girl, and always brought her toys, especially wild beasts made of wood or papier-mâché, about which Fanny insisted on having stories as if they had been real but enchanted animals. As for Frau Sommer every day she showed by word and look her increasing gratitude for the affection the doctor lavished on her fatherless child.

Less than a month had elapsed since Katharina's death when Dr Emil Graesler landed on the island of Lanzarote with little Fanny and her mother, who was now Frau Graesler. The hotel manager was standing beside the gangway, bareheaded as usual, his smoothly-plastered brown hair scarcely ruffled by the breeze.

'Welcome, my dear doctor,' was his greeting uttered in the American accent which had irked Graesler the year before. 'Welcome, indeed! You have given us a long wait, but we are all the happier to see you. The villa is ready for you, and I do hope Frau Graesler will find it to her taste.' He bowed over Frau Graesler's hand, and fondled the little girl's cheek.

The air was drenched in sunshine, as on a summer day. They walked up to the hotel, which faced them in its glaring whiteness, the manager leading the way in lively conversation with the young wife. Behind came Graesler and little Fanny, who was wearing a rather crumpled white linen frock, and whose black hair was tied with a white silk ribbon.

'Do you see that small white house,' said Graesler, 'the one with all the windows open? That's where you're going to live. Just behind it – you can't see it from here – there's a garden with wonderful trees such as you've never seen before. You'll play under those trees; and when it's snowing where you used to live, and when people are freezing there, the sun will shine in the garden just as it's shining today.'

He went on talking to her, holding her soft hand in his, its gentle pressure thrilling him with a happiness that no other such contact had ever brought him. Fanny looked up at him eagerly drinking in every word.

The manager continued to hold forth to the young wife.

'The season has opened auspiciously,' he said. 'Your husband will have plenty to do. On the fourth of next month we are expecting His Highness the Duke of Sigmaringen, with the Duchess, children, and suite ... Ah, this is a choice spot indeed. A perfect little paradise. As Herr Rüdenau-Hansen, the distinguished author who has visited our island regularly for twelve years in succession, remarked ...'

The wind, which stirs on these shores even on the calmest days, blew away the next words – and many more of the same nature.

The Spring Sonata

She was walking slowly down the hill; not by the broad high road which wound its way towards the town, but by the narrow footpath between the trellises of the vines. Her little boy was with her, hanging on to her hand and walking all the time a pace in front of her, because there was not room on the footpath for them to walk side by side.

The afternoon was well advanced, but the sun still poured down upon her with sufficient power to cause her to pull her dark straw hat a little further down over her forehead and to keep her eyes lowered. The slopes, at the foot of which the little town lay nestling, glimmered as though seen through a golden mist; the roofs of the houses below glistened, and the river, emerging yonder amongst the meadows outside the town, stretched, shimmering, into the distance. Not a quiver stirred the air, and it seemed as if the cool of the evening was yet far remote.

Bertha stopped for a moment and glanced about her. Save for her boy, she was all alone on the hill side, and around her brooded a curious stillness. At the cemetery, too, on the hilltop, she had not met anybody that day, not even the old woman who usually watered the flowers and kept the graves tidy, and with whom Bertha used often to have a chat. Bertha felt that somehow a considerable time had elapsed since she had started on her walk, and that it was long since she had spoken to anyone.

The church clock struck – six. So, then, scarcely an hour had passed since she had left the house, and an even shorter time since she had stopped in the street to chat with the beautiful Frau Rupius. Yet even the few minutes which had slipped away since she had stood by her husband's grave now seemed to be long past.

'Mamma!'

Suddenly she heard her boy call. He had slipped his hand out of hers and had run on ahead.

'I can walk quicker than you, mamma!'

'Wait, though! Wait, Fritz!' exclaimed Bertha. 'You're not going to leave your mother alone, are you?'

She followed him and again took him by the hand.

'Are we going home already?' asked Fritz.

'Yes; we will sit by the open window until it grows quite dark.'

Before long they had reached the foot of the hill and they began to walk towards the town in the shade of the chestnut trees which bordered the high-road, now white with dust. Here again they met but few people. Along the road a couple of wagons came towards them, the drivers, whip in hand, trudging along beside the horses. Then two cyclists rode by from the town towards the country, leaving clouds of dust behind them. Bertha stopped mechanically and gazed after them until they had almost disappeared from view.

In the meantime Fritz had clambered up on to the bench beside the road.

'Look, mamma! See what I can do!'

He made ready to jump, but his mother took hold of him by the arms and lifted him carefully to the ground. Then she sat down on the bench.

'Are you tired?' asked Fritz.

'Yes,' she answered, surprised to find that she was indeed feeling fatigued.

It was only then that she realized that the sultry air had wearied her to the point of sleepiness. She could not, moreover, remember having experienced such warm weather in the middle of May.

From the bench on which she was sitting she could trace back the course of the path down which she had come. In the sunlight it ran between the vine-trellises, up and up, until it reached the brightly gleaming wall of the cemetery. She was in the habit of taking a walk along that path two or three times a week. She had long since ceased to regard such visits to the cemetery as anything other than a mere walk. When she wandered about the well-kept gravel paths amongst the crosses and the tombstones, or stood offering up a silent prayer beside her husband's grave, or, maybe, laying upon it the few wild flowers which she had plucked on her way up, her heart was scarcely any longer stirred by the slightest throb of pain. Three years had, indeed, passed since her husband had died, which was just as long as their married life had lasted.

Her eyes closed and her mind went back to the time when she had first come to the town, only a few days after their marriage – which had taken place in Vienna. They had only indulged in a modest honeymoon trip, such as a man in humble circumstances, who had married a woman without any dowry, could treat himself to. They had taken the boat from Vienna, up the river, to a little village in Wachau, not far from their future home, and had spent a few days there. Bertha could still remember clearly the little inn at which they had stayed, the riverside garden in which they used to sit after sunset, and those quiet, rather tedious, evenings which were so completely different from those her girlish imagination had previously pictured to her as the evenings which a newly-married couple would spend. Of course, she had had to be content.

She was twenty-six years old and quite alone in the world when Victor Mathias Garlan had proposed to her. Her parents had recently died. A long time before, one of her brothers had gone to America to seek his fortune as a merchant. Her younger brother was on the stage; he had married an actress, and was playing comedy parts in third-rate German theatres. She was almost out of touch with her relations and the only one whom she visited occasionally was a cousin who had married a lawyer. But even that friendship had grown cool as years had passed, because the cousin had become wrapped up in her husband and children exclusively, and had almost ceased to take any interest in the doings of her unmarried friend.

Herr Garlan was a distant relation of Bertha's mother. When Bertha was quite a young girl he had often visited the house and made love to her in a rather awkward way. In those days she had no reason to encourage him, because it was in another guise that her fancy pictured life and happiness to her. She was young and pretty; her parents, though not actually wealthy people, were comfortably off, and her hope was rather to wander about the world as a great pianiste, perhaps, as the wife of an artist, than to lead a modest existence in the placid routine of the home circle. But that hope soon faded. One day her father, in a transport of domestic fervour, forbade her further attendance at the conservatoire of music, which put an end to her prospects of an artistic career and at the same time to her friendship with the young violinist who had since made such a name for himself.

The next few years were singularly dull. At first, it is true, she felt some slight disappointment, or even pain, but these emotions were certainly of short duration. Later on she had received offers of marriage from a young doctor and a merchant. She refused both of them; the doctor because he was too ugly, and the merchant because he lived in a country town. Her parents, too, were by no means enthusiastic about either suitor.

When, however, Bertha's twenty-sixth birthday passed and her father lost his modest competency through a bankruptcy, it had been her lot to put up with belated reproaches on the score of all sorts of things which she herself had begun to forget – her youthful artistic ambitions, her love affair of long ago with the violinist, which had seemed likely to lead to nothing, and the lack of encouragement which the ugly doctor and the merchant from the country had received at her hands.

At that time Victor Mathias Garlan was no longer resident in Vienna. Two years before, the insurance company, in which he had been employed since he had reached the age of twenty, had, at his own request, transferred him, in the capacity of manager, to the recently-established branch in the little town on the Danube where his married brother carried on business as a wine merchant. In the course of a somewhat lengthy conversation which took place on the occasion of his farewell visit to Bertha's parents, and which created a certain impression upon her, he had mentioned that the principal reasons for his asking to be transferred to the little town were that he felt himself to be getting on in years, that he had no longer any idea of seeking a wife, and that he desired to have some sort of a home amongst people who were closely connected with him. At that time Bertha's parents had made fun of his notion, which seemed to them somewhat hypochondriacal, for Garlan was then scarcely forty years old. Bertha herself, however, had found a good deal of common sense in Garlan's reason, inasmuch as he had never appeared to her as, properly speaking, a young man.

In the course of the following years Garlan used often to come to Vienna on business, and never omitted to visit Bertha's family on such occasions. After supper it was Bertha's custom to play the piano for Garlan's entertainment, and he used to listen to her with an almost reverent attention, and would, perhaps, go on to talk of his little nephew and niece – who were both very musical – and to whom he would often speak of Fräulein Bertha as the finest pianiste he had ever heard.

It seemed strange, and Bertha's mother could not refrain from commenting now and again upon it, that, since his diffident wooing in the old days, Herr Garlan had not once ventured so much as to make the slightest further allusion to the past, or even to a possible future. And thus Bertha, in addition to the other reproaches to which she had to listen, incurred the blame of treating Herr Garlan with too great indifference, if not indeed with actual coldness. Bertha, however, only shook her head, for at that time she had not so much as contemplated the possibility of marrying this somewhat awkward man, who had grown old before his time.

After the sudden death of her mother, which happened at a time when her father had been lying ill for many months, Garlan reappeared upon the scene with the announcement that he had obtained a month's holiday – the only one for which he had ever applied. It was clearly evident to Bertha that his sole purpose in coming to Vienna was to be of help to her in that time of trouble and distress. And when Bertha's father died a week after the funeral of her mother, Garlan proved himself to be a true friend, and one, moreover, blessed with an amount of energy for which she had never given him credit. He prevailed on his sister-in-law to come to Vienna, so that she could help Bertha to tide over the first few weeks of her bereavement, besides, in some slight degree, distracting her thoughts. He settled the business affairs capably and quickly. His kindness of heart did much to cheer Bertha during those sad days, and when, on the expiration of his leave, he asked her whether she would be his wife she acquiesced with a feeling of the most profound gratitude. She was, of course, aware of the fact that if she did not marry him she would in a few months' time have to earn her own living, probably as a teacher, and, besides, she had come to appreciate Garlan and had become so used to his company that she was able, in all sincerity, to answer 'Yes,' both when he led her to the altar and subsequently when, as they set off for their honeymoon, he asked her, for the first time, if she loved him.

It was true that at the very outset of their married life she discovered that she felt no love for him. She just let him love her and put up with the fact, at first with a certain surprise at her own disillusionment and afterwards with indifference. It was not until she found that she was about to become a mother that she could bring herself to reciprocate his affection. She very soon grew accustomed to the quiet life of the little town, all the more easily because even in Vienna she had led a somewhat secluded existence. With her husband's family she felt quite happy and comfortable; her brother-in-law appeared to be a most genial and amiable person, if not altogether innocent of an occasional display of coarseness; his wife was good-natured, and inclined at times to be melancholy. Garlan's nephew, who was thirteen years old at the time of Bertha's arrival at the little town, was a pert, good-looking boy; and his niece, a very sedate child of nine, with large, astonished eyes, conceived a strong attachment for Bertha from the very first moment that they met.

When Bertha's child was born, he was hailed by the children as a welcome plaything, and, for the next two years, Bertha felt completely happy. She even believed at times that it was impossible that her fate could have taken a more favourable shape. The noise and bustle of the great city came back to her memory as something unpleasant, almost hazardous; and on one occasion when she had accompanied her husband to Vienna, in order to make a few purchases and it so chanced, to her annoyance, that the streets were wet and muddy with the rain, she vowed never again to undertake that tedious and wholly unnecessary journey of three hours' duration.

Her husband died suddenly one spring morning three years after their marriage. Bertha's consternation was extreme. She felt that she had never taken into consideration the mere possibility of such an event. She was left in very straitened circumstances. Soon, however, her sister-in-law, with thoughtful kindness, devised a means by which the widow could support herself without appearing to accept anything in the nature of charity. She asked Bertha to take over the musical education of her children, and also procured for her an engagement as music teacher to other families in the town. It was tacitly understood amongst the ladies who engaged her that they should always make it appear as if Bertha had undertaken these lessons only for the sake of a little distraction, and that they paid her for them only because they could not possibly allow her to devote so much time and trouble in that way without some return. What she earned from this source was quite sufficient to supplement her income to an amount adequate to meet the demands of her mode of living, and so, when time had deadened the first keen pangs and the subsequent sorrow occasioned by her husband's death, she was again quite contented and cheerful. Her life up to then had not been spent in such a way as to cause her now to feel the lack of anything. Such thoughts as she gave to the future were occupied by scarcely any other theme than her son in the successive stages of his growth, and it was only on rare occasions that the likelihood of marrying a second time crossed her mind, and then the idea was always a mere fleeting fancy, for as yet she had met no one whom she was able seriously to regard in the light of a possible second husband. The stirrings of youthful desires, which she sometimes felt within her in her waking morning hours, always vanished as the day pursued its even course. It was only since the advent of the spring that she had felt a certain disturbance of her previous sensation of well-being; no longer were her nights passed in the tranquil and dreamless sleep of heretofore, and at times she was oppressed by a sensation of tedium, such as she had never experienced before. Strangest of all, however, was the sudden access of lassitude which would often come over her even in the daytime, under the influence of which she fancied that she could trace the course of her blood as it circled through her body. She remembered that she had experienced a similar sensation in the days when she was emerging from childhood. At first this feeling, in spite of its familiarity, was yet so strange to her that it seemed as though one of her friends must have told her about it. It was only when it recurred with ever-increasing frequency that she realized that she herself had experienced it before.

She shuddered, with a feeling as though she were waking from sleep. She opened her eyes.

It seemed to her that the air was all a-whirl; the shadows had crept halfway across the road; away up on the hilltop the cemetery wall no longer gleamed in the sunlight. Bertha rapidly shook her head to and fro a few times as though to waken herself thoroughly. It seemed to her as if a whole day and a whole night had elapsed since she had sat down on the bench. How was it, then, that in her consciousness time passed in so disjointed a fashion? She looked around her. Where could Fritz have gone to? Oh, there he was behind her, playing with Doctor Friedrich's children. The nursemaid was on her knees beside them, helping them to build a castle with the sand.

The avenue was now less deserted than it had been earlier in the evening. Bertha knew almost all the people who passed; she saw them every day. As, however, most of them were not people to whom she was in the habit of talking, they flitted by like shadows. Yonder came the saddler, Peter Nowak, and his wife; Doctor Rellinger drove by in his little country trap and bowed to her as he passed; he was followed by the two daughters of Herr Wendelein, the landowner; presently Lieutenant Baier and his fiancée cycled slowly down the road on their way to the country. Then, again, there seemed to be a short lull in the movement before her and Bertha heard nothing but the laughter of the children as they played.

Then, again, she saw that some one was slowly approaching from the town, and she recognized who it was while he was still a long way off. It was Herr Klingemann, to whom of late she had been in the habit of talking more frequently than had previously been her custom. Some twelve years ago or more he had moved from Vienna to the little town. Gossip had it that he had at one time been a doctor, and had been obliged to give up his practice on account of some professional error, or even of some more serious lapse. Some, however, asserted that he had never qualified as a doctor at all, but, failing to pass his examinations, had finally given up the study of medicine. Herr Klingemann, for his own part, gave himself out to be a philosopher, who had grown weary of life in the great city after having enjoyed it to satiety, and for that reason had moved to the little town, where he could live comfortably on what remained of his fortune.

He was now but little more than five-and-forty. There were still times when he was of a genial enough aspect, but, for the most part, he had an extremely dilapidated and disagreeable appearance.

While yet some distance away he smiled at the young widow, but did not hasten his steps. Finally he stopped before her and gave her an ironical nod, which was his habitual manner of greeting people.

'Good evening, my pretty lady!' he said.

Bertha returned his salutation. It was one of those days on which Herr Klingemann appeared to make some claim to elegance and youthfulness. He was attired in a dark grey frock coat, so tightly fitting that he might almost have been wearing stays. On his head was a narrow brimmed brown straw hat with a black band. About his throat, moreover, there was a very tiny red cravat, set rather askew.

For a time he remained silent, tugging his slightly grizzled fair moustache upwards and downwards.

'I presume you have come from up there, my dear lady?' he said.

Without turning his head or even his eyes, he pointed his finger over his shoulder, in a somewhat contemptuous manner, in the direction of the cemetery behind him.

Throughout the town Herr Klingemann was known as a man to whom nothing was sacred, and as he stood before her, Bertha could not help thinking of the various bits of gossip that she had heard about him. It was well known that his relations with his cook, whom he always referred to as his housekeeper, were of a somewhat more intimate nature than that merely of master and servant, and his name was also mentioned in connection with the wife of a tobacconist, who, as he had himself told Bertha with proud regret, deceived him with a captain of the regiment stationed in the town. Moreover, there were several eligible girls in the neighbourhood who cherished a certain tender interest in him.

Whenever these things were hinted at Herr Klingemann always made some sneering remark on the subject of marriage in general, which shocked the susceptibilities of many, but, on the whole, actually increased the amount of respect in which he was held.

'I have been out for a short walk,' said Bertha.

'Alone?'

'Oh, no, with my boy.'

'Yes – yes – of course, there he is! Good evening, my little mortal!' – he gazed away over Fritz's head as he said this – 'may I sit down for a moment beside you, Frau Bertha?'

He pronounced her name with an ironic inflection and, without waiting for her to reply, he sat down on the bench.

'I heard you playing the piano this morning,' he continued. 'Do you know what kind of an impression it made upon me? This: that with you music must take the place of everything.'

He repeated the word 'everything' and, at the same time, looked at Bertha in a manner which caused her to blush.

'What a pity I so seldom have the opportunity of hearing you play!' he went on. 'If I don't happen to be passing your open window when you are at the piano –'

Bertha noticed that he kept on edging nearer to her, and that his arm was touching hers. Involuntarily she moved away. Suddenly she felt herself seized from behind, her head pulled back over the bench and a hand clasped over her eyes.

For a moment she thought that it was Klingemann's hand, which she felt upon her lids.

'Why, you must be mad, sir,' she cried.

'How funny it is to hear you call me "Sir," Aunt Bertha!' replied the laughing voice of a boy behind her back.

'Well, do let me at least open my eyes, Richard,' said Bertha, trying to remove the boy's hands from her face. 'Have you come from home?' she added, turning round towards him.

'Yes, Aunt, and here's the newspaper which I have brought you.'

Bertha took the paper which he handed to her and began to read it.

Klingemann, meanwhile, rose to his feet and turned to Richard.

'Have you done your exercises already?' he asked.

'We have no exercises at all now, Herr Klingemann, because our final examination is to take place in July.'

'So you will actually be a student by this time next year?'

'This time next year! It'll be in the autumn!'

As he said this Richard drummed his fingers along the newspaper.

'What do you want, then, you ill-mannered fellow?' asked Bertha.

'I say, Aunt, will you come and visit me when I am in Vienna?'

'Yes, I should like to catch myself! I shall be glad to be rid of you!'

'Here comes Herr Rupius!' said Richard.

Bertha lowered the paper and looked in the direction indicated by her nephew's glance. Along the avenue leading from the town a maidservant came, pushing an invalid's chair, in which a man was sitting. His head was uncovered and his soft felt hat was lying upon his knees, from which a plaid rug reached down to his feet. His forehead was lofty; his hair smooth and fair and slightly grizzled at the temples; his eyes were peculiarly large. As he passed the bench on which Bertha was seated he only inclined his head slightly, without smiling. Bertha knew that, had she been alone, he would certainly have stopped; moreover, he looked only at her as he passed by, and his greeting seemed to apply to her alone. It seemed to Bertha that she had never before seen such a grave look in his eyes as on this occasion, and she was exceedingly sorry, for she felt a profound compassion for the paralysed man.

When Herr Rupius had passed by, Klingemann said:

'Poor devil! And wifie is away as usual on one of her visits to Vienna, eh?'

'No,' answered Bertha, almost angrily. 'I was speaking to her only an hour ago.'

Klingemann was silent, for he felt that further remarks on the subject of the mysterious visits of Frau Rupius to Vienna might not have been in keeping with his own reputation as a freethinker.

'Won't he really ever be able to walk again?' asked Richard.

'No,' said Bertha.

She knew this for a fact because Herr Rupius had told her so himself on one occasion when she had called on him and his wife was in Vienna.

At that moment Herr Rupius seemed to her to be a particularly pitiful figure, for, as he was being wheeled past her in his invalid's chair, she had, in reading the paper, lighted upon the name of one whom she regarded as a happy man.

Mechanically she read the paragraph again.

'Our celebrated compatriot Emil Lindbach returned to Vienna a few days ago after his professional tour through France and Spain, in the course of which he met with many a triumphant reception. In Madrid this distinguished artist had the honour of playing before the Queen of Spain. On the 24th of this month Herr Lindbach will take part in the charity concert which has been organized for the relief of the inhabitants of Vorarlberg, who have suffered such severe losses as a result of the recent floods. A keen interest in the concert is being shown by the public in spite of the fact that the season is so far advanced.'

Emil Lindbach! It required a certain effort on Bertha's part to realize that this was the same man whom she had loved – how many? – twelve years ago. Twelve years! She could feel the hot blood mount up into her brow. It seemed to her as though she ought to be ashamed of having gradually grown older.

The sun had set. Bertha took Fritz by the hand, bade the others good evening, and walked slowly homewards.

She lived on the first floor of a house in a new street. From her windows she had a view of the hill, and opposite were only vacant sites.

Bertha handed Fritz over to the care of the maid, sat down by the window, took up the paper and began to read again. She had kept the custom of glancing through the art news first of all. This habit had been formed in the days of her early childhood, when she and her brother, who was now an actor, used to go to the top gallery of the Burg-Theatre together. Her interest in art naturally grew when she attended the conservatoire of music; in those days she had been acquainted with the names of even the minor actors, singers and pianists. Later on, when her frequent visits to the theatres, the studies at the conservatoire and her own artistic aspirations came to an end, there still lingered within her a kind of sympathy, which was not free from the touch of home-sickness, towards that joyous world of art. But during the latter portion of her life in Vienna all these things had retained scarcely any of their former significance for her; just as little, indeed, as they had possessed since she had come to reside in the little town, where occasional amateur concerts were the best that was offered in the way of artistic enjoyment. One evening during the first year of her married life, she had taken part in one of these concerts at the 'Red Apple' Hotel. She had played two marches by Schubert as a duet with another young lady in the town. On that occasion her agitation had been so great that she had vowed to herself never again to appear in public, and was more than glad that she had given up her hopes of an artistic career.

For such a career a very different temperament from hers was necessary – for example, one like Emil Lindbach's. Yes, he was born to it! She had recognized that by his demeanour the very moment when she had first seen him step on to the daïs at a school concert. He had smoothed back his hair in an unaffected manner, gazed at the people below with sardonic superiority, and had acknowledged the first applause which he had ever received in the calm, indifferent manner of one long accustomed to such things.

It was strange, but whenever she thought of Emil Lindbach she still saw him in her mind's eye as youthful, even boyish, just as he had been in the days when they had known and loved each other. Yet not so long before, when she had spent the evening with her brother-in-law and his wife in a restaurant, she had seen a photograph of him in an illustrated paper, and he appeared to have changed greatly. He no longer wore his hair long; his black moustache was curled downwards; his collar was conspicuously tall, and his cravat was twisted in accordance with the fashion of the day. Her sister-in-law had given her opinion that he looked like a Polish count.

Bertha took up the newspaper again and was about to read on, but by that time it was too dark. She rose to her feet and called the maid. The lamp was brought in and the table laid for supper. Bertha ate her meal with Fritz, the window remaining open. That evening she felt an even greater tenderness for her child than usual; she recalled once more to memory the times when her husband was still alive, and all manner of reminiscences passed rapidly through her mind. While she was putting Fritz to bed, her glance lingered for quite a long time on her husband's portrait which hung over the bed in an oval frame of dark brown wood. It was a full-length portrait; he was wearing a morning coat and a white cravat, and was holding his tall hat in his hand. It was all in memory of their wedding day.

Bertha knew for a certainty, at that moment, that Herr Klingemann would have smiled sarcastically had he seen that portrait.

Later in the evening she sat down at the piano, as was a not infrequent custom of hers before going to bed, not so much because of her enthusiasm for music, but because she did not want to retire to rest too early. On such occasions she played, for the most part, the few pieces which she still knew by heart – mazurkas by Chopin, some passages from one of Beethoven's sonatas, or the Kreisleriana. Sometimes she improvised as well, but never pursued the theme beyond a succession of chords, which, indeed, were always the same.

On that evening she began at once by striking those chords, somewhat more softly than usual; then she essayed various modulations and, as she made the last triad resound for a long time by means of the pedal – her hands were now lying in her lap – she felt a gentle joy in the melodies which were hovering, as it were, about her. Then Klingemann's observation recurred to her.

'With you music must take the place of everything!'

Indeed he had not been far from the truth. Music certainly had to take the place of much.

But everything –? Oh, no!

What was that? Footsteps over the way . . .

Well, there was nothing remarkable in that. But they were slow, regular footsteps, as though somebody was passing up and down. She stood up and went to the window. It was quite dark, and at first she could not recognize the man who was walking outside. But she knew that it was Klingemann. How absurd! Was he going to haunt the vicinity like a love-sick swain?

'Good evening, Frau Bertha,' he said from across the road, and she could see in the darkness that he raised his hat.

'Good evening,' she answered, almost confusedly.

'You were playing most beautifully.'

Her only answer was to murmur 'really?' and that perhaps did not reach his ears.

He remained standing for a moment, then said:

'Good night, sleep soundly, Frau Bertha.'

He pronounced the word 'sleep' with an emphasis which was almost insolent.

'Now he is going home to his cook!' thought Bertha, to herself.

Then suddenly she called to mind something which she had known for quite a long time, but to which she had not given a thought since it had come to her knowledge. It was rumoured that in his room there hung a picture which was always covered with a little curtain because its subject was of a somewhat questionable nature.

Who was it had told her about that picture? Oh, yes, Frau Rupius had told her when they were taking a walk along the bank of the Danube one day last autumn, and she in her turn had heard of it from some one else – Bertha could not remember from whom.

What an odious man! Bertha felt that somehow she was

guilty of a slight depravity in thinking of him and all these things. She continued to stand by the window. It seemed to her as though it had been an unpleasant day. She went over the actual events in her mind, and was astonished to find that, after all, the day had just been like many hundreds before it and many, many more that were yet to come.

They stood up from the table. It had been one of those little Sunday dinner parties which the wine merchant Garlan was in the habit of occasionally giving his acquaintances. The host came up to his sister-in-law and caught her round the waist, which was one of his customs on an afternoon.

She knew beforehand what he wanted. Whenever he had company Bertha had to play the piano after dinner, and often duets with Richard. The music served as a pleasant introduction to a game of cards, or, indeed, chimed in pleasantly with the game.

She sat down at the piano. In the meantime the door of the smoking-room was opened; Garlan, Doctor Friedrich and Herr Martin took their seats at a small baize-covered table and began to play. The wives of the three gentlemen remained in the drawing-room, and Frau Martin lit a cigarette, sat down on the sofa and crossed her legs – on Sundays she always wore dress shoes and black silk stockings. Doctor Friedrich's wife looked at Frau Martin's feet as though fixed to the spot by enchantment. Richard had followed the gentlemen – he already took an interest in a game of taroc. Elly stood with her elbows leaning on the piano waiting for Bertha to begin to play. The hostess went in and out of the room; she was perpetually giving orders in the kitchen, and rattling the bunch of keys which she carried in her hand. Once as she came into the room Doctor Friedrich's wife threw her a glance which seemed to say: 'Just look how Frau Martin is sitting there!'

Bertha noticed all those things that day more clearly, as it were, than usual, somewhat after the manner in which things are seen by a person suffering from fever. She had not as yet struck a note. Then her brother-in-law turned towards her and threw her a glance, which was intended to remind her of her duty. She began to play a march by Schubert, with a very heavy touch.

'Softer,' said her brother-in-law, turning round again.

'Taroc with a musical accompaniment is a speciality of this house,' said Doctor Friedrich.

'Songs without words, so to speak,' added Herr Martin.

The others laughed. Garlan turned round towards Bertha again, for she had suddenly left off playing.

'I have a slight headache,' she said, as if it were necessary to make some excuse; immediately, however, she felt as though it were beneath her dignity to say that, and she added: 'I don't feel any inclination to play.'

Everybody looked at her, feeling that something rather out of the common was happening.

'Won't you come and sit by us, Bertha?' said Frau Garlan.

Elly had a vague idea that she ought to show her affection for her aunt, and hung on her arm; and the two of them stood side by side, leaning against the piano.

'Are you going with us to the "Red Apple" this evening?' Frau Martin asked her hostess.

'No, I don't think so.'

'Ah,' broke in Herr Garlan; 'if we must forgo our concert this afternoon we will have one in the evening instead – your lead, Doctor.'

'The military concert?' asked Doctor Friedrich's wife.

Frau Garlan rose to her feet.

'Do you really mean to go to the "Red Apple"? this evening,' she asked her husband.

'Certainly.'

'Very well,' she answered, somewhat flustered, and at once went off to the kitchen again to make fresh arrangements.

'Richard,' said Garlan to his son; 'you might make haste and run over and tell the manager to have a table reserved for us in the garden.'

Richard hurried off, colliding in the doorway with his mother, who was just coming into the room. She sank down on the sofa as though exhausted.

'You can't believe,' she said to Doctor Friedrich's wife; 'how difficult it is to make Brigitta understand the simplest thing.'

Frau Martin had gone and sat down beside her husband, at the same time throwing a glance towards Bertha who was still standing silently with Elly beside the piano. Frau Martin stroked her husband's hair, laid her hand on his knee and seemed to feel that she was under the necessity of showing the company how happy she was.

'I'll tell you what, Aunt,' said Elly suddenly to Bertha; 'let's go into the garden for awhile. The fresh air will drive your headache away.'

They went down the steps into the courtyard, in the centre of which a small lawn had been laid out. At the back, it was shut off by a wall, against which stood a few shrubs and a couple of young trees, which still had to be propped up by stakes. Away over the wall only the blue sky was to be seen; in boisterous weather the rush of the river which flowed close by could be heard. Two wicker garden chairs stood with their backs against the wall, and in front of them was a small table. Bertha and Elly sat down, Elly still keeping her arm linked in her aunt's.

'Won't you tell me, Aunt?'

'Tell you what, Elly?'

'See, I am quite a big girl now; do tell me about him.'

Bertha was somewhat alarmed, for it struck her at once that her niece's question did not refer to her dead husband, but to some one else. And suddenly she saw before her mind's eye the picture of Emil Lindbach, just as she had seen it in the illustrated paper; but immediately both the vision and her slight alarm vanished, and she felt a kind of emotion at the shy question of the young girl who believed that she still grieved for her dead husband, and that it would comfort her to have an opportunity for talking about him.

'May I come down and join you, or are you telling each other secrets?'

Richard's voice came at that moment from a window overlooking the courtyard. For the first time Bertha was struck by the resemblance he bore to Emil Lindbach. She realized, however, that it might perhaps only be the youthfulness of his manner and his rather long hair that put her in mind of Emil.

Richard was now nearly as old as Emil had been in the days of her studies at the conservatoire.

'I've reserved a table,' he said as he came into the courtyard. 'Are you coming with us, Aunt Bertha?'

He sat down on the back of her chair, stroked her cheeks, and said in his fresh, yet rather affected, way :

'You will come, won't you, pretty Aunt, for my sake?'

Mechanically Bertha closed her eyes. A feeling of comfort stole over her, as if some childish hand, as if the little fingers of her own Fritz, were caressing her cheeks. Soon, however, she felt that some other memory as well rose up in her mind. She could not help thinking of a walk in the town park which she had taken one evening with Emil after her lesson at the conservatoire. On that occasion he had sat down to rest beside her on a seat, and had touched her cheeks with tender fingers. Was it only once that that had happened? No – much oftener! Indeed, they had sat on that seat ten or twenty times, and he had stroked her cheeks. How strange it was that all these things should come back to her thoughts now!

She would certainly never have thought of those walks again had not Richard by chance – but how long was she going to put up with his stroking her cheek?

'Richard!' she exclaimed, opening her eyes.

She saw that he was smiling in such a way that she thought that he must have divined what was passing through her mind. Of course, it was quite impossible, because, as a matter of fact, scarcely anybody in the town was aware that she was acquainted with Emil Lindbach, the great violinist. If it came to that, was she really acquainted with him still? It was indeed a very different person from Emil as he must now be that she had in mind – a handsome youth whom she had loved in the days of her early girlhood.

Thus her thoughts strayed further and further back into the past, and it seemed altogether impossible for her to return to the present and chatter with the two children.

She bade them good-bye and went away.

The afternoon sun lay brooding heavily upon the streets of the little town. The shops were shut, the pavements almost deserted. A few officers were sitting at a little table in front of the restaurant in the market square. Bertha glanced up at the windows of the first story of the house in which Herr and Frau Rupius lived. It was quite a long time since she had been to see them. She clearly remembered the last occasion – it was the day after Christmas. It was then that she had found Herr Rupius alone and that he had told her that his affliction was incurable. She also remembered distinctly why she had not called upon him since that day: although she did not admit it to herself, she had a kind of fear of entering that house which she had then left with her mind in a state of violent agitation.

On the present occasion, however, she felt that she must go up; it seemed as though in the course of the last few days a kind of bond had been established between her and the paralysed man, and as though even the glance with which he had silently greeted her on the previous day, when she was out walking, had had some significance.

When she entered the room her eyes had, first of all, to become accustomed to the dimness of the light; the blinds were drawn and a sunbeam poured in only through the chink at the top, and fell in front of the white stove. Herr Rupius was sitting in an armchair at the table in the centre of the room. Before him lay stacks of prints, and he was just in the act of picking up one in order to look at the one beneath it. Bertha could see that they were engravings.

'Thank you for coming to see me once again,' he said, stretching out his hand to her. 'You see what it is I am busy on just now? Well, it is a collection of engravings after the old Dutch masters. Believe me, my dear lady, it is a great pleasure to examine old engravings.'

'Oh, it is, indeed.'

'See, there are six volumes, or rather six portfolios, each containing twenty prints. It will probably take me the whole summer to become thoroughly acquainted with them.'

Bertha stood by his side and looked at the engraving immediately before him. It was a market scene by Teniers.

'The whole summer,' she said absent-mindedly.

Rupius turned towards her.

'Yes, indeed,' he said, his jaw slightly set, as though it was a matter of vindicating his point of view; 'what I call being thoroughly acquainted with a picture. By that I mean: being able, so to speak, to reproduce it in my mind, line for line. This one here is a Teniers – the original is in one of the galleries at The Hague. Why don't you go to The Hague, where so many splendid examples of the art of Teniers and so many other styles of painting are to be seen, my dear lady?'

Bertha smiled.

'How can I think of making such a journey as that?'

'Yes, yes, of course, that's so,' said Herr Rupius; 'The Hague is a very beautiful town. I was there fourteen years ago. At that time I was twenty-eight, I am now forty-two – or, I might say, eighty-four' – he picked up the print and laid it aside – 'here we have an Ostade – "The Pipe Smoker". Quite so, you can see easily enough that he is smoking a pipe. "Original in Vienna".'

'I think I remember that picture.'

'Won't you come and sit opposite to me, Frau Bertha, or here beside me, if you would care to look at the pictures with me? Now we come to a Falkenborg – wonderful isn't it? In the extreme foreground, though, it seems so void, so cramped. Yes, nothing but a peasant lad dancing with a girl, and there's an old woman who is cross about it, and here is a house out of the door of which some one is coming with a pail of water. Yes, that is all – a mere nothing of course, but there in the background you see, is the whole world, blue mountains, green towns, the clouded sky above, and near it a tourney – ha! ha! – in a certain sense perhaps it is out of place, but on the other hand, in a certain sense it may be said to be appropriate. Since everything has a background and it is therefore perfectly right that here, directly behind the peasant's house, the world should begin with its tourneys, and its mountains, its rivers, its fortresses, its vineyards and its forests.'

He pointed out the various parts of the picture to which he was referring with a little ivory paper-knife.

'Do you like it?' he continued. 'The original also hangs in the Gallery in Vienna. You must have seen it.'

'Oh, but it is now six years since I lived in Vienna, and for many years before that I had not paid a visit to the museum.'

'Indeed? I have often walked round the galleries there, and

stood before this picture, too. Yes, in those earlier days I *walked*.'

He was almost laughing as he looked at her, and her embarrassment was such that she could not make any reply.

'I fear I am boring you with the pictures,' Herr Rupius went on abruptly. 'Wait a little, my wife will be home soon. You know, I suppose, that she always goes for a two hours' walk after dinner now. She is afraid of becoming too stout.'

'Your wife looks as young and slender as ... well, I don't think she has altered in the very least since I have come to live here.'

Bertha felt as though Rupius's countenance had grown quite rigid. Then suddenly he said, in a gentle tone of voice which was not by any means in keeping with the expression of his face:

'A quiet life in a little town such as this keeps one young, of course. It was a clever idea of mine and hers, for it occurred simultaneously to both of us, to move here. Who can say whether, had we stayed in Vienna, it might not have been all over already?'

Bertha could not guess what he meant by the expression 'all over'; whether he was referring to his own life, to his wife's youthfulness, or to something else. In any case, she was sorry that she had called that day; a feeling of shame at being so strong and well herself came over her.

'Did I tell you,' continued Rupius, 'that it was Anna who got these portfolios for me? It was a chance bargain, for the work is usually very expensive. A bookseller had advertised it and Anna telegraphed at once to her brother to procure it for us. You know, of course, that we have many relations in Vienna, both Anna and myself. Sometimes, too, she goes there to visit them. Soon after they pay us a return visit. I should be very glad indeed to see them again, especially Anna's brother and his wife, I owe them a great deal of gratitude. When Anna is in Vienna, she dines and sleeps at their house – but, of course, you already know all that, Frau Bertha.'

He spoke rapidly and, at the same time, in a cool, business-like tone. It sounded as though he had made up his mind to tell the same things to everyone who should enter the room that day. It was the first time that he had as much as spoken to Bertha of the journeys of his wife to Vienna.

'She is going again tomorrow,' he continued; 'I believe the matter in hand this time is her summer costume.'

'I think that is a very clever notion of your wife,' said Bertha, glad to have found an opening for conversation.

'It is cheaper, at the same time,' added Herr Rupius. 'Yes, I assure you it is cheaper even if you throw in the cost of the journey. Why don't you follow my wife's example?'

'In what way, Herr Rupius?'

'Why, in regard to your frocks and hats! You are young and pretty, too!'

'Heavens above! On whose account should I dress smartly?'

'On whose account! On whose account is it that my wife dresses so smartly?'

The door opened and Frau Rupius entered in a bright spring costume, a red sunshade in her hand and a white straw hat, trimmed with red ribbon, on her dark hair, which was dressed high. A pleasant smile was hovering around her lips, as usual, and she greeted Bertha with a quiet cheerfulness.

'Are you making an appearance in our house once more?' she said, handing her sunshade and hat to the maid who had followed her into the room. 'Are you also interested in pictures, Frau Garlan?'

She went up close behind her husband and softly passed her hand over his forehead and hair.

'I was just telling Frau Garlan,' said Rupius, 'how surprised I am that she never goes to Vienna.'

'Indeed,' Frau Rupius put in; 'why don't you do so? Moreover, you must certainly have some acquaintances there, too. Come with me one day – tomorrow, for example. Yes, tomorrow.'

Rupius gazed straight before him while his wife said this, as though he did not dare to look at her.

'You are really very kind, Frau Rupius,' said Bertha, feeling as though a perfect stream of joy was coursing through her being.

She wondered, too, how it was that all this time the possibility of making such a journey had not once entered her mind, the more so as it could be accomplished with so little trouble. It appeared to her at that moment that such a journey might be a remedy for the strange sense of dissatisfaction under which she had been suffering during the past few days.

'Well, do you agree, Frau Garlan?'

'I don't really know – I daresay I could spare the time, for I have only one lesson to give tomorrow at my sister-in-law's, and she, of course, won't be too exacting; but wouldn't I be putting you to some inconvenience?'

A slight shadow flitted across Frau Rupius's brow.

'Putting me to inconvenience! Whatever are you dreaming of! I shall be very glad to have pleasant company during the few hours of the journey there and back. And in Vienna – oh, we shall be sure to have much to do together in Vienna.'

'Your husband,' said Bertha, blushing like a girl who is speaking of her first ball, 'has told me ... has advised me ...'

'Surely, he has been raving to you about my dressmaker,' said Frau Rupius, laughing.

Rupius still sat motionless in his chair and looked at neither of them.

'Yes, I should really like to ask you about her, Frau Rupius. When I see you I feel as if I should like to be well dressed again, just as you are.'

'That is easily arranged,' said Frau Rupius. 'I will take you to my dressmaker, and by so doing I hope also to have the pleasure of your company on my subsequent visits. I am glad for your sake as well,' she said to her husband, touching his hand which was lying on the table. Then she turned to Bertha and added: 'and for yours. You will see how much good it will do you. Wandering about the streets without being known to a soul has a wonderful effect on one's spirits. I do it from time to time, and I always come back quite refreshed and –' in saying this she threw a sidelong glance, full of anxiety and tenderness, in the direction of her husband – 'and then I am as happy here as ever it is possible to be; happier, I believe, than any other woman in the world.'

She drew near her husband and kissed him on the temple. Bertha heard her say in a soft voice, as she did so:

'Dearest!'

Rupius, however, continued to stare before him as though he shrank from meeting his wife's glance.

Both were silent and seemed to be absorbed in themselves, as though Bertha was not in the room. Bertha comprehended vaguely that there was some mysterious factor in the relations of these two people, but what that factor was she was not clever, or not experienced, or not good enough to understand. For a whole minute the silence continued, and Bertha was so embarrassed that she would gladly have gone away had it not been necessary to arrange with Frau Rupius the details of the morrow's journey.

Anna was the first to speak.

'So then it is agreed that we are to meet at the railway station in time for the morning train – isn't it? And I will arrange matters so that we return home by the seven o'clock train in the evening. In eight hours, you see, it is possible to get through a good deal.'

'Certainly,' said Bertha; 'provided, of course, that you are not inconveniencing yourself on my account in the slightest degree.'

Anna interrupted her, almost angrily.

'I have already told you how glad I am that you will be travelling with me, the more so as there is not a woman in the town so congenial to me as you.'

'Yes,' said Herr Rupius, 'I can corroborate that. You know, of course, that my wife is on visiting terms with hardly anybody here – and as it has been such a long time since you came to see us I was beginning to fear that she was going to lose you as well.'

'However could you have thought such a thing? My dear Herr Rupius! And you, Frau Rupius, surely you haven't believed –'

At that moment Bertha felt an overwhelming love for both of them. Her emotion was such that she detected her voice to be assuming an almost tearful tone.

Frau Rupius smiled, a strange, deliberate smile.

'I haven't believed anything. As a matter of fact there are some things over which I do not generally ponder for long. I have no great need of friends, but you, Frau Bertha, I really and truly love.'

She stretched out her hand to her. Bertha cast a glance at Rupius. It seemed to her that an expression of contentment should now be observable on his features. To her amazement, however, she saw that he was gazing into the corner of the room with an almost terrified look in his eyes.

The parlourmaid came in with some coffee. Further particulars as to their plans for the morrow were discussed, and finally they drew up a tolerably exact time-table which, to Frau Rupius's slight amusement, Bertha entered in a little notebook.

When Bertha reached the street again, the sky had become overcast, and the increasing sultriness foretold the approach of a thunderstorm. The first large drops were falling before she reached home, and she was somewhat alarmed when, on going upstairs, she failed to find the servant and little Fritz. As she went up to the window, however, in order to shut it, she saw the two come running along. The first thunderclap crashed out, and she started back in terror. Then immediately came a brilliant flash of lightning.

The storm was brief, but unusually violent. Bertha went and sat on her bed, held Fritz on her lap, and told him a story, so that he should not be frightened. But, at the same time, she felt as though there was a certain connection between her experiences of the past two days and the thunderstorm.

In half an hour all was over. Bertha opened the window; the air was now fresh, the darkening sky was clear and distant. Bertha drew a deep breath, and a feeling of peace and hope seemed to permeate her being.

It was time to get ready for the concert in the gardens. On her arrival she found her friends already gathered at a large table beneath a tree. It was Bertha's intention to tell her sister-in-law at once about her proposed visit to Vienna on the morrow, but a sense of shyness, as though there was something underhand in the journey, caused her to refrain.

Herr Klingemann went by with his housekeeper towards their table. The housekeeper was getting on towards middle-age; she was a very voluptuous looking woman, taller than Klingemann, and, when she walked, always appeared to be asleep.

Klingemann bowed towards them with exaggerated politeness. The gentlemen scarcely acknowledged the salutation, and the ladies pretended not to have noticed it. Only Bertha nodded slightly and gazed after the couple.

'That is his sweetheart – yes, I know it for a positive fact,' whispered Richard, who was sitting near his aunt.

Herr Garlan's party ate, drank and applauded. At times various acquaintances came over from other tables, sat down with them for awhile, and then went away again to their places. The music murmured around Bertha without making any impression on her. Her mind was continuously occupied with the question as to how to inform them of her project.

Suddenly, while the music was playing very loudly, she said to Richard:

'I say, I won't be able to give you a music lesson tomorrow. I am going to Vienna.'

'To Vienna!' exclaimed Richard; then he called across to his mother; 'I say, Aunt Bertha is going to Vienna tomorrow!'

'Who's going to Vienna?' asked Garlan, who was sitting furthest away.

'I am,' answered Bertha.

'What's this! What's this!' said Garlan, playfully threatening her with his finger.

So, then, it was accomplished. Bertha was glad. Richard made jokes about the people who were sitting in the garden, also about the fat bandmaster who was always skipping about while he was conducting, and then about the trumpet-player whose cheeks bulged out and who seemed to be shedding tears when he blew into his instrument. Bertha could not help laughing very heartily. Jests were bandied about her high spirits and Doctor Friedrich remarked that she must surely be going to some rendezvous at Vienna.

'I should like to put a stop to that, though!' exclaimed Richard, so angrily, that the hilarity became general.

Only Elly remained serious, and gazed at her aunt in downright astonishment.

Bertha looked out through the open carriage window upon the landscape; Frau Rupius read a book, which she had taken out of her little travelling-bag very soon after the train had started. It almost appeared as though she wished to avoid any lengthy conversation with Bertha, and the latter felt somewhat hurt. For a long time past she had been cherishing a wish to be a friend of Frau Rupius, but since the previous day this desire of hers had become almost a yearning, which recalled to her mind the whole-hearted devotion of the friendships of the days of her childhood.

At first, therefore, she had felt quite unhappy, and had a sensation of having been abandoned, but soon the changing panorama to be seen through the window began to distract her thoughts in an agreeable manner. As she looked at the rails which seemed to run to meet her, at the hedges and telegraph poles which glided and leaped past her, she recalled to mind the few short journeys to the Salzkammergut, where she had been taken, when a child, by her parents, and the indescribable pleasure of having been allowed to occupy a corner seat on those occasions. Then she looked into the distance and exulted in the gleaming of the river, in the pleasant windings of the hills and meadows, in the azure of the sky and in the white clouds.

After a time Anna laid down the book, and began to chat to Bertha and smiled at her, as though at a child.

'Who would have foretold this of us?' said Frau Rupius.

'That we should be going to Vienna together?'

'No, no, I mean that we shall both – how shall I express it? – pass or end our lives yonder' – she gave a slight nod in the direction of the place from which they came.

'Very true, indeed!' answered Bertha, who had not yet considered whether there was anything really strange in the fact or not.

'Well, you, of course, knew it the moment you were married, but I –'

Frau Rupius gazed straight before her.

'So then your move to the little town,' said Bertha, 'did not take place until – until –'

She broke off in confusion.

'Yes, you know that, of course.'

In saying this Frau Rupius looked Bertha full in the face as if reproaching her for her question. But when she continued to speak she smiled gently, as though her thoughts were not occupied by anything so sad.

'Yes, I never imagined that I should leave Vienna; my husband had his position as a government official, and indeed he would certainly have been able to remain longer there, in spite of his infirmity, had he not wanted to go away at once.'

'He thought, perhaps, that the fresh air, the quiet –' began Bertha, and she at once perceived that she was not saying anything very sensible.

Nevertheless Anna answered her quite affably.

'Oh, no, neither rest nor climate could do him any good, but he thought that it would be better for both of us in every way. He was right, too – what should we have been able to do if we had remained in the city?'

Bertha felt that Anna was not telling her the whole story and she would have liked to beg her not to hesitate, but to open her whole heart to her. She knew, however, that she was not clever enough to express such a request in the right words. Then, as though Frau Rupius had guessed that Bertha was anxious to learn more, she quickly changed the subject of their conversation. She asked Bertha about her brother-in-law, the musical talent of her pupils, and her method of teaching; then she took up the novel again and left Bertha to herself.

Once she looked up from the book and said:

'You haven't brought anything with you to read, then?'

'Oh, yes,' answered Bertha.

She suddenly remembered that she had bought a newspaper;

she took it up and turned over the pages assiduously. The train drew near to Vienna. Frau Rupius closed her book and put it in the travelling bag. She looked at Bertha with a certain tenderness, as at a child who must soon be sent away alone to meet an uncertain destiny.

'Another quarter of an hour,' she remarked; 'and we shall be – well, I very nearly said, home.'

Before them lay the town. On the far side of the river chimneys towered up aloft, rows of tall yellow painted houses stretched away into the distance, and steeples ascended skywards. Everything lay basking in the gentle sunlight of May.

Bertha's heart throbbed. She experienced a sensation such as might come over a traveller returning after a long absence to a longed-for home, which had probably altered greatly in the meantime, and where surprises and mysteries of all kinds awaited him. At the moment when the train rolled into the station she seemed almost courageous in her own eyes.

Frau Rupius took a carriage, and they drove into the town. As they passed the Ring, Bertha suddenly leaned out of the window and gazed after a young man whose figure and walk reminded her of Emil Lindbach. She wished that the young man would turn round, but she lost sight of him without his having done so.

The carriage stopped before a house in the Kohlmarkt. The two ladies got out and made their way to the third floor, where the dressmaker's workroom was situated. While Frau Rupius tried on her new costume, Bertha had various materials displayed to her from which she made a choice. The assistant took her measure, and it was arranged that Bertha should call in a week's time to be fitted. Frau Rupius came out from the adjoining room and recommended that particular care should be given to her friend's order.

It seemed to Bertha that everybody was looking at her in a rather disparaging, almost compassionate manner, and, on looking at herself in the large pier glass she suddenly perceived that she was very tastelessly dressed. What on earth had put it into her head to attire herself on this occasion in the provincial Sunday-best, instead of in one of the simple plain dresses she usually wore? She grew crimson with shame. She had on a black and white striped foulard costume, which was three years out of date, so far as its cut was concerned, and a bright-coloured hat, trimmed with roses and turned up at an extravagant angle in front, which seemed to weigh heavily upon her dainty figure and made her appear almost ridiculous.

Then, as if her own conviction needed further confirmation by some word of consolation, Frau Rupius said, as they went down the stairs:

'You are looking lovely!'

They stood in the doorway.

'What shall be done now?' asked Frau Rupius. 'What do you propose?'

'Will you then . . . I . . . I mean . . .'

Bertha was quite frightened, she felt as though she was being turned adrift.

Frau Rupius looked at her with kindly commiseration.

'I think,' she said, 'that you are going to pay a visit to your cousin now, are you not? I suppose that you will be asked to stay to dinner.'

'Agatha will be sure to invite me to dine with her.'

'I will accompany you as far as your cousin's, if you would like me to; then I will go to my brother and, if possible, I will call for you at three in the afternoon.'

Together they walked through the most crowded streets of the central part of the town and looked at the shop windows. At first Bertha found the din somewhat confusing; afterwards, however, she found it more pleasant than otherwise. She gazed at the passers-by and took great pleasure in watching the well-groomed men and smartly-attired ladies. Almost all the people seemed to be wearing new clothes, and it seemed to her they all looked much happier than the people at home.

Presently she stopped before the window of a picture-dealer's shop and immediately her eyes fell on a familiar portrait; it was the same one of Emil Lindbach as had appeared in the illustrated paper. Bertha was as delighted as if she had met an acquaintance.

'I know that man,' she said to Frau Rupius.

'Whom?'

'That man there' – she pointed with her finger at the photograph – 'what do you think? I used to attend the conservatoire at the same time as he did!'

'Really?' said Frau Rupius.

Bertha looked at her and observed that she had not paid the slightest attention to the portrait, but was thinking of something else. Bertha, however, was glad of that, for it seemed to her that there had been too much warmth lurking in her voice.

All at once a gentle thrill of pride stirred within her at the thought that the man whose portrait hung there in the shop window had been in love with her in the days of his youth, and had kissed her. She walked on with a sensation of inward contentment. After a short time they reached her cousin's house on the Riemerstrasse.

'So it's settled then,' she said; 'you will call for me at three o'clock, won't you?'

'Yes,' replied Frau Rupius; 'that is to say – but if I should be a little late, do not on any account wait for me at your cousin's any longer than you want to. In any case, this much is settled: we will both be at the railway station at seven o'clock this evening. Good-bye for the present.'

She shook hands with Bertha and hurried away.

Bertha gazed after her in surprise. Once more she felt forlorn, just as she had done in the train when Frau Rupius had read the novel.

Then she went up the two flights of stairs. She had not sent her cousin word as to her visit, and she was a little afraid that her arrival might be somewhat inopportune. She had not seen Agatha for many years, and they had exchanged letters only at very rare intervals.

Agatha received her without either surprise or cordiality, as though it was only the day before that they had seen each other for the last time. A smile had been playing around Bertha's lips – the smile of those who think that they are about to give some one else a surprise – she repressed it immediately.

'Well, you are not a very frequent visitor, I must say!' said Agatha, 'and you never let us have a word from you.'

'But, Agatha, you know it was your turn to write; you have been owing me a letter these last three months.'

'Really!' replied Agatha. 'Well, you'll have to excuse me; you can imagine what a lot of work three children mean. Did I write and tell you that Georg goes to school now?'

Agatha took her cousin into the nursery, where Georg and his two little sisters were just having their dinner given them by the nursery-governess. Bertha asked them a few questions, but the children were very shy, and the younger girl actually began to cry.

'Do beg Aunt Bertha to bring Fritz with her next time she comes,' said Agatha to Georg at length.

It struck Bertha how greatly her cousin had aged during the last few years. Indeed, when she bent down to the children Agatha appeared almost like an old woman; and yet she was only a year older than Bertha, as the latter knew.

By the time they had returned to the dining-room they had already told each other all that they had to say, and when Agatha invited Bertha to stay to dinner, it seemed that she spoke only for the mere sake of making some remark. Bertha accepted the invitation, nevertheless, and her cousin went into the kitchen to give some orders.

Bertha gazed around the room, which was furnished economically and in bad taste. It was very dark, for the street was extremely narrow. She took up an album which was lying on the table. She found hardly any but familiar faces in it. At the very beginning were the portraits of Agatha's parents, who had died long ago; then came those of her own parents and of her brothers, of whom she scarcely ever heard; portraits of friends whom they both had known in earlier days, and of whom she now knew hardly anything; and, finally, there was a photograph, the existence of which she had long forgotten. It was one of herself and Agatha together, and had been taken when they were quite young girls. In those days they had been very much alike in appearance, and had been great friends. Bertha could remember many of the confidential chats which they had had together in the days of their girlhood.

And that lovely creature there with the looped plaits was now almost an old woman! And what of herself? What reason had she then, for still looking upon herself as a young woman? Did she not, perhaps, appear to others as old as Agatha had seemed to her? She resolved that, in the afternoon, she would take notice of the glances which passers-by bestowed upon her. It would be terrible if she really did look as old as her cousin! No, the idea was utterly ridiculous! She called to mind how her nephew Richard always called her his 'pretty aunt,' how Klingemann had walked to and fro outside her window the other evening – and even the recollection of her brother-in-law's attentions reassured her. And, when she looked in the mirror which was hanging opposite to her, she saw two bright eyes gazing at her from a smooth, fresh face – they were her face and her eyes.

When Agatha came into the room again Bertha began to talk of the far-away years of their childhood, but it seemed that Agatha had forgotten all about those early days, as though marriage, motherhood and weekday cares had obliterated both youth and its memories. When Bertha went on to speak of a students' dance they had both attended, of the young men who had courted Agatha, and of a bouquet which some unknown lover had once sent her, Agatha at first smiled rather absent-mindedly, then she looked at Bertha and said:

'Just fancy you still remembering all those foolish things!'

Agatha's husband came home from his Government office. He had grown very grey since Bertha had last seen him. At first sight he did not appear to recognize Bertha, then he mistook her for another lady, and excused himself by remarking that he had a very bad memory for faces. At dinner he affected to be smart, he inquired in a certain superior way about the affairs of the little town, and wondered, jestingly, whether Bertha was not thinking of marrying again. Agatha also took part in this bantering, although, at the same time, she occasionally glanced reprovingly at her husband, who was trying to give the conversation a frivolous turn.

Bertha felt ill at ease. Later on she gathered from some words of Agatha's husband that they were expecting another addition to their family. Usually Bertha felt sympathy for women in such circumstances, but in this case the news created an almost unpleasant impression upon her. Moreover there was not a trace of love to be discerned in the tone of the husband's voice when he referred to it, but rather a kind of foolish pride on the score of an accomplished duty. He spoke of the matter as though it was a special act of kindness on his part that, in spite of the fact that he was a busy man, and Agatha was no longer beautiful, he condescended to spend his time at home. Bertha had an impression that she was being mixed up in some sordid affair which did not concern her in the least. She was glad when, as soon as he had finished his dinner, the husband went off – it was his custom, 'his only vice,' as he said with a smile, to play billiards at the restaurant for an hour after dinner.

Bertha and Agatha were left together.

'Yes,' said Agatha, 'I've got that to look forward to again.'

Thereupon she began, in a cold business-like way, to talk about her previous confinements, with a candour and lack of modesty which seemed all the more remarkable because they had become such strangers. While Agatha was continuing the relation of her experiences, however, the thought suddenly passed through Bertha's mind that it must be glorious to have a child by a husband whom one loved.

She ceased to pay attention to her cousin's unpleasant talk; and her thoughts were only occupied by the infinite yearning for motherhood which had often come over her when she was quite a young girl, and she called to mind an occasion when that yearning had been more keen than it had ever been, either before or after. This had happened one evening when Emil Lindbach had accompanied her home from the conservatoire, her hand clasped in his. She still remembered how her head had begun to swim, and that at one moment she had understood what the phrase meant which she had sometimes read in novels: 'He could have done with her just as he liked.'

Then she noticed that it had grown quite silent in the room, and that Agatha was leaning back in the corner of the sofa, apparently asleep. It was three by the clock. How tiresome it was that Frau Rupius had not yet arrived! Bertha went to the window and looked out into the street. Then she turned towards Agatha, who had again opened her eyes. Bertha quickly tried to begin a fresh conversation, and told her about the new costume which she had ordered in the forenoon, but Agatha was too sleepy even to answer. Bertha had no wish to put her cousin out, and took her departure. She decided to wait for Frau Rupius in the street. Agatha seemed very pleased when Bertha got ready to go, she became more cordial than she had been at any time during her cousin's visit, and said at the door, as if struck by some brilliant idea:

'How the time does pass! I do hope you'll come and see us again soon.'

Bertha, as she stood before the door of the house, realized that she was waiting for Frau Rupius in vain. There was no doubt that it had been the latter's intention from the beginning to spend the afternoon without her. Of course, it did not necessarily follow that there was anything wicked in it; as a matter of fact there was nothing wicked in it, but it hurt Bertha to think that Anna had so little trust in her.

She walked along with no fixed purpose. She had still more than three hours to while away before she was to be at the station. At first, she took a walk in the inner town, which she had passed through in the morning. It was really a pleasant thing to wander about unobserved like this, as a stranger in the crowd. It was long since she had experienced that pleasure. Some of the men who passed her glanced at her with interest, and more than one, indeed, stopped to gaze after her. She regretted that she was dressed to so little advantage, and rejoiced at the prospect of obtaining soon the beautiful costume she had ordered from the Viennese dressmaker. She would have liked to find some one following her.

Suddenly the thought passed through her mind: would Emil Lindbach recognize her if she were to meet him? What a question! Such things never happened, of course. No, she was quite sure that she could wander about Vienna the whole day long without ever meeting him. How long was it since she had seen him? Seven – eight years ... Yes, the last time she had met him was two years before her marriage. She had been with her parents one warm summer evening in the Schweitzerhaus on the Prater, he had gone by with a friend and had stopped a few minutes at their table. Ah, and now she remembered also that amongst the company at their table there had been the young doctor who was courting her. She had forgotten what Emil had said on that occasion, but she re-

membered that he had held his hat in his hand during the
whole time he was standing before her, which had afforded her
inexpressible delight. Would he do the same now, she thought
to herself, if she were to meet him?

Where was he living now, she wondered? In the old days
he had a room on the Weiden, near St Paul's Church ... Yes,
he had pointed out the window as they passed one day, and
had ventured, as they did so, to make a certain remark – she
had forgotten the exact words, but there was no doubt that
they had been to the effect that he and she ought to be in that
room together. She had rebuked him very severely for saying
such a thing, she had even gone the length of telling him that
if that was the sort of girl he thought she was, all was over
between them. And, in fact, he had never spoken another
word on the subject.

Would she recognize the window again? Would she find it?
It was all the same to her, of course, whether she went for a
walk in this direction or that. She hurried towards the Weiden
as though she had suddenly found an object for her walk. She
was amazed at the complete change which had come over the
neighbourhood. When she looked down from the Elizabeth
Bridge she saw walls that rose from the bed of the Wien, half
finished tracks, little trucks moving to and fro, and busy workmen. Soon she reached St Paul's Church by the same road as
she had so often followed in the old days. But then she came
to a standstill; she was absolutely at a loss to remember where
Emil had lived, whether she had to turn to the right or to the
left. It was strange how completely it had escaped her memory.
She walked slowly back as far as the Conservatoire, then she
stood still. Above her were the windows from which she had
so often gazed upon the dome of St Charles' Church, and
longingly awaited the end of the lesson so that she might meet
Emil. How great had been her love for him, indeed; and how
strange it was that it should have died so completely!

And now, when she had returned to these scenes, she was a
widow, had been so for years, and had a child at home who
was growing up. If she had died, Emil would never have heard
of it, or perhaps not until years afterwards. Her eyes fell on
a large placard fixed on the entrance gates of the Conserva-

toire. It was an announcement of the concert at which he was going to play, and there was his name appearing among a number of other great ones, many of which she had long since admired with gentle awe.

'BRAHMS VIOLIN CONCERTO — EMIL
LINDBACH, VIOLINIST TO THE
COURT OF BAVARIA.'

'Violinist to the Court of Bavaria!' — she had never heard anything about that before.

Gazing up at his name, which stood out in glittering letters, it seemed to her as though the next moment Emil himself might come out through the gate, his violin case in his hand, a cigarette between his lips. Of a sudden it all seemed so near, and nearer still when all at once from the windows above came floating down the long-drawn notes of a violin, just as she had so often heard in the old days.

She thought she would like to come to Vienna for that concert — yes, even if she should be obliged to spend the night at an hotel! And she would take a seat right in front and see him quite close at hand. She wondered whether he, in his turn, would see her, and, if so, whether he would recognize her. She remained standing before the yellow placard, wholly absorbed in thought; until she felt that some young people coming out of the Conservatoire were staring at her, and then she realized that she had been smiling to herself the whole time, as if lost in a pleasant dream.

She proceeded to walk on. The district around the town-park had also changed, and, when she sought the places where she and Emil had often been for walks together, she found that they had quite disappeared. Trees had been felled, hoardings barred the way, the ground had been dug up, and in vain she tried to find the seat where she and Emil had exchanged words of love, the tone of which she remembered so well without being able to recall the actual phrases.

Presently she reached the trim well-kept part of the park, which was full of people. But she had a sensation that many were looking at her, and that some ladies were laughing at her. And once more she felt that she was looking very countrified. She was vexed at being embarrassed, and thought of the time when, as a pretty young girl, she had walked, proud and unconcerned, along these very avenues. It seemed to her that she had fallen off so much since then, and become so pitiable. Her idea of sitting in the front row of the concert hall appeared presumptuous, almost unfeasible. It seemed also highly' improbable now that Emil Lindbach would recognize her; indeed, it struck her as almost impossible that he should remember her existence. What a number of experiences he must have had! How many women and girls might well have loved him – and in a manner quite different from her own!

And whilst she continued her way, walking, now along the less frequented avenues and at length out of the park upon the Ringsstrasse again, she drew a mental picture of the beloved of her youth figuring in all manner of adventures, in which confused recollections of events depicted in the novels she had read and indistinctly formed ideas of his professional tours were strangely intermingled. She imagined him in Venice with a Russian princess in a gondola; then in her mind's eye she saw him at the court of the King of Bavaria, where duchesses listened to his playing, and fell in love with him; then in the boudoir of an opera singer; then at a fancy-dress ball in Spain, with crowds of alluring masqueraders about him. The further he seemed to soar away, unapproachable and enviable, the more miserable she felt herself to be, and all at once it seemed utterly inconceivable that she had so lightly surrendered her own hopes of an artistic career and given up her lover, in order to lead a sunless existence, and to be lost in the crowd. A shudder seemed to seize her as she recalled that she was nothing but the widow of an insignificant man, that she lived in a provincial town, that she earned her living by means of music lessons, and that she saw old age slowly approaching. Never had there fallen upon her way so much as a single ray of the brilliance which shone upon the road his footsteps would tread so long as he lived. And again the same shudder ran through her at the thought that she had always been content with her lot, and that, without hope and indeed, without yearning, she had passed her whole existence in a gloom, which, at that moment, seemed inexplicable.

She reached the Aspernbrücke without in the least giving heed to where her footsteps were taking her. She wished to cross the street at this point, but had to wait while a great number of carriages drove by. Most of them were occupied by gentlemen, many of whom carried field-glasses. She knew that they were returning from the races at the Prater.

There came an elegant equipage in which were seated a young man and a girl, the latter dressed in a white spring costume. Immediately behind was a carriage containing two strikingly dressed ladies. Bertha gazed long after them, and noticed that one of the ladies turned round, and that the object of her attention was the carriage which followed immediately behind, and in which sat a young and very handsome man in a long grey overcoat. Bertha was conscious of something very painful – uneasiness and annoyance at one and the same time. She would have liked to be the lady whom the young man followed; she would have liked to be beautiful, young, independent, and, Heaven knows, she would have liked to be any woman who could do as she wanted, and could turn round after men who pleased her.

And at that moment she realized, quite distinctly, that Frau Rupius was now in the company of somebody whom she loved. Indeed why shouldn't she? Of course, so long as she stayed in Vienna, she was free and mistress of her own time – besides, she was a very pretty woman, and was wearing a fragrant violet costume. On her lips there hovered a smile such as only comes to those who are happy – and Frau Rupius was unhappy at home. All at once, Bertha had a vision of Herr Rupius sitting in his room, looking at the engravings. But on that day, surely, he was not doing so; no, he was trembling for his wife, consumed with an immense fear that some one yonder in the great city would take her away from him, that she would never return, and that he would be left all alone with his sorrow. And Bertha suddenly felt a thrill of compassion for him, such as she had never experienced before. Indeed, she would have liked to be with him, to comfort and to reassure him.

She felt a touch on her arm. She started and looked up. A young man was standing beside her and gazing at her with an

impudent leer. She stared at him, full in the face, still quite
absentmindedly; then he said with a laugh:

'Well?'

She was frightened, and almost ran across the street, quickly
passing in front of a carriage. She was ashamed of her previous desire to be the lady in the carriage she had seen coming
from the Prater. It seemed as though the man's insolence had
been her punishment. No, no, she was a respectable woman,
in the depth of her soul she had an aversion to everything
that savoured of the insolent ... No, she could no longer stay
in Vienna, where women were exposed to such things! A
longing for the peace of her home came over her, and she
rejoiced in the prospect of meeting her little boy again, as in
something extraordinarily beautiful.

What time was it, though? Heavens, a quarter to seven! She
would have to take a carriage, there was no question about
that now, indeed! Frau Rupius had, of course, paid for the
carriage in the morning, and so the one which she was now
going to take would only cost her half, so to speak. She took
her seat in an open cab, leaned back in the corner, in almost
the same aristocratic manner as that of the lady she had seen
in the white frock. People gazed after her. She knew that she
was now looking young and pretty. Moreover, she was feeling
quite safe, nothing could happen to her. She took an indescribable pleasure in the swift motion of the cab with its rubber-
tyred wheels. She thought how splendid it would be if on the
occasion of her next visit she were to drive through the town,
wearing her new costume and the small straw hat which made
her look so young.

She was glad that Frau Rupius was standing in the entrance
to the station and saw her arrive. But she betrayed no sign of
pride, and acted as though it was quite the usual thing for her
to drive up to the station in a cab.

'We have still ten minutes to spare,' said Frau Rupius. 'Are
you very angry with me for having kept you waiting? Just
fancy, my brother was giving a grandchildren's party today,
and the little ones simply wouldn't let me go. It occurred to me
too late that I might really have called for you; the children

would have amused you so much. I have told my brother that, next time, I will bring you and your boy with me.'

Bertha felt heartily ashamed of herself. How she had wronged this woman again! She could only press her hand and say:

'Thank you, you are very kind!'

They went on to the platform and entered an empty compartment. Frau Rupius had a small bag of cherries in her hand, and she ate them slowly, one after another, throwing the stones out of the window. When the train began to move out of the station she leaned back and closed her eyes. Bertha looked out of the window; she felt very tired after so much walking, and a slight uneasiness arose within her; she might have spent the day differently, more quietly and enjoyably. Her chilly reception and the tedious dinner at her cousin's came to her mind. After all, it was a great pity that she no longer had any acquaintances in Vienna. She had wandered like a stranger about the town in which she had lived twenty-six years. Why? And why had she not made the carriage pull up in the morning, when she saw the figure that seemed to have a resemblance to Emil Lindbach? True, she would not have been able to run or call after him – but if it had been really he, if he had recognized her and been pleased to see her again? They might have walked about together, might have told each other all that had happened during the long time that had passed since they had last known anything about one another; they might have gone to a fashionable restaurant and had dinner; some would naturally have recognized him, and she would have heard quite distinctly people discussing the question as to who 'she' might really be. She was looking beautiful, too; the new costume was already finished; and the waiters served her with great politeness, especially a small youth who brought the wine – but he was really her nephew, who had, of course, become a waiter in that restaurant instead of a student. Suddenly Herr and Frau Martin entered the dining-hall; they were holding one another in such a tender embrace as if they were the only people there. Then Emil rose to his feet, took up the violin bow which was lying beside him, and raised it with a commanding gesture, whereupon the waiter turned Herr and Frau Martin out of the room. Bertha could not help laughing at the incident, laughing much too loudly indeed, for by this time she had quite forgotten how to behave in a fashionable restaurant. But then it was not a fashionable restaurant at all, it was only the coffee room at the 'Red Apple,' and the military band was playing somewhere out of sight. That, be it known, was a clever invention on the part of Herr Rupius, that military bands could play without being seen. Now, however, it was her turn that was immediately to follow. Yonder was the piano – but, of course, she had long since completely forgotten how to play; she would run away rather than be forced to play. And all at once she was at the railway station, where Frau Rupius was already waiting for her. 'It is high time you came,' she said. She placed in Bertha's hand a large book, which, by the way, was her ticket. Frau Rupius, however, was not going to take the train; she sat down, ate cherries and spat out the stones at the stationmaster, who took a huge delight in the proceedings. Bertha entered the compartment. Thank God, Herr Klingemann was already there! He made a sign to her with his screwed-up eyes, and asked her if she knew whose funeral it was. She saw that a hearse was standing on the other line. Then she remembered that the captain with whom the tobacconist's wife had deceived Herr Klingemann was dead – of course, it was the day of the concert at the 'Red Apple'. Suddenly Herr Klingemann blew on her eyes, and laughed in a rumbling way.

Bertha opened her eyes – at that moment a train was rushing past the window. She shook herself. What a confused dream! And hadn't it begun quite nicely? She tried to remember. Yes, Emil played a part in it ... but she could not recollect what part.

The dusk of evening slowly fell. The train sped on its way along by the Danube. Frau Rupius slept and smiled. Perhaps she was only pretending to be asleep. Bertha was again seized with a slight suspicion, and she felt rising within her a sensation of envy at the unknown and mysterious experiences which Frau Rupius had had. She, too, would gladly have experienced something. She wished that some one was sitting beside her now, his arm pressed against hers – she would fain have felt once more that sensation that had thrilled her on that occasion when she had stood with Emil on the bank of the Wien, and when she had almost been on the point of losing her senses and had yearned for a child ... Ah, why was she so poor, so lonely, so much in obscurity? Gladly would she have implored the lover of her youth:

'Kiss me but once again just as you used to do, I want to be happy!'

It was dark; Bertha looked out into the night.

She determined that very night before she went to bed to fetch from the attic the little case in which she kept the letters of her parents and of Emil. She longed to be home again. She felt as though a question had been wakened within her soul, and that the answer awaited her at home.

When, late in the evening, Bertha entered her room, the idea which she had taken into her head of going up to the attic at once, and fetching down the case with the letters seemed to her to be almost venturesome. She was afraid that some one in the house might observe her on her nocturnal pilgrimage, and might take her for mad. She could, of course, go up the next morning quite conveniently and without causing any stir; and so she fell asleep, feeling like a child who has been promised an outing into the country on the following day.

She had much to do the next forenoon; her domestic duties and piano lessons occupied the whole of the time. She had to give her sister-in-law an account of her visit to Vienna. Her story was that in the afternoon she had gone for a walk with her cousin, and the impression was conveyed that she had made an excuse to Frau Rupius at the request of Agatha.

It was not until the afternoon that she went up to the attic and brought down the dusty travelling-case, which was lying beside a trunk and a couple of boxes – the whole collection covered with an old and torn piece of red-flowered coffee-cloth. She remembered that her object on the last occasion on which she had opened the case had been to put away the papers which her parents had left behind. On her return to her room she opened the case and perceived lying on top of the other contents a number of letters from her brothers and other letters, with the hand-writing of which she was not familiar; then she found a neat little bundle containing the few letters which her parents had addressed to her; these were followed by two books of her mother's household accounts, a little copybook dating back to her own schooldays and containing entries of time-tables and exercises, a few programmes of the dances which she had attended when a young girl, and, finally, Emil Lindbach's letters, which were wrapped up in blue tissue paper, torn here and there. And now she was able to fix the very day on which she had last held those letters in her hand, although she had not read them on that occasion. It was when her father had been lying ill for some time and, for whole days, she had not once gone outside the door.

She laid the bundle aside. She wanted, first of all, to see all the other things which had been stored in the case, and concerning which she was consumed with curiosity. A number of letters lay in a loose heap at the bottom of the case, some with their envelopes and others without. She cast her eye over them at random. There were letters from old friends, a few from her cousin, and here was one from the doctor who had courted her in the old days. In it he asked her to reserve for him the first waltz at the medical students' dance. Here – what was it? Why, it was that anonymous letter which some one had addressed to her at the Conservatoire. She picked it up and read:

My Dear Fraulein,

Yesterday I again had the good fortune to have an opportunity of admiring you on your daily walk; I do not know whether I had also the good fortune to be observed by you.

No, he had not had that good fortune. Then followed three pages of enthusiastic admiration, and not a single wish, not a single bold word. She had, moreover, never heard anything more of the writer.

Here was a letter signed by two initials, 'M. G.' That was the impudent fellow who had once spoken to her in the street, and who in this letter made proposals – wait a minute, what were they? Ah, here was the passage which had sent the hot blood mounting to her brow when she had first read it:

Since I have seen you, and since you have looked on me with a glance so stern and yet seemingly so full of promise, I have had but one dream, but one yearning – that I might kiss those eyes!

Of course, she had not answered the letter, she was in love with Emil at the time. Indeed, she had even thought of showing him the letter, but was restrained by the fear of rousing his jealousy. Emil had never learned anything of 'M. G.'

And that piece of soft ribbon that now fell into her hands? ... A cravat ... but she had quite forgotten whose it was, and why she had kept it.

Here again was a little dance album in which she had written the names of her partners. She tried to call the young men to mind, but in vain. Though, by the way, it was at that very dance that she had met that man who had said such passionate words to her as she had never heard from any other. It seemed as though he suddenly emerged a victor from among the many shadows that hovered around her. It must have happened during the time when she and Emil had been meeting each other less frequently. How strange it was ... or had it only been a dream? This passionate admirer had clasped her closely in his arms during the dance – and she had not offered the slightest resistance. She had felt his lips in her hair, and it had been incredibly pleasant ... Well, and then? – she had never seen him again.

It suddenly seemed to her that, after all, in those days she had had many and strange experiences, and she was lost in amazement at the way in which all these memories had slumbered so long in the travelling-case and in her soul ... But no, they had not slumbered; she had thought of all these things many a time: of the men who had courted her, of the anonymous letter, of her passionate partner at the dance, of the walks with Emil – but only as if they had been nothing out of the common, as if they had been merely such things as go to constitute the past, the youth which is allotted to every young girl, and from which she emerges to lead the placid life of a woman. On the present occasion, however, it seemed to Bertha as if these recollections were, so to speak, unredeemed promises, as if in those experiences of distant days there lay destinies which had not been fulfilled; nay more, as if a kind of deception had long been practised upon her, from the very day on which she had been married until the present moment, as if she had discovered it all too late; and here she was, unable to lift a finger to alter her destiny.

Yet why should it seem so? ... She thought of all these futile things, and there beside her, wrapped up in tissue paper, still lay the treasure, for the sake of which alone she had rummaged in the case – the letters of the only man she had loved, the letters written in the days when she had been happy. How many women might there be now who envied her because that very man had once loved her – loved her with a different, better, chaster love than that which he had given any of the women who had followed her in his affections. She felt herself most bitterly deceived that she, who could have been his wife if ... if ... her thoughts broke off.

Hurriedly, as though seeking to rid her mind of doubt, or rather, indeed, of fear, she tore off the tissue paper and seized the letters. And she read – read them one after another. Long letters, short letters; brief, hasty notes, like: 'Tomorrow evening, darling, at seven o'clock!' or 'Dearest, just one kiss ere I go to sleep!' letters that covered many pages, written during the walking tours which he and his fellow students had taken in the summer; letters written in the evening, in which he had felt constrained to impart to her his impressions of a concert immediately on returning home; endless pages in which he unfolded his plans for the future: how they would travel together through Spain and America, famous and happy ... she read them all, one after another, as though tortured by a quenchless thirst. She read from the very first, which had accompanied a few pieces of music, to the last, which was dated two and a half years later, and contained nothing more than a greeting from Salzburg.

When she came to an end she let her hands fall into her lap and gazed fixedly at the sheets lying about. Why had that been the last letter? How had their friendship come to an end? How could it have come to an end? How had it been possible that that great love had died away? There had never been any actual rupture between Emil and herself, they had never come to any definite understanding that all was over between them, and yet their acquaintanceship had ended at some time or other – when? ... She could not tell, because at the time when he had written that card to her from Salzburg she had still been in love with him. She had, as a matter of fact, met him in the autumn – indeed, during the winter of the same year everything had seemed once more to blossom forth. She remembered certain walks they had taken over the crunching snow, arm in arm, beside St Charles' Church – but when was it that they had taken the last of these walks? They had, to be sure, never taken farewell of each other ... She could not understand it.

How was it that she had been able so easily to renounce a happiness which it might yet have been within her power to retain? How had it come about that she had ceased to love him? Had the dullness of the daily routine of her home life, which weighed so heavily upon her spirits ever since she had left the Conservatoire, lulled her feelings to sleep just as it had blunted the edge of her ambitions? Had the querulous remarks of her parents on the subject of her friendship with the youthful violinist – which had seemed likely to lead to nothing – acted on her with such sobering effect?

Then she recalled to mind that even at a later date, when some months had elapsed since she had last seen him, he had called at her parents' house, and had kissed her in the back room. Yes, that had been the last time of all. And then she remembered further that on that occasion she had noticed that his relations towards women had changed, that he must have had experiences of which she could know nothing – but the discovery had not caused her any pain.

She asked herself how it all would have turned out if in those days she had not been so virtuous, if she had taken life as easily as some of the other girls? She called to mind a girl at the Conservatoire with whom she had ceased to associate on finding that her friend had an intrigue with a dramatic student. She remembered again the suggestive words which Emil had spoken as they were walking together past his window, and the yearning that had come over her as they stood by the bank of the Wien. It seemed inconceivable that those words had not affected her more keenly at the moment, that that yearning had been awakened within her only once, and then only for so short a time. With a kind of perplexed amazement she thought of that period of placid purity and then, with a sudden agonized feeling of shame which drove the blood to her temples, of the cold readiness with which she had given herself afterwards to a man whom she had never loved. The consciousness that whatever happiness she had tasted in the course of her married life had been gained in the arms of the husband she had not loved made her shudder with horror, for the first time, in its utter wretchedness. Had that, then, been life such as her thoughts had depicted to her, had that been the mystic happiness such as she had yearned for? ... And a dull feeling of resentment against everything and everybody, against the living and the dead, began to smoulder within her bosom. She was angry with her dead husband and with her dead father and mother; she was indignant with the people amongst whom she was now living, whose eyes were always upon her so that she dared not allow herself any freedom; she was hurt with Frau Rupius, who had not turned out to be such a friend that Bertha could rely on her for support; she hated Klingemann because, ugly and repulsive as he was, he desired to make her his wife; and finally she was violently enraged with the man she had loved in the days of her girl-hood, because he had not been bolder, because he had with-held from her the ultimate happiness, and because he had bequeathed her nothing but memories full of fragrance, yet full of torment. And there she was, sitting in her lonely room amongst the faded mementoes of a youth that had passed unprofitably and friendlessly; there she was, on the verge of the time when there would be no more hopes and no more desires – life had slipped through her fingers, and she was thirty and poor.

She wrapped up the letters and the other things, and threw them, all crumpled as they were, into the case. Then she closed it and went over to the window.

Evening was at hand. A gentle breeze was blowing over from the direction of the vine-trellises. Her eyes swam with unwept tears, not of grief, but of exasperation. What was she to do? She, who had, without fear and without hope, seen the days, nights, months, years extending into the future, shuddered at the prospect of the emptiness of the evening which lay before her.

It was the hour at which she usually returned home from her walk. On that day she had sent the nursemaid out with Fritz – not so much as once did she yearn for her boy, indeed for one moment there even fell on her child a ray of the anger which she felt against all mankind and against her fate. And, in her vast discontent, she was seized with a feeling of envy against many people who, at ordinary times, seemed to her anything but enviable. She envied Frau Martin because of the tender affection of her husband; the tobacconist's wife because she was loved by Herr Klingemann and the captain; her sister-in-law, because she was already old; Elly, because she was still young; she envied the servant, who was sitting on a plank over there with a soldier, and whom she heard laughing. She could not endure being at home any longer. She took up her straw hat and sunshade and hurried into the street. There she felt somewhat better. In her room she had been unhappy; in the street she was no more than out of humour.

In the main thoroughfare she met Herr and Frau Mahlmann, to whose children she gave music-lessons. Frau Mahlmann was already aware that Bertha had ordered a costume from a dressmaker in Vienna on the previous day, and she began to discuss the matter with great weightiness. Later on, Bertha met her brother-in-law, who came towards her from the chestnut avenue.

'Well,' he said, 'so you were in Vienna yesterday! Tell me, what did you do with yourself there? Did you have any adventures?'

'What do you mean?' asked Bertha, looking at him in great alarm, as though she had done something she ought not, and had been found out.

'What? You had no adventures? But you were with Frau Rupius, all the men must surely have run after you?'

'What on earth has come into your head? Frau Rupius' conduct is irreproachable! She is one of the most well-bred ladies I know.'

'Quite so, quite so! I am not saying a word against Frau Rupius or you.'

She looked him in the face. His eyes were gleaming, as they often did when he had had a little too much to drink. She could not help recalling that somebody had once foretold that Herr Garlan would die of an apoplectic stroke.

'I must pay another visit to Vienna myself one of these days,' he said. 'Why, I haven't been there since Ash Wednes-

day. I should like to see some of my acquaintances once again.
The next time you and Frau Rupius go, you might just take
me with you.'

'With pleasure,' answered Bertha. 'I shall have to go again,
of course, before long, to have my costume tried on.'

Garlan laughed.

'Yes, and you can take me with you, too, when you try it
on.'

He sidled up closer to her than was necessary. It was a way
he had always to squeeze up against her, and, moreover, she
was accustomed to his jokes, but on the present occasion she
thought him particularly objectionable. She was very much
annoyed that he, of all men, always spoke of Frau Rupius in
such a suspicious way.

'Let us sit down,' said Herr Garlan; 'if you don't mind.'

They both sat down on a seat. Garlan took the newspaper
from his pocket.

'Ah!' said Bertha involuntarily.

'Will you have it?' asked Garlan.

'Has your wife read it yet?'

'Tut, tut!' said Garlan disdainfully. 'Will you have it?'

'If you can spare it.'

'For you – with pleasure. But we might just as well read it
together.'

He edged closer to Bertha and opened the paper.

Herr and Frau Martin came along, arm in arm, and stopped
before them.

'Well, so you are back again from the momentous journey,'
said Herr Martin.

'Ah, yes, you were in Vienna,' said Frau Martin, nestling
against her husband. 'And with Frau Rupius, too,' she added,
as though that implied an aggravation of the offence.

Once more Bertha had to give an account of her new
costume. She told them all about it in a somewhat mechanical
manner, indeed; but she felt, none the less, that it was long
since she had been such an interesting personage as she was
now.

Klingemann went by, bowed with ironical politeness, and
turned round to Bertha with a look which seemed to express

his sympathy for her in having to be friendly with such people.

It seemed to Bertha as though she were gifted that day with the ability to read men's glances.

It began to grow dark. They set off together towards the town. Bertha suddenly grew uneasy at not having met her boy. She walked on in front with Frau Martin, who turned the conversation on to the subject of Frau Rupius. She badly wanted to find out whether Bertha had observed anything.

'But what do you mean, Frau Martin? I accompanied Frau Rupius to her brother's house, and called for her there on my way back.'

'And are you convinced that she was with her brother the whole time?'

'I really don't know what you expect Frau Rupius to do! Where would she have been then?'

'Well,' said Frau Martin, 'really, you are an artless creature, I must say – or are you only putting it on? Do you quite forget then ...'

Then she whispered something into Bertha's ear, at which the latter grew very red. She had never heard such an expression from a woman. She was indignant.

'Frau Martin,' she said, 'I am not so old myself either and, as you see, it is quite possible to live a decent life in such circumstances.'

Frau Martin was a little taken aback.

'Yes, of course!' she said. 'Yes, of course! You must, I dare say, think that I am a little over-nice in such matters.'

Bertha was afraid that Frau Martin might be about to give her some further and more intimate disclosures and she was very glad to find that, at that moment, they had reached the street corner where she could say good-bye.

'Bertha, here's your paper!' her brother-in-law called after her.

She turned round quickly and took the paper. Then she hastened home. Fritz had returned and was waiting for her at the window. She hurried up to him. She embraced and kissed him as though she had not seen him for weeks. She felt that she was completely engrossed with love for her boy, a fact which, at the time, filled her with pride. She listened to his account of how he had spent the afternoon, where he had been, and with whom he had played. She cut up his supper for him, undressed him, put him to bed, and was satisfied with herself. Her state of mind of the afternoon, when she had rummaged among the old letters, had cursed her fate and had even envied the tobacconist's wife, seemed to her, at the thought of it, as an attack of fever. She ate a hearty supper and went to bed early. Before falling to sleep, however, it occurred to her that she would like to read the paper. She stretched her limbs, shook up the soft bolster so that her head should be higher, and held the paper as near the candle as possible.

As her custom was, she first of all skimmed through the theatrical and art news. Even the short announcements, as well as the local reports, had acquired a new interest for her, since her trip to Vienna. Her eyelids were beginning to grow heavy when all at once she observed the name of Emil Lindbach amongst the personal news. She opened her eyes wide, sat up in bed and read the paragraph.

Emil Lindbach, violinist to the Court of Bavaria, whose great success at the Spanish Court we were recently in a position to announce, has been honoured by the Queen of Spain, who has invested him with the Order of the Redeemer.

A smile flitted across her lips. She was glad, Emil Lindbach had obtained the Order of the Redeemer ... Yes ... the man whose letters she had been reading that very day ... the man who had kissed her – the man who had once written to her that he would never adore any other woman ... Yes, Emil – the only man in all the world in whom she really had still any interest – except her boy, of course. She felt as though this notice in the paper was intended only for her, as though, indeed, Emil himself had selected that expedient, so as to establish some means of communication with her. Had it not been he, after all, whose back she had seen in the distance on the previous day? All at once she seemed to be quite near to him; still smiling, she whispered to herself: 'Herr Emil Lindbach, violinist to the Court of Bavaria ... I congratulate you ...'

Her lips remained half open. An idea had suddenly come to

her. She got up quickly, donned her dressing-gown, took up
the light and went into the adjoining room. She sat down at
the table and wrote the following letter as fluently as though
some one were standing beside her and dictating it, word for
word:

Dear Emil,

I have just read in the newspaper that the Queen of Spain has
honoured you by investing you with the Order of the Redeemer. I
do not know whether you still remember me – she smiled as she
wrote these words – but, all the same, I will not let this opportunity
slip without congratulating you upon your many successes, of which
I so often have the pleasure of reading. I am living most contentedly
in the little town where fate has cast me; I am getting on very well!

A few lines in reply would make me very happy.

> Your old friend,
> Bertha.

P.S. – Kind regards also from my little Fritz (five years old).

She had finished the letter. For a moment she asked herself
whether she should mention that she was a widow; but even
if he had not known it before, it was quite obvious from her
letter. She read it over and nodded contentedly. She wrote the
address.

'Herr Emil Lindbach, violinist to the Court of Bavaria,
Holder of the Order of the Redeemer ...' Should she write all
that? He was certain to have many other Orders also ...
'Vienna ...'

But where was he living at present? That, however, was of
no consequence with such a celebrated name. Moreover the
inaccuracy in the address would also show that she did not
attach so very much importance to it all; if the letter reached
him – well, so much the better. It was also a way of putting
fate to the test ... Ah, but how was she to know for a
certainty that the letter had arrived or not? The answer might,
of course, quite easily fail to reach her if ... No, no, certainly
not! He would be sure to thank her. And so, to bed.

She held the letter in her hand. No, she could not go to bed
now, she was wide awake again. And, moreover, if she did not
post the letter until next morning it would not go before the

midday train, and would not reach Emil before the day after. That was an interminably long time. She had just spoken to him, and were thirty-six hours to be allowed to elapse before her words reached his ears? ... Supposing she did not wait, but went to the post now? ... no, to the station? Then he would have the letter at ten o'clock the next morning. He was certain to be late in rising, the letter would be brought into his room with his breakfast ... Yes, she must post the letter at once!

Quickly she dressed again. She hurried down the stairs – it was not yet late – she hastened along the main street to the station, put the letter in the yellow box, and was home again.

As she stood in her room, beside the tumbled bed, and she saw the paper lying on the floor and the candle flickering, it seemed as though she had returned from a strange adventure. For a long time she remained sitting on the edge of the bed, gazing through the window into the bright, starlit night, and her soul was filled with vague and pleasurable expectations.

My Dear Bertha!

I am wholly unable to tell you how glad I was to receive your letter. Do you really still think of me, then? How curious it is that it should have been an Order, of all things, that was the cause of my hearing from you again! Well, at all events, an Order has at least had some significance for once in a way! Therefore, I heartily thank you for your congratulations. But, apart from all that, don't you come to Vienna sometimes? It is not so very far, after all. I should be immensely pleased to see you again. So come soon!

With all my heart,

Your old

Emil.

Bertha was sitting at breakfast, Fritz beside her. He was chatting, but she was not listening to him. The letter lay before her on the table.

It seemed miraculous. Two nights and a day ago she had posted her letter, and here was his reply already. Emil had not allowed a day to pass, not even an hour! He had written to her as cordially as if they had only parted the previous day.

She looked out of the window. What a splendid morning it was! Outside the birds were singing, and from the hills came floating down the fragrance of the early summer-tide.

Bertha read the letter again and again. Then she took Fritz, lifted him up and kissed him to her heart's content. It was long since she had been so happy.

While she was dressing she turned things over in her mind. It was Thursday; on Monday she had to go to Vienna again to try on the costume. That was four long days, just the same space of time as had elapsed since she had dined at her brother-in-law's – what a long time it seemed to have to wait. No, she must see Emil sooner than that. She could, of course, go the very next morning and remain in Vienna a few days. But what excuse could she make to the people at home? ... Oh, she would be sure to find some pretext. It was more important to decide in what way she should answer his letter and tell him where she would meet him ... She could not write and say: 'I am coming, please let me know where I can see you ...' Perhaps he would answer: 'Come to my rooms ...' No, no, no! It would be best to let him have a definite statement of fact. She would write to the effect that she was going to Vienna on such and such a day and was to be found at such and such a place ...

Oh, if she only had some one with whom she could talk the whole thing over! ... She thought of Frau Rupius – she had a genuine yearning to tell her everything. At the same time she had an idea that, by so doing, she might become more intimate with her and might win her esteem. She felt that she had become much more important since the receipt of Emil's letter. Now she remarked, too, that she had been very much afraid that Emil might quite possibly have changed and become conceited, affected and spoiled – just as was the case with so many celebrated men. But there was not the slightest trace of such things in the letter; there was the same quick, heavy writing, the same warmth of tone, as in those earlier letters. What a number of experiences he might well have had since she had last seen him – well, had not she also had many experiences, and were they not all seemingly obliterated?

Before going out she read Emil's letter again. It grew more like a living voice; she heard the cadence of the words, and that final 'Come soon' seemed to call her with tender yearning. She stuck the letter into her bodice and remembered how, as a girl, she had often done the same with his notes, and how the gentle touch had sent a pleasant thrill coursing through her.

First of all, she went to the Mahlmanns', where she gave the twins their music lesson. Very often the finger exercises, to which she had to listen there, were positively painful to her, and she would rap the children on the knuckles when they struck a false note. On the present occasion, however, she was not in the least strict. When Frau Mahlmann, fat and friendly as ever, came into the room and inquired whether Bertha was satisfied, the latter praised the children and added, as though suddenly inspired:

'Now I shall be able to give them a few days' holiday.'

'Holiday? How will that be, then, dear Frau Garlan?'

'You see, Frau Mahlmann, I have no choice in the matter. What do you think, when I was in Vienna lately my cousin begged me so pressingly to be sure to come and spend a few days with her –'

'Quite so, quite so,' said Frau Mahlmann.

Bertha's courage kept rising, and she continued to add falsehood to falsehood, taking a kind of pleasure in her own boldness:

'I really wanted to put it off till June. But this very morning I had a letter from her, saying that her husband is going away for a time, and she is so lonely, and just now' – she felt the letter crackle, and had an indescribable desire to take it out; but yet restrained herself – 'and I think I shall perhaps take advantage of the opportunity ...'

'Well, to tell the truth,' said Frau Mahlmann, taking Bertha by both hands, 'if I had a cousin in Vienna, I would like to stay with her a week every fortnight!'

Bertha beamed. She felt as though an invisible hand was clearing away the obstacles which lay in her path; everything was going so well. And, indeed, to whom, after all, was she accountable for her actions? Suddenly, however, the fear flashed through her mind that her brother-in-law really intended to go with her to Vienna. Everything became entangled again; dangers cropped up and suspicion lurked even under the good-natured smile of Frau Mahlmann ...

Ah, she must on no account fail to take Frau Rupius into her confidence. Directly the lesson was over she went to call upon her.

It was not until she had found Frau Rupius in a white morning gown, sitting on the sofa, and had observed the surprised glance with which the latter received her, that it struck Bertha that there was anything strange in her early visit, and she said with affected cheerfulness:

'Good morning! I'm early today, am I not?'

Frau Rupius remained serious. She had not the usual smile on her lips.

'I am very glad to see you. The hour makes no difference to me.'

Then she threw her a questioning glance, and Bertha did not know what to say. She was annoyed, too, at the childish embarrassment of which she could not rid herself in the presence of Frau Rupius.

'I wanted,' she said, at length, 'to ask you how you felt after our trip.'

'Quite well,' answered Frau Rupius, rather stiffly. But all at once her features changed, and she added with excessive friendliness: 'Really, it was my place to have asked you. I am accustomed to those trips, you know.'

As she said this she looked through the window and Bertha mechanically followed her gaze, which wandered over to the other side of the market square to an open window with flowers on the sill. It was quite calm, and the repose of a summer day shrouded the slumbering town. Bertha would have dearly liked to sit beside Frau Rupius and be kissed upon the brow by her, and blessed; but at the same time she had a feeling of compassion towards her. All this puzzled her. For what reason, indeed, had she really come? And what should she say to her? ... 'I'm going tomorrow to Vienna to see the man who used to be in love with me when I was a girl?' ... In what way did all that concern Frau Rupius? Would it really interest her in the very slightest degree? There she sat as if surrounded by something impenetrable; it was impossible to approach her. *She* could not approach her, that was the trouble. Of course, there was a word by means of which it was possible to find the way to her heart, only Bertha did not know it.

'Well, how is your little boy?' asked Frau Rupius, without taking her eyes off the flowers in the opposite window.

'He is going on as well as ever. He is very well-behaved, and is a marvellously good child!'

The last word she uttered with an intentional tenderness as though Frau Rupius was to be won over by that means.

'Yes, yes,' answered the latter, her tone implying that she

knew he was good, and had not asked about that. 'Have you a reliable nursemaid?' she added.

Bertha was somewhat astonished at the question.

'My maid has, of course, many other things to attend to besides her nurse's duties,' she replied; 'but I cannot complain of her. She is also a very good cook.'

'It must be a great happiness to have such a boy,' said Frau Rupius very drily, after a short interval of silence.

'It is, indeed, my only happiness,' said Bertha, more loudly than was necessary.

It was an answer which she had often made before, but she knew that, on that day, she was not speaking with entire sincerity. She felt the sheet of paper touch her skin, and, almost with alarm, she realized that she had also deemed it a happiness to have received that letter. At the same time it occurred to her that the woman sitting opposite her had neither a child nor even the prospect of having one, and Bertha would have been glad to take back what she had said. Indeed, she was on the point of seeking some qualifying word. But, as if Frau Rupius was able to see into her soul, and as if in her presence a lie was impossible, she said at once:

'Your only happiness? Say rather, "a great happiness," and that is no small thing! I often envy you on that score, although I really think that, apart from such considerations, life in itself is a joy to you.'

'Indeed, my life is so lonely, so ...'

Anna smiled.

'Quite so, but I did not mean that. What I meant was that the fact that the sun is shining and the weather is now so fine also makes you glad.'

'Oh yes, very glad!' replied Bertha assiduously. 'My frame of mind is generally dependent on the weather. During that thunderstorm a few days ago I was utterly depressed, and then, when the storm was over –'

Frau Rupius interrupted her.

'That is the case with every one, you know.'

Bertha grew low-spirited. She felt that she was not clever enough for Frau Rupius, she could never do any more than follow the ordinary lines of conversation, like the other women of her acquaintance. It seemed as though Frau Rupius had arranged an examination for her, which she had not passed, and, all at once, she was seized with a great apprehension at the prospect of meeting Emil again. What sort of a figure would she cut in his presence? How shy and helpless she had become during the six years of her narrow existence in the little town!

Frau Rupius rose to her feet. The white morning gown streamed around her; she looked taller and more beautiful than usual, and Bertha was involuntarily reminded of an actress she had seen on the stage a very long time ago, and to whom at that moment Frau Rupius bore a remarkable resemblance. Bertha said to herself: If I were only like Frau Rupius I am sure I would not be so timid. At the same time it struck her that this exquisitely lovely woman was married to an invalid – might not the gossips be right then, after all? But here, again, she was unable to pursue further her train of thought; she could not imagine in what way the gossips could be right. And at that moment it dawned upon her mind how bitter was the fate to which Frau Rupius was condemned, no matter whether she now bore it or resisted it.

But, as if Anna had again read Bertha's thoughts, and could not tolerate that the latter should thus insinuate herself into her confidence, the uncanny gravity of her face relaxed suddenly, and she said in an innocent tone:

'Just fancy, my husband is still asleep. He has acquired the habit of remaining awake until late at night, reading and looking at engravings, and then he sleeps on until midday. As for that, it is quite a matter of habit; when I used to live in Vienna I was incredibly lazy about getting up.'

And thereupon she began to chat about her girlhood, cheerfully, and with a confiding manner such as Bertha had never before noticed in her. She told about her father, who had been an officer on the Staff, about her mother, who had died when she was quite a young woman; and about the little house in the garden of which she had played as a child. It was only now that Bertha learned that Frau Rupius had first become acquainted with her husband when he was just a boy; he had lived with his parents in the adjoining house, and had fallen in

love with Anna and she with him, while they were both
children. To Bertha the whole period of Frau Rupius' youth
appeared as if radiant with bright sunbeams, a youth replete
with happiness, replete with hope; and it seemed to her, moreover, that Frau Rupius' voice assumed a fresher tone when she
went on to relate about the travels which she and her husband
had undertaken in the early days of their married life.

Bertha let her talk and hesitated to interrupt her with a
word, as though she were a somnambulist wandering on the
ridge of a roof. But while Frau Rupius was speaking of her
past, a period through which the blessedness of being loved
ever beamed brightly as its chiefest glory, Bertha's soul began
to thrill with the hope of a happiness for herself such as she
had not yet experienced. And while Frau Rupius was telling
of the walking tours through Switzerland and the Tyrol, which
she had once undertaken with her husband, Bertha pictured
herself wandering by Emil's side on similar paths, and she was
filled with such an immense yearning that she would dearly
have liked at once to get up, go to Vienna, seek him out, fall
into his arms, and at last, at last to taste those delights which
had hitherto been denied her.

Her thoughts wandered so far that she did not notice that
Frau Rupius had long since fallen silent, and was sitting on the
sofa, staring at the flowers in the window of the house over
the way. The utter stillness brought Bertha back to reality; the
whole room seemed to her to be filled with some mysterious
atmosphere, in which the past and the future were strangely
intermingled. She felt that there existed an incomprehensible
connection between herself and Frau Rupius. She rose to her
feet, stretched out her hand, and, as if it were quite a matter of
course, the two ladies kissed each other good-bye like a couple
of old friends.

On reaching the door Bertha remarked:

'I am going to Vienna again tomorrow for a few days.'

She smiled as she spoke, like a girl about to be married.

After leaving Frau Rupius, Bertha went to her sister-in-law.
Her nephew was already sitting at the piano, improvising in a
very wild manner. He pretended not to have noticed her enter,

and proceeded to practise his finger exercises, which he played in an attitude of stiffness, assumed for the occasion.

'We will play a duet today,' said Bertha, endeavouring to find the volume of Schubert's marches.

She paid not the least attention to her own playing, and hardly noticed how, in using the pedals, her nephew touched her feet.

In the meantime Elly came into the room and kissed her aunt.

'Ah, just so, I had quite forgotten that!' said Richard, and, whilst continuing to play, he placed his lips close to Bertha's cheek.

Her sister-in-law came in with her bunch of keys rattling and a deep dejection on her pale and indistinct features.

'I have given Brigitta notice,' she said in a feeble tone. 'I couldn't endure it any longer.'

'Shall I get you a maid in Vienna?' asked Bertha with a facility which even surprised her.

And now for the second time she told the fiction which she had invented about her cousin's invitation, with even greater assurance than before, and, moreover, with a little amplification this time. Along with the secret joy which she found in the telling, she felt her courage increasing at the same time. Even the possibility of being joined by her brother-in-law no longer alarmed her. She felt, too, that she had an advantage over him, because of the way in which he was in the habit of sidling up to her.

'How long are you thinking of staying in the town then?' asked her sister-in-law.

'Two or three days; certainly no longer. And in any case, of course, I should have had to go on Monday – to the dressmaker.'

Richard strummed on the keys, but Elly stood with both arms resting on the piano, gazing at her aunt with a look almost of terror.

'Whatever is the matter with you?' asked Bertha involuntarily.

'Why do you ask that?' said Elly.

'You are looking at me,' said Bertha, 'as queerly as though –

well, as though you did not like the idea of missing your music
lessons for a couple of days.'

'No, it is not that,' replied Elly, smiling. 'But ... no, I can't
tell you.'

'What is it, though?' asked Bertha.

'No, please, I really can't tell you.'

She hugged her aunt, almost imploringly.

'Elly,' said her mother, 'I cannot permit you to have any
secrets.'

She sat down as though most deeply grieved and very tired.

'Well, Elly,' said Bertha, filled with a vague fear, 'if I were
to beg you –'

'But you mustn't laugh at me, Aunt.'

'Certainly not.'

'Well, you see, Aunt, I was so frightened when you were
away in Vienna that last time – I know very well it is silly –
but it is because ... because of the number of carriages in the
streets.'

Bertha drew a deep breath as of relief, and stroked Elly's
cheeks.

'I will be sure to take great care. You can be quite easy in
your mind.'

Her sister-in-law shook her head.

'I am afraid that Elly will turn out a most eccentric girl.'

Before Bertha left the house she arranged with her sister-in-
law that she would come back to supper, and that she would
hand over Fritz to the care of her relations while she was
away in Vienna.

After dinner, Bertha sat down at the writing table, read over
Emil's letter a few more times, and made a rough draft of her
reply.

'My dear Emil,

'It was very good of you to answer me so soon. I was very
happy' – she crossed out 'very happy' and substituted 'very
glad' – 'when I received your dear note. How much has
changed since we last saw each other! You have become a
famous virtuoso since then, which I, for my part, was always
quite sure that you would be' – she stopped and struck out
the whole sentence – 'I also share your desire to see me soon

again' – no, that was mere nonsense! This was better: 'I should be immensely delighted to have an opportunity of talking to you once more.' – Then an excellent idea occurred to her, and she wrote with great zest: 'It is really strange that we have not met for so long, for I come to Vienna quite often; for instance, I shall be there this week-end ...' Then she allowed her pen to drop and fell into thought. She was determined to go to Vienna the next afternoon, to put up at an hotel, and to sleep there, so as to be quite fresh the following day, and to breathe the air of Vienna for a few hours before meeting him. The next question was to fix a meeting place. That was easily done. 'In accordance with your kind wish I am writing to let you know that on Saturday morning at eleven o'clock ...' No, that was not the right thing! It was so businesslike, and yet again too eager – 'if,' she wrote, 'you would really care to take the opportunity of seeing your old friend again, then perhaps you will not consider it too much trouble to go to the Art and History Museum on Saturday morning at eleven o'clock. I will be in the gallery of the Dutch School' – as she wrote that she seemed to herself rather impressive and, at the same time, everything of a suspicious nature seemed to be removed.

She read over the draft. It appeared to her rather dry, but, after all, it contained all that was necessary, and did not compromise her in any way. Whatever else was to happen would take place in the Museum, in the Dutch gallery.

She neatly copied out the draft, signed it, placed it in an envelope, and hurried down the sunny street to post the letter in the nearest box. On arriving home again she slipped off her dress, donned a dressing-gown, sat down on the sofa, and turned over the leaves of a novel by Gerstäcker, which she had read half a score of times already. But she was unable to take in a word. At first, she attempted to dismiss from her mind the thoughts which beset her, but her efforts met with no success.

She felt ashamed of herself, but all the time she kept dreaming that she was in Emil's arms. Why ever did such dreams come to her? She had never, even for a moment, thought of such a thing! No ... she would not think of it, either ... she was not that sort of woman ... No, she could not be anyone's mistress – and even on this occasion ... Yes, perhaps if she were to go to Vienna once more and again ... and again ... yes, much later – perhaps. And besides, he would not even so much as dare to speak of such a thing, or even to hint at it ... It was, however, useless to reason like this, she could no longer think of anything else. Ever more importunate came her dreams and, in the end, she gave up the struggle. She lolled indolently in the corner of the sofa, allowed the book to slip from her fingers and lie on the floor, and closed her eyes.

When she rose to her feet an hour later a whole night seemed to have passed, and the visit to Frau Rupius seemed, in particular, to be far distant. Again she wondered at this confusion of time – in truth the hours appeared to be longer or shorter just as they chose.

She dressed in order to take Fritz for a walk. She was in the tired, indifferent mood which usually came over her after an unaccustomed afternoon nap. It was that mood in which it is scarcely possible to collect one's thoughts with any degree of completeness, and in which the usual appears strange, but as though it refers to some one else. For the first time, it seemed strange to Bertha that the boy, whom she was now helping into his coat, was her own child, whose father had long been buried, and for whom she had endured the pangs of motherhood.

Something within her urged her to go to the cemetery again that day. She had not, however, the feeling that she had a wrong to make reparation for, but that she must again politely visit some one to whom she had become a stranger for no valid reason. She chose the way through the chestnut avenue. There the heat was particularly oppressive that day. When she passed out into the sun again a gentle breeze was blowing and the foliage of the trees in the cemetery seemed to greet her with a slight bow. As she passed through the cemetery gates with Fritz the breeze came towards her, cool, even refreshing. With a feeling of gentle, almost sweet, weariness, she walked through the broad centre avenue, allowed Fritz to run on in front, and did not mind when he disappeared from her sight for a few seconds behind a tombstone, though at other times she would not have allowed such behaviour. She remained standing before her husband's grave. She did not, however, look down at the flower-bed, as was her general custom, but gazed past the tombstone and away over the wall into the blue sky. She felt no tears in her eyes, she felt no emotion, no dread; she did not even realize that she had walked over the dead, and that there beneath her feet he, who had once held her in his arms, had crumbled into dust.

Suddenly she heard behind her hurried footsteps on the gravel, such as she was not generally accustomed to hear in the cemetery. Almost shocked, she turned round. Klingemann was standing before her, in an attitude of greeting, holding in his hand his straw hat, which was fixed by a ribbon to his coat button. He bowed deeply to Bertha.

'What a strange thing to see you here!' she said.

'Not at all, my dear lady, not at all! I saw you from the street; I recognized you by your walk.'

He spoke in a very loud tone, and Bertha almost involuntarily murmured:

'Hush!'

A mocking smile at once made its appearance on Klingemann's face.

'He won't wake up,' he muttered, between his clenched teeth.

Bertha was so indignant at this remark that she did not attempt to find an answer, but called Fritz, and was about to depart.

Klingemann, however, seized her by the hand.

'Stop,' he whispered, gazing at the ground.

Bertha opened her eyes wide; she could not understand.

Suddenly Klingemann looked up from the ground and fixed his eyes on Bertha's.

'I love you, you see,' he said.

Bertha uttered a low cry.

Klingemann let go her hand, and added in quite an easy conversational tone:

'Perhaps that strikes you as rather odd.'

'It is unheard of! – unheard of!'

Once more she sought to go, and she called Fritz.

'Stop! If you leave me alone now, Bertha ...' said Klinge-mann, now in a suppliant tone.

Bertha had recovered her senses again.

'Don't call me Bertha!' she said, vehemently. 'Who gave you the right to do so? I have no wish to say anything further to you ... and here, of all places!' she added, with a down-ward glance, which, as it were, besought the pardon of the dead.

Meanwhile Fritz had come back. Klingemann seemed very disappointed.

'My dear lady,' he said, following Bertha, who, holding Fritz by the hand, was slowly walking away: 'I recognize my mistake. I should have begun differently and not said that which seems now to have frightened you, until I had come to the end of a well-turned speech.'

Bertha did not look at him, but said, as though she were speaking to herself:

'I would not have considered it possible; I thought a gentle-man ...'

They were at the cemetery gate. Klingemann looked back again, and in his glance there was something of regret at not having been able to play out his scene at the graveside to a finish. Hat in hand, and twisting the ribbon, by which it was fastened, round his finger, and still keeping by Bertha's side, he went on to say:

'All I can do now is to repeat that I love you, that you pursue me in my dreams – in a word, you must be mine!'

Bertha came to a standstill again, as if she were terrified.

'You will, perhaps, consider my remarks insolent, but let us take things as they are. You' – he made a long pause – 'are alone in the world. So am I –'

Bertha stared him full in the face.

'I know what you are thinking of,' said Klingemann. 'That is all of no consequence; that is all done with the moment you give the word. I have a dim presentiment that we two suit each other very well. Yes, unless I am very much deceived, the blood should be flowing in your veins, my dear lady, as warm ...'

The glance which Bertha now gave him was so full of anger

and loathing that Klingemann was unable to complete the sentence. He therefore began another.

'Ah, when you come to think of it, what sort of a life is it that I am now leading? It is even a long, long time since I was loved by a noble woman such as you are. I understand, of course, your hesitation, or rather, your refusal. Deuce take it, of course it needs a bit of courage – with such a disreputable fellow as I am, too . . . although, perhaps, things are not quite so bad. Ah, if I could only find a human soul, a kind, womanly soul!' – He emphasized the 'womanly soul' – 'Yes, my dear lady, it was as little meant to be my fate as it was yours to pine away and grow crabbed in such a hole of a town as this. You must not be offended if I . . . if I –'

The words began to fail him when he approached the truth. Bertha looked at him. He seemed to her at that moment to be rather ridiculous, almost pitiable, and very old, and she wondered how it was that he still had the courage, not so much as to propose to her, as even simply to court her favour.

And yet, to her own amazement and shame, there over-flowed from these unseemly words of a man who appeared absurd to her, the surge, so to speak, of desire. And when his words had died away she heard them again in her mind – but as though from the lips of another who was waiting for her in Vienna – and she felt that she would not be able to withstand this other speaker. Klingemann continued to talk; he spoke of his life as being a failure, but yet a life worth saving. He said that women were to be blamed for bringing him so low, and that a woman could raise him up again. Away back in his student days he had run away with a woman, and that had been the beginning of his misfortunes. He talked of his un-bridled passions, and Bertha could not restrain a smile. At the same time she was ashamed of the knowledge which seemed to her to be implied by the smile . . .

'I will walk up and down in front of your window this evening,' said Klingemann, when they reached the gate. 'Will you play the piano?'

'I don't know.'

'I will take it as a sign.'

With that he went away.

In the evening she supped, as she had so often done, at her brother-in-law's house. At the table she sat between Elly and Richard. Mention was made of her approaching journey to Vienna as though it was really nothing more than a matter of paying a visit to her cousin, trying on the new costume at the dressmaker's, and executing a few commissions in the way of household necessities, which she had promised to undertake for her sister-in-law. Towards the end of supper, her brother-in-law smoked his pipe, Richard read the paper to him, her sister-in-law knitted, and Elly, who had nestled up close beside Bertha, leaned her childish head upon her aunt's breast. And Bertha, as her glance took in the whole scene, felt herself to be a crafty liar. She, the widow of a good husband, was sitting there in a family circle which interested itself in her welfare so loyally; by her side was a young girl who looked up at her as on an older friend. Hitherto she had been a good woman, honest and industrious, living only for her son. And now, was she not about to cast aside all these things, to deceive and lie to these excellent people, and to plunge into an adventure, the end of which she could foresee? What was it, then, that had come over her these last few days, by what dreams was she pursued, how was it that her whole existence seemed only to aspire towards the one moment when she would again feel the arms of a man about her? She had but to think of it and she was seized with an indescribable sensation of horror, during which she seemed devoid of will, as if she had fallen under the influence of some strange power.

And while the words that Richard was reading beat monotonously upon her ear, and her fingers played with the locks of Elly's hair – she resisted for the last time; she resolved that she would be steadfast – that she would do no more than see Emil once again, and that, like her own mother who had died long ago, and like all the other good women she knew – her cousin in Vienna, Frau Mahlmann, Frau Martin, her sister-in-law, and ... yes, certainly Frau Rupius as well – she would belong only to him who made her his wife. As soon, however, as she thought of that, the idea flashed through her mind, like lightning: if he himself ... if Emil ... But she was afraid of the thought, and banished it from her. Not with such bold dreams as these would she go to meet Emil. He, the great artist, and she, a poor widow with a child ... no, no! – she would see him once again ... in the Museum of course, at the Dutch gallery ... once only, and that for the last time, and she would tell him that she did not wish for anything else than to see him that once. With a smile of satisfaction she pictured to herself his somewhat disappointed face; and, as if practising before-hand for the scene, she knitted her brow and assumed a stern cast of countenance, and had the words ready on her lips to say to him: 'Oh, no, Emil, if you think that ...' But she must take care not to say it in quite too harsh a tone, in order that Emil might not, as on that previous occasion ... twelve years before! ... cease to plead after only the one attempt. She intended that he should beg a second time, a third time – ah, Heaven knew, she intended that he should continue to plead until she gave way ... For she felt, there in the midst of all those good, respectable, virtuous people, with whom, indeed, she would soon no longer be numbered, that she would give way the moment he first asked her. She was only going to Vienna to be *his*, and after that, if needs must be, to die.

On the afternoon of the following day Bertha set off. It was very hot, and the sun beat down upon the leather-covered seats of the railway carriage. Bertha had opened the window and drawn forward the yellow curtain, which, however, kept flapping in the breeze. She was alone. But she scarcely thought of the place towards which she was travelling; she scarcely thought of the man whom she was about to see again, or of what might be in store for her – she thought only of the strange words she had heard, an hour before her departure. She would gladly have forgotten them, at least for the next few days. Why was it that she had been unable to remain at home during those few short hours between dinner and her departure? What unrest had driven her on this glowing hot afternoon out from her room, on to the street, into the market, and bade her pass Herr Rupius' house? He was sitting there upon the balcony, his eyes fixed on the gleaming white pavement, and over his knees, as usual, was spread the great plaid rug, the ends of which were hanging down between the bars of the balcony railings; in front of him was the little table with a bottle of water and a glass. When he perceived Bertha his eyes became fixed upon her, as though he were making some request to her, and she observed that he beckoned her with a slight movement of the head.

Why had she obeyed him? Why had she not taken his nod simply as a greeting and thanked him and gone upon her way? When, however, in answer to his nod, she turned towards the door of the house, she saw a smile of thanks glide over his lips and she found it still on his countenance when she went out to him on the balcony, through the cool, darkened room, and, taking his outstretched hand, sat down opposite to him on the other side of the little table.

'How are you getting on?' she asked.

At first he made no answer; then she observed from the working of his face that he wanted to say something, but seemed as if he was unable to utter a word.

'She is going to . . .' he broke out at length. These first words he uttered in an unnecessarily loud voice; then, as though alarmed at the almost shrieking tone, he added very softly: 'My wife is going to leave me.'

Bertha involuntarily looked around her.

Rupius raised his hands, as if to reassure her.

'She cannot hear us. She is in her room; she is asleep.'

Bertha was embarrassed.

'How do you know? . . .' she stammered. 'It is impossible – quite impossible!'

'She is going away – away, for a time, as she says . . . for a time . . . do you understand?'

'Why, yes, to her brother, I suppose.'

'She is going away for ever . . . for ever! Naturally she does not like to say to me: Good-bye, you will never see me again! So she says: I should like to travel a little; I need a change; I will go to the lake for a few weeks; I should like to bathe; I need a change of air! Naturally she does not say to me: I can endure it no longer; I am young and in my prime and healthy; you are paralysed and will soon die; I have a horror of your affliction and of the loathsome state that must supervene before it is at an end. So she says: I will go away only for a few weeks, then I will come back again and stay with you.'

Bertha's painful agitation became merged in her embarrassment.

'You are certainly mistaken,' was all that she could answer.

Rupius hastily drew up the rug, which was on the point of slipping down off his knees. He seemed to find it chilly. As he continued to speak, he drew the rug higher and higher, until finally he held it with both hands pressed against his breast.

'I have seen it coming; for years I have seen this moment coming. Imagine what sort of an existence it has been; waiting for such a moment, defenceless and forced to be silent! – Why are you looking at me like that?'

'Oh, no,' said Bertha, looking down at the market square.

'Well, I beg your pardon for referring to all this. I had no intention of doing so, but when I saw you walking past – well, thank you very much for having listened to me.'

'Please don't mention it,' said Bertha, mechanically stretching out her hand to him. He did not notice it, however, and she let it lie upon the table.

'Now it is all over,' said Herr Rupius; 'now comes the time of loneliness, the time of dread.'

'But has your wife ... she loves you, I'm sure of it! ... I am quite certain that you are giving yourself needless anxiety. Wouldn't the simplest course be, Herr Rupius, for you to request your wife to forgo this journey?'

'Request? ...' said Herr Rupius, almost majestically. 'Can I pretend to have the right to do so? All these last six or seven years have only been a favour which she has granted me. I beg you, consider it. During all these seven years not a word of complaint at the waste of her youth has passed her lips.'

'She loves you,' said Bertha, decisively; 'and that is the chief point.'

Herr Rupius looked at her for a long time.

'I know what is in your mind, although you do not venture to say it. But your husband, my dear Frau Bertha, lies deep in the grave, and does not sleep by your side night after night.'

He looked up with a glance that seemed to ascend to Heaven as a curse.

Time was getting on; Bertha thought of her train.

'When is your wife going to start?'

'Nothing has been said about that yet – but I am keeping you, perhaps?'

'No, not at all, Herr Rupius, only . . . Hasn't Anna told you? I'm going to Vienna today, you know.'

She grew burning red. Once more he gazed at her for a long time. It seemed to her as though he knew everything.

'When are you coming back?' he asked drily.

'In two or three days.'

She would have liked to say that he was mistaken, that she was not going to see a man whom she loved, that all these things about which he was worrying were sordid and mean, and really of not the slightest importance to women – but she was not clever enough to find the right words to express herself.

'If you come back in two or three days' time you may, perhaps, find my wife still here. So, good-bye! I hope you will enjoy yourself.'

She felt that his glance had followed her as she went through the dark, curtained room and across the market square. And now, too, as she sat in the railway carriage, she felt the same glance and still in her ears kept ringing those words, in which there seemed to lie the consciousness of an immense unhappiness, which she had not hitherto understood. The torment of this recollection seemed stronger than the expectation of any joys that might be awaiting her, and the nearer she approached to the great city the heavier she became at heart. As she thought of the lonely evening that lay before her she felt as though she were travelling, without hope, towards some strange, uncertain destination. The letter which she still carried in her bodice had lost its enchantment; it was nothing but a piece of crackling paper, filled with writing, the corners of which were beginning to get torn. She tried to imagine what Emil now looked like. Faces bearing a slight resemblance to his arose before her mind's eye; many times she thought that she had surely hit upon the right one, but it vanished immediately. Doubts began to assail her as to whether she had done the right thing in travelling so soon. Why had she not waited, at least, until Monday?

Then she was obliged, however, to confess to herself that

she was going to Vienna to keep an appointment with a young man, with whom she had not exchanged a word for ten years, and who, perhaps, was expecting a quite different woman from the one who was travelling to see him on the morrow. Yes, that was the cause of all her uneasiness, she realized it now. The letter which was already beginning to chafe her delicate skin was addressed to Bertha, the girl of twenty; for Emil, of course, could not know what she looked like now. And, although for her own part, she could assure herself that her face still preserved its girlish features and that her figure, though grown fuller, still preserved the contours of youth, might he not see, in spite of all, how many changes a period of ten years had wrought in her, and, perhaps, even destroyed without her having noticed it herself?

The train drew up at Klosterneuburg. Bertha's ears were assailed by the sound of many clear voices and the clatter of hurrying footsteps. She looked out of the window. A number of schoolboys crowded up to the train and, laughing and shouting, got into the carriages. The sight of them caused Bertha to call to mind the days of her childhood, when her brothers used to come back from picnics in the country, and suddenly there came before her eyes a vision of the blue room in which the boys had slept. She seemed to feel a tremor run through her as she realized how all the past was scattered to the wind; how those to whom she owed her existence had died, how those with whom she had lived for years under one roof were forgotten; how friendships which had seemed to have been formed to last for ever had become dissolved. How uncertain, how mortal, everything was!

And he ... he had written to her as if in the course of those ten years nothing had changed, as if in the meantime there had not been funerals, births, sorrows, illnesses, cares and – for him, at least – so much good fortune and fame. Involuntarily she shook her head. A kind of perplexity in the face of so much that was incomprehensible came over her. Even the roaring of the train, which was carrying her along to unknown adventures, seemed to her as a chant of remarkable sadness. Her thoughts went back to the time, by no means remote, in fact no more than a few days earlier, when she had been tranquil and contented, and had borne her existence without desire, without regret and without wonder. However had it happened that this change had come over her? She could not understand.

The train seemed to rush forward with ever-increasing speed towards its destination. Already she could see the smoke of the great city rising skywards as out of the depths. Her heart began to throb. She felt as if she was awaited by something vague, something for which she could not find a name, a thing with a hundred arms, ready to embrace her. Each house she passed knew that she was coming; the evening sun, gleaming on the roofs, shone to meet her; and then, as the train rolled into the station, she suddenly felt sheltered. Now for the first time, she realized that she was in Vienna, in *her* Vienna, the town of her youth and of her dreams, that she was home. Had she not given the slightest thought to that before? She did not come from home – no, now she had arrived home. The din at the station filled her with a feeling of comfort, the bustle of people and carriages gladdened her, everything that was sorrowful had been shed from her.

There she stood at the Franz Josef Station in Vienna, on a warm May evening, Bertha Garlan, young and pretty, free and accountable to no one, and on the morrow she was to see the only man whom she had ever loved – the lover who had called her.

She put up at a little hotel near the station. She had determined to choose one of the less fashionable, partly for the sake of economy, and partly, too, because she stood in awe, to a certain extent, of smart waiters and porters. She was shown to a room on the third floor with a window looking out on the street. The chambermaid closed the window when the visitor entered, and brought some fresh water, the boots placed her box beside the stove, and the waiter placed before her the registration paper which Bertha filled up immediately and unhesitatingly, with the pride that comes of a clear conscience.

A feeling of freedom as regards external circumstances, such as she had not known for a long time, encompassed her; there were none of the petty domestic cares of the daily round, there was no obligation to talk to relations or acquaintances; she was at liberty that evening to do just as she liked.

When she had changed her dress she opened the window. She had already been obliged to light the candles, but out of doors it was not yet quite dark. She leaned her elbows on the window-sill and looked down. Again she remembered her childhood, when she had often looked down out of the windows in the evenings, sometimes with one of her brothers, who had thrown his arm around his shoulders. She also thought of her parents with so keen an emotion that she was on the verge of tears.

Down below the street lamps were already alight. Well, at all events, she must find something to do. She thought of what might be happening the next day at that hour ... She could not picture it to herself. At that moment, it just happened that a lady and gentleman drove by the hotel in a cab. If things turned out in accordance with her wishes Emil and she should be going for a drive together into the country the next morning – yes, that would be nicest. Some quiet spot away from the town in a restaurant garden, a candle lamp on the table, and he beside her, hand in hand like a pair of young lovers. And then back again – and then ... No, she would rather not imagine anything further! Where was he now, she wondered. Was he alone? Or was he at that very instant engaged in talking with some one? And with whom – a man? – a woman? – a girl? But, after all, was it any concern of hers? For the present it was certainly not any concern of hers. And to Emil it mattered just as little that Herr Klingemann had proposed to her the previous day, that Richard, her precocious nephew, kissed her sometimes, and that she had a great admiration for Herr Rupius. She would be sure to ask him on the morrow – yes, she must be certain as regards all these points before she ... well, before she went with him in the evening into the country.

So then she decided to go out – but where? She stopped, irresolute, at the door. All she could do was to go for a short walk and then have supper ... but again, where? A lady alone ... No, she would have supper here in her room at the hotel and go to bed early so that she might have a good night's rest and look fresh, young and pretty in the morning.

She locked the door and went out into the street. She turned towards the inner town and proceeded at a very sharp pace, for she did not like walking alone in the evening. Soon she reached the Ring and went past the University, and on to the Town Hall. But she took no pleasure at all in this aimless rambling. She felt bored and hungry, and went back to her hotel in a tramcar. She had no great desire to seek her room. From the street she had already noticed that the dining-room of the hotel was barely lighted and evidently empty. She had supper there, after which she grew tired and sleepy and, with an effort, went up the three flights of stairs to her room. As she sat on the bed and undid her shoe laces, she heard ten o'clock chime in a neighbouring church steeple.

When she awoke in the morning she hurried, first of all, to the window and drew up the blinds with a great longing to see the daylight and the town. It was a sunny morning, and the air was as fresh as if it had come flowing down from a thousand springs in the forests and hills, into the streets of the town. The beauty of the morning acted on Bertha as a good omen; she wondered at the strange, foolish manner in which she had spent the previous evening – as if she had not quite correctly understood why she had come to Vienna. The certainty that the repose of a whole night no longer separated her from the longed-for hour, filled her with a sense of great gladness. All at once, she could no longer understand how it was that she could have come to Vienna, as she had done just recently, without daring to make even an attempt to see Emil. Finally, too, she wondered how it was that she had, for weeks, months, perhaps years, needlessly deferred availing herself of the opportunity of seeing him. The fact that she had scarcely thought of him during the whole time, did not occur to her at first, but, when at length she did realize it, she was amazed at that, most of all.

At last only four more hours were to be endured, and then she would see him. She lay down on the bed again; she reclined, at first, with her eyes wide open, and she whispered to herself, as though she wanted to intoxicate herself with the words: 'Come soon!' She heard Emil himself speak the words, no longer far away, no, but as though he were close by her side. His lips breathed them on hers: 'Come soon!' he said, but the words meant: 'Be mine! be mine!' She opened her arms as though making ready to press her beloved to her heart. 'I love you,' she said, and breathed a kiss into the air.

At length she got up and dressed. This time she had brought with her a simple grey costume, cut in the English fashion, which, according to the general opinion of her friends, suited her very well, and she was quite content with herself when she had completed her toilet. She probably did not look like a fashionable lady of Vienna, but, on the other hand, she had not the appearance of a fashionable lady from the country either; it seemed to her that she looked more like a governess in the household of some Count or Prince, than anything else. Indeed, as a matter of fact, there was something of the young unmarried lady in her aspect; no one would have taken her for a married woman and the mother of a five-year-old boy. She thought, with a slight sigh, that truly she would have done better to have remained unmarried. But, as to that, she was feeling that day very much like a bride.

Nine o'clock! Still two long hours to wait! What could she do in the meantime? She sat down at the table, ordered coffee and sipped it slowly. There was no sense in remaining indoors any longer; it was better to go out into the open air at once.

For a time she walked about the streets of the suburb, and she took a particularly keen pleasure in the wind blowing on her cheeks. She asked herself: What was Fritz doing at that moment? Probably Elly was playing with him. Bertha took the road which led towards the public gardens; she was glad to go for a walk through the avenues, in which, many years ago, she had played as a child. She entered the garden by the gate opposite the Burg-theater. At that early hour of the day there were but few people in the gardens. Children were playing on the gravel; governesses and nursemaids were sitting on the seats; little girls were running about along the steps of the Temple of Theseus and under its colonnade. Elderly people were walking in the shade of the avenues; young men, who were apparently studying from large writing books, and ladies, who were reading books, had taken their seats in the cool shade of the trees.

Bertha sat on a seat and watched two little girls who were jumping over a piece of string, as she had so often done herself, when a child – it seemed to her, in just the same spot. A gentle breeze blew through the foliage, from afar she heard the calls and laughter of some children playing 'catch'. The cries came nearer and nearer; and then the children ran trooping past her. She felt a thrill of pleasure when a young man in a long overcoat walked slowly by and turned round to look at her for a second time, when he reached the end of the avenue. Then there passed by a young couple; the girl, who had a roll of music in her hand, was neatly but somewhat strikingly dressed; the man was clean-shaven and was wearing a light summer suit and a tall hat. Bertha thought herself most experienced when she fancied that she was able with certainty to recognize in the girl a student of music, and in her companion a young man who had just gone on the stage. It was very pleasant to be sitting there, to have nothing to do, to be alone, and to have people walking, running and playing like this before her. Yes, it would be nice to live in Vienna and be able to do just as she liked. Well, who could say how everything would turn out, what the next few hours would bring forth, what prospects for her future life that evening would open out before her? What was it then, that really forced her to live in that dreadful little town? After all, in Vienna she would be able to supplement her income by giving music lessons just as easily as at home. Why not, indeed? Moreover, in Vienna, better terms were to be obtained for music lessons . . . Ah, what an idea! . . . if he came to her aid; if he, the famous musician, recommended her? Why, certainly it would only need one word from him. What if she were to speak to him on the subject? And would it not also be a most advantageous arrangement in view of her child? In a few years' time he would have to go to school, and then, of course, the schools were so much better in Vienna than at home. No, it was quite impossible for her to pass all her life in the little town – she would have to move to Vienna, and that, too, at no distant date. Moreover, even if she had to economize here, and – and . . . In vain she attempted to restrain the bold thoughts which now came rushing along . . . If she should take Emil's fancy, if she should again . . . if he should still be in love with her . . . if he should ask her to be his wife? If she could be a bit clever, if she avoided compromising herself in any way, and understood how to fascinate him – she felt rather ashamed of her craftiness ... But, after all, was it so bad that she should think of such things, considering that she was really in love with him, and had never loved any other man but him? And did not the whole tone of his letter give her the right to indulge in such thoughts?

And then, when she realized that in a few minutes she was to meet him who was the object of her hopes, everything began to dance before her eyes. She rose to her feet, and nearly reeled. She saw the young couple who had previously walked past her leave the gardens by the road leading to the Burgplatz. She went off in the same direction. Yonder, she saw the dome of the Museum, towering and gleaming. She decided to walk slowly, so as not to appear too excited or even breathless when she met him. Once more she was seized with a thrill of fear – suppose he should not come? But whatever happened, she would not leave Vienna this time without seeing him.

Would it not, perhaps, even be better if he did not come, she wondered. She was so bewildered at that moment ... and supposing she was to say anything silly or awkward ... So much depended on the next few minutes – perhaps her whole future ...

There was the Museum before her. Up the steps, through the entrance, and she was standing in the large cool vestibule. Before her eyes was the grand staircase and, yonder, where it divided to right and left, was the colossal marble statue of Theseus, slaying the Minotaur. Slowly she ascended the stairs and, as she looked round about her, she grew calmer. The magnificence of her surroundings captivated her. She looked up at the galleries which, with their golden railings, ran round the interior of the dome. She came to a stop. Before her was a door, above which appeared in gilt letters: 'Dutch School'.

Her heart gave a sudden convulsive throb. Before her eyes lay the row of picture galleries. Here and there she saw people standing before the pictures. She entered the first hall, and gazed attentively at the first picture hanging at the very entrance. She thought of Herr Rupius' portfolio. And then she heard a voice say:

'Good morning, Bertha.'

It was his voice. She turned round. He was standing before her, young, slim, elegant and rather pale. In his smile there was a suggestion of mockery. He nodded to Bertha, took her hand at the same time, and held it for a while in his own. It was Emil himself, and it was exactly as if the last occasion on which they had spoken to one another had been only the previous day.

'Good morning, Emil,' she said.

They gazed at each other. His glance was expressive of much: pleasure, amiability, and something in the nature of a scrutiny. She realized all this with perfect clearness, whilst she gazed at him with eyes in which nothing but pure happiness was shining.

'Well, then, how are you getting on, Bertha?' he asked.

'Quite well.'

'It is really funny that I should ask you such a question after eight or nine years. Things have probably gone very differently with you.'

'Yes, indeed, that's true. You know, of course, that my husband died three years ago.'

She felt obliged to assume an expression of sorrow.

'Yes, I know that, and I know, too, that you have a boy. Let me see, who could it have been that told me?'

'I wonder who?'

'Well, it'll come back to me presently. It is new to me, though, that you are interested in pictures.'

Bertha smiled.

'Well, it wasn't really on account of the pictures alone. But you mustn't think that I am quite so silly as all that. I do take an interest in pictures.'

'And so do I. If the truth must be told, I think I would rather be a painter than anything else.'

'Yet you ought to be quite satisfied with what you have attained.'

'Well, that's a question that can't be disposed of in one word. Of course, I find it a very pleasant thing to be able to play the violin so well, but what does it all lead to? Only to this, I think: that when I am dead my name will endure for a short time. That –' his eyes indicated the picture before which they were standing – 'that, on the other hand, is something different.'

'You are awfully ambitious, Emil!'

He looked at her, but without evincing the slightest interest in her.

'Ambitious? Well, it is not such a simple matter as all that. But let's talk about something else. What a strange idea to indulge in a theoretical conversation on the subject of art, when we haven't seen each other for a hundred years! So come, then, Bertha, tell me something about yourself! What do you do with yourself at home? How do you live? And what really put it into your head to congratulate me on getting that silly Order?'

She smiled a second time.

'I wanted to write to you again,' she answered; 'and, chiefly, I wanted to hear something of you once more. It was really very good of you to answer my letter at once.'

'Good? Not at all, my child! I was so pleased when, all of a sudden, your letter came – I recognized your writing at once. You know, you still have the same schoolgirl writing as ... Well, let us say, as in the old days, although I can't bear such expressions.'

'But why?' she asked, somewhat astonished.

He looked at her, and then said in a rapid voice:

'Well, tell me, how do you live? You must generally get very bored, I'm sure.'

'I haven't much time for that,' she replied gravely. 'I give lessons, you must know.'

'Oh!'

His tone was one of such disproportionate pity that she felt constrained to add quickly:

'Oh, not because there is really any pressing need for me to do so – although, of course, I find it very useful, because ...' she felt that it would be best to be quite frank with him ... 'I could scarcely live on the slender means that I possess.'

'What is it, then, that you are actually a teacher of?'

'What! Didn't I tell you that I give piano lesons?'

'Piano lessons? Really? Yes, of course ... you used to be very talented. If you hadn't left the Conservatoire when you did ... well, of course, you would not have become one of the great pianistes, you know, but for certain things you had quite a pronounced aptitude. For instance, you used to play Chopin and the little things of Schumann very prettily.'

'You still remember that?'

'After all, I dare say that you have chosen the better course.'

'In what way?'

'Well, if it is impossible to master everything, it is better no doubt to get married and have children.'

'I have only one child.'

He laughed.

'Tell me something about him, and all about your own life in general.'

They sat down on the divan in the little saloon in front of the Rembrandts.

'What have I to tell you about myself? There is nothing in it of the slightest interest. Rather, you tell me about yourself' – she looked at him with admiration – 'things have gone so splendidly with you, you are such a celebrated man, you see!'

Emil twitched his underlip very slightly, as if discontented.

'Why, yes,' she continued undaunted; 'quite recently I saw your portrait in an illustrated paper.'

'Yes, yes,' he said impatiently.

'But I always knew that you would make a name for yourself,' she added. 'Do you still remember how you played the Mendelssohn Concerto at that final examination at the Conservatoire? Everybody said the same thing then.'

'I beg you, my dear girl, don't, please, let us have any more of these mutual compliments! Tell me, what sort of a man was your late husband?'

'He was a good – indeed, I might say noble – man.'

'Do you know, though, that I met your father about eight days before he died?'

'Did you really?'

'Didn't you know?'

'I am certain he didn't tell me anything about it.'

'We stood chatting with one another in the street for a quarter of an hour, perhaps. I had just returned then from my first concert tour.'

'Not a word did he tell me – not a single word!'

She spoke almost angrily, as though her father had, at that time, neglected something that might have shaped her future life differently.

'But why didn't you come to see us in those days?' she continued. 'How did it happen at all that you had already suddenly ceased to visit us some considerable time before my father's death?'

'Suddenly? – Gradually!'

He looked at her a long time; and now his eyes glided down over her whole body, so that she mechanically drew in her feet under her dress and pressed her arms against her body, as though to defend herself.

'Well, how did it happen that you came to get married?'

She related the whole story. Emil listened to her, apparently with attention, but as she spoke on and remained seated, he rose to his feet and gazed out through the window ... When she had finished with a remark about the good-nature of her relations, he said:

'Don't you think that we ought to look at a few pictures now that we are here in the Museum?'

They walked slowly through the galleries, stopping here and there before a picture.

'Lovely! Exquisite!' commented Bertha many a time, but Emil only nodded.

It seemed to Bertha that he had quite forgotten that he was with her. She felt slightly jealous at the interest which the paintings roused in him. Suddenly they found themselves before one of the pictures which she knew from Herr Rupius' portfolio. Emil wanted to pass on, but she stopped and greeted it, as she might an old acquaintance.

'Exquisite!' she exclaimed. 'Emil, isn't it beautiful? On the whole I greatly admire Falckenborg's pictures.'

He looked at her, somewhat surprised.

She became embarrassed, and tried to go on talking.

'Because such an immense quantity – because the whole world –'

She felt that this was dishonest, even that she was robbing some one who could not defend himself; and accordingly she added, repentantly, as it were:

'You must know, there's a man living in our little town who has an album, or rather a portfolio, of engravings, and that's how I know the picture. His name is Rupius, he is very infirm; just fancy, he is quite paralysed.'

She felt obliged to tell Emil all this, for it seemed to her as though his eyes were unceasingly questioning her.

'That might be a chapter, too,' he said, with a smile, when she had come to an end; then he added more softly, as though ashamed of his indelicate joke: 'There must certainly also be gentlemen in that little town who are not paralysed.'

She felt that she had to take poor Herr Rupius under her protection.

'He is a very unhappy man,' she said, and, remembering how she had sat with him on the balcony the previous day, a feeling of great compassion seized her.

But Emil was following his own train of thought.

'Yes,' he said; 'that is what I should really like to know – what experiences you have had.'

'You know them, already.'

'I mean, since the death of your husband.'

She understood now what he meant, and was a little offended.

'I live only for my boy,' she said, with decision. 'I do not allow men to make love to me. I am quite respectable.'

He had to laugh at the comically serious way in which she made this confession of virtue. For her part, she felt at once that she ought to have expressed herself differently, and so she laughed, too.

'How long are you going to stay, then, in Vienna?' asked Emil.

'Till tomorrow, or the day after tomorrow.'

'So short a time as that? And where are you staying? I should like to know.'

'With my cousin,' she replied.

Something restrained her from mentioning that she had put up at an hotel. But immediately she was angry with herself for having told such a stupid lie, and she was about to correct herself. Emil, however, broke in quickly:

'Perhaps you will have a little time to spare for me, too? I hope so, at least.'

'Oh, yes!'

'So, then, we can arrange something now if you like' – he glanced at the clock – 'Ah!'

'Must you go?' she asked.

'Yes, by twelve o'clock I ought really to ...'

She was seized with an intense uneasiness at the prospect of having to be alone again so soon, and she said:

'I have plenty of time – as much as you like. But, of course, it must not be too late.'

'Is your cousin so strict then?'

'But –' she said, 'this time, as a matter of fact, I'm not staying with her, you see.'

He looked at her in astonishment.

She grew red.

'Usually I do stay with her ... I mean, sometimes ... She has such a large family, you know.'

'So you are staying at an hotel,' he said, rather impatiently. 'Well, there, of course, you are accountable to no one, and we can spend the evening together quite comfortably.'

'I shall be delighted. But I should like not to be too late ... even in an hotel I should like not to be too late ...'

'Of course not. We will just have supper and you can be in bed long before ten o'clock.'

They paced slowly down the grand staircase.

'So, if you are agreeable,' said Emil, 'we will meet at seven o'clock.'

She was on the point of replying: 'So late as that?' – but, remembering her resolution not to compromise herself, she refrained and answered instead:

'Very well, at seven.'

'Seven o'clock at ... where? ... Out of doors, shall we say? In that case we could go wherever we fancied, life would lie before us, so to speak ... yes.'

He seemed to her just then remarkably absent-minded. They went through the entrance hall, and at the exit they stopped for a moment.

'At seven o'clock, then – by the Elizabeth Bridge.'

'Very well, seven o'clock at the Elizabeth Bridge.'

Before them lay the square, with the Maria Theresa memorial, in the brilliant glare of the noonday sun. It was a warm day, but a very high wind had arisen. It seemed to Bertha that Emil was looking at her with a scrutinizing glance. At the same time, he appeared to her cold and strange, a very different man from what he had been when standing before the pictures in the Museum.

'Now we will say good-bye for the present,' he said, after a time.

It made her feel somewhat unhappy to think that he was going to leave her.

'Won't you ... or can't I come with you a little way?' she said.

'Well, no,' he answered. 'Besides, it is blowing such a gale. There's not much enjoyment to be had in walking side by side and having to hold your hat all the time, for fear it should blow away. Generally, it is difficult to converse if you are walking with a person in the street, and then, too, I have to be in such a hurry ... But perhaps I can see you to a carriage?'

'No, no, I shall walk.'

'Yes, you can do that. Well, good-bye till we meet again this evening.'

He stretched out his hand to her and walked quickly away across the square. She gazed after him for a long time. He had taken off his hat and held it in his hand, and the wind was ruffling his hair. He went across the Ring, then through the Town Gate, and disappeared from Bertha's view.

Mechanically and very slowly she had followed him. Why had he suddenly grown so cold? Why had he taken his departure so quickly? Why didn't he want her to accompany him? Was he ashamed of her? She looked down at herself, wondering whether she was not dressed, after all, in a countrified and ridiculous manner. Oh, no, it could not be that! Moreover, she had been able to remark from the way in which people gazed at her that she was not looking ludicrous, but, on the contrary, decidedly pretty. Why, then, this sudden departure? She called to mind the period of their previous acquaintance, and it seemed to her that she could remember his having this strange manner even then. He would break off a conversation quite unexpectedly, whilst he suddenly became as though his thoughts had been carried away, and his whole being expressed an impatience which he could not master. Yes, she was certain that he had been like that in those days also, though, perhaps, less strikingly so than now. She remembered, as well, that she had sometimes made jokes on the subject of his capriciousness, and had laid the responsibility at the door of his artistic temperament. Since then he had become a greater artist, and certainly more absent and irresponsible than ever.

The chimes of noon rang out from many a spire, the wind grew higher and higher, dust flew into her eyes. She had a whole eternity before her, with which she did not know what to do. Why wouldn't he see her, then, until seven o'clock? Unconsciously, she had reckoned on his spending the whole day with her. What was it that he had to do? Had he, perhaps, to make his preparations for the concert? And she pictured him to herself, violin in hand, by a cabinet, or leaning on a piano, just as, many years ago, he had played before the company at her home. Yes, that would be nice if she could only be with him now, sitting in his room, on a sofa, while he played, or even accompanying him on the piano. Would she, then, have gone with him if he had asked her? Why hadn't he asked her? No, of course, he could not have done so within an hour of seeing her again ... But in the evening – wouldn't he ask her that evening? And would she go with him? And, if she went, would she be able to deny him anything else that he might ask her? Indeed, he had a way of expressing everything so innocently. How easily he had managed to make those ten years seem as nothing! Had he not spoken to her as if they had seen each other daily all that time? 'Good morning, Bertha. How are you, then?' – just as he might have asked if, on the previous evening, he had wished her 'Good night!' and said 'Good-bye till we meet again!' What a number of experiences he must have had since then! And who could tell who might be sitting on the sofa in his room that afternoon, while he leaned against the piano and played the violin? Ah, no, she would not think of it. If she followed up such thoughts to the end, would she not simply have to go home again?

She walked past the railings of the public gardens, and could see the avenue where, an hour ago, she had sat, and through which clouds of dust were now sweeping. So, then, that for which she had so deeply yearned was over – she had seen Emil again. Had it been so lovely as she expected? Had she felt any particular emotion when walking by his side, his arm touching hers? No! Had his departure put her out of humour? Perhaps. Would she be able to go home again without seeing him once more? Good heavens, no! And a sensation almost of terror thrilled through her at the thought. Had not, then, her life during the past few days been, as it were, obsessed by him? And all the years that lay behind her, had they been meant for anything else, at all, than to lead her back to him at the right moment? Ah, if she only had a little more experience, if she were a little more worldly-wise! She would have liked to possess the capability of marking out for herself a definite course.

She asked herself which would be the wiser – to be reserved or yielding? She would gladly have known what she was to do that evening, what she ought to do in order to win his heart with greater certainty. She felt that any move on her part, one way or the other, might have the effect of gaining him, or, just as well, of losing him. But she also realized that all her meditation was of no avail, and that she would do just as he wished.

She was in front of the Votive Church, a spot where many streets intersected. The wind there was so violent as to be altogether intolerable. It was time to dine. But she decided that she would not go back to the little hotel that day. She turned towards the inner town. It suddenly occurred to her that she might meet her cousin, but that was a matter of supreme indifference to her. Or, supposing that her brother-in-law had followed her to Vienna? But that thought did not worry her either in the least. She had a feeling, such as she had never experienced before, that she had the right to dispose of her person and her time just as she pleased. She strolled leisurely along the streets, and amused herself by looking at the shop windows. On the Stephansplatz the idea came to her to go into the church for a while. In the dim, cool, and immense building a profound sensation of comfort came over her. She had never been of a religious disposition, but she could never enter a place of worship without experiencing a devotional feeling and, without clothing her prayers in definite form, she had yet always thought to find a way to send up her wishes to Heaven. At first she wandered round the church in the manner of a stranger visiting a beautiful edifice, then she sat down in a pew before a small altar in a side chapel.

She called to mind the day on which she had been married, and she had a vision of her late husband and herself standing side by side before the priest – but the event seemed to be so infinitely far away in the past, and it affected her spirit as little as if her thoughts were occupied by strangers. But suddenly, as a picture changed in a magic lantern, she seemed to see Emil, instead of her husband, standing by her side, and the picture appeared to stand out so completely, without any co-operation on the part of her will, that she almost had to regard as a premonition, even as a prediction from Heaven itself. Mechanically she folded her hands and said softly: 'So be it.' And, as though her will acquired thereby a further access of strength, she remained sitting in a pew a while longer and sought to hold the picture fast.

After a few minutes she went out again into the street, where the broad daylight and the din of the traffic affected her as something new, something which she had not experienced for a long time, as though she had spent whole hours in the church. She felt tranquil, and hopes seemed to hover about her.

She dined in the restaurant of a fashionable hotel in the Kärnthernstrasse ... She was not in the least embarrassed, and thought it very childish that she had not preferred to put up at a first-class hotel. On reaching her room again she undressed and, such was the state of languor into which she had fallen as the result of the unusually rich meal and the wine she had taken, that she had to stretch herself out on the sofa and fall asleep. It was five o'clock before she awoke. She had no great desire to get up. Usually at that time ... what would she probably have been doing at that moment if she had not come to Vienna? If he had not answered her letter – if she had not written to him? If he had not received that Order? If she had never seen his portrait in the illustrated paper? If nothing had called his existence back into her memory? If he had become an insignificant, unknown fiddler in some suburban orchestra? What strange thoughts were these! Did she, then, love him merely because he was celebrated? What did it all mean? Did she, indeed, take any interest in his violin playing? ... Wouldn't he be dearer to her if he was not famous and ad-mired? Certainly in that case she would have felt herself much nearer to him, much more allied to him; in that case, she would not have had this feeling of uncertainty about him, and also he would have been different in his manner towards her. As it was, of course, he was, indeed, very charming, and yet ... she realized it now ... something had come between them that day and had sundered them. Yes, and that was nothing else than the fact that he was a man whom the whole world knew, and she was nothing but a stupid little woman from the country. Suddenly she pictured him to herself as he had stood in the Rembrandt gallery at the Museum, and had looked out of the window while she had been telling him the story of her life in the little town; she remembered how he had scarcely bidden her good-bye, and how he had gone away from her, indeed absolutely fled away from her. But, then, had she her-self felt any emotion such as a woman would feel in the presence of the man she loved? Had she been happy when he had been speaking to her? Had she longed to kiss him when he was standing beside her? ... Not at all. And now – was she pleased at the prospect of the evening she was going to spend with him? Was she pleased at the idea of seeing him again in a couple of hours? If she had the power, simply by expressing the wish, to transport herself just where she pleased, would she not, perhaps, at that moment, rather be at home, with her boy, walking between the vine-trellises, without fear, without agitation, and with a clear conscience; as a good mother and a respectable woman, instead of lying in that uncomfortable room in the hotel, on a miserable sofa, restlessly, yet without longing, awaiting the next hours? She thought of the time, still so near, when all her concern was for nothing save her boy, the household, and her lessons – had she not been contented, almost happy? ...

She looked round her. The bare room with the ugly blue and white painted walls, the specks of dust and dirt on the ceiling, the cabinet with its half-open door, all seemed most repulsive to her. No, that was no place for her. Then she thought with displeasure, too, of the dinner in the fashionable hotel, and also of her strolling about in the town, her weariness, the wind and the dust. It seemed to her that she had been wandering about like a tramp. Then another thought came to her: what if something had happened at home! – Fritz might have caught the fever, they would telegraph to her cousin at Vienna, or they might even come to look for her, and they would not be able to find her, and all would know that she had lied like any disreputable person whose purpose it suits to do so ... It was terrible! How could she face them at home, her sister-in-law, her brother-in-law, Elly, her grown-up nephew Richard ... the whole town, which, of course, would hear the news at once ... Herr Rupius! No, in good truth, she was not intended for such things! How childishly and clumsily, after all, she had set about it, so that only the slightest accident was needed to betray her. Had she, then, failed to give the least thought to all these things? Had she only been obsessed with the idea of seeing Emil once more, and for that had hazarded everything ... her good name, even her whole future! For who could say whether the family would not renounce her, and she would lose her music lessons, if the truth came out? ... The truth ... But what could come out? What had happened, then? What had she to reproach herself with? And with the comforting feeling of a clear conscience she was able boldly to answer: 'Nothing.' And, of course, there was still time ... She could leave Vienna directly by the seven o'clock train, be back by ten in her own home, in her own cosy room, with her beloved boy ... Yes, she could; to be sure, Fritz was not at home ... but she could have him brought back ... No, she would not do it, she would not return at once ... there was no occasion to do so – tomorrow morning would be quite time enough. She would say good-bye to Emil that very evening ... Yes, she would inform him at once that she was returning home early next morning, and that her only reason in coming had been to press his hand once more. Yes, that would be best.

Oh, he could, of course, accompany her to the hotel; and, goodness knows, he could even have supper with her in the garden restaurant ... and she would go away as she had come. ... Besides, she would see from his behaviour what he really felt towards her; she would be very reserved, even cold, it would be quite easy for her to act in that way, because she felt completely at her ease. It seemed to her as if all her desires had fallen into slumber again, and she had a feeling akin to a determination to remain respectable. As a young girl she had withstood temptation, she had been faithful to her husband, her whole widowhood had hitherto passed without attack ... Well, the long and the short of it was: if he wished to make her his wife she would be very glad, but she would reject any bolder proposal with the same austerity as ... as ... twelve years before, when he had showed her his window behind St Paul's Church.

She stood up, stretched herself, held up her hands, and went to the window. The sky had become overcast, clouds were moving down from the mountains, but the storm had subsided.

She got ready to go out.

Bertha had hardly proceeded a few steps from the hotel when it began to rain. Under her open umbrella she seemed to herself to be protected against unwelcome attentions from people she might meet. A pleasant fragrance was diffused throughout the air, as if the rain brought with it the aroma of the neighbouring woods, shedding it over the town. Bertha gave herself up wholly to the pleasure of the walk, even the object of her outing appeared before her mind's eye only vaguely, as if seen through a mist. She had at last grown so weary as the result of the profusion of her changing feelings that she no longer felt anything at all. She was without fear, without hope, without purpose. She walked on past the gardens, across the Ring, and rejoiced in the humid fragrance of the elder-trees. In the forenoon it had completely escaped her notice that everything was beautiful in an array of violet blossoms. An idea brought a smile to her lips: she went into a flower shop and bought a little bunch of violets. As she raised the flowers to her lips, a great tenderness came over her; she thought of the train going homewards at seven o'clock, and she rejoiced, as if she had outwitted some one.

She walked slowly across the bridge, diagonally, and remembered how she had crossed it a few days ago in order to reach the neighbourhood of her former home, and to see Emil's window again. The throng of traffic at the bridge was immense; two streams, one coming from the suburb into the town, the other going in the opposite direction, poured by in confusion; carriages of all kinds rolled past; the air resounded with the jingling of bells, with whistling and with the shouts of drivers. Bertha tried to stand still, but was pushed forward.

Suddenly she heard a whistle quite close by. A carriage pulled up, a head leaned out of the window ... it was Emil.

He made a sign to her to come over to him. A few people immediately became attentive, and seemed very anxious to hear what the young man had to say to the lady who had gone up to his carriage.

'Will you get in?' Emil asked in a low voice.

'Get in ... ?'

'Why, yes, it is raining, you see!'

'Really, I would rather walk, if you don't mind.'

'Just as you like,' said Emil.

He got out quickly and paid the driver. Bertha observed, with some alarm, that about half a dozen people who were crowding round her were very anxious to see how this remarkable affair would turn out.

'Come,' said Emil.

They quickly crossed the road, and thereby got away from the whole throng. They then walked slowly along a less frequented street by the bank of the Wien.

'Why, Emil, you haven't brought your umbrella with you!'

'Won't you take me under yours? Wait a moment, it won't do like this.'

He took the umbrella out of her hand, held it over both of them, and thrust his arm under hers. Now she felt that it was *his* arm, and rejoiced greatly.

'The country, unfortunately, is out of the question,' he said.

'What a pity.'

'Well, what have you been doing with yourself all day long?'

She told him about the fashionable restaurant, in which she had had her dinner.

'Now, why on earth didn't I know about that? I thought you were dining with your cousin. We might, of course, have had such a pleasant lunch together!'

'You have had so much to do, I dare say,' she said, a little proud at being able to infuse a slight tone of sarcasm into her voice.

'Yes, that's true, in the afternoon, of course. I had to listen to half an opera.'

'Oh? How was that, then?'

'There was a young composer with me – a very talented fellow, in his own way.'

She was very glad to hear that. So that, then, was the way in which he spent his afternoons.

He stood still and, without letting go her arm, looked into her face.

'Do you know that you have really grown much prettier? Yes, I am quite serious about it! But, tell me, first of all, tell me candidly, how the idea came to you to write to me.'

'Why, I have already told you.'

'Have you thought of me, then, all this time?'

'A great deal.'

'When you were married, too?'

'Certainly, I have always thought of you. And you?'

'Often, very often.'

'But ...'

'Well, what?'

'You are a man, you see!'

'Yes – but what do you mean by that?'

'I mean that certainly you must have loved many women.'

'Loved ... loved ... yes, I suppose I have.'

'But I,' she broke out with animation, as though the truth was too strong to be restrained within her; 'I have loved no one but you.'

He took her hand and raised it to his lips.

'I think we might rather leave that undecided, though,' he said.

'Look, I have brought some violets with me for you.'

He smiled.

'Are they to prove that you have told me the truth? Anybody would think, from the way in which you said that, that you have done nothing else since we last met but pluck, or, at least, buy, violets for me. However, many thanks! But tell me, why didn't you want to get into the carriage?'

'Oh, but you know, a walk is so nice.'

'But we can't walk for ever ... We are having supper together, though?'

'Yes, I shall be delighted – for instance, here is an hotel,' she added hastily.

At that time they were walking through quieter streets, and it was growing dusk.

Emil laughed.

'Oh, no, we will arrange things a little more cosily than that.'

Bertha cast her eyes down.

'However, we mustn't sit at the same table as strangers,' she said.

'Certainly not. We will even go somewhere where there is nobody else at all.'

'What are you thinking of?' she asked. 'I don't do that sort of thing!'

'Just as you please,' he answered, shrugging his shoulders. 'Have you an appetite yet?'

'No, not at all.'

They were both silent for a time.

'Shall I not make the acquaintance of your boy some day?' he asked.

'Certainly,' she replied, greatly pleased; 'whenever you wish.'

She began to tell him about Fritz, and then went on to speak about her family. Emil threw in a question at times, and soon he knew all that happened in the little town, even down to the efforts of Klingemann, of which Bertha gave him an account, laughingly, but with a certain satisfaction.

The street lamps were alight; the rays glittered on the damp pavements.

'My dear girl, we can't stroll about the streets all night, you know,' said Emil suddenly.

'No ... but I cannot come with you ... into a restaurant ... Just think, if I should happen to meet my cousin or anyone else!'

'Make your mind easy, no one will see us.'

Quickly he passed through a gateway and closed the umbrella.

'What are you going to do, then?'

She saw a large garden before her. Near the walls, from which canvas shelters were stretched, people were sitting at tables, laid for supper.

'There, do you mean?'

'No. Just come with me.'

Immediately on the right of the gate was a small door, which had been left ajar.

'Come in here.'

They found themselves in a narrow lighted passage, on both sides of which were rows of doors. A waiter bowed and went in front of them, past all the doors. The last one he opened, allowed the guests to enter, and closed it again after them.

In the centre of the little room stood a small table laid for three, by the wall was a blue velvet sofa, and opposite that hung a gilt framed oval mirror, before which Bertha took her hat off and, as she did so, she noticed that the names 'Irma' and 'Rudi' had been scratched on the glass. At the same time, she saw in the mirror Emil coming up behind her. He placed his hands on her cheeks, bent her head back towards himself, and kissed her on the lips. Then he turned away without speaking and rang the bell.

A very young waiter came in at once, as if he had been standing outside the door. When he had taken his order he left them and Emil sat down.

'Well, Bertha!'

She turned towards him. He took her gently by the hand and still continued to hold it in his, when Bertha had taken a seat beside him on the sofa. Mechanically she touched her hair with her other hand.

An older waiter came in, and Emil made his choice from the menu. Bertha agreed to everything. When the waiter had departed Emil said:

'Mustn't the question be asked: How is it that all this hasn't happened before today?'

'What do you mean by that?'

'Why didn't you write to me long ago?'

'Well, I would ... if you had got your Order sooner!'

He held her hand and kissed it.

'But you come to Vienna fairly often!'

'Oh, no.'

He looked up.

'But you said something like that in your letter!'

She remembered then, and grew red.

'Well, yes ... often ... Monday was the last time I was here.'

The waiter brought sardines and caviare, and left the room.

'Well,' said Emil; 'it is probably just the right time.'

'In what way?'

'That we should have met again.'

'Oh, I have often longed for you.'

He seemed to be deep in thought.

'And perhaps it is also just as well that things *then* turned out as they did,' he said. 'It is on that very account that the recollection is so charming.'

'Yes, charming.'

They were both silent for a time.

'Do you remember ...' she said, and then she began to talk of the old days, of their walks in the town-park, and of her first day at the Conservatoire.

He nodded in answer to everything she said, held his arm on the back of the sofa, and lightly touched the lock of hair, which curled over the nape of her neck. At times he threw in a word. Then Emil himself recalled something which she had forgotten; he had remembered a further outing: a trip to the Prater one Sunday morning.

'And do you still recollect,' said Bertha, 'how we ...' she hesitated to utter it – 'once were almost in love with each other?'

'Yes,' he said. 'And who knows ...'

He was perhaps about to say: 'It would have been better for me if I had married you' – but he did not finish the sentence.

He ordered champagne.

'It is not so long ago,' said Bertha, 'since I tasted champagne. The last time was about six months ago, at the party which my brother-in-law gave on the occasion of his fiftieth birthday.'

She thought of the company at her brother-in-law's, and it was amazing how remote from the present time it all seemed – the entire little town and all who lived there.

The young waiter brought an ice-tub with the wine. At that moment it occurred to Bertha that Emil had certainly been there before, many a time, with other women. That, however, was a matter of tolerable indifference to her.

They clinked glasses and drank. Emil embraced Bertha and kissed her. That kiss reminded her of something ... what could it have been, though? ... Of the kisses she had received when a young girl? ... Of the kiss of her husband? ... No ... Then it suddenly occurred to her that it was exactly like the kisses which her young nephew Richard had lately given to her.

The waiter came in with fruit and pastry. Emil put some dates and a bunch of grapes on a plate for Bertha.

'Why don't you say something?' she asked. 'Why do you leave me to do all the talking? And you know you could tell me so much!'

'I? ...'

He slowly sipped the wine.

'Why, yes, about your tours.'

'Good Heavens, one town is just like all the others. You must not, of course, lose sight of the fact that I only rarely travel for my own pleasure.'

'Quite so, of course.'

During the whole time she had not given a thought to the fact that it was Emil Lindbach, the celebrated violin virtuoso, with whom she was sitting there, and she felt bound to say:

'By the way, you are playing in Vienna soon. I should be very glad to hear you.'

'Not a soul will hinder you from doing so,' he replied drily.

It passed through her mind that it would really be very much nicer for her to hear him play, not at the concert, but for herself alone. She had almost said so, but then it occurred to her that that would have meant nothing else than: 'I will come with you' – and, who could say, perhaps very soon she would go with him. It would be as easy for her as ever, if she had had some wine ... Yet, not so, the wine was affecting her differently from usual – it was not the soft inebriation which made her feel a little more cheerful; it was better, lovelier. It was not the few drops of wine that made it so, it was the touch of his dear hand, as he stroked her brow and hair. He had sat down beside her and he drew her head on to his shoulder. How gladly would she have fallen asleep like that ... Yes, indeed, nothing else did she desire ... Then she heard him whisper: 'Darling.' ... She trembled softly.

Why was this the first time? Could she not have had all this before? Was there a grain of sense in living as she did? ...

After all there was nothing wicked in what she was doing now
... And how sweet it was to feel the breath of a young man
upon her eyelids! ... No, not – not the breath of a young
man ... of a lover ...

She had shut her eyes. She made not the slightest effort to
open them again, she had not the least desire to know where
she was, or with whom she was ... Who was it after all? ...
Richard? ... No ... Was she falling asleep, then? ... She was
there with Emil ... With whom? ... But who was this Emil?
... How hard it was to be clear as to who it was! ... The
breath upon her eyelids was the breath of the man she had
loved when a girl ... and, at the same time, that of the
celebrated artist who was soon to give a concert ... and, at the
same time, of a man whom she had not seen for thousands
and thousands of days ... and, at the same time, of a gentleman with whom she was sitting alone in a restaurant, and
who, at that moment, could do with her just as he pleased ...
She felt his kiss upon her eyes ... How tender he was ... and
how handsome ... But what did he really look like, then? ...
She had only to open her eyes to be able to see him quite
plainly ... But she preferred to imagine what he was like,
without actually seeing him ... No, how funny – why, that was
not in the least like his face! ... Of course, it was the face of
the young waiter, who had left the room a minute or two
before ... But what did Emil look like, after all? ... Like this?
... No, no, of course, that was Richard's face ... But away ...
away ... Was she then so low as to think of nothing but other
men while she ... was with him? ... If she could only open
her eyes! ... Ah!

She shook herself violently, so that she almost pushed Emil
away – and then she tore her eyes wide open.

Emil gazed at her, smiling.

'Do you love me?' he asked.

She drew him towards her and kissed him of her own
accord ... It was the first time that day that she had given him
a kiss of her own accord, and in doing so she felt that she was
not acting in accordance with her resolve of the morning ...
She tried to think what that resolve had been ... To compromise herself in no way; to deny herself ... Yes, there had

certainly been a time when that had been her wish, but why? She was in love with him, really and truly; and the moment had arrived which she had been awaiting for days ... No, for years!

Still their lips remained pressed together ... Ah, she longed to feel his arms about her ... to be his, body and soul. She would not let him talk any more ... he would have to take her unto himself ... He would have to realize that no other woman could love him so well as she did ...

Emil rose to his feet and paced up and down the little room a few times. Bertha raised her glass of champagne to her lips again.

'No more, Bertha,' said Emil, in a low tone.

Yes, he was right, she thought. What was she really doing? Was she going to make herself drunk, then? Was there any need for that? After all, she was accountable to no one, she was free, she was young; she was determined to taste of happiness at last.

'Ought we not to be thinking of going?' said Emil.

Bertha nodded. He helped her to put on her jacket. She stood before the mirror and stuck the pin through her hat. They went. The young waiter was standing before the door; he bowed. A carriage stopped before the gate; Bertha got in; she did not hear what instructions Emil gave the driver. Emil took his seat by her side. Both were silent; they sat pressing closely against each other. The carriage rolled on, a long, long way. Wherever could it be, then, that Emil lived? But, perhaps, he had purposely told the driver to take a circuitous route, knowing, no doubt, how pleasant it was to drive together through the night like this.

The carriage pulled up. Emil got out.

'Give me your umbrella,' he said.

She handed it out to him and he opened it. Then she got out and they both stood under the shelter of the umbrella, on which the rain was rattling down. Was this the street in which he lived? The door opened; they entered the hall; Emil took a candle which the porter handed to him. Before them was a fine broad staircase. When they reached the first floor Emil opened a door. They passed through an ante-chamber into a drawing-room. With the candle which he held in his hand Emil lighted two others upon the table; then he went up to Bertha, who was still standing in the doorway, as though waiting, and led her further into the room. He took the pin out of her hat, and placed the hat upon the table. In the uncertain light of the two feebly-burning candles, Bertha could only see that a few coloured pictures were hanging on the wall – portraits of the Emperor and Empress, so it appeared to her – that, on one side, was a broad divan covered with a Persian rug and that, near the window, there was an upright piano with a number of framed photographs on the lid. Over the piano a picture was hanging, but Bertha was unable to make it out. Yonder, she saw a pair of red curtains hanging down beside a door, which was standing half open and through the broad folds something white and gleaming could be seen within.

She could no longer restrain the question:

'Do you live here?'

'As you see.'

She looked straight before her. On the table stood a couple of little glasses, a decanter containing liqueur and a small epergne, loaded with fruit and pastry.

'Is this your study?' asked Bertha.

Mechanically her eyes sought for a desk such as violin players use. Emil put his arm round her waist and led her to the piano. He sat down on the piano stool and drew her on to his knees.

'I may as well confess to you at once,' he said to her, simply and almost drily, 'that really I do not live here. It was only for our own sake ... that I have ... for a short while ... I deemed it prudent ... Vienna, you know, is a small town, and I didn't want to take you into my house at night-time.'

She understood, but was not altogether satisfied. She looked up. She was now able to see the outlines of the picture which was hanging above the piano ... It was a naked female figure. Bertha had a curious desire to examine the picture, close at hand.

'What is that?' she asked.

'It is not a work of art,' said Emil.

He struck a match and held it up, so as to throw the light on the picture. Bertha saw that it was merely a wretched daub, but at the same time she felt that the painted woman, with the bold laughing eyes, was looking down at her, and she was glad when the match went out.

'You might just play something to me upon the piano,' said Emil.

She wondered at the coldness of his demeanour. Didn't he realize that she was with him? ... But, on the other hand, did she herself feel any special emotion? ... No ... A strange sadness seemed to come welling forth from every corner of the room ... Why hadn't he rather taken her to his own house? ... What sort of a house was this, she wondered? ... She regretted now that she had not drunk more wine ... She wished that she was not so sober ...

'Well, won't you play something to me?' said Emil. 'Just think how long it is since I have heard you.'

She sat down and struck a chord.

'Indeed, I have forgotten everything.'

'Oh, do try!'

She played very softly Schumann's Albumblatt, and she remembered how, a few days before, late in the evening, she had improvised as she was sitting at home, and Klingemann had walked up and down in front of the window. She could not help thinking also of the report that he had a scandalous picture in his room. And involuntarily, she glanced up again at the picture of the naked woman over the piano, but now the figure seemed to be gazing into space.

Emil had brought a chair beside Bertha's. He drew her towards him and kissed her while her fingers first continued to play, and at length rested quietly upon the keys. Bertha heard the rain beating against the window-panes and a sensation as of being at home came over her.

Then she felt as though Emil was lifting her up and carrying her. Without letting her out of his arms he had stood up and was slowly bearing her out of the room. She felt her right arm graze against the curtain ... She kept her eyes closed; she could feel Emil's cool breath upon her hair ...

When they went out into the street the rain had left off, but the air was permeated with a wondrous mildness and humidity. Most of the street lamps had already been extinguished, the one at the street corner was the nearest that was alight; and, as the sky was still overcast with clouds, deep darkness hung over the city. Emil had offered Bertha his arm; they walked in silence. From a church tower a clock struck – one. Bertha was surprised. She had believed that it must be nearly morning, but now she was glad at heart to wander mutely through the night in the still, soft air, leaning on his arm – because she loved him very much.

They entered an open square, before them lay the Church of St Charles.

Emil hailed a driver who had fallen asleep, sitting on the footboard of his open carriage.

'It is such a fine night,' said Emil; 'we can still indulge in a short drive before I take you to your hotel – shall we?'

The carriage started off. Emil had taken off his hat; she laid it in her lap, an action which also afforded her pleasure. She took a sidelong glance at Emil, his eyes seemed to be looking into the distance.

'What are you thinking of?'

'I ... To tell the truth, Bertha, I was thinking of a melody out of the opera, which that man I was telling you about played to me this afternoon. But I can't get it quite right.'

'You are thinking of melodies now ...' said Bertha, smiling, but with a slight tone of reproach in her voice.

Again there was silence. The carriage drove slowly along the deserted Ringstrasse, past the Opera House, the Museum and the public gardens.

'Emil?'

'What do you want, my darling?'

'When shall I at last have an opportunity of hearing you play again?'

'I am playing at a concert today, as a matter of fact,' he said, as if it were a joke.

'No, Emil, that was not what I meant – I want you to play to me alone. You will do that just once ... won't you? Please!'

'Yes, yes.'

'It would mean so much to me. I should like you to know that there was no one in the room except myself listening to you.'

'Quite so. But never mind that now, though.'

He spoke in such a decided tone of voice that it seemed as if he was defending something from her. She could not understand for what reason her request could have been distasteful to him, and she continued:

'So then it is settled: tomorrow at five o'clock in the evening at your house?'

'Yes, I am curious to see whether you will like it there.'

'Oh, of course I shall. Surely it will be much nicer being at your house than at that place where we have been this evening. And shall we spend the evening together? Do you know, I am just thinking whether I ought not to see my cousin ...'

'But, my dearest one, please, don't let us map out a definite programme.'

In saying this he put his arm round her neck, as if he wanted to make her feel the tenderness which was absent from the tone of his voice.

'Emil!'

'Well?'

'Tomorrow we will play the Kreutzer Sonata together – the Andante at least.'

'But, my dear child, we've talked enough about music, do let us drop the subject. I am quite prepared to believe that you are immensely interested in it.'

Again he spoke in that vague way, from which she could not tell whether he really meant what he said or had spoken ironically. She did not, however, venture to ask. At the same time her yearning at that moment to hear him play the violin was so keen that it was almost painful.

'Ah, here we are near your hotel, I see!' exclaimed Emil; and, as if he had completely forgotten his wish to go for a drive with her before leaving her at her door, he called out the name of the hotel to the driver.

'Emil –'

'Well, dearest?'

'Do you still love me?'

Instead of answering he pressed her close to him and kissed her on the lips.

'Tell me, Emil –'

'Tell you what?'

'But I know you don't like anybody to ask much of you.'

'Never mind, my child, ask anything you like.'

'What will you ... Tell me, what are you accustomed to do with your forenoons?'

'Oh, I spend them in all sorts of ways. Tomorrow, for instance, I am playing the violin solo in Haydn's Mass in the Lerchenfeld Church.'

'Really? Then, of course, I won't have to wait any longer than tomorrow morning before I can hear you.'

'If you want to. But it is really not worth the trouble ... That is to say, the Mass itself, of course, is very beautiful.'

'However does it happen that you are going to play in the Lerchenfeld Church?'

'It is ... an act of kindness on my part.'

'For whom?'

'For whom ... well, for Haydn, of course.'

A thrill of pain seemed to seize Bertha. At that moment she felt that there must be some special connection between it and his taking part in the Mass at the Lerchenfeld Church. Perhaps some woman was singing in the Mass, who ... Ah, what did she know, after all? ... But she would go to the church, yes, she must go ... she could let no other woman have Emil! He belonged to her, to her alone ... he had told her so, indeed ... And she would find a way to hold him fast ... She had, she told herself, such infinite tenderness for him ... she had reserved all her love for him alone ... She would completely envelop him in it ... no more would he yearn for any other woman ... She would move to Vienna, be with him each day, be with him for ever.

'Emil –'

'Well, what is the matter with you, darling?'

He turned towards her and looked at her rather uneasily.

'Do you love me? Good Heavens, here we are already!'

'Really?' said Emil, with surprise.

'Yes – there, do you see? – that's where I am staying. So tell me, please, Emil, tell me once more –'

'Yes, tomorrow at five o'clock, my darling. I am very glad.'

'No, not that ... Tell me, do you –'

The carriage stopped. Emil waited by Bertha's side until the porter came out and opened the door, then he kissed her hand with the most ceremonious politeness, and said:

'Good-bye till we meet again, dear lady.'

He drove away.

Bertha's sleep that night was sound and heavy.

When she awoke, the light of the morning sun was streaming around her. She remembered the previous evening, and she was very glad that something which she had imagined to be so hard, and almost grievous, had been done and had proved to be quite easy and joyous. And then she felt a thrill of pride on recollecting her kisses, which had had nothing in them of the timidity of a first adventure. She could not observe the slightest trace of repentance in her heart, although it occurred to her that it was conventional to be penitent after such things as she had experienced. Words, too, like 'sin' and 'love affair' passed through her mind, without being able to linger in her thoughts, because they seemed to be devoid of all meaning. She believed herself certain that she replied to Emil's tenderness just like a woman accomplished in the art of love, and was very happy in the thought that all those things which came to other women as the result of the experiences of nights of drunkenness had come to her from the depth of her feelings. It seemed to her as though in the previous evening she had discovered in herself a gift, of the existence of which she had hitherto had no premonition, and she felt a slight emotion of regret stir within her at not having turned that gift to the best advantage earlier. She remembered one of Emil's questions as to her past, on account of which she had not been so shocked as she ought to have been, and now, as she recalled it to mind, the same smile appeared on her lips, as when she had sworn that she had told him the truth, which he had not wanted to believe. Then she thought of their next meeting, she pictured to herself how he would receive her and escort her through his rooms. The idea came to her that she would behave just as if nothing at all had yet happened between them. Not once would he be able to read in her glance the recollection of the previous evening; he would have to win her all over again, he would have to woo her – not with words alone, but also with his music ... Yes ... Wasn't she going to hear him play that very forenoon? ... Of course – in the Church ... Then she remembered the sudden jealousy which had seized her the previous evening ... Yes, but why? ... It seemed to her now to be so absurd – jealousy of a singer who perhaps was taking part in singing the Mass, or of some other unknown woman. She would, however, go to the Church in any case. Ah, how fine it would be to stand in the dim light of the Church, unseen by him and unable to see him, and to hear only his playing, which would float down to her from the choir. And she felt as though she rejoiced in the prospect of a new tenderness which should come to her from him without his apprehending it.

Slowly she got up and dressed herself. A gentle thought of her home rose up within her, but it was altogether without strength. She even found it a trouble to think of it. Moreover, she felt no penitence on that account, rather, she was proud of what she had done. She felt herself wholly as Emil's creature, all that had had part in her life previous to his advent seemed to be extinguished. If he were to demand of her that she should live a year, live the coming summer with him, but that then she should die – she would obey him.

Her dishevelled hair fell over her shoulders. Memories came to her which almost made her reel ... Ah, Heaven! why had all this come so late, so late? But there was still a long time before her – there were still five, still ten years during which she might remain beautiful ... Oh, there was even longer so far as he was concerned, if they remained together, since, indeed, he would change together with her. And again the hope flitted through her mind: if he should make her his wife, if they should live together, travel together, sleep together, night after night – but now she began to feel slightly ashamed of herself – why was it that these thoughts were for ever present in her mind? Yet, to live together, did it not mean something further – to have cares in common, to be able to talk with one another on all subjects? Yes she would, before all things, be his friend. And that was what she would tell him in the evening before everything else. That day he would have at last to tell her everything, tell her about himself, he would have to unfold his whole life before her, from the moment when they had parted twelve years ago until – and she could not help being amazed as she pursued her thoughts – until the previous morning ... She had seen him again for the first time the morning before, and in the space of that one day she had become so completely his that she could no longer think of anything except him; she was scarcely any longer a mother ... no, nothing but his beloved.

She went out into the brightness of the summer day. It occurred to her that she was meeting more people than usual, that most of the shops were shut – of course, it was Sunday! She had not thought of that at all. And now that, too, made her glad. Soon she met a very slender gentleman who was wearing his overcoat open and by whose side was walking a young girl with very dark, laughing eyes. Bertha could not help thinking that she and Emil looked just such another couple ... and she pictured to herself how beautiful it must be to stroll about, not merely in the darkness of the night, but, just as these two were doing, openly in the broad light of day, arm in arm, and with happiness and laughter shining in their eyes. Many a time, when a gentleman going past her looked into her face, she felt as though she understood the language of glances, like something new to her. One man looked at her with a sort of grave expression, and he seemed to say: Well, you are also just like the others! Presently came two young people who left off talking to each other when they saw her. She felt as though they knew perfectly well what had happened the previous night. Then another man passed, who appeared to be in a great hurry, and he cast her a rapid sidelong glance which seemed to say: Why are you walking about here as imposingly, as if you were a good woman? Yesterday evening you were in the arms of one of us. Quite distinctly she heard within her that expression 'one of us', and, for the first time in her life, she could not help pondering over the fact that all the men who passed by were indeed men, and that all the women were indeed women, that they desired one another, and, if they so wished, found one another. And she had the feeling as though only on the previous day at that time she had been a woman apart, from whom all other women had secrets, whilst now she also was included amongst them and could talk to them. She tried to remember the period which followed her wedding, and she recalled to mind that she had felt nothing beyond a slight disappointment and shame. Very vaguely there rose in her mind a certain sentence – she could not tell whether she had once read it or heard it – namely: 'It is always the same, indeed, after all.' And she seemed to herself much cleverer than the person, whoever it might have been, man or woman, who had spoken or written that sentence.

Presently she noticed that she was following the same route as she had taken on the previous morning. Her eye fell on an advertising column on which was an announcement of the concert in which Emil was one of those taking part. Delightedly she stopped before it. A gentleman stood beside her. She smiled and thought: if he knew that my eyes are resting upon the very name of the man who, last night, was my lover ... Suddenly, she felt very proud. What she had done she considered as something unique. She could scarcely imagine that other women possessed the same courage. She walked on through the public gardens in which there were more people than on the previous day. Once again she saw children playing, governesses and nursemaids gossiping, reading, knitting. She noticed particularly a very old gentleman who had sat down on a seat in the sun; he looked at her, shook his head and followed her with a hard and inexorable glance. The incident created a most unpleasant impression upon her, and she had a feeling of injury in regard to the old gentleman. When, however, she mechanically glanced back, she observed that he was gazing at the sunlit sand and was still shaking his head. She realized then that this was due to his old age, and she asked herself whether Emil, too, would not one day be just such an aged gentleman, who would sit in the sun and shake his head. And all at once she saw herself walking along by his side in the chestnut avenue at home, but she was just as young as she was now, and he was being wheeled in an invalid's chair. She shivered slightly. If Herr Rupius were to know ... No – never, never would he believe that of her! If he had supposed her capable of such things, he would not have called her to join him on the balcony and told her that his wife was intending to leave him ...

At that moment she was amazed at what seemed to her to be the great exuberance of her life. She had the impression that she was existing in the midst of such complex relations as no other woman did. And this feeling also contributed to her pride.

As she walked past a group of children, of whom four were dressed exactly alike, she thought how strange it was that she had not for a moment considered the fact that her adventure of the previous day might possibly have consequences. But a connection between that which had happened the day before, between those wild embraces in a strange room – and a being which one day would call her 'Mother' seemed to lie without the pale of all possibility.

She left the garden and took the road to the Lerchenfelder-strasse. She wondered whether Emil was now thinking that she was on her way to him. Whether his first thought that morning had been of her. And it seemed to her now that previously her imagination had pictured quite differently the morning after a night such as she had spent ... Yes, she had fancied it as a mutual awakening, breast on breast, and lips pressed to lips.

A detachment of soldiers came towards her. Officers paced along by the side on the pavement; one of them jostled her slightly, as he passed, and said politely:

'I beg your pardon.'

He was a very handsome man, and he gave himself no

further concern on her account, which vexed her a little. And the thought came to her involuntarily: had he also a beloved? And suddenly she knew for a certainty that he had been with the girl he loved the previous night; also that he loved her only, and concerned himself with other women as little as Emil did.

She was now in front of the church. The notes of the organ came surging forth into the street. A carriage was standing there, and a footman was on the box. How came that carriage there? All at once, it was quite clear to Bertha that some definite connection must have subsisted between it and Emil, and she resolved to leave the church before the conclusion of the Mass so as to see who might enter the carriage. She went into the crowded church. She passed forward between the rows of seats until she reached the High Altar, by which the priest was standing. The notes of the organ died away, the string orchestra began to take up the melody. Bertha turned her head in the direction of the choir. Somehow, it seemed strange to her that Emil should, incognito, so to speak, be playing the solo in a Haydn Mass here in the Lerchenfeld Church ... She looked at the female figures in the front seats. She noticed two – three – four young women and several old ladies. Two were sitting in the foremost row, one of them was very fashionably dressed in black silk, the other appeared to be her maid. Bertha thought that in any case the carriage must belong to that aristocratic old lady, and the idea greatly tranquillized her mind. She walked back again, half unconsciously keeping everywhere on the lookout for pretty women. There were still some who were passably good-looking; they all seemed to be absorbed in their devotions, and she felt ashamed that she alone was wandering about the church without any holy thoughts.

Then she noticed that the violin solo had already begun. He was now playing, he! he! ... And at that moment she was hearing him play for the first time for more than ten years. And it seemed to her that it was the same sweet tone as of old, just as one recognizes the voices of people whom one has not met for years. The soprano joined in. If she could only see the singer! It was a clear, fresh voice, though not very highly trained, and Bertha felt something like a personal connection between the notes of the violin and the song. It was natural that Emil should know the girl who was now singing ... But was there not something more in the fact of their performing together in the Mass than appeared on the surface? The singing ceased, the notes of the violin continued to resound, and now they spoke to her alone, as though they wished to reassure her. The orchestra joined in, the violin solo hovered over the other instruments, and seemed only to have that one desire to come to an understanding with her. 'I know that you are there,' it seemed to say, 'and I am playing only for you ...'

The organ chimed in, but still the violin solo remained dominant over the rest. Bertha was so moved that tears rose to her eyes. At length the solo came to an end, as though engulfed in the swelling flood of sound from the other instruments, and it arose no more. Bertha scarcely listened, but she found a wonderful solace in the music sounding around her. Many a time she fancied that she could hear Emil's violin playing with the orchestra, and then it seemed quite strange, almost incredible, that she was standing there by a column, down in the body of the church and he was sitting at a desk up in the choir above, and the previous night they had been clasped in each other's arms, and all the hundreds of people there in the church knew nothing at all about it ...

She must see him at once – she must! She wanted to wait for him at the bottom of the staircase ... She did not want to speak a word to him – no, but she wished to see him and also the others who came out – including the singer of whom she had been jealous. But she had got completely over that now; she knew that Emil could not deceive her ...

The music had ceased; Bertha felt herself thrust forward towards the exit; she wanted to find the staircase, but it was at a considerable distance from her. Indeed, it was just as well that it was so ... no, she would not have dared to do it, to put herself forward, to wait for him – what would he have thought of her? He certainly would not have liked it! No, she would disappear with the crowd, and would tell him in the evening that she had heard him play. She was now positively afraid of being observed by him. She stood at the entrance, walked down the steps, and went past the carriage, just as the old lady and her maid were getting into it. Bertha could not help smiling when she called to mind in what a state of apprehension the sight of that carriage had thrown her, and it seemed to her that her suspicion in regard to the carriage having been removed, all the others must necessarily flicker out. She felt as though she had passed through an extraordinary adventure and was standing now on the brink of an absolutely new existence. For the first time it seemed to her to have a meaning, everything else had been but a fiction of the imagination and became as nothing in comparison with the happiness which was streaming through her pulses, while she slowly sauntered from the church through the streets of the suburbs towards her hotel. It was not until she had nearly reached her destination that she noticed that she had gone the whole way as though lost in a dream and could scarcely remember which way she had taken and whether she had met any people or not.

As she was taking the key of her room the porter handed her a note and a bouquet of violets and lilac blossoms ... Oh, why had not she had a similar idea and sent Emil some flowers? But what could he have to write to her about? With a slight thrill of fear at her heart, she opened the letter and read:

Dearest,
I must thank you once again for that delightful evening. Today, unfortunately, it is impossible for me to see you. Don't be angry with me, my dear Bertha, and don't forget to let me know in good time on the next occasion when you come to Vienna.
> Ever your own
>> Emil.

She went, she ran up the stairs, into her own room ... Why was he unable to see her that day? Why did he not at least tell her the reason? But then, after all, what did she know of his various obligations of an artistic and social nature? ... It would certainly have been going too much into detail, and it would have appeared like an evasion if he had, at full length, given his reasons for putting her off. But in spite of that ... And then, why did he say: the next occasion when you came to Vienna? ... Had she not told him that she would be remaining there a few days longer? He had forgotten that – he must have forgotten it! And immediately she sat down and wrote:

My Dearest Emil,

I am very sorry indeed that you have had to put me off today, but luckily I am not leaving Vienna yet. Do please write to me at once, dearest, and tell me whether you can spare a little time for me tomorrow or the next day.

A thousand kisses from your

Bertha.

P.S. – It is most uncertain when I shall be coming to Vienna again, and I should be very sorry in any case to go away without seeing you once more.

She read the letter over. Then she added a further postscript:

I must see you again!

She hurried out into the street, handed the letter to a commissionaire, and impressed upon him strongly that he was on no account to come back without an answer. Then she went up to her room again and posted herself at the window. She wanted to keep herself from thinking, she wished only to look down into the street. She forced herself to fix her attention on the passers-by, and she recalled to mind a game, which she used to play as a child, and in which she and her brothers looked out of the window and amused themselves by commenting on how this or that passer-by resembled some one or other of their acquaintances. In the present circumstances, it was a matter of some difficulty for her to discover any such resemblances, for her room was situated on the third story; but, on the other hand, owing to the distance, it was easier for her to discover the arbitrary resemblances which she was looking for. First of all, came a woman who looked like her cousin Agatha; then some one who reminded her of her music teacher at the Conservatoire; he was arm in arm with a woman who looked like her sister-in-law's cook. Yonder was a young man who bore a resemblance to her brother, the actor. Directly behind him, and in the uniform of a captain, a person who was the image of her dead father came along the road; he stood still awhile before the hotel, glanced up, exactly as if he were seeking her, and then disappeared through the doorway. For a moment Bertha was as greatly alarmed as if it really had been her father, who had come as a ghost from the grave. Then she forced herself to laugh – loudly – and sought to continue the game, but she was not able to play it any longer with success.

Her sole purpose now was to see whether the commissionaire was coming. At length she decided to have dinner, just to while away the time. After she had ordered it, she again went to the window. But now she no longer looked in the direction from which the commissionaire had to come, but her glances followed the crowded omnibuses and trams on their way to the suburbs. Then the captain, whom she had seen a short time before, struck her attention again, as he was just jumping on to a tram, a cigarette in his mouth. He no longer bore the slightest resemblance to her dead father.

She heard a clatter behind her; the waiter had come into the room. Bertha ate but little, and drank her wine very quickly. She grew sleepy, and leaned back in the corner of the divan. Her thoughts gradually grew indistinct; there was a ringing in her ears like the echoes of the organ, which she had heard in the church. She shut her eyes and, all at once, as though evoked by magic, she saw the room in which she had been with Emil the previous evening, and behind the red curtains she perceived the gleaming whiteness of the coverlet. It appeared that she herself was sitting again before the piano, but another man was holding her in a close embrace – it was her nephew Richard. With an effort she tore her eyes open, she seemed to herself depraved beyond all measure, and she felt panic-stricken as though some atonement would have to be exacted from her, for these visionary fancies.

Once more she went to the window. She felt as if an eternity had passed since she had sent the commissionaire on his errand. She read through Emil's letter once again. Her glance lingered on the last words: 'Ever your own'; and she repeated them to herself aloud and in a tender tone, and called to mind similar words which he had spoken the previous evening. She concocted a letter which was surely on the point of arriving and would certainly be couched in these terms: 'My dearest

Bertha! Heaven be thanked that you are going to remain in Vienna until tomorrow! I shall expect you for certain at my house at three o'clock,' or: 'tomorrow we will spend the whole day together,' or even; 'I have put off the appointment I had, so we can still see each other today. Come to me at once, longingly I am waiting for you!'

Well, whatever his answer might be, she would see him again before leaving Vienna, although not that day perhaps. Indeed, anything else was quite unthinkable. Why, then, was she a prey to this dreadful agitation as though all were over between them? But why was his answer so long in coming? ... He had, in any case, gone out to dinner – of course, he had no one to keep house for him! So the earliest that he could be home again was three o'clock ... But if he were not to return home till the evening? ... She had, indeed, told the commissionaire to wait in any case – even till the night, if necessary ... But what was she to do? Of course, she could not stand there looking out of the window all the time! The hours, indeed, seemed endless! She was ready to weep with impatience, with despair!

She paced up and down the room; then she again stood at the window for a while, then she sat down and took up for a short time the novel which she had brought with her in her travelling bag; she attempted, too, to go to sleep – but did not succeed in doing so. At length four o'clock struck – nearly three hours had passed since she had begun her vigil.

There was a knock at the door. The commissionaire came into the room and handed her a letter. She tore open the envelope and with an involuntary movement, so as to conceal the expression of her features from the stranger, she turned towards the window.

She read the letter.

My Dearest Bertha,

It is very good of you still to give me a choice between the next few days but, as indeed I have already hinted to you in my former letter, it is, unfortunately, absolutely impossible for me to do just as I like during that time. Believe me, I regret that it is so, at least as much as you do.

Once more a thousand thanks and a thousand greetings and I trust that we will be able to arrange a delightful time when next we meet.

Don't forget me completely,

Your
Emil.

When she had finished reading the letter she was quite calm; she paid the commissionaire the fee he demanded and found that, for a person in her circumstances, it was by no means insignificant. Then she sat down at the table and tried to collect her thoughts. She realized immediately that she could no longer remain in Vienna, and her only regret was that there was no train which could take her home at once. On the table stood the half empty bottle of wine, bread crumbs were scattered beside the plate, on the bed lay her spring jacket, beside it were the flowers which he had sent her that very morning.

What could it all mean? Was it at an end?

Indistinctly, but so that it seemed that it must bear some relation to her recent experiences, there occurred to her a sentence which she had once read. It was about men who desire nothing more than 'to attain their object ...' But she had always considered that to be a phrase of the novelists. But, after all, it was surely not a letter of farewell that she was holding in her hand, was it? ... Was it really not a letter of farewell? Might not these kind words be also lies? ... Also lies – that was it! ... For the first time the positive word forced itself into her thoughts ... Lies! ... Then it was certain that, when he brought her home the previous night, he had already made up his mind not to see her again. And the appointment for the present day and his desire to see her again that day were lies ...

She went over the events of the previous evening in her mind, and she asked herself what could she have said or done to put him out of humour or disappoint him ... Really, it had all been so beautiful, and Emil had seemed so happy, just as happy as she had been ... was all that going to prove to have been a lie too? ... How could she tell? ... Perhaps, after all, she had put him out of humour without being aware that she was doing so ... She had, indeed, been nothing more or less than a good woman all her life ... Who could say whether she had not been guilty of something clumsy or stupid? ...

whether she had not been ludicrous and repellent in some moment when she had believed herself to be sacrificing, tender, enchanted and enchanting? ... But what did she know of all these things? ... And, all at once, she felt something almost in the nature of repentance that she had set out upon her adventure so utterly unprepared, that, until the previous day, she had been so chaste and good, that she had not had other lovers before Emil ... Then she remembered, too, that he had evaded her shy questions and requests on the subject of his violin playing, as if he had not wanted to admit her into that sphere of his life. He had thus remained strange to her, intentionally strange, so far as concerned the very things which were of the deepest and most vital importance to him. All at once she realized that she had no more in common with him than the pleasures of a night, and that the present morning had found them both as far apart from one another as they had been during all the years in which they had each led a separate existence.

And then jealousy again flared up within her ... But she felt as though she was always thus, as though every conceivable emotion had always been present within her ... love and distrust, and hope and penitence, and yearning and jealousy ... and, for the first time in her life, she was so stirred, even to the very depths of her soul, that she understood those who in their despair have hurled themselves out of a window to meet their death ... And she perceived that the present state of affairs was impossible, that only certainty could be of any avail to her ... She must go to him and ask him ... but she must ask in the manner of one who is holding a knife to another's breast ...

She hurried away through the streets, which were almost deserted, as though all Vienna had gone off into the country ... But would she find him at home? ... Would he not, perhaps, have had a presentiment that the idea might come to her to seek him, to take him to task, and would he not have taken steps to evade the chance of such an occurrence? ... She was ashamed of having had to think of that, too ... And if he was at home would she find him alone? ... And if he was not alone, would she be admitted into his house?

And if she found him in the arms of some other woman, what should she say? ... Had he promised her anything? Had he sworn to be true to her? Had she even so much as demanded loyalty of him? How could she have imagined that he was waiting for her here in Vienna until she congratulated him on his Spanish Order? ... Yes, could he not say to her: 'You have thrown yourself on my neck and have desired nothing more than that I should take you as you are ...' And if she asked herself – was he not right? ... Had she not come to Vienna to be his beloved? – and for no other reason ... without any regard to the past, without any guarantee as to the future? ... Yes, that was all she had come for! All other hopes and wishes had only transiently hovered around her passion, and she did not deserve anything better than that which had happened to her ... And if she was candid to herself, she must also admit that of all that she had experienced this had still been the best ...

She stopped at a street corner. All was quiet around her, the summer air about her was heavy and sultry. She retraced her steps back to her hotel. She was very tired, and a new thought rose up convulsively within her: was it not possible that he had written to put her off only because he also was tired? ... She seemed to herself very experienced when that idea occurred to her ... And yet another thought flashed through her mind: that he could also love no other woman in the way in which he had loved her ... And suddenly she asked whether, after all, the previous night would remain her only experience – whether she herself would belong to no other man save him? And she rejoiced in the doubt, as if, by cherishing it, she was taking a kind of revenge on his compassionate glance and mocking lips.

And now she was back again in the cheerless room away up in the third storey of the hotel. The remains of her dinner had not yet been cleared away, her jacket and the flowers were still lying on the bed. She took the flowers in her hand and raised them to her lips, as though about to kiss them. Suddenly, however, as though her whole anger burst forth again, she flung them violently to the ground. Then she threw herself on the bed, her face buried in her hands.

After lying for some time in this position she felt her calmness gradually returning. It was perhaps just as well that she could return home that very day. She thought of her boy, how he was accustomed to lie in his little cot with his whole face beaming with laughter, if his mother leaned over the railings. She yearned for him. Also she yearned in some slight degree for Elly and for Frau Rupius. Yes, it was true – Frau Rupius, of course, was going to leave her husband ... What could there be at the bottom of it all? ... A love affair? ... But, strangely enough, she was now still less able than before to picture to herself the answer to that question.

It was growing late, it was time for her to get ready for her departure ... So, then, she would be home again by Sunday evening.

She sat in the carriage; on her lap lay the flowers, which she had picked up from the floor ... Yes, she was now travelling home, leaving the town where she ... had experienced something – that was the right expression, wasn't it? ... Words which she had read or heard in connection with similar circumstances kept recurring continually to her mind ... such words as: 'bliss' ... 'transports of love' ... 'ecstasy' ... and a gentle thrill of pride stirred within her at having experienced what those words denoted. And yet another thought came to her which caused her to grow singularly calm: if he also – maybe – had an affair with another woman at that very time ... she had taken him from *her* ... not for long indeed, but yet as completely as it was possible to take a man from a woman. She grew calmer and calmer, almost cheerful.

It was, indeed, clear to her that she, Bertha, the inexperienced woman, could not, with one assault, completely obtain possession of her beloved ... But might she not be successful on a second occasion, she wondered? She was very glad that she had not carried out her determination to hasten to him at once. Indeed, she even formed the intention of writing him such a cold letter that he would fall into a mild fit of anger; she would be coquettish, subtle ... But she must have him again ... of that she was certain ... soon, and, if possible, for ever! ... And so her dreams went on and on as the train carried her homewards ... Ever bolder they grew as the humming of the wheels grew deeper and deeper, lulling her into a semi-slumberous state.

On her arrival she found the little town buried in a deep sleep – she reached home and told the maidservant to fetch Fritz from her sister-in-law's the first thing in the morning. Then she slowly undressed herself. Her glance fell on the portrait of her dead husband, which hung over the bed. She asked herself whether it should remain in that position. Then the thought occurred to her that there are some women who come from their lovers and then are able to sleep by the side of their husbands, and she shuddered ... She could never have done such a thing while her husband had been alive! ... And, if she *had* done it, she would never have returned home again ...

The next morning Bertha was wakened by Fritz. He had jumped on to her bed and had breathed softly on her eyelids. Bertha sat up, embraced and kissed him, and he immediately began to tell her how well he had fared with his uncle and aunt, how Elly had played with him, and how Richard had once had a fight with him without being able to beat him. On the previous day, too, he had learned to play the piano, and would soon be as clever at it as mamma.

Bertha was content just to listen to him.

'If only Emil could hear his sweet prattle now!' she thought.

She considered whether, on the next occasion, she should not take Fritz with her to Vienna to see Emil, by doing which she would at once remove anything of a suspicious nature in such a visit.

She thought only of the pleasant side of her experiences in Vienna, and of the letters which Emil had written to put her off scarcely anything remained in her memory, other than those words which had reference to a future meeting.

She got up in an almost cheerful frame of mind and, whilst she was dressing herself, she felt a quite new tenderness for her own body, which still seemed to her to be fragrant with the kisses of her beloved.

While the morning was yet young, she went to call on her relations. As she walked by the house of Herr Rupius she deliberated for a moment whether she should not go up and see him there and then. But she had a vague fear of being immediately involved again in the agitated atmosphere of the household, and she deferred the visit until the afternoon.

At her brother-in-law's house Elly was the first to meet her, and she welcomed her as boisterously as if Bertha had returned from a long journey. Her brother-in-law, who was on the point of going out, jestingly shook a threatening finger at Bertha and said:

'Well, have you had a good time?'

Bertha felt herself blushing crimson.

'Yes,' he continued; 'these are pretty stories that we hear about you!'

He did not, however, notice her embarrassment and, as he went out of the door, greeted her with a glance which plainly meant: 'You can't keep your secrets from me.'

'Father is always making jokes like that,' said Elly. 'I don't like him doing that at all!'

Bertha knew that her brother-in-law had only been talking at random, as his usual manner was, and that, if she had told him the truth, he would not have believed her for a moment.

Her sister-in-law came into the room, and Bertha had to relate all about her stay in Vienna.

To her own surprise she succeeded very well in cleverly blending truth with fiction. She told how she had been with her cousin to the public gardens and the picture gallery; on Sunday she had heard Mass at St Stephen's Church; she had met in the street a teacher from the Conservatoire; and finally she even invented a funny married couple, whom she represented as having had supper one evening at her cousin's. The further she proceeded with her lies, the greater was her desire to tell all about Emil as well, and to inform them how she had met in the street the celebrated violinist Lindbach, who had formerly been with her at the Conservatoire, and how she had had a conversation with him. But a vague fear of not being able to stop at the right time caused her to refrain from making any reference to him.

Frau Albertine Garlan sat on the sofa in an attitude of profound lassitude, and nodded her head. Elly stood, as usual, by the piano, her head resting on her hands, and she gazed open-eyed at her aunt.

From her sister-in-law's Bertha went on to the Mahlmanns' and gave the twins their music lesson. The finger exercises and scales which she had to hear were at first intolerable to her, but finally she ceased to listen to them at all, and let her thoughts wander at will. The cheerful mood of the morning had vanished, Vienna seemed to her to be infinitely distant, a strange feeling of disquietude came over her and suddenly the fear seized her that Emil might go away immediately after his concert. That would indeed be terrible! He might go away all of a sudden without her having seen him once more – and who could say when he would return?

She wondered whether it would not be well to arrange to be in Vienna in any case on the day of the concert. She had to admit to herself that she had not the slightest longing to hear him play. Indeed, it seemed to her that she would not in the least mind if he was not a violin virtuoso at all, if he was not even an artist, but just an ordinary kind of man – a bookseller, or something like that! If she could only have him for herself, for herself alone! ...

Meanwhile the twins played through their scales. It was surely a terrible doom to have to sit there and give these untalented brats music lessons. How was it that she had been in good spirits only just a little earlier that day? ...

Ah, those beautiful days in Vienna! Quite irrespective of Emil – the entire freedom, the sauntering about the streets, the walks in the public gardens ... To be sure, she had spent more money during her stay than she could afford; two dozen lessons to the Mahlmann twins would not recoup her the outlay. ... And now, here she had to come back again to her relations, to give music lessons, and really it might even be necessary to look about for fresh pupils, for her accounts would not balance at all that year! ... Ah, what a life! ...

In the street Bertha met Frau Martin, who asked her how she had enjoyed herself in Vienna. At the same time she threw Bertha a glance which clearly said:

'I'm quite sure you don't enjoy life so much as I do with my husband!'

Bertha had an overwhelming desire to shriek in that person's face:

'I have had a much better time than you think! I have been with an enchanting young man who is a thousand times more charming than your husband! And I understand how to enjoy life quite as well as you do! You have only a husband, but I have a lover! – a lover! – a lover!' ...

Yét, of course, she said nothing of the kind, but related how she had gone with her cousin and the children for a walk in the public gardens.

Bertha also met with some other ladies with whom she was superficially acquainted. She felt that her mental attitude towards those ladies had undergone a complete change since her visit to Vienna – that she was freer, superior. It seemed to her that she was the only woman in the town with any experience, and she was almost sorry that nobody knew anything about it, for although, publicly, they would have despised her, in their hearts all those women would have been filled with unutterable envy of her.

And if, after all, they *had* known who ... Although in that hole of a town there were certainly many who had not so much as heard Emil's name! If only there was some one in the world to whom she could open her heart! Frau Rupius – yes, there was Frau Rupius! ... But, of course, she was in the habit of going away, of taking trips! ... And, to tell the truth, thought Bertha, that was also a matter of indifference to her. She would only like to know how things would eventually turn out as far as she and Emil were concerned, she would like to know how matters actually stood. It was the uncertainty that was causing her that terrible uneasiness ... Had she only had a love affair with him, after all? ... Ah, but why had she not gone to him once again? ... But, of course, that was quite impossible! ... That letter ... He didn't want to see her, that was it! ... But then, on the other hand, he had sent her flowers ...

And now she was back again with her relations. Richard was going to meet her and to embrace her in his playful manner. She pushed him away.

'Impudent boy!' she thought to herself. 'I know very well what he means by doing that, although he himself does not know. I understand these things – I have a lover in Vienna! ...'

The music lesson took its course and, at the end of it, Elly and Richard played as a duet Beethoven's* 'Festival Overture' which was intended to be a birthday surprise for their father.

Bertha thought only of Emil. She was nearly being driven

* Query – Brahms (translator's note).

out of her mind by this wretched strumming ... no, it was not possible to live on like that, whichever way she looked at it! ... She was still a young woman, too ... Yes, that was the secret of it all, the real secret ... She would not be able to live on like that any more ... And yet it would not do for her ... any other man ... How could she ever think of such a thing! ... What a very wicked person she must be, after all! Who could tell whether it had not been that trait in her character which Emil, with his great experience of life, had perceived in her, and which had been the cause of his being unwilling to see her any more? ... Ah, those women surely had the best of it who took everything easily, and, when abandoned by one man, immediately turned to another ... But stay whatever could it be that was putting such thoughts as these into her head? Had Emil, then, abandoned her? ... In three or four days she would be in Vienna again; with him; in his arms! ... And had she been able to live for three years as she had done? ... Three? – Six years – her whole life! ... If he only knew that, if he only believed that!

Her sister-in-law came into the room and invited Bertha to have supper with them that evening ... Yes, that was her only distraction: to go out to dinner or supper occasionally at some other house than her own!

If only there was a man in the town to whom she could talk! ... And Frau Rupius was going off on her travels and leaving her husband ... Hadn't a love affair maybe, something to do with that, Bertha wondered.

The music lesson came to an end and Bertha took her leave. In the presence of her sister-in-law, too she noticed that she had that feeling of superiority, almost of compassion, which had come over her when she had seen the other ladies. Yes, she was certain that she would not give up that one hour with Emil for a whole life such as her sister-in-law led. Moreover, as she thought to herself as she was walking homewards, she had not been able to arrive at a complete perception of her happiness, which, indeed, had all slipped by so quickly. And then that room, that whole house, that frightful picture ... No, no, it was all really hideous rather than anything else. After all, the only really beautiful moments had been those which had followed, when Emil had accompanied her to her hotel in the carriage, and her head had rested on his breast ...

Ah, he loved her indeed; of course, not so deeply as she loved him; but how could that be possible? What a number of experiences he had had in his life! She thought of that now without any feeling of jealousy; rather, she felt a slight pity for him in having to carry so much in his memory. It was quite evident from his appearance that he was not a man who took life easily ... He was not of a cheerful disposition ... All the hours which she had spent with him seemed in her recollection as if encompassed by an incomprehensible melancholy. If she only knew all about him! He had told her so little about himself ... nothing, indeed, absolutely nothing! ... But how would that have been possible on the very first day that they had met again? Ah, if only he really knew her! If she were only not so shy, so incapable of expressing herself!

She would have to write to him again before seeing him ... Yes, she would write to him that very day. What a stupid concoction it was, that letter which she had sent him on the previous day! In truth, he could not have sent her any other answer than that which she had received. She would not write to him either defiantly or humbly ... No, after all, she was his beloved! She who, as she walked along the streets here in the little town, was regarded by every one who met her as one of themselves ... she was the beloved of that magnificent man whom she had worshipped since her girlhood. How unreservedly and unaffectedly she had given herself to him — not one of all the women she knew would have done that! ... Ah, and she would do so still more! Oh, yes! She would even live with him without being married to him, and she would be supremely indifferent to what people might say ... she would even be proud of her action! And later on he would marry her, after all ... of course he would. She was such a capable housekeeper, too ... And how much good it would be sure to do him, after the unsettled existence which he had been leading during the years of his wanderings, to live in a well-ordered house, with a good wife by his side, who had never loved any man but him.

And now she was home again. Before dinner was served she

had made all her preparations for writing the letter. She ate her dinner with feverish impatience, she scarcely allowed herself time to cut up Fritz's dinner and give it to him. Then, instead of undressing him herself and putting him to bed for his afternoon sleep, as she was always accustomed to do, she told the maid to attend to him.

She sat down at the desk and the words flowed without effort from her pen, as though she had long ago composed in her head the whole letter.

My Emil, my beloved, my all!

Since I have returned home again I have been possessed by an overwhelming desire to write to you, and I should like to say to you over and over again how happy, how infinitely happy you have made me. I was angry with you at first when you wrote and said you could not see me on Sunday, I must confess that to you as well, for I feel that I am under the necessity of telling you everything that passes in my mind. Unfortunately, I could not do so while we were together; I had not the power of expressing myself, but now I can find the words and you must, I fear, put up with my boring you with this scribble. My dearest, my only one – yes, that you are, although it seems to me that you were not quite so certain of it as you ought to have been. I beseech you to believe that it is true. You see, I have no means, of course, wherewith to tell you this, other than these words. Emil, I have never, never loved any man, but you – and I will never love any other. Do with me as you will. I have no ties in the little town where I am living now – on the contrary, indeed, I often find it a terrible thing to be obliged to live my life here. I will move to Vienna, so as to be near you. Oh, do not fear that I will disturb you! I am not alone, you see, I have my boy, whom I *idolize*. I will cut down my expenses and, in the long run, why shouldn't I succeed in finding pupils even in a large town like Vienna just as I do here, perhaps, indeed, even more easily than here, and in that way improve my position? Yet that is a secondary consideration, for I may tell you that it has long been my intention to move to Vienna if only for the sake of my dearly loved boy, when he grows older.

You cannot imagine how stupid the men are here! And I can no longer bear to look at any one of them at all, since I have again had the happiness of being in your company.

Write to me, my dearest! Yet you need not trouble to send me a whole long letter. In any case I shall be coming to Vienna again this week. I would have had to do so in any event, because of some pressing commissions, and you will then be able to tell me everything, just what you think of my proposal, and what you consider best for me to do. But you must promise me this, that, when I live in Vienna, you will often visit me. Of course, no one need know anything about it, if you do not care that they should. But you may believe me – every day on which I may be allowed to see you will be a red-letter day for me and that, in all the world, there is nobody who loves you in such a true and life-long manner as I do.

Farewell, my beloved!

Your
Bertha.

She did not venture to read over what she had written, but left the house at once so as to take the letter herself to the railway station. There she saw Frau Rupius, a few paces in front of her, accompanied by a maid who was carrying a small valise.

What could that mean?

She caught up Frau Rupius, just as the latter was going into the waiting room. The maid laid the valise on the large table in the centre of the room, kissed her mistress's hand, and departed.

'Frau Rupius!' exclaimed Bertha, a note of inquiry in her voice.

'I heard that you had returned already. Well, how did you get on?' said Frau Rupius, extending her hand in a friendly way.

'Very well – very well indeed, but –'

'Why, you are gazing at me as though you were quite frightened! No, Frau Bertha, I am coming back again – no later than tomorrow. The long journey that I had in view came to nothing, so I have had to – settle on something else.'

'Something else?'

'Why, of course, staying at home. I shall be back again tomorrow. Well, how did you get on?'

'I told you just now – very well.'

'Yes, of course, you did tell me before. But I see you are going to post that letter, are you not?'

And then for the first time Bertha noticed that she was still holding the letter to Emil in her hand. She gazed at it with such enraptured eyes that Frau Rupius smiled.

'Perhaps you would like me to take it with me? It is to go to Vienna, I presume?'

'Yes,' answered Bertha, and then she added resolutely, as though she was glad to be able to say it out at last: 'to him.'

Frau Rupius nodded her head, as if satisfied. But she neither looked at Bertha nor made any reply.

'I am so glad that I have met you again!' said Bertha. 'You are the only woman here, you know, whom I trust; indeed, you are the only woman who could understand anything like this.'

'Ah, no,' said Frau Rupius to herself, as though she were dreaming.

'I do envy you so, because today in a few short hours you will see Vienna again. How fortunate you are!'

Frau Rupius had sat down in one of the leather arm-chairs by the table. She rested her chin on her hand, looked at Bertha, and said:

'It seems to me, on the other hand, that it is you who are fortunate.'

'No, I must, you see, remain here.'

'Why?' asked Frau Rupius. 'You are free, you know. But go and put that letter into the box at once, or I shall see the address, and so learn more than you wish to tell me.'

'I will, though not because of that – but I should be glad if the letter went by this train and not later.'

Bertha hurried into the vestibule, posted the letter and at once returned to Anna, who was still sitting in the same quiet attitude.

'I might have told you everything, you know,' Bertha went on to say; 'indeed I might say that I wished to tell you before I actually went to Vienna ... but – just fancy, isn't it strange? I did not venture to do so.'

'Moreover at that time, too, there probably had not been anything to tell,' said Frau Rupius, without looking at Bertha.

Bertha was amazed. How clever that woman was! She could see into everybody's thoughts!

'No, at that time there had not been anything to tell,' she repeated, gazing at Frau Rupius with a kind of reverence. 'Just think – you will probably find it hard to believe what I am going to tell you now, but I should feel a liar if I kept it secret.'

'Well?'

Bertha had sat down on a seat beside Frau Rupius, and she spoke in a lower tone, for the vestibule door was standing open.

'I wanted to tell you this, Anna: that I do not in the least feel that I have done anything wicked, not even anything immoral.'

'It wouldn't be a very clever thing, either, if you had.'

'Yes, you are quite right ... What I really meant to say was rather that it seems to me as though I had done something quite good, as if I had done something outstanding. Yes, Frau Rupius, the fact of the matter is, I have been proud of myself ever since.'

'Well, there is probably no reason for that either,' said Frau Rupius, as if lost in thought, stroking Bertha's hand which lay upon the table.

'I am aware of that, of course, and yet I am so proud and seem quite different from all the women whom I know. You see if you knew ... if you were acquainted with him – it is such a strange affair! You mustn't think, let me tell you, that it is an acquaintanceship which I have made recently – quite the contrary; I have been in love with him, you must know, ever since I was quite a young girl, no less than twelve years ago. For a long time we had completely lost sight of one another, and now – isn't it wonderful? – now he is my ... my ... my ... lover!'

She had said it at last. Her whole face was radiant.

Frau Rupius threw her a glance in which could be detected a little scorn and a great deal of kindliness.

'I am glad that you are happy,' she said.

'How very kind you are indeed! But then, you see, on the other hand again, it is a dreadful thing that we are so far apart from one another; he, in Vienna; I, here – I don't think I shall ever be able to endure that. Moreover, I have ceased to feel that I belong to this place, least of all to my relations. If they knew ... no, if they knew! However, they would never be able to bring themselves to believe it. A woman like my sister-in-law, for instance – well, I am perfectly certain that she could never imagine such a thing to be in any way possible.'

'But you are really very ingenuous!' said Frau Rupius suddenly, almost with exasperation. Then she listened for a moment. 'I thought I could hear the train whistling already.'

She rose to her feet, walked over to the large glass door leading on to the platform, and looked out. A porter came and asked for the tickets in order to punch them.

'The train for Vienna is twenty minutes late,' he remarked, at the same time.

Bertha had stood up and gone over to Frau Rupius.

'Why do you consider that I am ingenuous?' she asked shyly.

'But, indeed, you know absolutely nothing about men,' replied Frau Rupius, as if she were annoyed. 'You haven't, you know, the slightest idea among what kind of people you are living. I can assure you, you have no reason at all to be proud.'

'I know, of course, that it is very stupid of me.'

'Your sister-in-law – that is delightful! – your sister-in-law!'

'What do you mean, then?'

'I mean that she has had a lover too!'

'Whatever put such an idea as that into your head!'

'Well, she is not the only woman in this town.'

'Yes, there are certainly women who ... but, Albertine –'

'And do you know who it was? That is very amusing! It was Herr Klingemann!'

'No, that is impossible!'

'Of course, it is now a long time ago, about ten or eleven years.'

'But at that time, by the way, you yourself had not come to live here, Frau Rupius!'

'Oh I have heard it from the best source. It was Herr Klingemann himself who told me about it.'

'Herr Klingemann himself! But is it possible for a man to be so base as all that!'

'I don't think there's the least doubt about that,' answered Frau Rupius, sitting down on a seat near the door, whilst Bertha remained standing beside her, listening in amazement to her friend's words. 'Yes, Herr Klingemann himself ... As soon as I came to the town, you must know, he did me the honour of making violent love to me, neck or nothing, so to speak. You know yourself, of course, what a loathsome wretch he is. I laughed him to scorn, which probably exasperated him a great deal, and evidently he thought that he would be able conclusively to prove to me how irresistible he was by recounting all his conquests.'

'But perhaps he told you some things which were not true.'

'A great deal, probably, but this story, as it happens, is true ... Ah, what a rabble these men are!'

There was a note of the deepest hatred in Frau Rupius' voice. Bertha was quite frightened. She had never thought it possible that Frau Rupius could have said such things.

'Yes, why shouldn't you know what kind of men they are amongst whom you are living?' continued Frau Rupius.

'No, I would never have thought it possible! If my brother-in-law knew about it! –'

'If he knew about it? He knows about it as well as you or I do!'

'What do you say! No, no!'

'Indeed, he caught them together – you understand me! Herr Klingemann and Albertine! So that, however much inclined he might have been to make the best of things, there was no doubt possible!'

'But, for Heaven's sake – what did he do, then?'

'Well, as you can see for yourself, he has not turned her out!'

'Well, yes, the children ... of course!'

'The children – pooh-pooh! He forgave her for the sake of convenience – and chiefly because he could do as he liked after that. You can see for yourself how he treats her. When all is said and done, she is but little better than his servant; you know as well as I do in what a miserable, browbeaten way she slinks about. He has brought it to this, that, ever since that moment, she has always had to look upon herself as a woman who has been treated with mercy. And I believe she has even a perpetual fear that he is reserving the punishment for some future day. But it is stupid of her to be afraid of that, for he wouldn't look out for another housekeeper for anything ...

Ah, my dear Frau Bertha, we are not by any means angels, as you know now from your own experiences, but men are infamous so long' – she seemed to hesitate to complete the phrase – 'so long as they are men.'

Bertha was as though crushed; not so much on account of the things which Frau Rupius had told her, as on account of the manner in which she had done so. She seemed to have become a quite different woman, and Bertha was pained at heart.

The door leading to the platform was opened and the low, incessant tinkling of the telegraph was heard. Frau Rupius stood up slowly, her features assumed a mild expression, and, stretching out her hand to Bertha, she said:

'Forgive me, I was only a little bit vexed. Things can be also very nice; of course, there are certainly decent men in the world as well as others. Oh, yes, things can be very nice, no doubt.'

She looked out on to the railway lines and seemed to be following the iron track into the distance. Then she went on to say with that same soft, harmonious voice which appealed so strongly to Bertha:

'I shall be home again tomorrow evening ... Oh, yes, of course, my travelling case!'

She hurried to the table and took her valise.

'It would have been a terrible catastrophe if I had forgotten that! I cannot travel without my ten bottles! Well good-bye! And don't forget, though, that all I have been telling you happened ten years ago.'

The train came into the station. Frau Rupius hurried to a compartment, got in, and, looking out of the window, nodded affably to Bertha. The latter endeavoured to respond as cheerfully, but she felt that her wave of the hand to the departing Frau Rupius was stiff and forced.

Slowly she walked homewards again. In vain she sought to persuade herself that all that she had heard was not the least concern of hers; the long past affair of her sister-in-law, the mean conduct of her brother-in-law, the baseness of Klingemann, the strange whims of that incomprehensible Frau Rupius; all had nothing to do with her. She could not explain it to herself, but somehow, it seemed to her as though all these things were mysteriously related to her own adventure.

Suddenly the gnawing doubts appeared again ... Why hadn't Emil wanted to see her again? Not on the following day, or on the second or on the third day? How was it? He had attained his object, that was sufficient for him ... However had she been able to write him that mad, shameless letter?

And a thrill of fear arose within her ... If he were to show her letter to another woman, maybe ... make merry over it with her ... No, how on earth could such an idea come into her head? It was ridiculous even to think of such a thing! ... It was possible, of course, that he would not answer the letter and would throw it into the wastepaper basket – but nothing worse than that ... No ... However, she must just have patience, and in two or three days all would be decided. She could not say anything with certainty, but she felt that this unendurable confusion within her mind could not last much longer. The question would have to be settled, somehow.

Late in the afternoon she again went for a walk amongst the vine-trellises with Fritz, but she did not go into the cemetery. Then she walked slowly down the hill and sauntered along under the chestnut trees. She chatted with Fritz, asked him about all sorts of things, listened to his stories and, as her frequent custom was, instilled some knowledge into his head on several subjects. She tried to explain to him how far the sun is distant from the earth, how the rain comes from the clouds, and how the bunches of grapes grow, from which wine is made. She was not annoyed, as often happened, if the boy did not pay proper attention to her, because she realized well enough that she was only talking for the sake of distracting her own thoughts.

Then she walked down the hill, under the chestnut trees, and so back to the town. Presently she saw Herr Klingemann approaching, but the fact made not the slightest impression upon her. He spoke to her with forced politeness; all the time he held his straw hat in his hand and affected a great and almost gloomy gravity. He seemed very changed, and she observed, too, that his clothes in reality were not at all elegant, but positively shabby. Suddenly she could not help picturing him tenderly embracing her sister-in-law, and she felt extremely disgusted.

Later on she sat down on a bench and watched Fritz playing with some other children, all the time making an effort to keep her attention fixed on him so that she would not have to think of anything else.

In the evening she went to her relatives. She had a sensation as though she had had a presentiment of everything long before, for otherwise how could she have failed to have been struck before this by the kind of relations which existed between her brother-in-law and his wife? The former again made jocular remarks about Bertha's visit to Vienna. He asked when she was going there again, and whether they would not soon be hearing of her engagement. Bertha entered into the joke, and told how at least a dozen men had proposed to her, amongst others, a Government official; but she felt that her lips alone were speaking and smiling, while her soul remained serious and silent.

Richard sat beside her, and his knee touched hers, by chance. And as he was pouring out a glass of wine for her and she seized his hand to stop him, she felt a comforting glow steal up her arm as far as her shoulder. It made her feel happy. It seemed to her that she was being unfaithful to Emil. And that was quite as she wished; she wanted Emil to know that her senses were on the alert, that she was just the same as other women, and that she could accept the embraces of her nephew in just the same way as she did his ... Ah, yes, if he only knew it! That was what she ought to have written in her letter, not that humble, longing letter! ...

But even while these thoughts were surging through her mind, she remained serious in the depths of her soul, and a feeling of solitude actually came over her, for she knew that no one could imagine what was taking place within her.

Afterwards, when she was walking homewards through the deserted streets, she met an officer whom she knew by sight. With him he had a pretty woman whom she had never seen before.

'Evidently a woman from Vienna!' she thought, for she knew that the officers often had such visitors.

She had a feeling of envy towards the woman, she wished that she was also being accompanied by a handsome young officer at that moment ... And why not? ... After all, everybody was like that ... And now she herself had ceased to be a respectable woman. Emil, of course, did not believe that, any more than anybody else, and anyhow it was all just the same!

She reached home, undressed and went to bed. But the air was too sultry. She got up again, went to the window and opened it. Outside, all was dark. Perhaps somebody could see her standing there at the window, could see her skin gleaming through the darkness ... Indeed, she would not mind at all if anybody did see her like that! ... Then she lay down on the bed again ... Ah, yes, she was no better than any of the others! And there was no good reason either why she should be ...

Her thoughts grew indistinct ... Yes, he was the cause of it all, he had brought her to this, he had just taken her like a woman of the street – and then cast her off! ... Ah, it was shameful, shameful! – how base men were! And yet ... it was delightful ...

She fell asleep.

A warm rain was gently falling the next morning. Thus Bertha was able to endure her immense impatience more easily than if the sun had been blazing down. She felt as though during her sleep much had been smoothed out within her. In the soft grey of the morning everything seemed so simple and so utterly commonplace. On the morrow she would receive the letter she was expecting, and the present day was just like a hundred others.

She gave her pupils their music lessons. She was very strict with her nephew that day and rapped him on the knuckles when he played unbearably badly. He was a lazy pupil – that was all.

In the afternoon she was struck by an idea which seemed to herself to be extremely praiseworthy. She had for a long time past intended to teach Fritz to read, and she would make a start that very day. For a whole hour she slaved away, instilling a few letters into his head.

The rain still kept falling; it was a pity that she could not go for a walk. The afternoon would be long, very long. Surely she ought to go and see Herr Rupius without further delay. It was too bad of her that she had not called on him since her return from Vienna. It was quite possible that he would feel somewhat ashamed of himself in her presence, because just lately he had been using such big words, and now Anna was still with him, after all ...

Bertha left the house. In spite of the rain she walked, first of all, out into the open country. It was long since she had been so tranquil as she was that day; she rejoiced in the day without agitation, without fear, and without expectation. Oh, if it could be always like that! She was astonished at the indifference with which she could think of Emil. She would be more than content if she should not hear another word from him, and could continue in her present state of tranquillity for ever ... Yes, it was good and pleasant to be like that – to live in the little town, to give the few music lessons, which, after all, required no great effort, to educate her boy, to teach him to read, to write, and to count! Were her experiences of the last few days, she asked herself, worth so much anxiety – nay, so much humiliation? No, she was not intended for such things. It seemed as though the din of the great city, which had not disturbed her on her last visit, was now for the first time ringing in her ears, and she rejoiced in the beautiful calm which encompassed her in her present surroundings.

Thus the state of profound lassitude into which her soul had fallen after the unaccustomed agitations of the last few days appeared to Bertha as a state of tranquillity that would be final. ... And yet, only a short time later, when she was wending her way back to the town, the internal quietude gradually disappeared, and vague forebodings of fresh agitations and sorrows awoke within her.

The sight of a young couple who passed her, pressed close to one another under an open umbrella, aroused in her a yearning for Emil. She did not resist it, for she already realized that everything within her was in such a state of upheaval that every breath brought some fresh and generally unexpected thing on to the surface of her soul.

It was growing dusk when Bertha entered Herr Rupius' room. He was sitting at the table, with a portfolio of pictures before him. The hanging lamp was lighted.

He looked up and returned her greeting.

'Let me see; you, of course, came back from Vienna on the evening of the day before yesterday,' he said.

It sounded like a reproach, and Bertha had a sensation of guilt.

'Well, sit down,' he continued; 'and tell me what happened to you in Vienna.'

'Nothing at all,' answered Bertha. 'I went to the Museum, and I have seen the originals of several of your pictures.'

Herr Rupius made no reply.

'Your wife is coming back this very evening?'

'I believe not' – he was silent for a time, and then said, with intentional dryness: 'I must ask your pardon for having told you recently things which I am sure could not possibly have been of any interest to you. For the rest, I do not think that my wife will return today.'

'But . . . She told me so herself, you know . . .'

'Yes, she told me also. She simply wanted to spare me the farewell, or rather the comedy of farewell. By that I don't mean anything at all untruthful, but just the things which usually accompany farewells: touching words, tears . . . However, enough of that. Will you be good enough to come and see me at times? I shall be rather lonely, you know, when my wife is no longer with me.'

All this he said in a tone the sharpness of which was so little in keeping with the meaning of his words that Bertha sought in vain for a reply.

Rupius, however, continued at once:

'Well, and what else did you see besides the Museum?'

With great animation Bertha began to tell all sorts of things about her visit to Vienna. She also mentioned that she had met an old friend of her schooldays, whom she had not seen for a long time. Strangely, too, the meeting had taken place exactly in front of the Falckenborg picture.

While she was speaking of Emil in this way without mentioning his name, her yearning for him increased until it seemed boundless, and she thought of writing to him again that day.

Then she noticed that Herr Rupius was keeping his gaze fixed intently on the door. His wife had come into the room. She went up to him, smiling.

'Here I am, back again!' she said, kissing him on the forehead; and then she held out her hand to Bertha.

'Good evening, Frau Rupius,' said Bertha, highly delighted.

Herr Rupius spoke not a word, but signs of violent agitation could be seen on his face. His wife, who had not yet taken off her hat, turned away for a moment, and then Bertha noticed how Herr Rupius had rested his face on both his hands and had begun to sob inwardly.

Bertha left them. She was glad that Frau Rupius had returned, it seemed to be something in the nature of a good omen. By an early hour on the morrow she might receive the letter which would, perhaps, decide her fate. Her sense of restfulness had again completely vanished, but her being was filled with a different yearning from that which she had experienced before. She wished only to have Emil there, near her; she would have liked only to see him, to walk by his side.

In the evening, after she had put her little boy to bed, she stopped on for a long time alone in the dining-room; she went to the piano and played a few chords, then she walked over to the window and gazed out into the darkness. The rain had ceased, the earth was imbibing the moisture, the clouds were still hanging heavily over the landscape.

Bertha's whole being became imbued with yearning; everything within her called to him; her eyes sought to see him before her in the darkness; her lips breathed a kiss into the air, as though it could reach his lips; and, unconsciously, as if her wishes had to soar aloft, away from all else that surrounded her, she looked up to Heaven and whispered:

'Give him back to me! ...'

Never had she been as at that moment. She had an impression that for the first time she now really loved him. Her love was free from all the elements which had previously disturbed it; there was no fear, no care, no doubt. Everything within her was the purest tenderness, and now, when a faint breeze came blowing and stirring the hair on her forehead, she felt as though it was a breath from the lips of Emil.

The next morning came, but no letter. Bertha was a little disappointed, but not disquieted. Soon Elly, who had suddenly acquired a great liking for playing with Fritz, made her appearance. The servant, on returning from the market, brought the news that the doctor had been summoned in the greatest haste to Herr Rupius' house, though she did not know whether it was Herr Rupius or his wife who was ill. Bertha decided to go and inquire herself without waiting until after dinner.

She gave the Mahlmann twins their music lesson, feeling very absent-minded and nervous all the time, and then went to Herr Rupius' house. The servant told her that her mistress was ill in bed, but that it was nothing dangerous, although Doctor

Friedrich had strictly forbidden that any visitors should be admitted. Bertha was frightened. She would have liked to speak to Herr Rupius, but did not wish to appear importunate.

In the afternoon she made an attempt at continuing Fritz's education, but, do what she could, she met with no success. Again, she had the impression that her own hopes were influenced by Anna having been taken ill; if Anna had been well, it would have surely happened also that the letter would have arrived by that time. She knew that such an idea was utter nonsense, but she could not resist it.

Soon after five o'clock she again set out to call on Herr Rupius. The maid admitted her. Herr Rupius himself wanted to speak to her. He was sitting in his easy-chair by the table.

'Well?' asked Bertha.

'The doctor is with her just at this moment – if you will wait a few minutes ...'

Bertha did not venture to ask any questions, and both remained silent. After a few seconds Doctor Friedrich came out from the bedroom.

'Well, I cannot say anything definite yet,' he said slowly, then, with a sudden resolution, he added: 'Excuse me, Frau Garlan, but it is absolutely necessary for me to have a few words with Herr Rupius alone.'

Herr Rupius winced.

'Then I won't disturb you,' said Bertha mechanically, and she left them.

But she was so agitated that it was impossible for her to go home, and she walked along the pathway leading between the vine-trellises to the cemetery. She felt that something mysterious was happening in that house. The thought occurred to her that Anna might perhaps have made an attempt to commit suicide. If only she did not die, Bertha said to herself. And immediately the thought followed: if only a nice letter were to come from Emil!

She seemed to herself to be encompassed by nothing but dangers. She went into the cemetery. It was a beautiful warm summer's day, and the flowers and blossoms were fragrant and fresh after the rain of the previous day. Bertha followed her accustomed path towards her husband's grave, but she felt that she had absolutely no object in going there. It was almost painful to her to read the words on the tombstone; they had no longer the least significance for her:

'Victor Mathias Garlan, died the 6th June, 1895.'

It seemed to her, then, that any of her walks with Emil which had happened ten years before were nearer than the years she had spent by the side of her husband. Those years were as though they had not even existed ... she would not have been able to believe in them if Fritz had not been alive ... Suddenly the idea passed through her mind that Fritz was not Garlan's son at all ... perhaps he was really Emil's son ... Were not such things possible after all? ... And she felt at that moment that she could understand the doctrine of the Holy Ghost ... Then she was alarmed at the madness of her own thoughts.

She looked at the broad roadway, stretching straight from the cemetery gate to the opposite wall, and all at once she knew, for a positive fact, that in a few days a coffin, with the corpse of Frau Rupius within it, would be borne along that road. She wanted to banish the idea, but the picture was there in full detail; the hearse was standing before the gate; the grave which two men were digging yonder just at that moment was destined for Frau Rupius; Herr Rupius was waiting by the open grave. He was sitting in his invalid chair, his plaid rug across his knees, and was staring at the coffin which the black-garbed undertakers were slowly carrying along ... The vision was more than a mere presentiment; it was a precognition ... But whence had this idea come to her?

Then she heard people talking behind her. Two women walked past her, one was the widow of a lieutenant-colonel who had recently died, the other was her daughter. Both greeted Bertha and walked slowly on. Bertha thought that these two women would consider her a faithful widow who still grieved for her husband, and she seemed to herself to be an impostor, and she retired hastily.

Possibly there would be some news awaiting her at home, a telegram from Emil perhaps – though that indeed would be nothing extraordinary ... after all, the two things were closely connected ... She wondered whether Frau Rupius still thought of what Bertha had told her at the railway station, and whether perhaps she would speak of it in her delirium ... however, that was a matter of indifference, indeed. The only matters of importance were that Emil should write and that Frau Rupius should get better ... She would have to call again and see Herr Rupius; he would be sure to tell her what the doctor had had to say ... And Bertha hastened homewards between the vine-trellises down the hill ...

Nothing had arrived, no letter, no telegram ... Fritz had gone out with the maid. Ah, how lonely she was! She hurried to Herr Rupius' house once more, and the maid opened the door to her. Things were progressing very badly, Herr Rupius was unable to see anyone ...

'But what is the matter with her? Don't you know what the doctor said?'

'An inflammation, so the doctor said.'

'What kind of an inflammation?'

'Or it might even be blood poisoning, he said. A nurse from the hospital will be here immediately.'

Bertha went away. On the square in front of the restaurant a few people were sitting, and one table, right in front, was occupied by some officers, as was usual at that time of the day.

They didn't know what was going on up yonder, thought Bertha, otherwise they wouldn't be sitting there and laughing ... Blood poisoning – well, what could that mean? ... Obviously Frau Rupius had attempted to commit suicide! ... But why? ... Because she was unable to go away – or did not wish to? – but she wouldn't die – no, she must not die!

Bertha called on her relatives, so as to pass the time. Only her sister-in-law was at home; she already knew that Frau Rupius had been taken ill, but that did not affect her very much, and she soon began to talk of other things. Bertha could not endure it, and took her departure.

In the evening she tried to tell Fritz stories, then she read the paper, in which amongst other things, she found another announcement of the concert at which Emil was to play. It struck her as very strange that the concert was still an event which was announced to take place, and not one long since over.

She was unable to go to bed without making one more inquiry at Herr Rupius' house. She met the nurse in the anteroom. It was the one Doctor Friedrich always sent to his private patients. She had a cheerful-looking face and a comforting expression in her eyes.

'The doctor will be sure to pull Frau Rupius through,' she said.

And although Bertha knew that the nurse was always making such observations, she felt more reassured.

She walked home, went to bed, and fell quietly asleep.

The next morning Bertha was late in waking up. She was fresh after her good night's rest. A letter was lying beside the bed. And then, for the first time that morning, everything came back into her mind; Frau Rupius was very ill, and here was a letter from Emil. She seized it so hurriedly that she set the little candlestick shaking violently; she opened the envelope and read the letter.

My dear Bertha,

Many thanks for your nice letter. I was very pleased to get it. But I must tell you that your idea of coming to live permanently in Vienna requires again to be carefully considered by you. Circumstances here are quite different from what you seem to imagine. Even the native, fully accredited musicians have the greatest difficulty in obtaining pupils at anything like decent fees, and for you it would be – at the beginning, at least – almost a matter of impossibility. Where you are now you have your assured income, your circle of relations and friends, your home; and, finally, it is the place where you lived with your husband, where your child was born, and so it is the place where you ought to be.

And apart from all these considerations it would be a very foolish procedure on your part to plunge into the exhausting struggle for a livelihood in the city. I purposely refrain from saying anything about the part which your affection for me (you know I return it with all my heart) seems to play in your proposals; to bring that in would carry the whole question over to another domain, and we must not let that happen. I will accept no sacrifice from you, under any condition. I need not assure you that I would like to see you again, and soon, too, for there is nothing I desire so much as to spend another such hour with you as that which you recently gave me (and for which I am very grateful to you).

So, then, arrange matters, my child, in such a way that, say, every four or six weeks you can come to Vienna for a day and a night. We will often be very happy again, I trust. I regret I cannot see you during the next few days, and, moreover, I start off on a tour immediately after the concert. I have to play in London during the season there, and after that I am going on to Scotland. So I look forward to the joyful prospect of meeting you again in the autumn.

I greet you and kiss that sweet spot behind your ear, which I love best of all.

Your
Emil.

When Bertha had read the letter to the end, for some little time she sat bolt upright in the bed. A shudder seemed to pass through her whole body. She was not surprised, she knew that she had expected no other kind of letter. She shook herself ...

Every four or six weeks ... excellent! Yes, for a day and a night ... It was shameful, shameful! ... And how afraid he was that she might go to Vienna ... And then that observation right at the end, as if his object had been, while he was still at a safe distance, so to speak, to stimulate her senses, because that, forsooth, was the only kind of relations he desired to keep up with her ... It was shameful, shameful! ... What sort of a woman had she been! She felt a loathing – loathing! ...

She sprang out of bed and dressed herself ... Well, what was going to happen after that? ... It was over, over, over! He had not time to spare for her – no time at all! ... One night every six weeks, after the autumn ... Yes, my dear sir, I at once accept your honourable proposals with pleasure. Indeed, for myself, I desire nothing better! I will go on turning sour, I will go on giving music lessons and growing imbecile in this hole of a town ... You will fiddle away, turn women's heads, travel, be rich, famous and happy – and every four or six weeks I may hope to be taken for one night to some shabby room where you entertain your women of the street ... It was shameful, shameful, shameful! ...

Quick! She would get ready to go to Frau Rupius – Anna was ill, seriously ill – what mattered anything else?

Before she went out Bertha pressed Fritz to her heart and she recalled the passage in Emil's letter: it is the place where your child was born ... Indeed that was quite right, too; but

Emil had not said that because it was true, but only to avoid the danger of having to see her more than once in six weeks.

She hurried off ... How was it, then, that she did not feel any nervousness on Frau Rupius' account? ... Ah, of course, she had known that Frau Rupius had been better the previous evening. But where was the letter, though? ... She had again thrust it quite mechanically into her bodice.

Some officers were sitting in front of the restaurant having breakfast. They were all covered with dust, having just returned from the manoeuvres. One of them gazed after Bertha. He was a very young man, and could only have obtained his commission quite recently ...

Pray, don't be afraid, thought Bertha, I am altogether at your disposal, I have an engagement which takes me into Vienna only once every four or six weeks ... please, tell me when you would like ...

The balcony door was open, the red velvet piano cover was hanging over the balustrade. Well, evidently order had been restored again – otherwise, would the cover have been hanging over the balustrade? ... Of course not, so forward then, and upstairs without fear ...

The maid opened the door. There was no need for Bertha to ask her any questions, in her wide-open eyes there was an expression of terrified amazement, such as is only called forth by the proximity of an appalling death.

Bertha went in, she entered the drawing-room first, the door leading to the bedroom was open to its full extent. The bed was standing in the middle of the room, away from the wall, and free on all sides. At the foot was sitting the nurse, looking very tired, with her head sunk upon her breast. Herr Rupius was sitting in his invalid's chair by the head of the bed. The room was so dark that it was not until Bertha had come quite close that she could see Anna's face clearly. Frau Rupius seemed to be asleep. Bertha came nearer. She could hear the patient's breathing; it was regular, but inconceivably rapid – she had never heard a human being breathe like that before. Then Bertha felt that the eyes of the two others were fixed upon her. Her surprise at having been admitted in this unceremonious manner lasted only for a moment, since she understood that all precautionary measures had now become superfluous; the matter had been decided.

Suddenly another pair of eyes turned towards Bertha. Frau Rupius opened her eyes and was watching her friend attentively. The nurse made room for Bertha and went into the adjoining room. Bertha sat down, moving her chair closer to the bed. She noticed that Anna was slowly stretching out her hand towards her. She grasped it.

'Dear Frau Rupius,' she said, 'you are already getting on much better now, are you not?'

She felt that she was again saying something awkward, but she knew she could not help doing so. It was just her fate to say such things in the presence of Frau Rupius, even in her last hour.

Anna smiled; she looked as pale and young as a girl.

'Thank you, dear Bertha,' she said.

'But whatever for, my dear, dear Anna?'

She had the greatest difficulty in restraining her tears. At the same time, however, she was very curious to hear what had actually happened.

A long interval of silence ensued. Anna closed her eyes again and appeared to sleep. Herr Rupius sat motionless in his chair. Bertha looked sometimes at Anna and sometimes at him.

In any case, she must wait, she thought. She wondered what Emil would say if *she* were suddenly to die. Ah, surely it would cause him some slight grief if he had to think that she whom he had held in his arms a few days before now lay mouldering in the grave. He might even weep. Yes, he would weep if she were to die ... wretched egoist though he was at other times ...

Ah, but where were her thoughts flying to again? Wasn't she still holding her friend's hand in her own? Oh, if she could only save her! ... Who was now in the worse plight – this woman who was doomed to die, or Bertha herself – who had been so ignominiously deceived? Was it necessary, though, to put it so strongly as that, because of one night? ... Ah, but that had much too fine a sound! ... for the sake of one hour – to humiliate her so – to ruin her so – was not that unscrupulous and shameless? ... How she hated him! How she hated him! ... If only he were to break down at his next concert, so that all the people would laugh him to scorn, and he would be put to shame and all the papers would have the news – 'The career of Herr Emil Lindbach is absolutely ended.' And all his women would say: 'Ah, I don't like that a bit, a fiddler who breaks down!' ...

Yes, then he would probably remember her, the only woman who had loved him since the days of her girlhood, who loved him truly ... and whom he was now treating so basely! ... Then he would be sure to come back to her and beg her to forgive him – and she would say to him: 'Do you see, Emil; do you see, Emil' ... for, naturally, anything more intelligent than that would not occur to her ...

And there she was thinking again of him, always of him – and here somebody was dying, and she was sitting by the bed, and that silent person there was the husband ... It was all so quiet; only from the street, as though wafted up over the balcony and through the open door, came a confused murmur – men's voices, the rumble of the traffic, the jingle of a cyclist's bell, the clattering of a sabre on the pavement, and, now and then, the twitter of the birds – but it all seemed so far away, so utterly unconnected with actuality.

Anna became restless and tossed her head to and fro – several times, quickly, quicker and quicker ...

'Now it's beginning!' said a soft voice behind Bertha.

She turned round. It was the nurse with the cheerful features; but Bertha now perceived that that expression did not denote cheerfulness at all, but was only the result of a strained effort never to allow sorrow to be noticeable, and she considered the face to be indescribably fearful ... What was it the nurse had said? ... 'Now it's beginning.' ... Yes, like a concert or a play ... and Bertha remembered that once the same words had been spoken beside her own bed, at the time when she began to feel the pangs of childbirth ...

Suddenly Anna opened her eyes, opened them very wide, so that they appeared immense; she fixed them on her husband, and, vainly striving, meanwhile, to raise herself up, said in a quite clear voice:

'It was only you, only you ... believe me, it was only you whom I have ...'

The last word was unintelligible, but Bertha guessed it.

Then Herr Rupius bent down and kissed the dying woman on the forehead. Anna threw her arms around him; his lips lingered long on her eyes.

The nurse had gone out of the room again. Suddenly Anna pushed her husband away from her; she no longer recognized him; delirium had set in.

Bertha rose to her feet in great alarm, but she remained standing by the bed.

'Go now!' said Herr Rupius to her.

She lingered.

'Go!' he repeated, this time in a stern voice.

Bertha realized that she must go. She left the room quietly on tip-toes, as though Anna might still be disturbed by the sound of footsteps. Just as she entered the adjoining room she saw Doctor Friedrich, who was taking off his overcoat and, at the same time, was talking to a young doctor, the assistant at the hospital.

He did not notice Bertha, and she heard him say:

'In any other case I would have notified the authorities, but, as this affair falls out as it does ... Besides, there would be a terrible scandal, and poor Rupius would be the worst sufferer –' then he saw Bertha – 'Good day, Frau Garlan.'

'Oh, doctor, what is really the matter, then?'

Doctor Friedrich threw his colleague a rapid glance.

'Blood poisoning,' he replied. 'You are, of course, aware, my dear Frau Garlan, that people often cut their fingers and die as a result; the wound cannot always be located. It is a great misfortune ... Yes, indeed!'

He went into the room, followed by the assistant.

Bertha went into the street like one stupefied. What could be the meaning of the words which she had overheard – 'information?' – 'scandal?' Yes, had Herr Rupius, perhaps, murdered his own wife? ... No, what nonsense! But some injury had been done to her, it was quite obvious ... and it must have been, in some way, connected with the visit to Vienna; for she had been taken ill during the night subsequent to her journey ... And the words of the dying woman recurred to Bertha: 'It was only you, only you whom I have loved! ...' Had they not sounded like a prayer for forgiveness? 'Loved only you' – but ... another ... of course, she had a lover in Vienna ... Well, yes, but what followed? ... Yes, she had wished to go away, and had not done so after all ... What could it have been that she said on that occasion at the railway station? ... 'I have made up my mind to do something else.' ... Yes, of course, she had taken leave of her lover in Vienna, and, on her return – had poisoned herself? ... But why should she do that, though, if she loved only her husband? ... And that was not a lie, certainly not!

Bertha could not understand ...

Why ever had she gone away, then? ... What should she do now, too? ... She could not rest. She could neither go home nor to her relatives, she must go back again ... She wondered, too, whether Anna would have to die if another letter from Emil came that day? ... In truth, she was losing her reason ... Of course these two things had not the least connection between them ... and yet ... why was she unable to dissociate them one from the other? ...

Once more she hurried up the steps. Not a quarter of an hour had elapsed since she had left the house. The hall door was open, the nurse was in the ante-room.

'It is all over,' she said.

Bertha went on. Herr Rupius was sitting by the table, all alone; the door leading to the death-chamber was closed. He made Bertha come quite close to him, then he seized the hand which she stretched out to him.

'Why, why did she do it?' he said. 'Why did she do *that*?'

Bertha was silent.

'It wasn't necessary,' continued Herr Rupius, 'Heaven knows, it wasn't necessary. What difference could the other men make to me – tell me that?'

Bertha nodded.

'The main point is to live – yes, that is it! Why did she do that?'

It sounded like a suppressed wail, although he seemed to be speaking very quietly. Bertha burst into tears.

'No, it wasn't necessary! I would have brought it up – brought it up as my own child!'

Bertha looked up sharply. All at once she understood everything, and a terrible fear ran through her whole being. She thought of herself. If in that night she also ... in that one hour? ... So great was her terror that she believed that she must be losing her reason. What had hitherto been scarcely more than a vague possibility floating through her mind now loomed suddenly before her, an indisputable certainty. It could not possibly be otherwise, the death of Anna was an omen, the pointing of the finger of God.

At the same time there arose within her mind the recollection of the day, twelve years ago, when she had been walking with Emil on the bank of the Wien, and he had kissed her and for the first time she had felt an ardent yearning for a child. How was it that she had not experienced the same yearning when, recently, she felt his arms about her? ... Yes, she knew now, she had desired nothing more than the pleasures of the moment, she had been no better than a woman of the streets. It would be only the just punishment of Heaven if she also perished in her shame, like the poor woman lying in the next room.

'I would like to see her once more,' she said.

Rupius pointed towards the door. Bertha opened it, went up slowly to the bed on which lay the body of the dead woman, gazed upon her friend for a long time, and kissed her on both eyes. Then a sense of unequalled restfulness stole over her. She would have liked to have remained beside the corpse for hours together, for, in proximity to it her own sorrow and disappointment became as nothing to her. She knelt down by the bed and clasped her hands, but she did not pray.

All at once everything danced before her eyes. Suddenly a well-known attack of weakness came over her, a dizziness which passed off immediately. At first she trembled slightly, but then she drew a deep breath as one who had been rescued, because, indeed, with the approach of that lassitude, she felt at the same time that, at that moment, not only her previous apprehensions, but all the illusion of that confused day, the last tremors of the desires of womanhood, everything which she had considered to be love, had begun to merge and to fade away into nothingness. And kneeling by the death-bed, she realized that she was not one of those women who are gifted with a cheerful temperament and can quaff the joys of life without trepidation. She thought with disgust of that hour of pleasure that had been granted her, and, in comparison with the purity of that yearning kiss, the recollection of which had beautified her whole existence, the shameless joys which she then had tasted seemed to her like an immense falsehood.

The relations which had existed between the paralysed man in the room beyond and this woman, who had had to die for her deceit, seemed now to be spread out before her with wonderful clearness. And, while she gazed upon the pallid brow of the dead woman she could not help thinking of the unknown man, on account of whom Anna had had to die, and who, exempt from punishment, and, perhaps, remorseless, too, dared to go about in a great town and to live on, like any other – no, like thousands and thousands of others who had stared at her with covetous, indecent glances. Bertha divined what an enormous wrong had been wrought against the world in that the longing for pleasure is placed in woman just as in man; and that with women that longing is a sin, demanding expiation, if the yearning for pleasure is not at the same time a yearning for motherhood.

She rose, threw a last farewell glance at her dearly loved friend, and left the death-chamber.

Herr Rupius was sitting in the adjoining room, exactly as she had left him. She was seized with a profound desire to speak some words of consolation to him. For a moment it seemed to her as though her own destiny had only had this one purpose: to enable her fully to understand the misery of that man. She would have liked to have been able to tell him so, but she felt that he was one of those who desire to be alone with their sorrow. And so, without speaking, she sat down opposite to him.

More about Penguins and Pelicans

Penguinews, which appears every month, contains details of all the new books issued by Penguins as they are published. From time to time it is supplemented by *Penguins in Print*, which is a complete list of all available books published by Penguins. (There are well over four thousand of these.)

A specimen copy of *Penguinews* will be sent to you free on request. For a year's issues (including the complete lists) please send 30p if you live in the United Kingdom, or 60p if you live elsewhere. Just write to Dept EP, Penguin Books Ltd, Harmondsworth, Middlesex, enclosing a cheque or postal order, and your name will be added to the mailing list.

Note: *Penguinews* and *Penguins in Print* are not available in the U.S.A. or Canada

Hermann Hesse

Hermann Hesse (1877–1962), novelist and poet, won many literary awards including the Nobel prize (1946). He was interested in both psychology and Indian mysticism and his novels explore different attempts to find a 'total reality' in life.

Steppenwolf

This Faust-like, poetical and magical story of the humanization of a middle-aged misanthrope was described in the *New York Times* as 'a savage indictment of bourgeois society'. But, as the author notes in this edition, *Steppenwolf* is a book which has been violently misunderstood. This self-portrait of a man who felt himself to be half-human and half-wolf can also be seen as a plea for rigorous self-examination and an indictment of intellectual hypocrisy.

Narziss and Goldmund

Narziss is a teacher at Mariabronn, a monastery in medieval Germany. Brilliant and severe, he feels that Goldmund, his favourite pupil, will never be a scholar or a monk.

So Narziss helps Goldmund realize that they must each fulfil themselves in different ways: Narziss retiring from the world into a patterned order of prayer and philosophy while Goldmund quits the cloisters to plunge into a sea of blood and lust; cutting a picaresque swathe through plague, storm and murder; always chasing a fugitive vision of artistic perfection, its form 'the mother of all things'.

In a sense, both Narziss and Goldmund – the ascetic and the Dionysian – are what Hesse himself might have been. This element of conjectural autobiography gives to this masterpiece a ripe wisdom, an insight into universal dilemmas and man's role on earth, unique in the fiction of our time.

Not for sale in the U.S.A.

Also available
The Glass Bead Game